CORSAIR MENACE

JAMIE MCFARLANE

FICKLE DRAGON PUBLISHING

CONTENTS

PREFACE

FREE DOWNLOAD

Sign up for the author's New Releases mailing list and get free copies of the novellas; *Pete, Popeye and Olive* and *Life of a Miner*.

To get started, please visit:

http://www.fickledragon.com/keep-in-touch

PROLOGUE

While *Privateer Tales* is a series, each story is crafted to stand alone. That said, many of the crew, locations and even governments show up in multiple stories and readers have requested a reminder they can reference in case memory has lapsed.

I enjoy interacting with readers and sharing inside information about myself and the characters I create. When a new story is available, or I'm otherwise inspired, I send out an email newsletter. If you are interested in joining my newsletter distribution, please visit http://fickledragon.com/keep-in-touch/ to sign up.

On with the list of characters.

Liam Hoffen – our hero. With straight black hair and blue eyes, Liam is a lanky one hundred seventy-five centimeters tall, which is a typical tall, thin spacer build. His parents are Silver and Pete Hoffen, who get their own short story in *Big Pete*. Raised as an asteroid miner, Liam's destiny was most definitely in the stars, if not on the other end of a mining pick. Our stories are most often told from Liam's perspective and he, therefore, needs the least introduction.

Nick James – the quick-talking, always-thinking best friend who is usually five moves ahead of everyone and the long-term planner of the team. At 157 cm, Nick is the shortest human member of the crew.

He, Tabby, and Liam have been friends since they met in daycare on Colony-40 in Sol's main asteroid belt. The only time Nick has trouble forming complete sentences is around Marny Bertrand, who by his definition is the perfect woman. Nick's only remaining family is a brother, Jack, who now lives on Lèger Nuage. The boys lost their mother during a Red Houzi pirate attack that destroyed their home in the now infamous Battle for Colony-40.

Tabitha Masters – fierce warrior and loyal fiancé of our hero, Liam. Tabby lost most of her limbs when the battle cruiser on which she was training was attacked by the dreadnaught *Bakunawa*. Her body subsequently repaired, she lives for the high adrenaline moments of life and engages life's battles at one hundred percent. Tabby is a lithe, 168 cm tall bundle of impatience.

Marny Bertrand – former Marine from Earth who served in the Great Amazonian War and now serves as guardian of the crew. Liam and Nick recruited Marny from her civilian post on the Ceres orbital station in *Rookie Privateer*. Marny is 180 cm tall, heavily muscled and the self-appointed fitness coordinator — slash torturer — on the ship. Her strategic vigilance has safeguarded the crew through some rather unconventional escapades. She's also extraordinarily fond of Nick.

Ada Chen – ever-optimistic adventurer and expert pilot. Ada was first introduced in *Parley* when Liam and crew rescued her from a lifeboat. Ada's mother, Adela, had ejected the pod from their tug, *Baux-201*, before it was destroyed in a pirate attack. Ada is a 163 cm tall, ebony-skinned beauty and a certified bachelorette. Ada's first love is her crew and her second is sailing into the deep dark.

Jonathan – a collective of 1,438 sentient beings residing in a humanoid body. Communicating as Jonathan, they were initially introduced in *A Matter of Honor* when the crew bumped into Thomas Phillipe Anino. Jonathan is intensely curious about the human condition, specifically how humanity has the capacity to combine skill, chance, and morality to achieve a greater result.

Sendrei Buhari – a full two meters tall, dark skinned and heavily muscled. Sendrei started his military career as a naval officer only to be captured by the Kroerak while on a remote mission. Instead of killing him outright, the Kroerak used him as breeding stock, a decision he's dedicated his life to making them regret.

Felio Species – an alien race of humanoids best identified by its clear mix of human and feline characteristics. Females are dominant in this society. Their central political structure is called the Abasi, a governing group consisting of the most powerful factions, called houses. An imposing, middle-aged female, Adahy Neema, leads House Mshindi. Her title and name, as is the tradition within houses, is Mshindi First for as long as she holds the position.

Strix Species – A vile alien species that worked their way into power within the Confederation of Planets. Spindly legs, sharp beaks, feathery skin and foul mouthed, most representatives of this species have few friends and seem to be determined to keep it that way.

Aeratroas Region – located in the Dwingeloo galaxy and home to 412 inhabited systems occupying a roughly tubular shape only three hundred parsecs long with a diameter of a hundred parsecs. The region is loosely governed by agreements that make up The Confederation of Planets.

Planet Zuri – located in the Santaloo star system and under loose Abasi control. One hundred fifty standard years ago, Zuri was invaded by Kroerak bugs. It was the start of a bloody, twenty-year war that left the planet in ruins and its population scattered. Most Felio who survived the war abandoned the planet, as it had been seeded with Kroerak spore that continue to periodically hatch and cause havoc.

York Settlement – located on planet Zuri. York is the only known human settlement within the Aeratroas region. The settlement was planted shortly before the start of the Kroerak invasion and survived, only through considerable help from House Mshindi.

MARQUE RESTORED

Chapter 1

NOTHING VENTURED

I lifted the battered, boxy, gray ship *Fleet Afoot* from the loading platform of Loose Nuts corporation's hastily assembled shipping yard. It was only a day since my crew and I returned to our new home in the York settlement, having barely survived an alien attack on planet Earth.

"Never gets old, does it?" Tabby asked, seated in the starboard pilot's chair next to me. Her face, the only skin showing outside of her vac-suit, bore the scars of battle - as did mine - but she was as beautiful as always. Her copper-colored hair was braided into a thick pony tail that curled around her neck and rested over her shoulder.

"All hands; check in for hard burn." The AI would transmit my message to the other two crew we'd brought along: Roby, a young, ebony-skinned man who'd grown up in York, and Semper, an equally young Felio female and native to the planet Zuri.

"Engineering is green," Roby answered almost immediately. It was quite a change for the young man who'd been forced to grow up quickly during our last adventure. I wished it wasn't true, but there was nothing like combat to teach the uninitiated the value of professionalism. Roby's training had been cemented when he survived a direct strike to the engine room and come through the ordeal a better man for it.

"Cargo has a green color," Semper responded. The young Felio had made impressive strides in her understanding of humanity's common language and preferred not to use the AI's translator circuits. The Felio species, like so many in the Dwingeloo galaxy, closely resembled humans (a fact I still struggle to comprehend). For sake of brevity, a Felio can best be described as a favorable mixture of feline and human traits. They have four fingers and toes, fur over their entire bodies, cat eyes, quick reflexes and uncanny balance.

"*Hard Burn in ten seconds.*"

We'd successfully installed wormhole drive engines into *Fleet Afoot* in response to Earth's planned shutdown of the TransLoc system used to jump between systems and galaxies. It had been a hard decision to leave our families behind, but it would have been even harder to leave unexplored an entire galaxy teeming with alien worlds. We held out hope that someday we'd find a wormhole that led home, but there was no guarantee of this.

"I'm showing seventy-two hour burn to Tamu gate," Tabby said.

"Copy," I acknowledged and engaged *Fleet Afoot's* powerful engines. The ship's gravity and inertial systems struggled while laboring to bleed off and redirect the crushing g-forces of acceleration.

We sailed in silence as Zuri slowly shrank behind us. Both Tabby and I enjoyed the quiet of space travel. I reached over and grabbed her hand as we shared the moment.

"What do you think of Nick's new venture?" Tabby asked.

Nick was our best friend from childhood and the brains behind our business. His latest project was the load of grav-sled components he'd manufactured with the help of the York settlement. The components were destined for a company on Kapik that would manufacture and distribute a batch of stevedore bots based on adaptations Nick made to technology we'd brought from earth.

"A lot of people are relying on this deal," I said. "I hope we don't have any trouble delivering."

Chapter 2

TRAP SPRUNG

"I'm picking up two ships," Tabby said.

We were eight hundred fifty kilometers from the cosmic anomaly most people called a wormhole. Nick and Roby liked to argue that *wormhole* wasn't technically an accurate description as it didn't involve a black hole. Some referred to the anomaly as a gate. Also, not correct. There was no required structure at the wormhole site. Turns out, only three things are required to move a ship through the wormhole: physical proximity, delta-v not in excess of a hundred meters-per-second, and engines tuned to the correct frequency.

"What are they doing?" I asked.

"Looks like they're on approach to the gate," she said.

Perhaps the most uncomfortable thing about the gates – at least the ones we'd been through – was that they were only a few dozen kilometers across, which would put us closer to the other ships than I liked.

"We could hold up," I said.

"We'll lose over an hour; they're moving ridiculously slow. There's plenty of room for us all if we just take the outside edge." She flicked a display onto my screen showing the predicted paths of the two ships and how we could slide past them, still leaving ten kilometers between us and the nearest ship.

"Roby, prepare for transition through the gate," I said.

"Aye, Captain," he replied. "Engines are attuned. Just need your word once we're in range."

I read the names of the two ships we were quickly overtaking. *Maguyuk* and *Tuuq.*

"Transmit our navigation plan to Maguyuk and Tuuq." My ever-listening AI initiated the communication. I waited a few minutes to receive a response, but soon grew impatient. An acknowledgment at least, was standard protocol.

"I'll take that as agreement," Tabby said.

I felt uneasy, but it was hard to argue. If they didn't want to respond, we certainly weren't going to wait. I pushed forward, engaging the nav-plan that would put us at the gate well before either ship arrived.

"Cap, I'm picking up acceleration vectors from both ships," Roby informed me over the comm.

When we were physically close to other ships, it was our practice to keep an open channel while executing maneuvers. Roby had heard our conversation and watched the situation with us.

"Any idea what they're doing?" I asked. I had an idea, but wanted a second opinion.

"If they keep at it, they'll arrive at the gate slightly after we do," he said.

"How much after?" I asked.

"Thirty seconds, max."

"Copy that, Roby. Semper, would you come forward?"

"Aye, aye, Liam Captain," she replied. Like all Felio she tended to place the name first and rank second as was common for their species.

The two ships were both about the size of *Fleet Afoot* and sensors showed they were reasonably well armed with what looked like particle blasters. We had better than average armor and much better than average acceleration.

It crossed my mind that the ships might have been waiting for us, but that felt paranoid and I didn't see how they could have known our schedule. I considered turning around, but neither ship had done anything overly provocative so I pushed forward.

This is where I feel I should mention that the nature of traps hasn't changed since the beginning of time. There's always that point you can look back to where you had an inkling of what was about to happen and pushed forward anyway.

"Roby, go ahead and engage wormhole engines."

"Aye, aye," he replied.

Unlike travel with TransLoc engines, the trip from one end of the wormhole to the other was instantaneous.

"Three more ships," Tabby exclaimed. "They're firing."

Chapter 3

DELICACY

Trying to get somewhere quickly from a dead stop is misery, especially when being fired upon. It was one of the things I most disliked about the gates. It took a patient pirate to hang out and wait for the occasional independent like us, as there was very little non-military traffic between Santaloo and Tamu systems.

"Strap in for combat burn." I gave the crew as much warning as possible and hoped they were already seated, then pushed hard on the stick just as heavy rounds impacted the stern of the ship.

I took it as a good sign that I was jammed into the back of my pilot's chair by our acceleration. Whoever was firing was targeting our engines and I was grateful they hadn't successfully taken them out.

"Starboard – energy net!" Tabby exclaimed.

Anyone else would probably have sailed to port in response to her information. We'd worked together enough that I knew better. She'd told me the information in the order I needed it. I pushed the stick hard right and we banked starboard. She'd done the necessary calculation and was giving an order, not just information. It was simple and efficient – that is, as long as you trusted your partner.

We'd never run into an energy net before, although I'd heard of them. The nets were designed to disrupt the electronics of any ship that ran into them. Good luck with that against a warship, but against *Fleet Afoot,* it would be plenty effective.

Our sensors picked up the two ships that'd been trailing us as they entered the system through the gate. We were severely outnumbered and substantially outgunned.

"What's the play here, Liam?" Tabby asked.

My mind spun with ideas. We could attempt to jump back into Santaloo and hope they couldn't or wouldn't follow us. Fact is, at least two of the ships could and I'd bet the rest of them could as well.

"*Incoming hail, Sangilak,*" the ship's AI announced.

I dodged as one of the unidentified ships cut off our escape route.

"Semper, you're with me," Tabby said as she fought against the several-g gravity my combat burn was generating. She disappeared through a hatch in the deck, making her way to one of two crow's nests on the bottom of the ship where she could control our weapons.

"*Accept hail.* What the frak are you pulling, *Sangilak*?" I asked. "You're firing, unprovoked on a civilian freighter."

"My apologies, Liam Hoffen." The rich voice sounded just before a pasty, white-skinned Pogona female appeared on the screen. "I should have more formally announced our intentions." Her mocking tone accompanied the AI translation of her words. "I am Belvakuski, leader of Genteresk. I am here to relieve you of your burdens."

Like all Pogona, she was the most human looking of the aliens we'd run into. The main difference in the species was a significant amount of loose skin beneath the chin, causing them to resemble lizards. This Pogona had thin, platinum blonde hair tightly pulled back. As her chin moved, the colorful jewelry attached to her loose jowls clinked together, distractingly.

"Pirates?"

"Such a lovely word. I do so enjoy the human tongue," she said. "It is talented at many things and a delicacy, I hear."

"Ass," Tabby said over internal comms.

Flashes of light erupted from *Fleet Afoot's* midsection as Tabby fired at a small ship closing on us. I leveled our flight as she stitched a line of blaster fire along the ship's skeg, fouling its propulsion. I pushed *Fleet Afoot* toward the weakened ship as Semper and Tabby took the opportunity to reduce it to scrap.

A message appeared on my vid-screen in response to our automated distress signal. An Abasi cruiser was four hours out and sailing in our direction. Instinctively, I answered affirmatively to the Abasi ship's request for a combat data-stream.

"How brave you look while you focus on your task. I will add you to my harem. You must be a thorough lover," Belvakuski said, apparently unbothered by our destruction of the smaller ship.

Too late, I realized the smaller ship had been bait as an energy mesh wrapped around the nose of *Fleet Afoot*.

Sparks flew from my console in my attempt to regain control of the ship.

"Roby, I'm dead stick," I announced. When he didn't reply, I pulled at the stick again and got no response. I jumped from my seat just as my vac-suit intoned a warning chime. Having grown up on a space station, I was more than familiar with the tone. It was telling me I'd entered a space next to vacuum – or Lo, meaning there were zero additional bulkheads before vacuum - and my helmet was not in place. Technically, all spaceships were Lo space, but armor and powered systems satiated the warnings. If the alarm was going off, the ship was good and truly dead in space.

Chapter 4

GHOST SHIP

"What the frak?" Tabby sailed up into the bridge from the gunner's nest.

"That small ship we took out was a bait-ship. I sailed right into one of those energy nets," I said with a growl.

"Get to the hold," Tabby said. "They're going to board us."

"What will we do?" Semper asked, following closely on Tabby's heals.

"They'll take our cargo," I said. "Nothing we can do about it. Our job is to stay alive."

"How?"

"Come." I jetted down the passageway to the lock separating Deck-1 from the hold. I spun the circular handle and manually opened the hatch, slid through and repeated the process on the second hatch. "Semper, get Roby and bring him to the hold."

"What are you thinking?" Tabby asked.

"Abasi cruiser is four hours out," I said. "We just need to survive. Open up your Popeye."

Popeye was slang for a mechanized infantry suit. Almost on a whim, we'd brought our suit along for ease in offloading our cargo on Kapik. The company we were delivering to manufactured stevedore equipment and, ironically, required shippers to do their own unloading.

"What's the play, Liam?" Roby asked as he found us in the hold, pulling open the shipping containers that held the Popeyes. "Are you seriously going to use those?"

"We're not leaving without a fight," I said. "Vent atmo from the hold."

I jumped up into the box, pushed my legs into the mechanized armor legs and waited for the foam to expand, sealing me tightly in. I laid back into the rest of the suit and stretched my fingers into the gloves. Once my hands were secure, the armor shell closed around my chest and equalized pressure, just as it had with my legs. The thing about wearing the mechanized armor was that while you ended up being almost seventy percent larger in every dimension, it felt like you were just wearing a normal vac-suit. Tactile sensors provided feedback, tricking your mind into accepting a new normal.

For Tabby and me, taking our spinach (an idiom I still didn't understand, but simply meant donning the suit) had become second nature. Since the energy net had broken the ship's gravity generator, I brought myself around with only a few micro gestures to control the suit's arc-jets.

"What should we do?" Roby asked, standing next to Semper. I had to give them both credit; we were in a pickle and neither of them were panicking.

"Right before we hit that energy net, we were nearly zero delta-v with the ship we destroyed. Tabby and I are going to make some noise when the Pogona send their boarding party. When that happens, you take the forward bilge hatch and make for that ship. Don't use your arc-jets until you're at least two kilometers away from *Fleet Afoot*.

For a moment, we all watched as Roby worked through some sort of calculation on his suit's HUD.

"That could work. What about you guys?"

"This only works if those pirates get what they came for," I said. "Otherwise, they'll just blow the ship."

Semper and Roby disappeared up the ladder and into the tween deck that would take them to the bilge hatch.

For the second time in my life, I opened the cargo hold of my ship and pushed our precious cargo into space. I couldn't imagine just how far back I was setting Nick's venture, not to mention the town of York. So much had relied on us getting these parts delivered. I had a difficult time believing the pirate's presence was merely a coincidence. Someone was getting in the way of technological advancement and I was afraid I knew just who it was.

Chapter 5

GILA MONSTER

I pushed a crate of parts away from the main bulk.

"*Incoming comm request*," the AI announced, not unexpectedly. I unstrapped the grenade launcher tube from my thigh, popped it open and affixed it beneath the barrel of my weapon. The Popeyes could manufacture a variety of ammunition and while not completely necessary, I found it easier to aim the RPG with the optional tube. I fired and the crate exploded brilliantly.

"*Accept comm.* Hello Belvakuski," I said, as I pushed another crate away from pile and into the deep dark.

"What are you doing? You can't hope to defeat us in those silly suits." She was right. *Sangilak* was fifty percent bigger than *Intrepid* and there was nothing a mechanized infantry suit could do if it got down to fisticuffs.

Once the crate reached twenty meters from our position, I fired a second round and blew it up. A little piece of me enjoyed the destruction, even though I knew I was destroying something valuable to my future.

"Did you really waste all that time setting up a trap for us, just to return empty handed?" I asked, tossing a third crate.

"You understand that once you're out of crates, there is no reason to keep you alive?" Belvakuski answered, her jewelry annoyingly clinking over the comms.

I fired at the third crate and blew it up.

"I've been down this road before, my dear," I said, pushing another crate away. I was gambling that she actually wanted what was in the crates. If she was just here to stop their delivery, she could blow the two of us up with the cargo and I was making a bad play. Although the fact that she hadn't blown up the ship as soon as she netted it gave me a certain amount of comfort. "You plan to kill us either way. I might as well buy us some time."

"Two hours, nineteen minutes," she replied, with my AI translating. "We are quite aware of the Abasi cruiser and will be gone well before it arrives."

I fired another shot and pushed another crate into space. We had almost thirty-two crates. At this rate, I'd run out in fifteen minutes and we'd get to play a new, less fun game.

"Stop it! What do you propose?"

"It's not hard," I said. "Leave your smallest ship behind. Twenty minutes before the Abasi arrive, we'll load the crates into your hold. If we don't, your people can shoot us."

"What prevents my ship from opening fire - killing you - once we have the crates? Even my smallest ship can destroy humans in their toys."

"That's the fun part," I said. "If your crew can take us out, then you win. If we live, we win."

"You are very calm for the position you find yourself in."

"Compartmentalization," I said. "It's a male thing. Saves on multi-tasking."

"You are very strange, Liam Hoffen. I will enjoy having you in my bed if you survive this," she said. "I accept your bargain."

Tabby fired at the crate that was floating away.

"What are you doing!? You must not destroy the crates or our deal is off," she said.

"He's spoken for, Gila monster," Tabby retorted.

"Delightful," Belvakuski said.

Chapter 6

DESPERATE TIMES

Three ships slowly pulled away. The remaining ship turned so its single turret lined up on us. In preparation, the pirates opened their hold and three suited figures appeared.

"What's your plan?" Tabby asked.

"What the heck?" I asked. "I got rid of four out of five. Shouldn't this one be yours?"

"It's a good point," she agreed. It wasn't as if she didn't know as well as I did, that the plan was to utilize *Fleet Afoot* to avoid fire from the Pogona ship for long enough that the Abasi cruiser would show up in time to pull our bacon from the fire.

When a ship has its turret pointed at you, patience is difficult. Tabby and I positioned ourselves on the back side of the pile of crates and were nervously passing the time. Finally, at thirty minutes out, we received an incoming message request.

"You're early," I said.

"It will take time to load and you are in no position to negotiate," a pirate said, not showing his face on the comm.

"Get ready to play catch, then," I said and pushed a crate toward their ship.

"*Secure communications request, Roby Bishop.*" Involuntarily, I swiveled my head, looking for the source. A secure comm would need to be line-of-sight to be undetectable. Roby knew this. Therefore, he was in my field of vision somewhere in the inky black of space.

"*Accept.*" Roby joined the comm that Tabby and I already shared.

"Get them to come to the pile," Roby said.

"What are you up to?"

"Desperate times, Captain," he said.

I had to trust him. "Time for hide and seek, Tabbs."

"Three. Two. One," Tabby counted us down. When she hit one, we both peeled away from the pile. I kicked my foot on one of the middle crates as I scooted away, scattering the remaining boxes. If the ship's gunner was getting an itchy trigger finger, I wanted a better screen.

Blaster fire pelted *Fleet Afoot's* hull next to me as I sailed behind one of the engines. A second round blew the engine shroud off and I found myself tumbling through space. I reached out just in time to grab a piece of the ship's tail, my suit straining as I rotated and brought myself around to the back side.

"Now, Semper," Roby said, just as I moved out of communications line-of-sight. I laid into my suit's arc-jets. Whatever was happening would be resolved in short order and my bet was that Roby and Semper were in big trouble. Another blaster bolt struck *Fleet Afoot* but missed me by a substantial margin.

Just as Tabby and I were no match against a warship, the suited figures loading the crates were no match for a mechanized infantry suit. As a younger man, I might have figured out some way to disable the pirates as we closed on them. But I'd seen too much carnage and too many good people die to care what happened to pirates who threatened me and mine.

The pirates raced back to their ship. They had no warning when my rounds found them. I winced. I'd never shot someone in the back before. It felt wrong and I wondered where my previous bravado had gone. A voice in my head urged me to stay in the moment.

Suddenly, the ship turned and the engines lit, even though the cargo bay door was still open. With a final burst of energy, I grabbed the retracting ramp and pulled myself forward, but the opening was no longer wide enough to slide through. The ship lurched and I felt myself being tugged forward as it tried to accelerate away from my grasp.

"Not today, bastards." Tabby pulled the pry bar from the calf of her mech-suit and stabbed it into the skin of the ship. It was just the idea I needed and I followed suit with my own bar. "Help me," she said as she worked to lever open the cargo ramp. The powerful hydraulic pistons were attempting to squeeze us out and my suit strained against them as we struggled, machine against suit.

"Hold it, one second," I said.

Tabby screamed in exertion as I released my grip on the ramp, giving her the entire load. I pulled my weapon up and fired into the cargo bay. My suit was still on RPG mode and debris from the explosion tore past us. I fired a second shot and must have hit something because the ramp suddenly fell, almost dislodging me as it did.

Tabby needed no prompting and neatly rolled into the cargo bay. Not quite as agile, I followed behind her. Not in play mode, Tabby leveled her gun at a door that separated the cargo hold from the crew and fired.

"Roby and Semper might be in there," I said.

"Shite," Tabby said as she pulled the ruined hatch off with her suit's powerful arms.

We were too big to fit through the now open hatch, so I hit my quick eject. I jumped from the suit and raced through the door carrying the pistol I'd brought.

"Stand down, Cap," Roby said as I raced down the passageway to the sealed bridge entrance.

"What's your sit-rep, Roby?" I asked.

"Semper is hurt, but okay," he said. "The captain has surrendered."

"Let me in."

"We're decompressing now."

I walked in to find two Pogona crumpled on the floor, dead. A third knelt with his hands over his head; Roby pointing a blaster pistol at him. Poor Roby's hands were shaking.

"Semper." I knelt and checked my youngest crew member's wound. Her vac-suit had healed around the wound and her eyes were glassy with shock. "We were brave," she said.

"You were brave," I agreed. "Tabbs, we're under control, but I need you."

"What happened?" I asked, taking Roby's gun.

"Cargo bay was empty," Roby said. "We cycled through and Semper caught one of the pirates trying to go back to bring in crates. She shredded his wattle with her claws. Did you know Felio vac-suits allow their claws to extend through little ports? I sure didn't."

Roby was understandably excited and adrenaline was making him talk too fast.

"I don't understand then. Why did they keep accelerating after you took control?" I asked.

"Captain had a gun," Roby looked at his feet. "He shot Semper after she killed the gunner. Captain only surrendered after Tabby ripped the door from the airlock."

"Captain. If you'd like to remain breathing, you'll turn over control of the helm to my associate."

Chapter 7

MARQUE RESTORED

I couldn't have been more relieved when the Abasi cruiser, *Cold Mountain Stream* came into view. Idly, I wondered if the Abasi had ever considered giving their ship's names that were more macho.

"We're receiving a hail," Roby said. I'd given him the honor of sailing the ship, *Tuuq*, back to where *Fleet Afoot* sat.

"This is Captain Liam Hoffen," I answered.

"Greetings, Hoffen Captain, and warm salutations." A Felio I recognized showed on the *Tuuq's* vid-screen.

"Mshindi Tertiary. Are congratulations in order? Is *Cold Mountain Stream* your first commission?" I asked.

"I have joined my mother and sister in command rank," she replied proudly, brushing a paw along her whiskered face.

"Well deserved! And it makes me doubly glad to see you today," I said. "We ran into a bit of a problem out here with pirates."

"Yes. It is a common problem for merchants now that we are in conflict with Strix," she said.

"We have taken a prisoner," I said. "Could we transfer him to your custody?"

"Yes. We will take your prisoner. Bumha engineer has informed that *Fleet Afoot* suffers repairable damage. Mshindi offers aid."

"LET ME GET THIS STRAIGHT," Nick said. He lay against his girlfriend, the thickly muscled Marny Bertrand and rested his feet on the arm of the couch. "The only parts lost to the pirates were the ones you blew up?"

I handed a beer to Tabby and sat on her lap in the chair adjacent to Marny and Nick.

"Hey. We delivered most of your parts," I said. "How pissed is Bakira Corporation that we didn't deliver everything?"

"Apparently, pirate activity is up in the sector. Once I explained what happened, they were fine," Nick said. "We won't make anything on this round. They'll build prototypes and send them out to the distributors. If all goes well, we'll get orders in half a stan, maybe sooner."

A knock at the front door got our attention. I stood to answer it, but Ada, the fifth managing member of our team, walked in, as was customary for crew while we were on the ground.

"We have a visitor," she said. It was always easy to tell what Ada was thinking; her face tended to reveal every emotion. In this case, her face was bright with excitement.

I followed her out and saw that a shuttle had landed in the field next to where we now kept both *Intrepid* and *Fleet Afoot*. From the shuttle, Mshindi Second emerged and walked briskly in our direction with an honor guard in tow.

"Mshindi Second. You honor us with your presence," I said as Tabby, Nick and Marny joined Ada and me.

"My time is minor," she said. I rolled my eyes. For some reason the translator for Mshindi Second gave the weirdest possible words.

"You have traveled a great distance," I said. "Surely we could offer refreshments."

The middle-aged Felio, who was first in line for the powerful House Mshindi, bowed slightly at the waist. "Your offer is acceptable."

"If we'd known you were coming, we'd have cleaned up," I said as we entered the main room of the bungalow Tabby, Marny, Nick and I shared. Suddenly self-conscious, I removed some of the dishes we had sitting out.

"Your accommodations are adequate." She sat on the edge of a chair, accepted a bottle of beer, and placed it on the table next to her.

"What brings you to Zuri, Mshindi Second?" Ada asked.

Mshindi cocked her head quizzically at Ada. "Loose Nuts Corporation brings Mshindi to Zuri. I would have thought this transparent."

Ada turned and raised her eyebrows at me.

"How can we help you?" I asked.

"We have returned the ship identified as *Tuuq*," she said.

"Mshindi Tertiary made it clear the captured ship would be seized by House Mshindi, but we gratefully accept it," I said. "The return of a ship seems a small matter for Mshindi Second. We would have gladly come to pick it up."

"True your words are. An alternate idea was delivered by a human comrade I converse with on schedule."

"You are talking about more than giving us *Tuuq*," Nick said.

Mshindi Second pulled a rolled piece of paper from beneath her tunic and handed it to me. "It was the idea of a human, LaVonne Sterra. She communicated the idea of Privateers. It is an idea the Abasi Council embraces hotly."

"You're making us Privateers?" I asked, unwrapping it. My eyes immediately glazed over at the fine print on the page and I handed it to Nick.

"You speak clearly. I deliver to you a Letter of Marque."

CORSAIR MENACE

Chapter 1

IT'S CALLED COERCION

Santaloo System, Planet Zuri, Loose Nuts enclave outside of York township

---

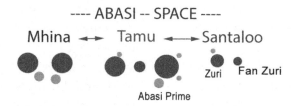

"What do you make of this pirate named Belvakuski?" I asked, projecting the Pogona's face onto the wall in our bungalow on Zuri.

Pogona were the most human-looking of all the aliens we'd run into. The most striking difference was loose, wrinkled skin beneath their chin that caused them to resemble lizards. Belvakuski's loose jowls had been pierced through with colorful jewelry.

"A powerful adversary is the Genteresk." Mshindi Second sat primly on the edge of her chair.

House Mshindi had honored us by sending the Felio, second only to her mother, to bestow on us the Letter of Marque and deliver the cutter-sized ship *Tuuq* as our first prize. The Abasi had learned of our previous status as privateers from contacts they'd made on Earth and were willing to extend a similar offer for the Santaloo star system. The task seemed well below Mshindi Second's station, but I wasn't about to let her leave without gathering whatever intel she might be willing to share.

"Genteresk operates a base on the moon Cenaki which creases the sky of Fan Zuri," she continued. "Belvakuski is not pursued within Pogona territory."

Zuri, where we were currently located, and Fan Zuri, were the only inhabitable planets in the Santaloo system. I'd learned Fan Zuri was controlled by lizard chins (our slang for Pogona) and it was news to me the Abasi didn't consider the planet to be their territory.

"Confederation of Planets just lets the Genteresk hijack other ships?" I asked.

"House Mshindi does not favor the politic that allows Genteresk free operation. The Confederation of Planets' judiciary requires matters relating to Genteresk be prosecuted by Nijjar government," Mshindi Second explained and then stood.

Out of respect, we stood with her.

"Seriously?" Nick, my best friend and business partner, was always one step ahead in every conversation. "Isn't Nijjar the Pogona government? We're dozens of lightyears from their home planet. How did they gain standing here?"

"For three-hundred-fifty spans, Nijjar occupy Fan Zuri. Abasi treaty becomes strained, resulting from separation with Strix," Mshindi Second said. "Loose Nuts is sharp sword of reprisal. Mshindi Second desists." With a bow, Mshindi Second nodded to the guard who stood at the front door.

"Reprisal?" Nick asked, following her closely.

"Yes, Nicholas James. Sterra Admiral illuminated that a privateer achieves where government lacks will. I anticipate with moist tongue your arrival at prize court."

We followed her into the front yard of our humble bungalows. Without looking over her shoulder, she and her guard loaded into the shuttle in which she'd arrived and took off.

"Moist tongue?" Tabby asked, lifting an eyebrow.

"Felio idiom for salivating in anticipation of prey," Nick answered.

Tabby rolled her eyes. "My interpreter AI needs an interpreter AI."

A glint of sunlight caught my attention. A caravan of vehicles was moving at high speed on the road from York. It was late in the day and Nick's employees had all returned home for the night.

"What the frak is that about?" Tabby asked.

"They're not from York," Nick observed. My AI locked in on the vehicles and steadied the view. The wheeled and heavily armored vehicles bounced along, their speed not well suited to the narrow road.

"Everyone inside," Marny commanded. "There's no time to make for the ships."

She was right. While *Fleet Afoot* sat only a hundred meters from our position, the vehicles were hurtling toward us at too great a speed.

"Jonathan, we have trouble. Don't come out until we have it resolved. We're taking cover in the bungalows."

Jonathan was a collection of non-biological sentients that resided in a humanoid body. The host had been provided to them by the extraordinarily wealthy inventor, Thomas Anino. Aside from being interested in all things new, Jonathan often had his own agenda. We were glad to have him as part of the crew whenever he was willing to join us.

"We will batten down the hatches," Jonathan replied. Strangely, Jonathan had the ability to construct sentences that were indistinguishable from those spoken by their human counterparts, something our AIs weren't even capable of.

"Incoming comm," Nick said.

"Goboble," we said together, as I'd received the same comm.

I pulled a blaster pistol and holster from the closet where we stored our weapons and strapped it around my waist.

"They're pulling up," Tabby said, looking through the front window.

The bungalows were designed to withstand the hostilities of the often-spawning Kroerak, but I doubted they'd hold up to the force I'd seen rolling down the hill. I longed for the mechanized suits that sat in the hold of *Fleet Afoot*.

"*Accept comm request*," I instructed my ever-listening AI. "This is Hoffen."

"Come outside. We have items to discuss." Goboble's voice rumbled over the comm channel and his dark gray, stone-textured face filled my HUD.

I muted comms and looked to Nick. "Any idea what this is about?"

"Could be any number of things," said he replied. "Can't be good, though. My best guess is he's calling in the note."

"I thought we'd been making payments." We were in to Goboble for four hundred thousand Abasi credits after he'd purchased the bond we lost when we'd been forced to abandon our cargo.

"Goboble is charging a vig," Nick said. "We're barely staying afloat."

"Vig?"

"Vigorish," Nick said, as if that explained it to me.

My AI recognized my confusion and displayed a definition. Best I could tell, Goboble was charging us illegal interest.

"We didn't agree to that," I said.

"He's pretty sore about you handing over his guy to the Abasi," Nick said.

"Well, frak."

We'd made tough decisions when the fate of Earth hung in the balance. It might be time to pay the piper.

"What's our balance?" I asked.

"Four hundred fifty-eight thousand," Nick said. "He's adding ten thousand a week."

"Stay here," I said, giving him a quick nod.

"Probably not." Tabby strapped grenade marbles to her lapel and grabbed a heavy blaster rifle.

I knew better than to argue with her.

"You cannot hide in there, Liam Hoffen," Goboble said. The Golenti smuggler had a flat affect to his voice.

I opened the comm channel and walked to the front door. "I'm coming."

"Be careful, Cap," Marny said. "We've got your backs with the house turrets."

"Let's hope it doesn't come to that." I pushed through the front door. "What's this about, Goboble?" I asked, resting the palm of my hand on the butt of the blaster.

From the largest of the three vehicles, an IFV (Infantry Fighting Vehicle, or Stryker as Marny would later name it), a rear hatch lifted and metal stairs rotated out, flopping onto the hard-packed ground. Goboble's Felio guards, Charena and Hakenti, slunk out and surveyed the area. The two Felio were deadly fighters.

"It seems we have come to a conflict in our operating agreement," Goboble said as he emerged from the back of the vehicle. The Golenti's skin was rich with calcium and gave the appearance of being made of rock. I'd heard rumor that flechette darts and light blaster fire had little effect on that natural armor. "Loose Nuts is not living up to the payment schedule of our bond and your flow of liquid currency is negative. I find you in default in both contracts."

"We just delivered parts to Kapik," I said. "We're expecting payment within five days. We should be able to pay you eighty thousand then."

"Goboble is businessman first," he said, stepping closer so he stood at arms-length. "If Loose Nuts was capable of making payments, I would not be here today."

I swallowed, choosing to exercise patience. "You're our business partner, Goboble. You thrive if we thrive. Give us the week."

"There is no point. Your shipment was rejected by Bakira Corporation," he said. "You will have no payment."

"Bilge water," I said. "I delivered the parts myself."

"Hold on, Liam." Nick's voice cut through on what I knew to be a private channel. "I just got a comm from Bakira."

"A minute?" I asked. Goboble nodded his head in agreement.

One minute turned into ten and Nick finally got back to me. "I just talked to my Bakira rep. Strix are putting pressure on them not to deal with us."

My face must have given away the conversation.

"Unfortunate that you learn of your fate in this way," Goboble chided.

"What's the bottom line, Nick?" I asked.

"Bakira is backing out of the deal. They're going to pay us twenty thousand for restocking."

I looked at Goboble accusingly.

He cracked a thin smile. "A good businessman anticipates events. I would prefer currency to our current predicament, but my capital is a premium and I find you to be untrustworthy."

"That's ridiculous," I said. "We've treated you more fairly than you are treating us."

"A strange interpretation," he said. "You handed my business partner to Abasi. It is no secret that you lay with the furry cowards. Did you not think word would get back to me of Ferin's capture?"

Goboble had me. Our predicament with him had started when we'd dropped the cargo he was shipping and handed a slimy pirate named Ferin over to the Abasi.

"You validate the truth of my statement with your eyes." His words appeared to be a cue to Hakenti and Charena as they raised their weapons threateningly. "Your actions are punishable by death on my homeworld of Golenti. A deal is sacred and you lack honor."

In response to the twin Felio guard's actions, Tabby aimed her blaster rifle at Goboble's head. "You have a lot of nerve talking honor, shite-stain. Every time you talk, you change our deal."

I winced inwardly. The ten thousand a week vig was something new, but we'd mostly signed up for the problems we were having.

There were extenuating circumstances, but he was within his right to hold us to our contracts.

"Guns aren't necessary," I said, placing my hand on the barrel of Tabby's rifle, unsuccessful in my attempt to push it down.

The sound of vehicle brakes caught my attention. I'd been so focused on the conversation with Goboble that I hadn't noticed the stream of two and four-person carriages pulling up on our position.

Hakenti and Charena shifted as three additional armed men exited from Goboble's vehicle and twin turrets popped up from its roof. A dozen York citizens piled out of their carriages, formed up around us and aimed a collection of older weaponry at Goboble's group. Their armaments were the equivalent of pitchforks and clubs compared to Goboble's, but they helped level the field — if only slightly.

"You okay, Liam?" Jackson 'Hog' Hagarson called.

"Heya, Hog," I said. "Goboble and I were just talking some things through."

"You should not be here, Jackson Hagarson," Goboble said, raising his voice. "We are not friends, but we are not enemies. My quarrel is with this human who is incapable of paying his debts."

"I know all about your debts, Goboble. You take advantage of people in need and then screw them when you get the chance," Hog retorted. "Hoffen and crew are part of York now. You mess with them, you mess with us."

I felt a mix of pride and fear at the big man's words. He shouldn't be squaring off with Goboble for us.

"Your bravado endangers your people, Jackson Hagarson," Goboble said evenly. "Do not make the mistake of joining with such as these. It will bring only ruin."

Things were rapidly spinning out of control and I needed to get us back on track. "Your argument is with me, Goboble. What do you want?"

"Four hundred, sixty-five thousand Abasi credits," he said.

"You know we don't have that on hand."

"I will take *Fleet Afoot* and you will owe me two hundred thousand," he said.

"That's rat piss," I said. "*Fleet Afoot* is worth eight hundred thousand to a million."

"Have you a buyer then? I have come to call your debt," he said.

"He'll never give in," Tabby shifted forward, still aiming her weapon at Goboble. "I say we do this. I'll pop his head like a fudge-pot tick. I don't care if his skin is made of diamonds. I guarantee he's never been hit by a full charge from one of these babies."

"The only reason you still live is that your finger has not yet contacted the trigger mechanism of your weapon, Tabitha Masters," Goboble said in that low, patient voice I was beginning to dearly hate. As he spoke, turrets from the other vehicles popped up and aimed at the people of York.

"Nick?" I asked. "What are you thinking, buddy?"

"Cap," Marny cut in. "We're looking at high casualties. Those mini-turrets on Goboble's vehicles are state-of-the-art."

"Stall him, Liam," Nick said.

I lowered my voice to a mere whisper. "You've got to be kidding."

"Four minutes."

I closed my eyes and shook my head. Four minutes was an eternity.

"*Fleet Afoot* and we're even," I said. "No bond. No vig. No agreements. We'll get our gear out of the hold and she's all yours."

"Liam, are you nuts?" Tabby asked.

"You have offered nothing new," Goboble said. "Why would I negotiate from my position of power? You will place many deaths on your side of the ledger."

"Two things," I said. "First. You're using the wrong value for *Fleet Afoot*. You think she's the ship you sold us. It's just not the case. Abasi repaired her weapon systems, put in new fold-space drives, and upgraded the living spaces. She's first class all the way. Plus, she's the fastest ship we've seen in this galaxy, at least with anything near her weight."

"I know of these things," Goboble replied. "My offer is to reduce your debt to two-hundred seventy-five thousand and we will remain business partners in Zug Enterprises."

I wanted to roll my eyes at the mention of Zug. It was a corporation he'd formed so that we could share a seventy-five, twenty-five split of the profits from operating *Fleet Afoot*. I resisted the urge.

"That's a horrible deal," I said. "Why would I take that?"

"You have no choice."

"You're negotiating at the end of the gun barrel," I said. "Back home we call that coercion and it's not legal."

"We are a significant distance from your home, human," Goboble said. "We stand in the wilds of Zuri. Coercion is a common negotiating tactic."

"You do understand my AI won't allow me to turn over control of a ship if I'm under duress, right? *Fleet Afoot* might as well be a pile of rocks where you're concerned if we don't come to terms."

"I am prepared for this," he said. "Hakenti, if you will."

Hakenti walked to the lead vehicle, an APC (Armored Patrol Craft), which was smaller than the Stryker, yet big enough to hold a maximum of five. From the back seat, he pulled two of our crew — Sempre and Roby Bishop. Sempre, a Felio female, was unconscious and her arm hung at an odd angle as she was tossed onto the ground. Roby stumbled forward and fell next to her, moaning.

"You're dead, Goboble," I growled.

"Careful with your words, Captain," Goboble said. "My guard found this pair in Azima. Let it be known we can find you anywhere."

"You beat kids?" I spat. "This is how you negotiate?"

"A useful demonstration," he said. "You have delayed enough, Captain Hoffen. You will agree to my terms. You will turn over *Fleet Afoot* immediately or we will discover if my head indeed bursts like a fudge-pot tick as your mate has indicated."

The faint sound of the whirring of gears caught my attention just before an orange blaster bolt tore through the air a meter above the Stryker and its twin turrets. The bolt embedded itself in the hillside some forty meters away, brilliantly exploding a tree and triggering a shower of rocks. Without thinking, I ducked and instinctively pulled my pistol from my belt.

Without hesitation, Goboble's troops turned toward *Intrepid*, where the blast had come from, and opened fire. The APC's twin turrets rapidly returned fire.

"Stop!" I yelled, but Goboble had already scrambled for cover and there was no slowing the assault by his team.

A second turret on *Intrepid* synced up with the first and twin bolts ripped through the air. Only one of the bolts struck the APC, but the force was enough to cause the vehicle to jump to the side. As the APC's wheels caught in the road, it bounced and teetered precariously, as if it might tip completely over. The action stopped the operator inside from continuing to fire.

Two more rounds from *Intrepid* plowed a furrow in front of Goboble's troops, pelting them with rocks and debris.

Another blast from *Intrepid* ripped a chunk from the back end of the heavy APC, causing it to tip precariously again. The vehicle finally bounced back onto all four wheels as smoke rolled out of its rear hatch.

"Goboble, tell your men to stop firing!" I yelled again over the chaos.

"Cease fire!" Goboble responded immediately. He looked at me, tipping his head to the side and waited as weapons were dropped on the ground. "I understood the ship was a burned-out hulk. You have been busy, Liam Hoffen."

Fortunately, I've played enough cards and talked to enough psychopaths that I wasn't about to let him know I had no idea what he was talking about. As far as I knew, *Intrepid's* turrets were nonfunctional, having just been returned a few days before by the Abasi. Moreover, the collective inside Jonathan were all pacifists.

"We finish this," I said, ignoring his implied question. "I will trade you *Fleet Afoot* for our bond debt. You will return our grav-suits and we will dissolve our partnership."

"You make an enemy today, Liam Hoffen," Goboble said.

"There's an old Earth saying I think you should learn."

"What is that?"

"'That ship has sailed.' You made us your enemy when you decided to coerce us into unfavorable conditions."

"As did your ship sail when you turned over our compatriot to Abasi," he said. "Do not let your victory today give you false security."

"Do you want your ship or not?" Anger started to cloud my thinking. "If we're going to be enemies, maybe I'd be better off burying the lot of you and keeping your cool trucks."

Goboble glared. It was the first indication of emotion I'd seen from the alien. I had him. He knew it and I knew it. "I accept your deal, but I will not forget this day."

"Nick, write that up, please?" I asked.

A moment later my AI chimed as a contract arrived.

Goboble reviewed the contract, signed it and narrowed his eyes as he looked at me. "I look forward to our next meeting."

Chapter 2

PATRIOT'S CALL

"*Hail from Silver Hoffen,*" my AI intoned.

Goboble must have heard something as he turned back to me after stepping into the damaged APC. Hate simmered behind his eyes and he stared me down for a long minute before ordering the hatch closed.

"Mom?" I asked, confused, turning away from the angry little golem. "Are you on Zuri?"

A sonic boom announced the arrival of a fast approaching ship.

"Sorry we couldn't make it more quickly," she said. "We received an urgent message from Nicholas, but it looks like you have things cleaned up."

"What are you doing here?" I asked.

"Long story," she said. "Everything okay down there?"

"Bad guys are just leaving. Maybe you could follow them out and make sure they don't stop in that little town back over the hill," I said.

"Copy that," she answered as I finally caught a glimpse of the ship she'd arrived in. My AI identified it as a stealth-armored small sloop made by Renaissance Airframes.

"Ada, we need med kits," I said as Tabby and I rushed to help the injured Roby and Sempre.

Ada Chen was the fifth member of our crew. While she'd been quiet up to this point, I knew she'd been following the encounter. She still bore the scars of our last battle with the Kroerak, an injury which had taken one of her eyes.

"They really tuned him up," Tabby said, gently rolling Roby onto his back. The ebony skin of his face was covered with purple bruises and his eyes were swollen shut.

"Help Sempre," Roby gurgled.

"We have her, Roby." Jonathan had already exited *Intrepid* and was helping the unconscious young Felio female. "You're safe," they said, helping her into a more comfortable position. My HUD displayed the initial diagnosis, indicating broken bones in her face and left arm.

"Jonathan, you fired at Goboble," I said. "You're pacifists."

"Not strictly true, Liam. We strongly desire peaceful outcomes. Firing on inanimate vehicles seemed a reasonable compromise."

"I'd like to think I'm rubbing off on you," I said.

"Indeed you have, Liam," Jonathan said. "As we have on you."

"Hug it out, already," Tabby said. "Did you know your mom was in-system?"

"No, and I think Nick has some explaining to do."

"What a brute," Ada complained as she knelt next to Tabby and placed two med-scanner patches on Sempre's bloodied fur. My AI connected to the med-scanner and confirmed multiple fractures of her cheek bones and considerable swelling in her cranium. We'd programmed a Felio specific set of patches into our replicator and made them part of our standard emergency kit, so my HUD outlined the small squares as I reached into the bag. Ada and I worked together quickly to activate and apply them to the soft orange and white fur of Sempre's bloodied face.

It would take a few days to repair the bone damage, but the most critical issue was the brain swelling. For a human, our technology easily dealt with concussions, but our understanding of Felio physiology wasn't nearly as advanced. I'd already transmitted Sempre's scan data for review to a medical center in Manetra, an Abasi city twenty-two hundred kilometers away.

"You kids doing okay over here?" Hog Hagarson interrupted, jumping from the electric vehicle the townsfolk called a carriage. Hog was the barrel-chested, bigger-than-life mayor of the York settlement.

"Roby?" From the other side of Hog's carriage, Bish, Roby's potbellied father rushed toward us. "I told you all not to get involved with that gangster. This is what I was talking about. You're endangering us all by going against Goboble."

"Now, Bish," Hog defended. "You can't be blaming Hoffen for Goboble. And, darn it! I'm done cowering. We can't just keep living hand-to-mouth. We finally have hope for the future prosperity of York and our people."

"Is *this* the hope you're looking for?" Bish gestured to Roby.

"Stop it, Dad," Roby grunted.

"Well, I don't like it," Bish said.

"You're right not to like it, Mr. Bishop," I said. "We can't underestimate Goboble. Our crew has run into his kind before. He will be trouble."

"And you're okay with our young being hurt or killed, Hog?" Bish asked as he and others transferred Roby and Sempre to a flat-bed carriage.

The body language of several of the gathered men and women of York clearly indicated that Bish wasn't the only one having concerns about the confrontation with Goboble.

"We can't take losses, Hagarson. We're barely holding on as it is. We don't need a new war." The speaker was a farmer we'd met before, Curtis Long. The tall, thin man was plain-speaking, hardworking and always pessimistic.

"We have to stick together," Hog said. "If we've learned anything, it's that."

"There's an alternative," Nick said. It wasn't like Nick to step into the middle of a heated conversation.

"What's that?" Long stepped toward Nick, still angry.

The action got Marny's attention and before Nick could respond, she'd stepped in next to him and placed a shoulder between the two men.

"It's okay, Marny. Curtis is scared. We know what that feels like." Nick rested his hand on her thickly muscled bicep and moved around her. "The alternative is that you ask us to leave. We've learned that Bakira is rejecting our parts. If ever there was a time for us to move on, this is it."

As he considered Nick's words, a range of emotions played across the normally stoic man's face.

Hog, on the other hand, had no conflict and wasn't about to let either Bish or Long speak for the community. "Hold on there. Hoffen, James, and all of you are part of York now. We'll not be asking anyone to leave. Long, weren't you just saying the other day how much you appreciated these young-bloods pumping energy and credits into our community? Bish, weren't you going on about how James' anti-grav technology could revolutionize industry? We're ready to drop all that because of one angry Golenti?"

"Goboble is more than that and you know it," Bish said, standing up to his life-long friend.

"And the citizens of York once stood against a tide of Kroerak when they invaded. Are you really suggesting Goboble is worse than that?"

Bish looked down and then back at Hog. "No. Damn it. Don't make me the bad guy here. We're getting pulled into this thing and we don't have anything to say about it."

"*Incoming comm, Silver Hoffen.*"

"Go ahead, Mom." I touched my ear and stepped away from the conversation.

"I noticed a landing pad outside that little town we passed. Do they have fuel?" Mom asked.

"That's York," I said. "Go ahead and set down there; we'll meet you. And you are so busted for not telling me you were coming."

"We have a lot to talk about," Mom said. "See you in a few minutes. Hoffen out."

"Did she hang up on you?" Tabby asked.

I rolled my eyes. "Yes. Only my family would do that."

"At least your family talks to you," Tabby said.

I turned to the group that had congregated around Nick just as Bish climbed into the vehicle that carried Sempre and Roby.

Ada had positioned herself on the flatbed between the two injured youths. "Let's go, Bish," she said.

"Where are you taking them?" I asked.

"Bish will take 'em home," Hog said. "And don't you all be worrying about Curtis and Bish. They're nervous nellies. The good folk of York know a good thing when it comes along. We hope you'll stay with us, warts and all."

"You sure about that, Hog?" Nick asked. "My read was that most of that group was very nervous."

"They have a right to be. Goboble has a reputation. Thing is, worry don't get you nowhere," Hog replied. I flinched as I attempted to unwind his grammar. "Now, did I get it right? Your mom was sailing that sleek looking ship?"

"That was Mom." I turned to Nick. "And ... you had to know Mom was coming. What gives? You holding that back from me?"

"Think I could get a ride to town?" Hog asked, interrupting. "Patty said a ship just set down on the pad and people are getting nervous. Apparently, there's a whole load who've disembarked."

"A whole load of people?" I looked back to Nick with a raised eyebrow. Something more than a visit from Mom was up. "What do you know about this?"

Nick, anticipating the question, was already jogging toward the bungalow he'd turned into his workshop. "Don't ask me," he called over his shoulder. "Ask your Mom."

"Chicken," I called after him. "Marny, you know anything about this?"

"I might," she said, smiling. "Not that I'm going to spill the beans, though. Hog, why don't you tell Patty we're coming over to the diner and we're going to need a lot of tables."

A moment later, Nick emerged from the workshop in the four-wheeled hauler he used to ferry parts and equipment. As there was only room for three in the cab, Tabby and I hopped into the bed as he pulled up.

"What's going on?" Tabby asked.

"I don't know how much more I can take today," I said. "I feel like I need a score card."

"Your mom wouldn't come out this far just for a social visit. She knows there's a short timeframe before TransLoc is shut down for good," Tabby said. "She'd be risking a lot if she got caught on this side."

Once we crested the hill, Tabby and I stood to look over the top of the hauler's cab. As we wound down the hill, York and the landing pad came into view.

"Something is seriously up," Tabby said. "That's Merrie, Amon, Sendrei Buhari, and Ortel Licht. Is that Priloe? That kid has really grown and Milenette has too."

"Who are all those military types?" I asked.

"Commander Munay is one of them," Tabby said.

There had been a rumor that Mom and Munay had some interest in each other. She denied it, but hearing that he was aboard made me wonder if there might be truth to the story.

I waved as the red-haired Ortel Licht tapped Mom on the shoulder and pointed up the hill at us. A few moments later, we arrived and Nick pulled to a stop. When Tabby and I jumped out we were drawn into hugs, handshakes and introductions.

"Mom, I'd like to introduce you to Hog Hagarson," I said. "Hog, Silver Hoffen." In turn, I introduced Hog to each of those I knew.

"Hog?" Mom asked.

"Pleasure to meet you," Hog said, smiling broadly. "Jackson Hagarson — but your boy is right. People around here call me Hog."

"Liam said there were good people on Zuri," she said. "I can see he wasn't exaggerating."

"Aren't you just the sweetest little thing. No sense standing around," Hog said. "Your ship'll be plenty safe on the pad there. My sweet little gal is throwing together a spread as we speak."

"Lieutenant." Munay turned to one of the Mars Protectorate Naval officers he'd brought along. "I want this bird in the air, first sign of those armored vehicles."

"Aye, aye, Commander." A uniformed lieutenant snapped to attention.

I gave Mom an inquisitive look. Munay was obviously here in an official capacity.

"Walk with me," she said, holding out her hand.

As we walked toward the open main gates, we laughed as Ortel and Priloe ran ahead, chased by Priloe's sister Milenette and a dark-haired girl named Demetria that I had only met once.

"Sendrei is huge," I observed, smiling as we passed several York citizens I either knew or at least recognized.

I'd first met Sendrei Buhari on the Kroerak controlled planet called The Cradle. He'd been mute, leading me to believe he was just a simple Kroerak-raised human slave. As it turned out, after being captured by Kroerak scouts, they'd removed his tongue. At the time, he'd been a sizeable man, four centimeters taller than Marny and leanly muscled. It shouldn't have been a surprise that with proper nutrition, he'd filled out significantly. I had trouble taking my eyes off his impressive, heavy earther body with thickly muscled arms and shoulders.

"He's gorgeous," Mom said. I found her admission a little embarrassing.

"That's Flaer, right?" I asked.

Sendrei walked next to a petite, frail looking woman with short-cropped red hair. I knew her looks to be deceiving. She had strength in that small body and would use it in the defense of her friends.

Mom nodded. "They married a few months back. Sendrei has been helping with security on Petersburg Station. Flaer runs our commissary."

"You're killing me, Mrs. H.," Tabby said, using the title Mom had earned as our secondary school teacher. The term took me back to when we'd grown up on Colony 40. "What's this all about?"

"Not completely mine to say," Mom said. "We'll have plenty of time to talk."

"We're here," I said. "This is Patty's restaurant." The glass-fronted restaurant occupied a single building that was basically a rectangle, twenty meters across and ten deep. "She makes all the dishes from scratch and gets her produce from local farmers. York is almost completely self-sufficient."

"It is a pretty town," Mom said just a little louder than was necessary. It didn't escape me that Patty had just pushed the front door open as we'd arrived and Mom was speaking in a stage whisper.

"Welcome, welcome," Patty said as we filed in. "Sit anywhere at the big table in the middle."

"Thank you, Patty," I said as we passed.

She gave me a warm smile. "Nonsense. A full house is my pleasure."

For the next forty minutes, we were distracted by the business of the meal and greeting York citizens who were both curious and bold enough to find us.

"Where's Ada?" Mom asked about halfway through.

"She was tending to a couple of our friends who were hurt," I said. "I'll send her a message. I'm sure she won't want to miss talking with you."

"I'll send someone over," Hog said, overhearing the exchange.

"I was thinking, Hog. How about we see if Bish wants to join us? I feel like we're going to be working through some issues here and I think having both of you at the table might be a good idea."

"You sure?" Hog asked. "Seems like this is your party."

"This," I gestured to the assembled group, "is more than a party. I'm not exactly sure what's going on, but I'm positive you'll want to be here."

"I would see to the injured," Flaer said, standing. "Such is my gift."

Hog looked at me, perplexed.

"Flaer is a doctor." I was stretching the truth as Flaer had no formal training. She did, however, have a long history of healing people under horrible conditions and I'd seen firsthand how quickly she'd adapted to new technologies.

"I'll take you," Hog said.

Sendrei stood with Flaer, who placed her hand on his chest to stop him. "Drei, you will sit and make plans. Such is *your* gift. I will remain safe in this community."

"As you wish." The sound of his voice reminded me of the first time I'd heard his soft baritone after his tongue had been restored in the med-tank on *Intrepid*.

Fifteen minutes later Ada, Bish and Hog arrived.

"How are Roby and Sempre?" I asked.

"Healing," Ada said. "Goboble is an ass."

"A dangerous ass," Bish agreed, not yet ready to concede his earlier point.

"Let's get to this, shall we?" I asked. "Why did a dozen of my favorite people take an intergalactic flight for dinner?"

"Our trip is not social," Commander Munay started.

"Glad you were able to give Mom a ride out to Zuri," I said.

"A decision not of my making," he said. "Powerful entities required dangerously cramped conditions aboard our ship."

Mom didn't look at Munay as she smiled in a way I knew to be less than genuine. "Greg worked diligently to be a wonderful host. Twelve days in the deep dark at max capacity is difficult with younger passengers."

"Why the trip?" I asked.

Munay cleared his throat. "I'm not sure this is the time or place."

Bish caught my eye as he rocked back in his chair and crossed his arms. His ire was rising at the hint of secret plans.

"I'm done holding secrets for Mars," I said. "Don't share anything with me privately that you don't want everyone at this table to know about."

"Admiral Sterra said you would feel this way," Munay said, frowning slightly. "She sends her warmest wishes, by the way."

I smiled at hearing of Sterra's promotion. Of all the military I'd met within Mars Protectorate, she was one who still held my respect.

"What's going on?" I asked.

"A small group of ships are on a mission to locate the Kroerak homeworld, but as you know, there's little information on the origin of the Kroerak species. Our objective is to put humanity into a position where we can strike back."

"So you want to chase the Kroerak," I said.

"There are ten ships like our sloop, *Gaylon Brighton*, currently on mission. We have lost contact with three of them. It is Admiral Sterra's belief that your crew should be briefed on this mission and that outcome."

He reached into his front pocket and extracted a quantum communication crystal and set it on the table in front of me. We'd used similar crystals in the past and I knew they allowed for virtually instantaneous communication over galactic distances.

"Mars requests your aid," he said. "When the gates are shut down, we'll be physically cut off from Mars. You are literally our last hope if *Gaylon Brighton* is lost."

"Again," Tabby added.

"What's that, Lieutenant?"

"Maybe you haven't read news feeds," Tabby growled. "We've been putting our asses on the line for Mars and humanity since we started flying. And, I'm not *your* frakking Lieutenant. Mars Protectorate discharged me."

A flush rose on his neck. "We paid for your tank transplants."

"Dumbass." Tabby pushed away from the table abruptly.

"What?" Munay asked defensively, either unaware or unwilling to admit what Loose Nuts had done to make M-Pro restore Tabby's limbs.

I picked up the comm crystal. "Just drop it. What do you think we can do that ten crews of the best and brightest can't?"

"Up to me, we wouldn't be having this conversation. You and your crew are loose cannons. There are many who believe your rash actions brought the Kroerak to Earth."

Sendrei's calm voice cut through Munay's rant. "Your view of history conveniently neglects a Kroerak visit to Sol ten years before this crew bravely rescued my people — the same people who were being bred as livestock to feed Kroerak."

"Tens of billions of people were killed in their invasion of Earth," Munay said. "Do you really believe your antics didn't impact the Kroerak schedule?"

"I don't know," I said, choking back doubt. The thing was, I blamed myself more than he ever could. Rationally, I knew there was no good choice to be made. The fact was, billions of people had died and I'd been part of it.

"I don't see how you can live with yourself."

"Greg!" Mom admonished.

He pushed back from the table. "You're right. I've said more than I should have."

I lifted my glass of water to him in a sarcastic salute. "Safe travels."

"Indeed," he said. "I'll need your answer in the morning."

"That's a ballsy ask, Munay," I said, leaving off his honorific title. "Especially considering your diatribe."

"Liam," Mom said. "Be respectful."

"That'd be new," Tabby said. "Mars Protectorate has lied to us, threatened us and pushed us around. Now, Munay chastises Liam for doing the only right thing — conveniently forgetting that it was Liam who literally carried mankind's salvation from the Kroerak all the way from Zuri. I'd say it is Commander Munay who should learn respect."

"Tabitha," Mom said, using her best disappointed voice.

"No, Silver, she is right," Munay said, turning to Tabby. "I acknowledge the potential legitimacy of your argument. There are many within Mars Protectorate who are unwilling to face the truth of this threat. It was Admiral Sterra who said we should enlist your help. She said that despite poor treatment, you would place the benefit of society above your own well-being. And to answer your question, it is Admiral Sterra who believes you and your crew can do things that ten Mars Protectorate crews of the best and brightest can't."

"I hate to be a blemish on her record in that case," I said. "I'm tired of being M-Pro's whipping boy."

"The stakes are too high, Liam Hoffen," Munay said. "It is not Mars Protectorate that needs your help. It is humanity."

I closed my eyes and tried to block the anger that clouded my vision. He was a masterful negotiator, saving his heaviest punch for last. "No promises. I want everything you have on the lost ships."

Chapter 3

ZERO LIQUIDITY

Hog alternately raised and lowered his hands, pretending to compare the weight of two sizeable objects he wasn't actually holding. "And I thought my Patty served a genuinely fantastic huevo dish."

Munay stiffened in his chair and looked at Hog. "It is my impression that young Hoffen can be reasoned with."

"You guys are all the same," Bish interjected. "You fill a boy's head with visions of being a hero, dump all the blame on him when things get tough, and then you pull this crap?"

"Hold on, Bish," I said. "He's right. Kroerak will come right back to Earth if they figure out a way around the selich poisoning."

Bish screwed his face into a disbelieving frown. "You can't be serious, Hoffen. This guy is handing you a load of chicken shit. Don't fall for it."

At that moment, something clicked. I looked around the table. I'd missed a detail, but now it was becoming clear.

"Petersburg Station is the carrot," I said.

The people around the table were the clues I'd been ignoring. Merrie and Amon had been Ophir residents and the first to take up residence on the asteroid I'd renamed Petersburg Station, in memory of my dad. They had helped restart the mining and smelting operations. Ortel Licht had been put in charge of all ore-related services. The only person missing was Katherine LeGrande, Mom's partner.

"During the Kroerak conflict, Petersburg Station was commandeered by Mars Protectorate," Munay said.

"There it is," I said. "You might have led with that and saved us all a bunch of time."

Munay pushed on without looking up. "We believe Petersburg Station, especially considering the upgrades that were made by our great nation, is of considerable value. The station could help significantly in effecting repairs of *Intrepid*."

"What upgrades?"

"An anonymous donor paid to install considerable defensive capabilities into the station. There is a full medical bay, including a grade three medical tank. We also fully integrated the portable armor repair platforms you purchased from Freedom Station into two new repair bays," he said.

"We even upgraded the pod-ball court. It's regulation," Ortel said, unable to contain himself. "It's frap."

"Frap?" I asked. My AI immediately displayed that frap was slang for good.

"Just to be clear. You'll trade me my own asteroid station for a loose agreement that I'll come looking for you if you get into trouble? I don't feel like I'm getting the whole story."

"I can't say anything more," Munay said.

"The station affects you, Mom. What would you want me to do?"

"The station is my home, Liam," she said. "It's my responsibility to look after the people on it."

"Mom, Mars Protectorate is using you to leverage me."

"That's not fair, Hoffen," Munay said.

"It's completely fair, Greg," Mom replied. "Liam, do what you need. We'll figure this out."

"Let's get it on the table, Mom. What about you and Munay?" I asked. "Are you willing to leave him behind?"

"I have told you before. Greg and I are friends. If anything, our dealings here have pointed out deficiencies in our relationship." Her words were frosty and I caught a rising blush on Munay.

"Loose Nuts, want to give me a vote?" I looked from Nick to Tabby to Ada and Marny.

Instead of answering, I saw green ready-check pings on my HUD. None of them wanted to answer out loud, but they all seemed to think it was workable.

"We're privateers, Munay. If you want my word, you'll provide full IP for every component of *Intrepid*, including frame and armor. If I want to make a fleet of them, then so be it. And I want zero spyware on my ship."

"Done." Munay agreed so quickly that I wondered what else I should have asked for.

"Fine. We're your backup and will come to your aid if called. What am I missing?" I looked to Nick.

"Commander Munay doesn't have the leverage he's implying," Nick said. "This deal has Anino's fingerprints all over it."

"You can't possibly know that," Munay spluttered.

Mom pursed her lips in disapproval but held in whatever she intended to say.

"Doesn't matter. Sterra knows we'll chase down the Kroerak with our last breath," I said, tipping my glass to the flustered officer. "To be of use to you, the asteroid will have to be dragged to this side of the gate. Nick, I imagine you have an idea where to place Petersburg Station?"

"I do. There's a group of celestial objects — technically moons — that orbit Zuri. I used the criteria Big Pete used when we analyzed the Descartes asteroid belt survey in the Tipperary System. I recommend we set the station in geo-sync with Zuri and seed mining missions in the Kafida cluster."

"Kafida cluster? I thought you were looking at moons."

"The Kafida cluster is a moon that had a collision at some point in its history. It's composed of ten large asteroids locked together in orbit over Zuri. Kafida asteroids show significant iron on the surface. It looks ideal. We'd just need to recruit miners."

"Would the Abasi allow that?" Tabby asked.

"Per Abasi law, the claims on those moons have expired," Nick said. "The process for filing a claim isn't difficult. We just need to provide a survey of the claim we want to make and then prove we have an ongoing, commercial presence. There isn't even an approval process unless we intersect with another claim and then we move into arbitration."

"When do you leave, Munay?" I asked.

"Contracts have been sent," he said. "We'll make way at your earliest convenience. I formally request an escort out of the system."

"Commander Munay and anyone who will be traveling back with the commander, I'd request that you retire. I'd like time to confer with my family and friends," I said.

"That is acceptable," Munay said, standing.

Mom stood and pulled him into a hug. "Good luck, Greg. For what it's worth, I understand the choices you've made."

Stiffly, he returned her hug and gave us all a quick nod before walking out. He was followed by his engineer and one other lieutenant who hadn't spoken the entire afternoon.

"Do you have anything stronger to drink, Patty?" I asked.

"We sure do," she said. "I wonder if I could get a couple of these strapping young lads to help me."

The four youngest, Ortel, Priloe, Milenette, and Demetria, all jumped at the chance to move and followed her into the back.

"I've been saving these," Patty said as they returned more quickly than I'd expected. She and the kids were carrying oddly shaped bottles. "It's the last of a batch of sparkling wine we've been slowly doling out. Feels like today is the right day for it."

She passed out the liquor and we poured drinks.

"What a day," I said, raising my glass. "I can't fathom adding one more thing to it."

"DID you pay Hagarsons for the soiree?" I asked Nick. We were back at our shared bungalow. Mom and the group from Ophir had been put up in town by Hog late the previous night. Even with the patch that removed the effects of alcohol, I felt sluggish.

"Hog didn't want anything. He's worried we're broke after losing that deal to Bakira Corporation. I told him we were in good shape," Nick said. "And soiree? Are you going French on me?"

"We are out of funds, aren't we?" I asked.

"We have a lot invested in those stevedore parts," he said. "Yeah. Our liquidity is at an all-time low. I've taken out a short-term note from a Manetra bank."

"Any chance Goboble is going to pick up that note too?" I asked. I'd been surprised at how easily Goboble had transferred our failed bond and didn't want to repeat past errors.

"No, we put collateral up against the note." Nick squirmed uneasily in his chair as he said it and I knew I was in for something bad. "*Fleet Afoot* was collateral. I contacted the bank this morning and they've agreed to transfer the note's collateral assignment to *Intrepid*."

"How big of a note?"

"Two hundred twenty thousand credits," Nick said. "Before you ask, we have twenty-three thousand credits. And in ten days we have a twenty thousand credit payment due."

"Before or after Bakira pays the order cancellation fee?"

"They've paid," Nick said. He shook his head as he breathed hard out loud. "I know what you're thinking. I overstepped and risked the whole company. You're right. I thought I had this. The technology is superior in every possible way to what they're using right now. It was a slam dunk."

I laughed humorously. "It's reassuring, you know."

"Reassuring?" Nick asked.

"I'm always the one risking everything and getting our shite blown up."

"I don't find this reassuring. What I really need is ten million in credits and six months."

"Doubling down," I coughed, choking on my synth coffee. "You really are taking one from the Hoffen school of crazy. What in galactic commerce do you need with ten million credits?"

Nick tapped the side of his head and projected a scene on the wall. It was an overhead of our current location complete with Nick's workshop, our bungalow, the road that ran in front, and the ships parked in the field directly across.

"The field is perfect for a manufacturing plant," Nick said, sweeping his hand across the projection. As he did, the ships disappeared and in their place a hundred-meter square, steel-framed warehouse was rapidly assembled. "We could buy steel and glass from Petersburg Station and hire construction work from York."

"We already have parts we can't sell," I said.

"Eff the parts," Nick said, gesturing again. As he did, manufacturing stations popped up on the floor, filling only a small section. "It would be slow at first, ten million doesn't buy as much as you think, but we could manufacture the entire stevedore bot. Think about it — when you make trade deals, who are you doing business with?"

"Everyone and no one in particular," I said. "Shipping and trading is all about finding people who either need something transported or something located."

"But those people all have one thing in common. They need to load and unload material from transports. The fact is, you're in contact with my target market every time you pick up or drop off goods."

"They'll have established contracts with equipment suppliers," I said. "They're not going to want to buy from us."

"They will when they see how a real stevedore bot works," Nick said. "The current state-of-the-art around here takes four to five times as long to load and unload. For a big shipper, this is real savings. At a minimum, we create demand and get our foot back in the door at places like Bakira."

"What are you boys talking about?" Marny asked as she joined us, dabbing at the back of her neck with a towel.

I pointed at Nick's manufacturing plant plans on the wall, which earned me an understanding smile.

"Good run?" Nick asked.

"Weightlifting this morning. I let Tabbs go for a run with Munay's crew," Marny replied. "Sure was great seeing everyone last night, don't you think?"

"Talk about a day full of surprises," I said. "I'd have thought you'd jump at the chance to go out with Tabby."

"Too much blind *Ooh-rah* in that group," Marny said. "With Munay twisting the knife on us, I just didn't have interest."

"Tabbs wanted to give Mom a heads-up about the Kroerak spawn in the region. None of the folks who came in from Ophir have been inoculated and their scent will draw in the hatchlings."

"They should stay in town behind the wall until they're acclimated," Marny said. "I'll talk to Hog."

"Have you surveyed *Tuuq*?" I asked, changing the subject.

"No," Nick answered. "What are you thinking?"

"We need cash. We could sell *Tuuq*. Isn't that the point of a prize?"

"Plenty of folks who need something to do. I'll talk to Merrie and Amon," Nick said.

"She's worth two hundred thousand and that would give us some breathing room," I said. "I'll work on a buyer. Also, I contacted Goboble about our exchange of *Fleet Afoot* for the grav-suits in Azima. We're going to run over there this afternoon."

Marny planted her feet. "Goboble will bring a crew. We'll have to go in strong."

"I'm thinking Ada follows *Fleet Afoot* with *Tuuq* for backup."

"We'll put my little man here on the *Tuuq's* turret, Ada in the pilot's chair, and I'll hang out in the cargo hold in a Popeye as backup."

Of course, a Popeye is just slang for the three mechanized infantry suits we'd brought with us from home.

"What do you think about recruiting Sendrei?"

"For what?"

"He's good in a pinch. What if Tabby doubled up in a Popeye and Sendrei came with me for the hand-off?"

"He's seen his share of tough situations. If he's in, I'd say that's a solid plan."

The perimeter alert for the bungalow chimed and I jumped off the couch. The tone indicated friendlies so I skipped the blaster rifle and pushed through the front door.

On the lawn stood Tabby, Sendrei, Munay and five uniformed Mars Protectorate officers. Except for Tabby, they were all expelling long, frosty vapor clouds as they fought to catch their breath. Tabby gave me a quick smile and a waggle of her eyebrows.

"Good morning, Commander. Did you enjoy the scenery on your jog?" I asked.

"You call this place civilized, Hoffen?" he puffed. I noticed he was holding a blaster pistol in his hand.

"It's a little rough around the edges, but I like it."

"I believe the commander wasn't impressed with the local fauna," Tabby said. "We collected quite a pile of hatchlings this morning and left 'em up the road next to Hogback trail."

"Didn't the Navy inoculate all of its officers during the war?" I asked.

"We are," Munay answered.

I looked to Sendrei, who was not obviously armed, but had the telltale stains of Kroerak hatchling blood on his vac-suit. "How about you, Sendrei? I don't suppose anyone thought to inoculate the good folks from Ophir before running through the mountains?"

"No inoculation, but I found the morning's activities to be refreshing," Sendrei said, his voice calm as ever. "While I do not enjoy the idea of killing, I will admit I harbor resentment toward that species as a whole. I am at peace with my actions."

I nodded. There wasn't much to say. Sendrei had watched the Kroerak slaughter many of his friends and family as if they were livestock.

"You knew this would happen, Masters?" Munay asked.

"I told you to bring weapons," she answered. "It all worked out."

"Indeed," Munay answered, frowning. I suspected bad things would have already been meted out to Tabby had she been in his chain of command. "Mr. Hoffen, if you are amenable, we have supplies to offload and then we will be on our way."

The sound of a ship passing overhead using only arc-jets caught my attention as the M-Pro sloop slowly dropped from the sky and settled next to *Intrepid*. She landed such that the cargo bays were directly adjacent.

"Agreed, Commander. I'll be along in a moment," I said and turned to Sendrei. "Flaer and the kids are in town?"

"That is correct. Tabitha was very clear about the danger posed to visitors," he said. "She also assured us we were adequately protected within town walls."

"I suspect that's why Tabby ran you around the mountain this morning. She was using you to flush the bugs out. How many did you run into?"

"A total of eight. They attacked in small, unorganized groups — nothing like mature warriors. I almost felt pity for them."

"Don't be surprised if chili is on the lunch menu today," I said, as we walked across the road and into the field where the ships rested. "I hope you don't have a sensitive stomach."

"I have heard of selich root," he said. "I particularly enjoy spicy foods — as does Flaer."

"Were you and Flaer together while on Cradle?" I asked. "I don't recall."

"Flaer was from a different village and we met after settling on Ophir. She brings me joy that I thought I had lost forever," he said.

I patted the big man on the back and smiled. "She has a passion for life, Sendrei. The fiery ones are always the best."

"Your Tabby is an accomplished warrior," he said. "I had not realized this when our paths crossed before. I feel she would provide a challenge if we were to spar. I find this intriguing."

"Don't take this the wrong way, but do you really think you could stand up to her?" I asked. "I'd be careful saying that in front of her."

"You are serious?" Sendrei asked. "Or are you making a joke? I admit to having lost some of my ability to understand humor."

"Oh, he's serious, big man," Tabby said, joining in. "And you'd best prepare your A-Game if you're going to talk smack."

"I wasn't looking to be provocative," Sendrei said, his face flushing with embarrassment. "I was impressed with your speed and conditioning this morning and intended a compliment."

"Tabbs is used to being top-dog around here," I explained.

"I look forward to training with you, Tabby," Sendrei placed his hands together as if praying and bowed slightly to her.

Instead of smarting off, she echoed his gesture, including the bow. "I'll admit, I'm curious about your moves this morning. Is that a specific form or just something you picked up?"

"Before I was captured by Kroerak, I was North American armed forces martial arts champion three years running. My skills are rusty, but I have been working on conditioning my body. The Kroerak are not human form, so many of my skills must be adapted when engaging their unique physiology. This morning was primarily Tae Kwon Do as it allowed me to maintain distance and to control more than one target."

"We'll be disembarking shortly," Munay interrupted, returning from overseeing the transfer of supplies from *Gaylon Brighton* to *Intrepid.*

Over his shoulder, I saw Mom exit the sloop's hold and approach. While I hadn't seen her arrive, I wasn't surprised she wanted to oversee the transfer of the Ophir group's belongings. Unexpectedly, she handed me a writing pad which had a contract loaded on it.

"What's this?"

"Contract for the transfer of Petersburg Station to Loose Nuts Corporation," Mom said.

I nodded at the prudent precaution. I took the pad and waited a moment for my AI to process the legalese. A positive chime sounded, prompting me to sign and hand it to Munay for his signature.

Munay looked skeptically at the pad. "Son, that rock has been in transit for almost twenty days. I don't believe a contract will change much. M-Pro would have no ability to maintain their claim on that rock once TransLoc is shut down."

"Why you dirty dog," I said, looking from Munay to Mom. "Just like Nick said — you had no control over what was being done with Petersburg Station."

"It was beneficial that you believed I did," he said.

"Honor in all things," Sendrei said quietly, as if to himself. It was a phrase I'd heard Marny use more than once.

"Excuse me, Lieutenant?" Munay challenged, using Sendrei's old Naval rank.

Sendrei nodded and smiled tightly.

"Tell me, Commander," I said. "If I hadn't agreed to your deal, what would you have done?"

He signed the contract. A flurry of details scrolled across my HUD, including acknowledgement of Petersburg Station and a release of claim on *Intrepid* by the Navy.

"Good luck to you, Captain." Munay thrust his hand forward as he held my gaze and ignored my question. "On behalf of a grateful nation, I extend my warmest thanks to you and your crew."

Chapter 4

TWISTED

"Can you believe that guy?" I asked from the port-side pilot's chair in *Tuuq's* cockpit. I'd brought Tabby, Sendrei and Mom along, mostly because they'd been close by when it was time to leave.

I had to accelerate hard to keep pace with the *Gaylon Brighton's* ascent from Zuri's surface. I'd agreed to accompany Munay out of orbit, but it didn't look like his pilot considered that particularly valuable.

"He underestimated you, but his heart is in the right place," Mom said. "Greg is very much a patriot."

I chuffed a harsh laugh. "That's an optimistic view. He was prepared to seize *Intrepid*."

"Mars Protectorate and the Earth governments are scrambling in light of heavy military losses. After the war ended, Greg refused to return control of Petersburg station and I thought I'd made a critical mistake in not following you to Zuri. You have Admiral Sterra to thank for Greg being as civil as he was. He lobbied to bring multiple ships and even more troops so they could retrieve *Intrepid*."

"Mars acknowledged our ownership of *Intrepid* well before the war," I said.

"People find ways to justify their behavior, Liam. The war brought out both the best and the worst in people."

"You liked him," I said. "You know, I'd have been okay with that."

She reached across the aisle that separated us and laid her hand on my forearm. "Your father casts a long shadow, Liam. There was a time I might have considered Greg. He was enjoyable to talk with and share dinners with, but his ambition is greater than his capacity for love. I am too old to compete for a man's affection."

"I'm glad you joined us," I said. "This place is wide open for opportunity. It's like we're back in the days of the wild west from those old vids I used to watch."

Mom's laugh caused me to smile. "I hear House Mshindi gave you a shiny new deputy badge."

Our business might be on the edge of ruin, but there was something about having Mom's approval that made me feel like everything was going to be just fine.

"It'll be interesting to see how that works out," I said as we broke through the upper atmosphere. Our sensors showed there were no ships within range. "The Abasi government is different from Sol governments. Houses claim what they control. The central government cedes power to those houses and only fills in where there are gaps."

"What house controls Zuri?"

"The big four houses all have claims," I said. "But they're limited to smaller regions. York and Azima are outside of house control and fall under the general government. Manetra is the biggest city and that falls under House Gundi. Bottom line is there's not much oversight."

"It is that type of loose control which allows for thugs like Goboble to rise up," she said.

"And make for a lot of opportunity for folks like us."

"You've a lot of your dad in you, Liam Hoffen. Where other people saw danger, he only saw opportunity."

"Incoming hail."

"This is *Tuuq*, go ahead," I replied.

Commander Munay's voice came over the comm. "Captain Hoffen. Silver. I wish you all the best."

"Safe travels, Commander. Pass along my best wishes to Admiral Sterra if you cross paths," I said.

"Godspeed, Greg," Mom said.

"Munay out." Munay closed the comm channel.

I pointed through the armor glass of the cockpit. "There they go." Along the path where the sloop had been accelerating slowly away from us, we could see only a faint orange trail that quickly faded.

"Welcome to Dwingeloo, Mom," I said.

"Thank you, Liam."

"Sendrei, what do you think of our little ship?" I asked. While we were close enough for him to hear me, the AI chose to pipe my voice back to the gunnery station where he sat.

"I am surprised at how limited Pogona technology is. There is much that could be improved, but the ship is quite workable. How offensive would it be if I were to unlimber the turrets?"

"*Grant Sendrei Buhari full weapons control,*" I directed *Tuuq.* "You have control. Tabby, you want to toss out some targets? You should try to keep in mind he was talking trash about you earlier."

Tabby guffawed at my undisguised attempt to cause trouble. "You're a bad man, Hoffen." She used the distraction of the conversation to launch three melon-sized targets all on different trajectories and at different speeds.

Tuuq responded with a staccato *thwup-thwup-thwup* as her turrets spun and chased down each target in turn. The period between each blaster bolt was shorter than *Intrepid's* turrets.

"Too easy, small one," he said. "You would not respect me if I were to miss those."

"You really are a trash talker," Tabby said, her interest piqued. "Put some stick to it, Hoffen. Let's give him something to work for."

"Mom, you feel like running a ghost attack against *Tuuq?*"

Soft amber lights pulsed around the ceiling, simulating the general quarters warning that showed in red when we were under attack. I resisted the urge to look out the cockpit; I knew the attacking ships on the forward vid-screen weren't really there.

Mom's job was more difficult than mine, as she had to ignore everything she was feeling and seeing as a passenger on *Tuuq*. She flew the ghost ships while relying entirely on information within her HUD.

Apparently, Mom thought we were most vulnerable to light ships, as a squadron of darts launched from the sloop that had appeared only ten kilometers from our position. The squadron split into two attack wings and raced at us while the frigate slowly turned.

"Now, prepare for combat burn." My announcement required everyone aboard ship to acknowledge the order once they were safely strapped in. Green acknowledgements checked off on my HUD and I tipped the stick and accelerated hard on an angle that would keep both attack wings to one side.

"We're taking fire," Tabby said. "Armor is holding."

The smaller ships were extremely fast and I pushed the sluggish *Tuuq* to evade their lines of fire. Apparently, I wasn't perfect in my execution, as the AI was recording hits along our belly on portside.

Thwuppity-thwup-thwup-thwup. The energy gauge showed the batteries dipping as Sendrei responded. I would love to have paid attention to his accuracy, but Mom was really handing it out and I had to focus to work around the smaller craft. Mom could multi-task better than I could, but I was annoyed at how easily she used the small ships to herd me toward the larger sloop.

"Two down," Tabby exclaimed excitedly. "Nice shooting!"

I flipped *Tuuq* end for end just as we grazed the frigate's firing range. I knew Mom wouldn't be able to resist and wondered if Sendrei would see the opportunity. Neither of them disappointed me as a neat line leapt from *Tuuq's* turret at just the moment the sloop opened fire with two of its own turrets.

It's not like ordnance becomes useless when it hits optimum range. The range is much more about aim than effective punch, although in the case of blaster bolts, it's a little of both. My HUD lit up the tail of *Tuuq* as imaginary bolts struck the stern. I attempted to expand the distance between the smaller ship I sailed and the bigger sloop.

Mom pressed her advantage and brought her fighters in close, laying into us with fire. One by one Sendrei popped them off us, but damage to *Tuuq* mounted. Finally, we pulled far enough away from the phantom sloop that I gained full maneuverability. Arcing to the side, I snapped around unexpectedly. The g-forces within the cabin pushed me against my flight harness and I fought to keep my wits about me as I raced back toward the pursuing fighters. In quick succession, Sendrei destroyed the remaining fighters.

"I think we'll leave that sloop alone," I said, pulling back on the throttle. We were a third the size of our heavy opponent and I'd need missiles to end the match.

"I'm claiming mother abuse," Mom said, rubbing where the combat harness had dug into her shoulders.

"Your reputation as pilots are well earned, Captains Hoffen," Sendrei said.

"Thanks," I laughed. "How'd he do, Tabbs?"

"High forties," Tabby said. "No recorded lost opportunities. Marny will want to see this."

"The controls are surprisingly responsive. It took a few moments to get used to the mechanical nature of their action," Sendrei said. "It is a joy to work again with this equipment. I have missed being in the chair."

I swung *Tuuq* around. Zuri filled the view screen in front of us and I set a navigation plan back to York. "I was hoping to talk to you about that."

"I can't believe you're recruiting my people already." Mom's voice conveyed that she wasn't entirely serious, but she wasn't completely joking either.

"Technically, I think Munay transferred the station to Loose Nuts," I said, raising my eyebrow in mock challenge.

"And you are my son," she said, as if that was the end of the matter.

Tabby's laughter rang through the bridge. "I'm not sure you want

68

JAMIE MCFARLANE

to open this can of worms, Liam. Even I know better than to get on the wrong side of Mrs. H."

"I am quite satisfied with my position on Petersburg Station," Sendrei said, unconvincingly.

"Oh Sendrei, please don't listen to our family squabble," Mom said. "There are many ways to fill the security role on Petersburg. I just know if I don't lay down the law with my boy, he'll make decisions without my approval."

"Is this something you would consider, Mrs. Hoffen?" he asked.

"I see no reason to stand in your way," Mom said. "I'm confident we can work out security once the station arrives."

"I would very much like to join the Loose Nuts crew again," Sendrei said. "I will need to talk with Flaer, though."

I slowed our descent through Zuri's atmosphere using the gravity systems. Munay's arrival had been punctuated by sonic booms which I could avoid by decelerating beneath the speed of sound before the sonic waves reached York.

"You know," Mom began. We jiggled and bumped as *Tuuq*'s anemic gravity and inertial systems attempted to adjust to the atmosphere. "Sometimes men and women get married after they've been engaged."

"Really? You're starting that up already?" I asked.

"Well, I'd like to be a grandmother someday," she said.

Tabby coughed. "No way."

"Mom, can you take the helm?"

"Copy that. I have the helm," Mom said, smirking.

I turned and snaked my hand out around Tabby's narrow waist, pulling her toward me. "Baby doll, do you have something you want to tell me? Don't you want to get married and have five kids like the Lichts?"

"Married, yes. Babies, absolutely not. I'm not ready for that," she said, furiously. "My family is so screwed up, I don't think I'll ever be ready for those."

"Damn," Mom said.

"I just. Well. Frak. Why do you have to be so difficult, Hoffen?" Tabby asked.

"You're my girl, Tabbs. I promise that when you are ready, you'll be a great mom," I said.

"You're full of crap, Hoffen."

I pulled her over on top of me and we wrestled for a few minutes while Mom set *Tuuq* down next to *Fleet Afoot*.

"Sendrei, are you up for another trip today?" I asked.

"I promised Flaer I would share midday meal with her."

"We're going to Azima, right?" Tabby said. "We should take them to Koosha's. Ada wanted to go to the bazaar to find fabric for a bed cover she has in mind."

"We're dropping off *Fleet Afoot*, but that shouldn't take long," I said. "You want to go, Mom?"

"Not today," she said. "I have lessons with the kids this afternoon and Patty roped me in to visiting York's school tomorrow. I'd like to do a little prep work."

"Where are you staying?"

She flicked an address to me. "I should have told you. Hog offered me and the kids a home on Fanta Blossom Street."

"Well, bilge water. He put us on the other side of Quail Hill, but he gives you a house?" I said.

"Patty thinks Hog's overprotective because of the children. They've had a few taken by Kroerak spawn over the years. If it makes you feel any better, he offered Merrie and Amon and Sendrei and Flaer homes even further out than yours. But when I told him we'd soon be in orbit, he said he could find in-town accommodations until then."

One thing about sailing in the *Tuuq* was that every change made by the pilot was obvious to everyone on board, and landing was no different. We all jostled to the side as the ship's antiquated gravity system released and Zuri's natural gravity took over.

"I'll run Silver and Sendrei into town and if Flaer wants to go to Azima I'll bring 'em back," Tabby said, pushing off my lap. "You get *Fleet Afoot* ready to sail. Make sure you unload the extra fuel and O2."

"Nick already removed all but one turret," I said.

"That's my boy."

The sound of whirring activators alerted me to the presence of Popeyes as I stepped through the starboard pressure barrier and slid down the ladder's rails to the grassy meadow.

"Any issues, Cap?" Marny asked, opening the armor glass face-plate of her mechanized suit.

"She's sloppy," I said. "Not complaining; just takes a little focus to accept the slow system responses. It's kind of fun after you get used to it, though."

"Tabby sent me Sendrei's weapon performance report," Marny said.

The conversation felt awkward, given Sendrei was climbing out of the ship just as she said it.

"What's your read on my skill, Sergeant Bertrand?" Sendrei asked, looking sincerely to Marny. With her mechanized suit on, Marny stood a meter taller than both of us.

"I saw better from you when we sailed *Intrepid*," she said. "It looks like you're more comfortable with the capabilities of larger ships."

"That's my assessment as well, although I'm not partial to excuses," he said.

"You'd be hard pressed to find another pilot who sails like our Cap," Marny said. "Don't beat yourself up. Truth is, I don't think I could score seventies consistently under combat conditions."

"This mean you're signing off on Sendrei in a gunner's seat?" I asked.

"Oh, Jupiter's moons, yes," Marny chortled. "Maybe I'll even get a break once in a while."

"You get the irony, right Marny?" I asked.

"I do not, Cap."

"You're talking about taking a break while sitting in a Popeye that I know for a fact was two clicks away not more than a few minutes ago. What kind of break is that?" I asked.

"The kind that doesn't have me floating in space, thinking my best answer is to board a hostile ship."

Tabby pulled up in a carriage she'd fetched from Nick's shop. "Hop in, guys," she said. "Back in about an hour, Love."

"Where's Nick?" I asked as Tabby pulled away and I started toward *Fleet Afoot*. As much as I appreciated the quick little ship, she gave up too much armor and teeth for my liking. I wasn't thrilled about letting her go, but Goboble's claim on our lost bond was legitimate and I looked forward to retrieving our grav-suits.

"York. He's talking with Mez Rigdon," Marny responded.

"Mez? Sounds familiar, who's that?"

"You've seen her. Younger gal. She's always on the wall when we're coming and going. Turns out she's the sheriff," Marny said.

"Dark hair, big smile?" I asked.

"That's her."

"What's going on?"

"Nick is negotiating a patrol schedule with her," Marny said.

"She up for that?"

"Not until Nick offered training and the use of one of the Popeyes."

"That's a lot of firepower."

"She's the one who raised the alarm when Goboble came after us," Marny said. "And the Popeyes sure didn't do us any good sitting in *Fleet Afoot's* hold."

We'd arrived at the little ship and I lowered the cargo elevator. "That's true. It would have been a different conversation if Rigdon had arrived in a Popeye instead of with a bunch of farmers holding pea shooters. As for our trip to Azima today, I think Sendrei and Flaer are thinking of coming along."

"I'll put Flaer in *Tuuq* with Ada and Nick," Marny said.

"What about you and Tabby? I'm not really expecting trouble." As soon as the words left my mouth I knew I was about to be chastised.

"It's not what we expect, Cap," Marny said. "We plan for worse case and are pleased when it doesn't go that way. I want Ada at *Tuuq's* helm with Nick on the turret."

"Are you sitting this one out?" I asked.

"Not hardly. I'll put Sendrei on the ground with you. Tabby and I will be on standby in *Tuuq's* cargo bay just in case Goboble tries something. Otherwise, I'd prefer we avoid an escalation."

"Let me guess. You and Tabby will be in Popeyes?"

Marny grinned. "I wouldn't have it any other way. We should get to work — only have an hour before we depart. What's first?"

"I want to get the kitchen equipment and suit cleaners removed," I said. "If we have time, we'll take linens and any spare supplies." As I spoke, my AI projected a work list onto my HUD. I swiped at the virtual display, splitting the tasks between Marny and myself.

For the next forty-five minutes, we worked in relative quiet as we removed items from *Fleet Afoot* in descending order of ease of removal and value.

"Knock, knock," Ada said. I was lying on my back in the tween deck working on a fitting. "Are you doing what I think you're doing, Liam?"

"I'm not giving that granite-faced turd my septic bugs," I said.

"Get out of there," she reprimanded. "You're better than that."

I closed my toolbox and slid out. "Okay, okay," I conceded.

"How do you want to do this?" she asked, handing me a rag.

As usual, I hadn't escaped from the tween deck unscathed.

"Did Sendrei clear things with Flaer?" I asked.

"Flaer's so cute. Did you know she's never been to a city other than Yishuv?" she said, referring to another failed Belirand mission on the planet Ophir.

"The Yishuv settlement is hardly a city, any more than York is," I said. "I wonder what she'd think of Puskar Stellar?"

"Probably best to break her in slowly. I told her to prepare for hard-core shopping today," Ada said.

I chuckled. I had no doubt of that.

"You're flying *Tuuq.* Just follow *Fleet Afoot* over," I said. "Sendrei and I will handle the exchange and if all goes well, we can get changed and head into town. If things go less than well, Tabby and Marny will be in your hold, hanging out in Popeyes."

"Do you think that's necessary?"

"I hope not, but you know Marny."

"That I do. And she's kept us alive this long so I say we keep listening to her," she said. "Give me a minute to get loaded onto *Tuuq* and we can get going."

I waited for her to clear the ladder that led down to *Fleet Afoot's* empty cargo hold. I climbed to the top deck where I met Tabby coming out of our old quarters.

"What were you doing in the tween deck?" Tabby asked, stepping onto the ladder so she could transfer to *Tuuq*.

I opened the toolbox and held up the septic junction I'd removed.

"Frak, put it away," she said, pulling her arm over her nose and scrunching her face. "You're twisted, Hoffen."

Chapter 5

PUSH COMES TO SHOVE

"Azima ground control, this is Liam Hoffen. We're on approach with two craft and will be landing at 1350 in Green Zone Two," I said. My AI would take care of the necessary translations as it conveyed my message.

Azima, a city of twenty thousand, had been given the designation of 'frontier' by the Confederation of Planets, just as had York. Frontier status basically meant the city could form its own government as long as it upheld a minimum of sentient rights. While Azima had a diverse population, it had been redeveloped by Pogona after the Felio pulled out during the Kroerak invasion of Zuri.

The vid-screen embedded into the forward bulkhead of *Fleet Afoot* showed a lizard-chinned controller who I recalled talking to at least once before. "Be advised, Captain Hoffen, an armed convoy currently occupies Green Zone One. We recommend redirecting to Violet."

The indicated violet landing zone was on the opposite side of town from the green one we were approaching.

Azima's landing zones had originally been built to surround the core of the town. As the population grew, building had continued in circular rings out away from the center, past the landing pads until significantly more of the population lived and worked on the outside rings. The war, however, had caused Azima's population to implode to roughly a twentieth of its former glory. The zones were now considered the outside edge of the town again.

"Understood, control," I said. "I believe we've a meeting with said convoy."

"Received, Captain Hoffen." The Pogona's chin quivered as was common when they felt stress. "In that you're new to the area, you should know that Azima does not interfere in private transactions. Any property destruction will result in an assessed fee to all involved parties. There will be no *proper course* given if hostilities extend to populated regions."

My AI popped up and highlighted the term 'proper course.' It was a legal term, defined by the Confederation of Planets, meaning due process. Ultimately, Azima ground control was telling me they'd shoot first and worry about who was to blame later if negotiations with Goboble turned violent and we endangered city residents.

"Copy that, Azima. Hoffen out," I said and closed the comm.

Though Sendrei and I were alone in *Fleet Afoot*, the entire team was linked on a tactical channel Marny commanded.

"Ada, we're headed in."

"Sounds good, Liam," Ada answered.

I was going to miss *Fleet Afoot*. She was a sluggish flier in atmosphere, given the general state of anti-grav technology in the galaxy, but she was ridiculously fast otherwise. Not even *Intrepid* could catch her outside of the gravity well of a planet.

Tipping the stick over, I dropped to a hundred meters as we approached. Flying at twenty meters per second, *Fleet Afoot* shuddered, struggling to remain aloft as I inspected Goboble's small army.

"Your adversary has added to his forces," Sendrei said. "These are not the actions of one who seeks peace."

Instead of three armed vehicles, Goboble had a total of five — one of which was closer to a tank. If my sensors were right, *Tuuq's* blasters would have difficulty disabling the heavy vehicle if it came to that. A cocky Pogona sat in the open armored hatch and lifted his hand, making a crude gesture. Additionally, twenty heavily armed, uniformed Pogona and Felio stood next to the Stryker that still bore the scars of our last encounter.

"Why does it always come to this?" I muttered and arced *Fleet Afoot* — as gently as she'd allow — over to a cement pad that was separated from Goboble's army by a shallow ravine. If push came to shove, the gap would slow the fighters by a few seconds. It was the best I could come up with.

"Goboble might be sabre rattling," Sendrei said. "I do not know enough about Golenti to tell you how they posture."

I stood and looked around the bridge. We were losing *Fleet Afoot* as the result of choices I'd made — choices I believed contributed to the Kroer-ak's defeat on Earth. I just wasn't a big fan of the payment end of sacrifice. That was just how it worked, as my late dad, Big Pete, often pointed out.

After climbing down the ladder into the cargo hold, I palmed my way through the airlock with Sendrei close behind. We'd worn our Mars Protectorate, Marine-issued armored vac-suits which provided additional armor, not to mention bulked up our profiles. Sendrei, who was at least ten percent larger than Marny, looked unbelievably intimidating. He handed me my favorite heavy blaster pistol and we exited the ship, I imagined for the last time.

"No rifle?" I asked, noticing that Sendrei had also strapped a single heavy blaster pistol to his chest. He had chosen to use my favorite combat holster position which allowed us to simply lift a hand to our chests to free the weapon.

"We will initially negotiate in close quarters," Sendrei said. "A rifle is a strong deterrent in a protracted fight but would be a liability close-in."

"Copy that."

We approached Goboble, next to whom stood his two Felio guards, Hakenti and Charena, and a lanky Pogona.

"This might be trouble," I said.

"What's up, Liam?" Tabby asked over our tactical comm.

"That Pogona next to Goboble is Ferin." Ferin was the Pogona smuggler we'd turned over to the Abasi. I was shocked to see he'd been released.

"How do you know that?" she asked.

"Look through Liam's suit feed," Nick said.

"Oh, frak," she responded.

"Surprised to see you here, Ferin," I said. He wore pistols loosely holstered on each hip. "Are we going to have a problem?"

"Our trouble is for another day," Ferin replied.

"Captain Hoffen!" Chills ran down my spine as I recognized the woman's voice. I turned just in time to see the pirate, Belvakuski, step from the back of the Stryker vehicle.

One of the problems with a holo projector image is that it can't communicate the size of a person. I knew Belvakuski by her reputation as a criminal and a pirate, by her severe face and lizard jowls, and by her deep alto voice. I'd made the mistake of creating a mental image of a large, imposing and powerful female Pogona. Belvakuski, in the flesh, couldn't have been any further from that image and only came up to about chest height.

"What's going on, Goboble?" I said. "This wasn't part of the bargain. You brought an army and now her?"

"Even I have a boss and when last we were together, a human ship fired its weapons and substantially damaged my property," Goboble said. "I will not allow the same today."

"Your memory is short, Goboble," I said. "You were attempting to coerce me into an unfavorable deal when your henchmen opened fire."

"I do not deny your assessment. I will not be disadvantaged this day."

"Negotiation is done. This is just a drop-off," I said. "Bring out our suits so I can inspect them, and we'll be on our way."

"You made no provision for inspection," he said.

"Even in the Dwingeloo galaxy, inspection of goods before delivery is implied, unless you'd like us to drop a few blaster rounds through *Fleet Afoot*, pre-delivery."

Belvakuski laughed aloud and stepped around the guard. "Plenty of vigor in this one. Finish the deal, Goboble."

Goboble was hard to read as his face rarely changed affect. I'd learned to look for other tells such as finger twitches, foot shuffling, and nervous coughing. As far as I could tell, Goboble had no discernable signs of nervousness or deceit.

"Bring the suits," he demanded, without turning.

Two Felio in loose armored suits broke from the group that stood watching us uneasily. When the two returned, they carried a crate between them that contained what looked like our grav-suits. A pungent smell struck me as the crate was set down between Goboble and Ferin.

"Now you will transfer control of the ship," Ferin said.

"What have you done to our suits?" I asked.

"They are in perfect working order," he said.

"I'll inspect them."

He gestured to the crate.

I reached for the first suit and my gloved hand met a charged field, which my suit easily grounded. My AI displayed a reading of one hundred thousand volts at a moderate amperage. If I'd touched the field with bare hands, it might have killed me.

It occurred to me that Goboble might be trying to test our technology. The armor worn by his thugs was nothing like the high-tech vac-suits Sendrei and I wore, but rather armor pieces laid over ordinary clothing.

I could just pick up on the sound of a recharging capacitor.

"Liam?" Sendrei asked, placing his hand on the butt of his pistol.

"We're fine, Sendrei," I said. "Must have been a small static buildup."

Tabby harrumphed through tactical comm. "Didn't look so small to me."

I pulled the first suit from the pile. It was covered with a smelly liquid that rolled off onto the suit beneath. The material was heavier that it should have been and I realized the suit was holding fluid, so I turned it upside down and drained it. I choked back a gag as I realized the liquid was waste from the Pogona or Felio.

"*Run diagnostic.*" My HUD showed the results. The suit I was holding and the others in the crate were in good working order, albeit heavily soiled.

"A signature," Ferin said, once again handing the thick tablet to me.

I took the tablet and ran my contract subroutine against the provided, alien contract. It was the contract we'd originally provided him — with a few gotchas added, including not dissolving our partnership.

"I'm disappointed, Goboble," I said. "You originally impressed me as a professional. Maybe this crap works when you're doing business with others, but not me. This is not the contract we agreed on." I pulled a pad from a thigh pocket.

I caught a momentary flicker in his eye as I handed across the pad. My AI picked up on my scrutiny and slowly replayed a slight contraction in what amounted to the pupil of his eye. I'd found his tell. I wasn't sure what it indicated, but I'd definitely seen it.

"You have made a mistake, Liam Hoffen," he said. "I control Azima. On my word, my fighters will fire upon you and your large companion. Azima will defend me and mine from your ship's weapons. You will lose everything."

My AI replayed another micro contraction of his pupil.

"Liam?" Sendrei asked, getting edgy.

"Let me make this easy." I tossed his thick reading pad on top of the grav-suits. Upon contact, the pad sparked noisily and caught fire.

In response, his troops adjusted their weapons so they were at the ready.

"Sign our agreement or we can just have this out now. I believe if you were as powerful in Azima as you say, you wouldn't be forced to live twenty kilometers out of town."

"You will risk your life and that of your companion on your estimate?" Goboble asked.

"Sign it, Goboble," Belvakuski said.

Goboble accepted the pad and signed. My HUD showed the transfer of suit controls to me and ship controls to a Goboble, immediately followed by another change as it shifted to a Genteresk interest.

"You may kill them now," Belvakuski said as she turned and jogged off in the direction of *Fleet Afoot*.

"Any last words, Liam Hoffen?" Goboble asked.

I pointed over his shoulder at Tabby and Marny in their Popeyes, falling from *Tuuq* two hundred meters from our position. "You might reconsider your stance."

"Take them," Goboble ordered, a blaster pistol appearing in his hand a moment before he fired.

My torso burned and I was pushed to the side by the impact of Goboble's blaster round. I accepted the force and turned with it, pulling my blaster pistol from its holster and rolling onto the ground. I brought my weapon up as I turned back to where Goboble and Ferin had been standing. The bright orange flash of a long nano-blade wielded by Sendrei, arced across Goboble. Surreally, the stone-like skin split with ease and Goboble's head toppled from his body in slow motion.

Instead of returning fire, Ferin turned from the fight. He ran toward the line of fighters who were moving to get a clear line of fire. Hakenti and Charena both drew swords and engaged with Sendrei. Expertly, he adjusted to the two and sparks flew as his nano-blade deflected their weapons.

I lined up on Hakenti and fired just as two bone-jarring *thawhumps* shook the ground. A pair of grenades had exploded next to the heavy mini-tank, lifting its front end from the ground. Sendrei, Hakenti and Charena were separated as a wave of debris swept out from the explosions. My suit hardened against chunks of rock and metal and my ears rang from the blast wave that impacted just before my suit's helmet closed.

Without missing a beat, Sendrei broke from his fight with the twin Felio. Incomprehensibly, he turned and rushed toward the mini-tank, jumping atop it. His rush toward the enemy caught those fighters who were still on their feet off-guard. Their stunned condition wouldn't last, so I laid down covering fire with my blaster pistol.

I was disappointed to realize the Felio armor I'd dismissed earlier as crude, was actually quite cleverly constructed. It had some property that drew blaster rounds away from the seams of the armor and allowed the thick plates to absorb the shot. I was, however, rewarded with a loud *pa-ting* — almost the sound of a hammer on steel — as my round found its home. The Felio I'd struck stumbled backward, but it was clear I'd done no permanent damage.

The mini-tank Sendrei now stood atop, spun to orient on the Popeyes, the soldiers inside having recovered from the grenade blasts. Sendrei seemed to have a crazy strategy. Tabby and Marny couldn't engage the tank while he was on top and its rounds were certainly big enough to damage the mechanized suits if it successfully landed a shot with its thirty-millimeter turret.

I felt useless as I fired my heavy blaster. Time and time again the rounds were absorbed by the strange armor on Goboble's thugs. Fortunately, the constant barrage from Tabby and Marny's Popeyes kept them from turning on me. Unlike my pistol rounds, the Popeye's ammo had no trouble penetrating the armor. Squishies were dropping quickly.

Thud-thud-thud. Tuuq's turret lined up on one of the patrol vehicles sitting outside the action. A half dozen shots later, it exploded and *Tuuq* spun to line up on another vehicle.

A well-aimed round from the tank caught Tabby's shoulder and she was lifted and spun around, disappearing into the crowd of troops. My attention was forced away as small-arms fire erupted from the tank and Sendrei leapt off and to the side. The Pogona who'd greeted us when we first arrived clawed at the hatch opening, trying desperately to get out of the vehicle. He was quickly swallowed by a cylinder of smoke and flame that erupted from within the still open hatch.

"*Armistice has been requested by Ferin of Enalti,*" my AI intoned.

"Accept. Cease Fire! Cease Fire!" I called over the tactical channel.

As quickly as it started, the shooting stopped. I pulled myself up from the ground and inspected the round I'd taken to my abdomen. The armored vac-suit had absorbed most of the blaster's impact, but I still had a small amount of bleeding. I'd have a fantastic bruise to show for my troubles.

Uneasily, Goboble's troops held their weapons ready and looked to Ferin. The weaselly Pogona waved his hands up and down to calm the tensions.

Someone whined loudly. "He killed Goboble."

I wasn't immediately able to make out who said it, but it became obvious when a Pogona fired, striking me in the shoulder. My suit absorbed much of the shot, as it hit well centered on the chest plate. I was forced to step back, and stumbled to a knee as I fought against the pain.

A dark shape filled my vision as Tabby landed heavily in front of me in her Popeye. More blaster fire ricocheted off her suit, but the armor held easily against the squishy assault.

Fire erupted from Marny's weapon as she stomped into the midst of Goboble's remaining troops. Without mercy, she fired into the crowd and swung her great arms at those who attempted to close in on her, flinging them into the nearby field.

Finally, the firing ceased and the remaining half dozen of Goboble's thugs raised their arms in defeat.

"Where's Ferin?" I asked, walking up next to where Marny prowled angrily, looking for any who would challenge her. The bloodlust of combat was still coursing through her veins.

I looked down at Goboble's dead body. His head had been trampled in the chaos. It seemed such a waste.

"I am here, Captain Hoffen," Ferin picked himself up from a shallow swale between the empty lots.

"Where are you going?" Tabby growled, bounding quickly after Hakenti and Charena, who were attempting to slink off.

"Did you know this is what Belvakuski planned?" I asked as Ferin approached. I had to give him credit for walking into our group, given how we'd just torn apart the army sent to kill us.

"I suspected, as you should have. I can think of no other reason to bring so much firepower to an exchange," he said. "However, I would not have anticipated this outcome. You are to be commended."

"The rest of you," I said. "Clean up this mess and I'll let you go."

"What about me?" Ferin asked.

"How about you and I call it even?" I said. "I feel I owe you one after we handed you over to the Abasi. I have no quarrel with you."

His eyes narrowed as he considered me. "You are not what I expected, Liam Hoffen. I accept. You and I are even today. Hakenti, Charena and I would take Goboble's body back to his estate."

"Knock yourselves out," I said.

"That sounds unproductive."

"Sorry, Human idiom."

"Not at all what I expected," he said, nodding to Hakenti, who picked up Goboble's body and slung it over his shoulder.

"*Hail Azima ground control,*" I said, watching the three depart with Goboble's parts. My goal was to let Azima know we were done fighting so they wouldn't send an army our way.

"Azima Municipal Control." The Pogona who appeared on my HUD was someone new. The male was older with a heavy, protruding chin and high, arched eyebrows. "Captain Hoffen, per Confederation of Planets articles on Frontier Government, I hereby assess damages in the amount of eighty-five thousand credits. It is my judgement that hostilities could have been avoided and I therefore assess an additional fifty thousand in penalties. This matter is closed."

"Are you saying I owe this?" I asked, incredulously.

"As a primary surviving participant, it is your responsibility to pay damages and penalties," he replied.

"I don't suppose you're in the market for some lightly used military equipment?"

Chapter 6

EVENING PRAYERS

Ada set *Tuuq* on the pavement in the midst of chaos.

"There was no way I thought you'd put us into more debt with a simple exchange," Nick said, shaking his head as he walked down *Tuuq's* still-damaged loading ramp which doubled as her transom when retracted.

"Sendrei, you're hurt." Flaer, with our portable med-kit in hand, hurried down the ramp and raced to where Sendrei was kneeling over a fallen Pogona. I wiped at my bruised side, instinctively trying to find the blood I'd felt running down the inside of my suit. One of the advantages of the armored suits was that they sealed almost immediately if breached. I came up with nothing.

Nick saw my reaction and chuckled. "Good luck competing with Sendrei on that. How bad is it?"

"I'll live. What do you suppose we're supposed to do with the bodies?" I asked. I was a little off-put with just how easily Azima washed their hands of everything but assessing fees.

"Azima has a morgue," Nick said. "If we drop them off, it's two-fifty a body. They'll make next-of-kin notifications."

"What if they pick up?"

"Five hundred. And before you ask, there's no bulk discount. They did say they'd send a guy out with bags, no additional charge."

"How did we get to this point in our lives?" I asked. We'd lined up the dead on the concrete pad. Flaer and Sendrei were tending to the remaining who were too injured to slink off.

"Why would Goboble pull that trigger?" Nick asked. "He had to see it would be a bloodbath."

"Belvakuski put him up to it. That crate was rigged with enough voltage to put me on my ass three times over. The contract he tried to get me to sign had us staying in business together. He also upped his percentage of ownership to seventy-five percent. And what in Neptune's seas is Ferin doing out of jail? I thought he was a wanted criminal. He sure didn't act like one of Goboble's henchmen."

"I have a feeling this isn't over," Nick said.

"By my count, we thoroughly wrecked one patrol vehicle and Sendrei toasted that mini-tank." I gestured to the still smoking vehicle. "The personnel carrier looks like it's still up and so are those two four-wheeled, armored vehicles."

"Mini-tank, Stryker and Armored Patrol Craft or APCs. Marines have clever names for everything. You might as well learn them," Marny said, having approached in her Popeye.

"It's worth the extra money to have Azima morgue pick up the bodies." I changed subjects. "I can't deal with that duty right now." While I didn't have moral objections to killing people trying to do the same to me, the finality of it still weighed on me. Once again, we'd been faced with the consequences of resisting corruption and greed, which was apparently not just a human condition.

Nick was about to argue when Marny stepped in. "Cap's right. Let's focus on the living. We've collected more than enough equipment to cover a few thousand for body recovery."

"What in the frak did they get all over these suits?" Tabby asked, carrying in the crate that held our old grav-suits. She set the box down a little too hard and it broke open on the deck of *Tuuq's* hold. The device that had created a high-voltage charge fell out and arced wildly upon contact with the steel deck. Tabby stomped on it, causing a small explosion beneath her heavily armored boot, which threw her back onto her butt in the middle of the smelly suits.

At first, no one spoke. Nick, Marny and I looked at each other wide eyed. Tabby wasn't prissy by any means, but icky wasn't her speed.

"You have to be frakking ... This is just great!" Tabby slammed her hands against the deck, sending a shudder through the ship.

"Liam. I'm registering an explosion in the cargo hold," Ada called over the tactical channel. "And something else; it's like we got hit. Is there something underneath us? I'm not picking up anything but the four of you down there right now."

I raised my eyebrows while exchanging a look with Nick and Marny. It was more than any of us could take and we burst out laughing.

"It's not funny, Ada," Tabby called. "Goboble did something bad to these suits and I fell in it."

Her admission sent us into gales of laughter as a red flush rose in her face.

"You're all horrible," Ada chastised us. "Liam, help her out of that."

"She's in a Popeye," I defended. "I can't even move her."

Marny stepped over to Tabby and held out her hand. Tabby lightly backhanded her offer and popped up. Her foot slid on one of the suits until she reached equilibrium.

"I'll get some bags," I said. I had no doubt it would fall to me to deal with the suits as I was the resident person for all-things-disgusting.

It took an hour to clean up the battle debris. The Stryker we damaged in our first confrontation with Goboble was still operational. The mini-tank rolled fine, but the internal controls were completely fried. We'd have to tow it.

We'd just loaded the burned-out patrol vehicle into *Tuuq's* hold when two vehicles arrived on the main road from Azima.

"Nick James?" a middle-aged Pogona asked, jumping from the cab of a large flat-bed.

"Yup," Nick said.

I walked with him as we greeted the morgue representative. The second Pogona was someone I recognized. We'd dealt with the trader, Mangusi before.

"Sign here," the first man said. I looked over Nick's shoulder at the receipt for picking up the bodies of the fallen. It seemed such a mundane process for the dead. Upon receipt of the signature, he gestured to two younger Pogona who jumped from the back of the truck and unloaded body bags.

We were just about to turn back to our cleanup effort when Mangusi stopped us. "Many pardons, my friends. I am not here in the service of the dead."

"Oh?" I asked.

"It has come to my attention that you have damaged equipment you might be interested in parting with."

"That's fast," I said. "Let me guess. For a significant discount, you'd be interested in helping us unburden ourselves from an unwanted load."

"Fair words, my friend. I am very interested in providing to you a bid that would convenience you greatly," he said.

"You're welcome to look. I'd take thirty-five thousand for the ruined patrol vehicle." I pointed at the four-wheel APC that could comfortably hold five, had a small mounted turret and was sitting in Tuuq's hold. "I'm afraid the others aren't currently for sale, but I'd consider selling the personnel armor. I'll give you a small break due to wear and tear, but realize, we're prepared to clean it and sell it."

"Thirty-five thousand is a good price for an operational vehicle," the Pogona argued. "I believe that value drops significantly after it has been — as you say — ruined."

"You know as well as do I, the four-wheel patrol vehicles are worth upwards of ninety-thousand when new. We won't have any difficulty repairing these and getting twice what I've offered."

"Twenty-five thousand," he said. "And if you include the small arms you've captured, I should be able to convince my brother in Azima Judiciary to drop the punitive fine and reduce the damages to sixty thousand."

I shook my head. Azima's assessment of damage had seemed awfully high and now I understood why. Abuse of power wasn't new to me. The fact remained, under Confederation law, the Azima judiciary was free to make the laws as they saw fit. We were in a bind.

"I think we can work something out," I said. "I'm convinced I could take this gear to Manetra and do better, but I'm all about convenience today. How about you take your pick of the two patrol vehicles and I'll throw in the personnel armor and small arms? You pay us twenty-five thousand in hard currency and convince Azima to give us a pass on damages and fines."

"If you would settle for twenty thousand, I believe we could reach an agreement." Mangusi pulled a pouch from his pocket and handed it to me.

When I opened it, I found it contained the same platinum fingers I'd traded with him so many months ago for replicator parts.

"Have your brother send notification of our release from debt to Azima and we have a deal," I said, pocketing the platinum.

No sooner had the words left my mouth than my HUD pinged with the arrival of a communication — the requested release from Azima.

We'd been swindled, but I was smart enough to know when I'd been outmaneuvered.

"Mangusi, your reputation as a trader remains intact," I said and extended my hand.

"I'm not getting in that thing," Tabby said.

"Just smell it." I handed the clean grav-suit to her. We'd borrowed *Tuuq's* tiny captain's quarters to change in. Fortunately, Nick had the foresight to install a suit cleaner and I'd run both of our suits through. When asked, Nick admitted to being squeamish about wearing grav-suits after they'd been worn by others, even if they had been taken care of properly.

Things had settled down. We'd cleaned the mess off the green landing zone and chained the mini-tank to the Stryker that Goboble had used as his command center.

Sitting on the edge of the bed, I pulled on my own grav-suit. It had taken considerable work on Nick's part to get the suits to recognize Goboble's death and allow us admin control, but he was clever and finally found the right answer.

I'd run all the suits through the suit cleaner three times and set the deodorizer cycle each time. My suit had a slight cinnamon smell, as that was my preference. I caught no whiff of the previously pungent waste smells and sealed myself in.

"*Reinitialize grav-suit with my last backup,*" I ordered.

Someone or something had seriously messed with the suit's systems and the control code was in shambles. While they were mechanically sound, their software was in bad shape. Fortunately, the smart-clothing I wore kept a backup and it would be an easy matter for my AI to reinitialize and restart the systems.

My HUD blanked as the suit's myriad systems rebooted after being asynchronously initialized. A red list of damages appeared on a projected screen to my right. The suit was fully capable of repairing itself and soon items turned from red to yellow and finally to green before disappearing from the list. Other items would take longer to repair and would perhaps require the use of the industrial replicator we'd brought back from Earth.

From the corner of my eye I caught Tabby bending over as she pulled off her suit liner. She was an amazing sight — long legs ending in a perfect bottom. I was a sucker for the sporty, tight black shorts she wore and the lacy camisole that held her perfectly shaped breasts in place. She startled when I reached out and stroked her bare waist with my ungloved hand, then turned and gave me that smile reserved just for me.

"Thanks for coming to my rescue out there," I said.

"I don't like it when things come between us." She pushed me back onto the bed and lightly jumped across to straddle me. "Well, only a very few things." She tugged at my suit's seal and I allowed her to pull it down.

"Did you lock the door?" I asked.

"Live a little." Tabby coaxed my grav-suit to the ground and caught my attention in an entirely new way.

Twenty minutes later, the two of us joined the rest of the crew who were waiting in the shade of *Tuuq's* hull.

"Trouble with the suits, Cap?" Marny asked, winking at Tabby.

I shook my head, sure my cheeks had reddened. "Anyone still interested in a late lunch?"

Tabby slapped my butt and gave it a good squeeze. "I'm famished."

"You kids," Ada said, smiling. It was a funny remark, as she was the youngest aboard.

"I would have expected the attack to have changed our plans," Flaer said. She sat rigidly next to the much larger Sendrei, who'd changed into a normal vac-suit. He looped his large arm around her protectively.

"If you would prefer," Ada said, "I'd be happy to take a group back to York. It *has* been a stressful afternoon."

Flaer looked at the ground demurely. "I would enjoy seeing Azima, but I want to be sensitive to the wishes of the group."

"I've been looking forward to lunch at Koosha's," I said. "It's a quick trip back, though, so I could drop folks off too."

"I wouldn't mind getting back," Nick said. "I'd like to see what can be salvaged between the mini-tank and the Stryker. Can you guys bring back the patrol vehicle and *Tuuq*?"

"We've got it," I said, having already verified we had full control of the vehicles.

"See you at home," Marny said. "And don't split up. There are bound to be those who'd like to make their bones on our group."

Ada nodded. "We'll be careful."

I felt a twinge of guilt at not following Nick and Marny back, but quickly dismissed it. Today had been a significant win. We'd survived against heavy odds, and gained equipment we could sell for a considerable gain.

"Bring us some of those spicy wraps," Marny said. "I feel like I could eat ten of them."

I smiled. Hungry she might be, but I'd only ever successfully finished one. "You want the yellow sauce or the red?"

"Red," she said. "Make sure Flaer and Sendrei get the red, it's made from selich root."

"Good to know," I said. Selich root was, of course, the spicy tuber that caused humans and many other species to become poisonous to Kroerak.

"If we have time, I'll see about a buyer for the vehicles," I said.

"Do you believe there's a possibility that if you sell them locally, they might be used to re-arm those who attacked us today?" Sendrei asked.

"It's possible," I said. "But, they'll rearm one way or another and Azima has a strong market."

"The man, Bishop, was not incorrect when he suggested you are causing an escalation in tensions," Sendrei continued. "I do not say this to place blame, but simply to recognize the shift in power dynamics in our new home. The York militia was substantially under-armed when they came to your aid. It may be to your long term financial benefit to contribute these captured vehicles to York."

"Marny?"

"Mez Rigdon would certainly put them to good use," she said. "Consider this — Goboble significantly underestimated our capabilities today. The Popeyes were an unknown quantity, without which we'd have had a different outcome. We're not sure who will be coming for us next, but it's reasonable to believe they won't make the same mistake."

"Well, frak, we're going to have to sell something," I said, a little frustrated. "I live with a bunch of hoarders."

"We should get going," Ada said, standing. "I don't want to miss the ladies and their fabrics at the bazaar."

"Can we at least eat first?" I complained, following her aft through the translucent pressure barrier. We'd closed the aft cargo bay so we exited the ship through the starboard hatch.

It was only a two kilometer walk to Azima's bazaar. In my mind, the marketplace was a sad parody of the one in the Mars city of Puskar Stellar. That said, it was the very definition of a free market. Most items had no price and haggling was both acceptable and expected.

"Ooh, there it is," Ada said, drawn to a booth we'd stopped at before. An older Pogona woman smiled toothily at her as we approached.

"You make deal today, Ms. Ada Chen?" The woman's voice was high and screechy.

"Zabdali thinks Ada Chen has much wealth," Ada replied. "I might have to settle for just admiring your beautiful weavings." Ada pulled a bright blue fabric from beneath a pile of similarly bright materials and ran her hand beneath to show it off.

"It would make a pretty wrap," Flaer said, stepping up next to Ada. Ada smiled and wrapped it around Flaer's shoulders.

"A beautiful woman, this short human. Why has Zabdali not see her before?"

"Flaer," she identified herself, extending her hand as if to shake.

Zabdali looked at her as if she had grown a second head.

I recognized her predicament. "Hold your hands with palms up."

Flaer did as I said. The old woman smiled and rubbed the backs of her fingers across Flaer's open palms. I'd found it interesting how both gestures had their origin in a demonstration of empty hands.

"Will you be here in a short-span?" Ada asked. A short-span on Zuri was about an hour. "We missed lunch."

"Has Ms. Ada Chen decided to make proper offer to Zabdali today?"

"Zabdali knows my price." Ada smiled knowingly at the old woman. "The question is if Zabdali will part with her fine woven cloth for Ada Chen's more than fair offer."

"Were you to add one stone in ten, I would give you the entire lot," Zabdali countered.

I liked her style; she was upping both price and volume.

"I will add one stone in twenty," Ada countered. "And I only need eight meters, Zabdali."

"What would Zabdali do with only a meter? Take the lot, and I will accept one stone in twenty," she said.

"You have ten meters, Zabdali," Ada said, raising her eyebrows and trying to shame the old woman. The effort was likely a lost cause on the old haggler, who simply smiled innocently, as if she didn't understand why Ada's statement might cause a problem. "Okay, fine, wrap up the lot."

The old woman thrust a thick merchant's pad into Ada's hand before any of us could bat an eye. "Eleven point three meters," she said. "Please sign."

Ada rolled her eyes. She'd wanted eight meters and had finally acquiesced to buy ten only to discover she'd be purchasing slightly more than ten. She signed and tapped the merchant on her slatted nose. "You are a wily one, Zabdali."

"You will have enough to make a covering for the small, red haired one." Zabdali reached out and carefully felt Flaer's hair with her gnarled fingers. "Tell me star child, would you sell your wool to Zabdali?"

Flaer gently reached up and removed Zabdali's hand from her head. "I would not."

"Zabdali means no offense. Yours is a color not seen on Pogona. It would be highly desirable."

"Koosha, Koosha," Tabby chanted. Like me, she was quickly bored with shopping and had even less patience for dickering.

Zabdali quickly wrapped Ada's fabric with a rough, brown covering and handed it to her.

"Remember my offer," she called after Flaer as we left.

We covered the hundred meters to the food vendors past booths, many of which were displaying items we could easily replicate with our least sophisticated Class-A replicators.

"The beautiful Tabitha Masters." We were still ten meters from where Koosha typically set up his cart when a Pogona woman approached. She had alabaster skin and straight white hair that hung to her shoulder blades.

Tabby turned just as the woman reached out to grab her shoulder. If not for the wrinkled skin beneath their necks and slatted nose, Jala, Koosha's wife, was quite beautiful, almost elegant if you could over-look the differences. To be honest, the neck skin really threw me off.

"Jala," Tabby turned to greet the woman. Jala pulled her into an uncomfortably close embrace, which I felt was held too long.

"Liam Hoffen." She acknowledged me by extending her palm and I brushed my fingertips along the surface. "And new friends I have not yet met." She traced the back of her long, reptilian fingers down Sendrei's chest and along Flaer's cheek, then turned to embrace Ada. I wasn't sure if I was being petty, but Jala didn't hold Ada for anywhere near as long as she had Tabby.

"Sendrei and Flaer," Ada explained as Jala released her. "They are of York now."

"And you have brought them to enjoy a meal with Koosha. He will be so honored," she said. "I will go ahead of you so we might prepare."

With that she turned and sliced her way through the throng of people milling around the bazaar. By the time we made it to where Koosha's tables were set up, Jala had arranged a table with six chairs. It was a forgone conclusion that Koosha would join us — as seemed his custom during our other meals with him.

"Will our new friends, Sendrei and Flaer, prefer yellow or red today?" Koosha asked. He made only one type of dish from his cart, but for me it never got old.

"We would try the red," Sendrei answered. "I am concerned that it might be uncomfortable for our untrained palettes."

It took Koosha's translator a moment to communicate what Sendrei had said and he finally smiled. "Ah, yes. Humans have deli-cate tongues. With our own young, we provide rich milk which reduces the feeling of fire."

"Um. I'm not sure that's a good idea," I said, placing my hand on Sendrei's arm.

"That is right," Flaer said. "We will eat of nothing that is gathered from captive animals."

"Our proteins come in a selection of vat grown or natural," he said. "It is your choice that we will respect."

"I will not drink milk from a domesticated animal." Her feelings were understandable. When we'd found humans on the Kroerak controlled world, called The Cradle, it was the humans who were held as animals for slaughter by the Kroerak.

"Our milks come from only the healthiest Pogona. It is not moral to keep one of our own captive for purpose of her body's produce."

"Yeah, that," I said. "Sorry. I should have warned you."

"I do not understand human hesitance in this matter. Our suppliers quite willingly give of themselves and the money they earn is used to raise their young families," he said.

"That is acceptable," Flaer said, interrupting the conversation.

This must have struck Sendrei as oddly as it did me, because we both looked at Flaer, mouths agape.

"Do not be prudes. If it is freely given I find no conflict."

I looked back to Tabby and we exchanged a scandalized look. I wasn't sure what my hang-up was, but something felt wrong.

"Koosha, share with me what you know of the planet Fan Zuri and its moon Cenaki," I said.

Fan Zuri was the only other inhabitable planet in the Santaloo solar system. It had multiple moons, although only Cenaki had any real population on it.

"Fan Zuri is much warmer than is Zuri. It is primarily populated by my people," he said. "I think you would find it to be very much to your liking. The peoples are friendly and trade is abundant."

"You should avoid Cenaki at all costs," Jala added. She set square wooden slabs in front of us, each holding a tightly wrapped mix of proteins and local vegetables. Within the slabs, wells had been gouged out and filled with a paste. Personally, I preferred the green, but that didn't appear to be an option.

"My sparkling gem speaks with truth," Koosha agreed. "Word of your encounter with Goboble will travel to Cenaki quickly. You must remain vigilant when traveling near Fan Zuri. The Nijjar government will not protect our friends against Genteresk."

"Goboble is Golenti," I said. "What does that have to do with Fan Zuri?"

"Goboble was in employ of Genteresk family that control the northern region of Cenaki. Even the Nijjar defensive forces of Fan Zuri will not broach hostility with Genteresk outside of their borders."

"Didn't Belvakuski identify herself as Genteresk?" Tabby asked.

"You speak that name so loudly," Koosha warned. "This Pogona is a revered outlaw."

"Those words don't make sense together," Ada said.

"Pogona do not define morality in the same way as humans and Felio," Jala said, setting a creamy liquid in front of Flaer. "It is possible to respect the audacity and free spirit of one that has embraced the rogue's lifestyle. This does not detract from a Pogona's own moral sense."

"I heard rumor that *Belvakuski* ran afoul of a lone group of humans," Koosha whispered the pirate's name as he said it. "I pray this was not you, Liam Hoffen."

"Why?" I asked.

"Such interaction could lead to dire consequences," he said, somberly.

"You want to see dire, pull a gun on Sendrei," Tabby said, breaking the tension that had built at the table. "I didn't even see you draw that nano-blade and then frakking Goboble was down. Quick as all that. You know, there's a saying — don't bring a knife to a gunfight. And that tank fight? I'm sure protocol suggests ground troops should take cover from mounted turrets, right? Or did you skip that day in tactics at the academy?"

"The soldiers we faced today were not professional," Sendrei replied. "It was a fatal mistake to leave open the hatch of the vehicle that gave them such an advantage. Bold action was required and as is often true in battle, it was rewarded."

"You don't think tossing an entire strip of grenade balls was overkill?" I asked. "I'm pretty sure you scrapped the interior."

"My dear, naive children. I will lift you in evening prayers." Koosha said, placing his hands together and bowing his head.

Chapter 7

BUGS

One look at the armored patrol vehicle and neither Flaer nor Ada wanted anything to do with driving it back to York. Sendrei's eyes showed the conflict in his emotions. He was torn between traveling with his wife or joining Tabby and me in what was sure to be a liver-jarring race of death through the wilds of Zuri. Chivalry won out.

Tabby and I waved goodbye as they boarded *Tuuq*. Ada lifted the ship from the landing pad and headed for home, which was a short eighty kilometers by air and a hundred twenty by ground.

"Best four out of seven?" Tabby asked after I beat her at rock-paper-scissors three times in a row.

"Whatever," I said and we went again. She was too predictable for her own good and chose rock on her opener, once again. It was in her nature to be the hammer and I wasn't about to let her know why I found it so easy to guess her actions.

Each of the four pneumatic wheels of the six-meter-long vehicle stood at a meter and had aggressive knobs of a semi-pliable black material that I was sure gave them excellent grip on all kinds of surfaces. The cab, while too small for any type of habitation, was split into two rows with access doors on either side. The front row had only two seats — the driver on the left and gunner on the right. The back row had room for three more passengers and five cubic meters of storage behind the seats. Except for the wheels, every exterior surface was armored.

"These panels pop out," Tabby said, exposing windows next to the passenger seats. I looked on the driver's side and discovered the same. We hauled the heavy panels to the back of the vehicle and laid them on a tarp, beneath which I hadn't yet looked. Similarly, we could lay down the front-facing armor to give us a much wider view from the cockpit.

"This thing better have a lot of power to be pushing around all this weight," Tabby said as we ran through the vehicle's simple controls.

There wasn't much to it: interior climate controls, fuel levels and a mechanism for turning the lights on and off.

"How much ammunition do you have?" I asked.

"It's a slug thrower," Tabby said. "Not very heavy, either. It has about a thousand rounds left, which is twenty-five percent. Hang on a sec."

She reached up, twisted a manual latch in the roof and pushed. Tabby followed the hatch up, stood on her seat and locked it open against the roof of the vehicle.

"Manual turret control. I'm in love," she said as I watched the turret's barrel swing back and forth.

"Ready to roll?" I'd always wondered about the saying, but suddenly the idea made a lot more sense.

"Hit it."

Unlike any machine I'd previously navigated, this vehicle had a round wheel for steering. Throttle and direction control was a single t-bar stick that sat between the two seats. "Hang on. I've never driven one of these."

I pushed the throttle forward and the vehicle leapt to life. Tabby, still standing on the seat, struggled to maintain her balance. Having to worry about objects in my path was something I'd only just started to learn with the carriages back in York. To say I was bad at predicting how quickly we'd run up on obstacles was something of an understatement.

"Port!" Tabby hollered.

I veered just in time to avoid a cement block at the edge of the parking area. Apparently, we were only supposed to leave through a few narrow corridors.

"*Show navigation path to York.*"

A blue contrail that curved in several places stretched out in front of me and directed me to turn again. I slowed on the throttle and followed it around. For some reason, driving the vehicle wasn't anywhere near as fun as I'd thought it would be. I really had to be vigilant to avoid crashing into debris that littered the area.

"A little pep already," Tabby chided.

I pushed the throttle forward and we leapt ahead. Whatever power source the vehicle possessed, it was well-matched to the heavy bulky frame; I was able to accelerate faster than I was comfortable with. At twenty-five meters per second, I barely had enough time to navigate the turns in the poorly maintained road. Finally, I missed a turn entirely and bumped up over a large block of cement. The impact was jarring and I scraped the bottom of the vehicle as we passed over the object. I wasn't sure which was more impressive: the screeching sound of metal on concrete or the fact that the vehicle just powered over the top — even though we bounced like a ball in low-g.

Tabby slid down into her seat once we leveled out. "Damn, Hoffen, is it that hard to drive?"

"AI says I'm going too fast for the road. I think it might be on to something."

"The road straightens out up ahead," she said.

I turned back onto the road and accelerated again. We were finally coming to the edge of Azima and the road was turning less and had widened such that it could accommodate several vehicles side by side.

"Whoo hooo!" Tabby yelled, standing up and sticking her head through the hatch in the vehicle's roof again.

Acclimating to the requirements of the road, we were soon

bouncing along at thirty meters per second, which was about as fast as I dared, given the terrain.

"Not very practical," Tabby said as she slid back into the seat.

"Sure is fun, though. If you aren't looking to travel into space, it's a lot cheaper. The only reason this vehicle would be expensive is because it's armored and all the mechanical parts have to be enhanced to deal with the weight."

"Are these really ninety thousand credits new?"

"I've already received an offer in Manetra on this one for fifty-two," I said.

"That's crazy. What's that mini-tank worth?"

"Eight hundred thousand — in pre-Sendrei shape, that is. I have an offer for the shell at one hundred twenty thousand."

"Shite, he knocked six-hundred-fifty thousand credits out of it?"

"Good thing too," I said. "I saw you get hit. How many of those could you have taken?"

"Not too many. Glad Goboble hadn't loaded that tank with armor piercing shells. Marny says there's an armor piercing loadout the Popeyes use for hunting tanks. The goal is to get something through that armor and have it bounce around inside, making scrambled eggs of the crew."

"Nice picture," I said.

"Her words, not mine. I'm pretty sure I never want to be a ground pounder," she said.

After a few minutes, driving became routine as we flew across terrain that had turned from urban to completely wild.

"Hey. Shortcut — turn right," Tabby said.

My AI had shown me the same route, which would take us around the back side of Quail Hill, just north of Kuende Run. I took a tight turn onto the new road. There was something thrilling about how the vehicle's knobby wheels bit into the road and threw chunks of gravel in response to our acceleration.

"They say there's a Kroerak hatchery in Kuende," I said,

Two of the most insidious things about Kroerak were the rapid reproductive cycles and the instinctive behavior of the hatchlings.

The young bugs' first act was almost always to plant more eggs. Kroerak hatcheries tended to be in remote locations where concentrations of spawn ended up planting their eggs before they moved out into the world to mature. Left unchecked, the vigorous aliens could easily take over a planet.

The city of Kuende had failed due to its own success. As the city grew, the natural environment had been razed and replaced by urban sprawl. Zuri's natural defense, the selich root, was nowhere to be found and cities like Kuende had thus been turned into natural hatcheries.

"I have a thousand rounds," Tabby said. "I hope we see something."

We finally arrived on the edge of the ancient city about an hour after Santaloo's star disappeared behind Zuri.

"Kind of spooky, don't you think?" Tabby asked, as an adolescent Kroerak darted in front of the vehicle.

"Shite," I said. "That's no hatchling."

"I'm going to see if I can get one," Tabby said and stood back up.

"Are you sure that's a good idea?" I asked.

Tabby answered by firing a few rounds, filling the cab of the vehicle with the rat-tat-tat sound of the turret firing. "Frak. They're fast."

"I'm not sure it's such a good idea to call attention to ourselves," I said.

"What are they going to do? Eat us?" Tabby asked.

"Probably not, but I'm not sure I want to find out," I said.

Two more adolescent Kroerak jumped onto the road and made a dash toward the heart of the city. We really should have turned away from the area already.

"Follow them!" Tabby said and responded by firing. The turret's bullets were certainly sufficient and she cut them down easily.

"You know what Abasi are paying for the big boys?" Tabby asked and then answered her own question. "Five-grand apiece."

There was a bounty for Kroerak on Zuri. When delivered, hatchlings earned us three hundred credits each and larger adolescents were more valuable. Catching sight of another adolescent further ahead, I gunned the accelerator and we flew over the bumps in the road.

The bugs had become wary and stayed back as we drove down the long-abandoned roads. Tabby was having difficulty pinpointing them now. In the back of my mind, I considered that, at our current speed, we could be getting deeper into the city — and deeper into trouble — than we might want.

"Uh, Tabbs," I said and pulled on her belt to get her back into the vehicle.

"Frak, Hoffen," she said, resisting me as she saw what I had. Up to the right, the powerful lights of the patrol vehicle had fallen on a hole in the side of a hill. Hatchlings and adolescent Kroerak boiled out and down the hill.

"This is shite," I said and slid the vehicle to a halt as Tabby poured fire into what looked like a never-ending supply of the bugs. "Frak!" I pulled back on the throttle and attempted to turn around, but bumped up over a thick log and my rear wheels became suspended in the air. When I tried to pull forward, I was unable to free us.

"Anytime, Hoffen," Tabby said, only letting off her firing for a moment. "I'm burning ammo like there's no tomorrow."

I jammed the throttle forward and back. The front wheels bit into the loose gravel but I was unable to dislodge us.

The turret stopped firing.

"What are you doing?" I asked. "We're stuck."

"We're out of ammo," Tabby said, pulling the hatch down and locking it.

"They'll come through the windows," I lurched forward and slammed shut the armor that covered the front glass.

"I know," Tabby said, annoyed. "I've got it."

She scrabbled over the seats and easily hefted the passenger side armor panel into place, locking it down just before the side of the vehicle was impacted.

I'd tried to do the same on my side, but the panel weighed at least fifty kilograms and I'd only been able to drag it into the back seat. "Damn, it's too heavy."

"Cover me," she said as she kicked at a hatchling that had discovered the open driver's side window and tried to jump in with us.

Pulling my heavy blaster from my chest, I slid to the side, out of her way. She was more than strong enough, but I didn't think she'd have sufficient time.

I fired across her back as she reached for the armor. An adolescent was reaching for her and jabbed a claw into the back of her calf. "Frak!" she screamed, but didn't drop the panel.

It took a dozen shots and Tabby slamming the armored plate onto its clawed arm, but we finally got the bug to fall away.

"This feels familiar," she said. "Help me."

She'd placed the panel where it needed to go, but the buffeting of the bugs prevented her from locking it down. I fired again at a claw that had snaked beneath the panel and then jammed my back against the armor as we strained to lock it in.

"It's just like being back in that gymnasium in Morris, Minnesota," Tabby said.

"Your leg. Doesn't it hurt?"

"I'll live," Tabby sounded more annoyed than in pain. "The suit stopped the bleeding, but I need to get a patch on it soon or there'll be serious rehab ahead."

The vehicle rocked as more and more bugs hit the sides.

"Think the armor will hold?" I asked. "We could call Marny."

"It'll hold," she said, sitting back in the chair. Though pain filled her face, she wasn't ready to admit or give in to it. "It'd take a full-sized warrior to come close to piercing this armor."

It was one of those surreal moments that would later become memorable. I swear — a person should be careful of what they think and say. The very next moment the vehicle was rocked by something hitting hard, just behind the passenger's seat. The armor buckled but didn't allow it through.

"Like that?" I asked.

"No way! That's something else," Tabby said. "If there were

warriors here, we'd know. The Abasi would never let that situation stand."

For a moment, everything went quiet. I lifted and twisted a latch that held in place a chunk of armor covering a finger sized slit. I peered through the opening into the darkness, unable to see anything.

"Shite, there's more ammo back here," Tabby said. I turned and saw the crate of ammunition she'd uncovered.

"How many rounds?" I asked.

"Two thousand at least," she said. "Interface our suits with the truck. We'll have to operate the turret remotely and I'll figure out how to reload."

When I peered out of the tiny window, the sensors in my suit picked up what I couldn't see with the naked eye, projecting the images onto my HUD. Where there had previously been a flood of Kroerak, now nothing moved aside from a couple of bugs Tabby had winged.

I closed the slit and pushed my AI to interface with the vehicle's sensors. We were still locked out of the vehicle's sensor, targeting and automated weapons control systems.

"*Recommend rebuilding and remapping of control systems,*" my AI indicated.

"*Predict success ratio and time to complete,*" I requested.

"*Seventy-eight percent overall. Two minutes forty seconds.*"

"We're going to reboot, Tabbs."

"Think that's a good idea?"

"AI's having trouble hacking the software, but it can wipe and rebuild easily enough."

"I almost have this loaded," she said.

"*Approved. Load with standard Loose Nuts administrative authorization.*"

The interior of the patrol vehicle blacked out.

"Frak, Hoffen," Tabby complained as she popped on her suit lamps. "Not like I'm working with explosive ordnance or anything."

The stillness of the night was eerie. The only sound was that of

Tabby maneuvering rope-lines of ammunition into tracks that ran the length of the vehicle. She finished with a final snap of the hardened covers that enclosed the ammo and slid into the passenger seat next to me.

"What's up with the systems?" Her face glowed from the dim lighting around her suit's collar.

"One minute," I flicked the timer from my HUD to her.

"Why do you think they stopped attacking?"

"Wish I knew. Maybe they're waiting for us to get out of the vehicle."

"That's a lot of patience for Kroerak."

"How's your leg?" I asked.

"Hurts a lot like getting stabbed by a bug."

I smiled. Tabby wasn't one to complain. "Wish I knew what was going on out there."

A chime in my ear sounded as the interior lights turned back on. My HUD showed a view from the exterior of the vehicle. I acknowledged my AI's request to fill my entire field of view. As I turned my head, it was as if there was no canopy on the patrol vehicle, although it rendered Tabby in real time, next to me.

The scene outside hadn't changed much from the view I remembered right before we'd seen the swarm of bugs, except for the twenty Kroerak hulls leading down the hill. The surrounding area looked clear, but I knew better than to rely on mechanical sensors to pick up bugs that were hunkered down. It was very possible they were lying in wait in the thick brush on either side of the road.

"We need to retrieve those adolescents," Tabby said.

"Are you serious? We need to free this truck from whatever I ran over."

"Cover me," Tabby said and swung open the door. "I saw a come-a-long on the front of this thing."

"Tabby! Get back in here," I called while sliding into her seat and grabbing the manual turret controls. I quickly rescanned the area.

"I'm just going to hook this up to a tree," she said, pulling a cable from the front of the vehicle and walking toward the brush on the other side of the road. She limped as she spooled out the cable.

"Don't, Tabbs. Kroerak could be in there. I'll call Marny."

"I got this," she said.

"Frak." I felt like I'd seen a small amount of movement in the brush two meters north of where she was headed. "I've got movement, Tabbs."

"Almost there."

Tabby was bowled over by an adolescent that rushed out of the thick undergrowth. I tracked the two with the turret, but had no shot. The bug slammed its razor-sharp talons into the concrete as Tabby furiously avoided them.

Two more medium-sized bugs burst from cover. I had no choice but to swing the turret over and pick them up. *Thup-thup-thup.* The patrol vehicle's slug thrower might not penetrate mechanized armor very well, but it splattered immature bugs like ... well ... bugs.

Tabby squirted out from beneath the bug. Just as it swiped at her, she lifted into the air, using her grav-suit's primary capability. She cried out as blood spray arced across the patrol vehicle's beams, glittering in the night air as it fell. The bug had cut Tabby's thigh.

Now that the two were separated, I only had to tamp down my fear and rage long enough to drill the pointy frak-bastard back to whatever hell it came from.

"Tabbs?"

"I'm okay," she called.

"That's shite! Get back here."

Her bio scan reported that she was still losing blood and her suit no longer had the right meds to staunch the bleeding in her artificially grown limb.

Still in the air, Tabby looped the cable around a tree and tied it off. If she'd only flown over there in the first place, she would have avoided the entire problem. Hindsight, however, wasn't particularly helpful and Marny's voice in the back of my head prompted me to stay in the moment.

I engaged the come-a-long, or winch as my HUD identified it, and we slowly pulled forward and off whatever I'd hit. Tabby slid back into the seat and closed the door.

"We can't leave all those corpses," she said, weakly. "We need that bounty."

"Bilge water we do!" I shouted, adrenaline pumping as the rear wheels struck gravel. "You're bleeding."

Her suit compressed around the gash in her leg, providing a tourniquet and slowing blood loss. The problem was, she'd lose the leg if the flow was stopped for too long. The suit only bought us a short amount of time.

I aimed the patrol vehicle's gun at the cable, shot it off the tree and jammed the throttle forward. We threw gravel as I spun around. I straightened her up and we barreled down the road toward home.

Chapter 8

CALL TO BATTLE

"What possessed the two of you to go to Kuende Run without backup?" Ada asked, wrapping Tabby's leg with a med-patch calibrated with nano-bots designed to repair the synthetic tissues of her leg. One of the advantages of synth technology was that it worked like DNA; the cells of the synthetic tissue contained enough information to fully repair any damage. The only requirement was application of the correct nano-bots and materials, all of which we could now replicate.

"My fault." Tabby had regained consciousness. "Liam saw the problem before I did and I pushed him to keep going."

"Explain this, Cap," Marny said, holding up a ten-centimeter-long barb that was broken at one end. My AI virtually projected the rest of the beast; a two and a half meter tall Kroerak warrior now connected to the broken shard.

"Where'd you get that?" I asked, looking over to the patrol vehicle that sat on the floor of Nick's crowded workshop, only a few meters from where Ada had met us with medical supplies.

Marny's eyes followed my own. "That's right, Cap. I pulled it from just behind the passenger seat. Not sure why the warrior stopped, either. A couple more hits and it would have broken through."

"It was weird," I said. "One minute the bugs were swarming us and the next, they were gone."

"Is that when you got out of the vehicle?" Ada asked.

"Yes. I high-centered us on a log. Tabbs went out to tie the come-a-long to a tree," I said.

"Winch." Nick corrected.

"Right. Winch. A couple adolescents jumped her."

"That's disturbing," Ada said. "They shouldn't have come anywhere near you with that selich root in your veins."

"Natural selection," Nick said. "It was bound to happen. The hatchlings reproduce at a ridiculous rate and seemed to be programmed to spread out fast. Most of them die because they can't find food or they're poisoned by the naturally occurring selich. It stands to reason, however, that a few of the Kroerak could find a way to survive and mature, maybe by staying put after they hatch."

"That doesn't explain why they attacked us," Tabby said, sitting up.

"I don't know. But what if just one in all of those generations had even the slightest resistance to selich?" Nick asked.

"I liked your first answer better," I said.

"What? The idea that there are a few warriors walking around because they're lazy and don't leave home or because they're immune and we're all screwed?" Tabby asked.

"Either way, we need to see what's going on," I said.

"And collect those adolescent corpses," Tabby added. "By my count, we dropped five adolescents and a dozen hatchlings. That's thirty thousand credits lying on the ground."

The lights of an approaching vehicle on the road from York momentarily interrupted our conversation.

"Who's that?" I asked.

"Sheriff Rigdon," Nick said. "I pinged her earlier."

"Why?"

"If you stirred up a nest, it might affect York," Marny answered.

"I hear you've had some excitement," Sheriff Mez Rigdon called out as she approached the workshop's open doors. Rigdon had a medium, earth-type build with dark brown hair and deeply tanned skin. She wore a new-looking brown uniform shirt that sported a shiny badge, dark blue pants, and heavy-soled tactical boots. At her waist, she carried a heavy blaster pistol which I was certain had come from our cache.

"Cap and Tabby ran into a nest of Kroerak over in Keundo Run," Marny said. "I was just getting ready to review the combat data-stream."

"The what?" Rigdon asked.

"Video," Marny said. "Our suits record all pertinent sensor data. We call the exciting bits data-streams. We'll run it from first contact."

"What were you doing over there after dark? Locals know better than that. More than one has gone missing over the years," she said.

A second set of lights on the road announced another visitor.

"Who now?" I asked, looking to Nick.

"Sendrei, Bish, and Hog, if I'm not mistaken," he replied. "We promised we'd be more open with information. I figured this would be a good time to share."

"Mind if I get some clothing on before we invite the entire town over?" Tabby asked. We'd pulled off her grav-suit and suit liner when we'd applied med-patches. As a result, she was sitting in her undies — a sight I never tired of.

Ada hurriedly helped Tabby pull the ruined suit liner back on and she hopped off the table, still favoring her injured right leg.

"How bad is it?" I asked, looping an arm around her shoulder.

"Frakking going to need rehabilitation," Tabby said. "AI says the bots will take the better part of a week stitching everything back together and another week of heavy PT."

"You took Goboble's equipment?" Bish asked suspiciously as he joined what was becoming a sizeable group. All three of the armored vehicles we'd retained were either in the workshop or parked just outside.

"That an issue, Bish?" I asked. I was getting tired of his bitch-first attitude.

"It is if it causes escalation," he answered.

"Seems like you would have heard already, but Goboble tried to take us out today," I said. "Didn't work so well for him and we did exactly what privateers do; we claimed the spoils of war."

"You can't just pick a fight with someone and take their stuff. That makes you no better than Goboble," Bish said.

"Bish," Hog warned, trying to calm his friend.

"That is a poor representation of the conflict," Sendrei said, stepping between us. "Goboble arrived with a large crew and initiated the fight. I believe we were summoned here for another purpose. Perhaps we could see to that, first."

"Thank you, Sendrei," Sheriff Rigdon said. "Tabby and Liam were attacked by a large group of Kroerak in Kuende Run. Marny was preparing to show us video of the events."

Bish started to complain, but stopped when Hog wrapped a large arm around his shoulders. "Appreciate being included," Hog warned.

The replay wasn't anywhere near as nice as I was used to. The AI pieced together data from my suit's feed and tied it into Tabby's. To call it video, was a simplification that Marny used for the group, since the AI showed the scene from a bird's eye view up and behind the patrol vehicle. It wasn't lost on me just how cool the vehicle looked while it aggressively dug into the road and threw clods of dirt and gravel into the air as I took the corners at speed.

"What is that?" Bish asked, stabbing a finger into the projection.

Marny's AI, hearing his question, froze the scene and backed up to roughly the time when he'd started asking the question. Instinctively, Bish brushed his hand to the side — a gesture he'd just started to learn with the tech we'd been supplying to the town — and the scene reversed in time.

I had to give it to the crotchety old guy, he had a sharp eye for detail. He pushed his hands apart and we zoomed in on the opening in the ground that I knew would get even more exciting in the next minute or two.

"That's trouble, Bish," I said, hoping my acknowledgement might ease some of the tension between us.

He turned to look at me, eyes alight. He was in the moment and petty differences were set aside. "It's active?"

"You recognize it?" I asked.

"Let it play out," Tabby said. "The good stuff is yet to come."

Bish nodded and turned back.

We picked back up with Tabby clipping a couple of hatchlings just before all hell broke loose and the mouth of what was obviously a tunnel erupted with hatchlings and adolescents. Tabby's efficacy with the mounted turret was substantial. Her previous estimate of a dozen hatchlings wasn't even close, as my AI tallied a body count well over forty.

"Did you catch that?" Nick asked, jumping up and grabbing onto a scene. We'd gotten to the point where Tabby and I had closed the vehicle and were battening down the hatches. I'd just opened the slit in the window and was peering out.

"Warriors," I said. There were at least ten of them clearly racing toward the vehicle.

"No. That," he said.

At the top of the screen a flash of color appeared and then disappeared. Nick worked to focus on the color, but it was at the edge of my suit sensor's capability, especially through such a small opening.

"What is it?" Hog asked. Nick had frozen the scene and zoomed in as far as he could. Between two warriors we could see the reflection of metallic red and a small, underdeveloped claw.

"Frak, Cap," Marny said.

"Someone want to share?" Bish asked impatiently.

I found the image of a Kroerak noble and threw it up on the wall. A bug, no bigger than an adolescent was shown with its bright red and green metallic carapace. When we'd invaded The Cradle, Mars Protectorate had taken three Kroerak nobles back to Earth. There had been speculation that this had always been the Kroerak's plan and that the nobles had wanted to be captured so they could learn more of Earth's defenses. My own experience with the nobles was nothing less than creepy, as they had demonstrated the ability to communicate telepathically through solid walls.

"Think of them as generals, Bish," I said. "As a rule, warriors have great tactical capacity. Point 'em at a hill, tell them to capture or clear it and you should consider it done. Strategically, they can't think their way out of a bag. That's the noble's job."

"Tell 'em about the mind-reading thing," Tabby said.

"We don't know how the nobles communicate with their troops. We thought it was chemical. During the invasion, the nobles directed troops from orbit with no obvious comm gear. I had one talk to me from a locked room like it was standing next to me."

"It was in your head?" Bish asked.

"Yes."

"We have to inform the Abasi about this," Hog said.

"I've already sent the data-streams to House Mshindi." Nick was always steps ahead. "I haven't heard back."

"We need to close up that hole." Bish was obviously worried.

"We need more information," Marny said. "We can't afford to blow that hole. We have no idea how deep it is or if there's a noble."

"You just can't leave well enough alone, can you!" Bish yelled. "If you go poking around in there, what's to prevent them from running over York?"

"Sticking our heads in the sand won't help either," Marny said. "Those bugs pulled off when they had more than enough to overwhelm Tabby and Liam. That kind of restraint isn't something warriors, much less hatchlings, are capable of. We need to know why. If there's a noble in Kuende Run, the situation is bigger than all of us can handle."

"Our ancestors successfully withstood the Kroerak invasion many decades ago," Rigdon said. "We can do it again, if it comes to that. What's our next step?"

"Rigdon, you don't speak for York. Hog, can you believe this?" Bish asked.

Hog, normally quick with a smile and a response, contemplatively stroked his chin as if he had a beard. "Seems like we should hear them out."

"We'll roll hard two hours pre-dawn," Marny said. "You should lock down York tonight. Kroerak aren't averse to night attacks, but they prefer daylight — as we do. If there is threat to York it'll happen immediately. We'll include Sheriff Rigdon on our tactical channel. That way we can adjust resources if necessary."

"I assume my invitation extends to your action in the morning," Sendrei said.

"Lieutenant, aside from Flaer, you have more knowledge of Kroerak than anyone alive. I'd be honored if you'd run tactical from the Stryker," Marny said.

"Can do, Sergeant." Sendrei said.

***

"YOU'RE NOT LEAVING ME BEHIND." Tabby rolled over, waking me up. I checked the time, it was 0329 and my alarm had only a minute before it would start chiming.

"You think you can run a Popeye?"

"No, but Sendrei needs a driver and a gunner if he's running tactical."

I squelched my alarm just as it rang. "You're not very mobile if things get crazy."

"I'll be fine. My leg is feeling better. Besides, I'll have my grav-suit on and best I remember, I didn't see any flying bugs."

"If you think you're up for it," I said, pulling on a fresh suit liner. Tabby stepped gingerly from our bed and hobbled to where her grav-suit lay over a chair. I watched for a moment as she struggled, realizing she was having trouble pulling it on over her still-swollen calf.

"Don't say a word," she said, grimacing as she pushed her leg into the freshly repaired suit.

"Everyone would understand if you sat this one out," I said. "You're injured."

"Suck it."

I chuckled at her expected response and ran water in the sink to tame my morning hair. I knew better than to push the conversation further. After getting dressed, Tabby and I joined Marny and Nick in the main room. Sendrei and Ada were already there, but the presence of Jonathan and Bish caught me off guard.

"Morning, folks," I said, accepting a plate of eggs and sausage from Marny. I'd have been okay with a meal bar, but wasn't about to turn down a fresh breakfast.

"Cap, Jonathan and Bish are looking for a ride-along," Marny said, broaching the elephant in the room.

"Bish, I guess I'm surprised to see you this morning."

"I know you all think I'm an angry lunatic," he said. "At least, I would in your shoes. Fact is, I understand the value of what you're trying to accomplish here, not just with Kuende Run, but James' factory, standing up to Goboble, and all that. I just think you'd do better if you had a little oversight, someone who thinks about the big picture, especially where it relates to York."

"If you come, you'll respect chain of command," I said. "There is no place for argument once we're in the field."

"I can live with that," he said.

"You'll need to wear armor and carry a rifle."

"Not really my style and I'm not expecting to get out of the armored vehicle."

"Wasn't a request," I said. "And it's not what we expect that worries me. It's when the metaphorical bilge pump breaks that causes me the most concern."

He nodded curtly, which I took as assent.

"I worked on the Stryker's rear hatch last night," Nick said. "I have more cosmetic work to do, but it's solid."

"Sounds like we're ready, then. We'll put Sendrei, Tabby, Jonathan, and Bish in the Stryker. Ada, you and Nick are on over-watch in *Tuuq*. Marny and I will take point with the Popeyes. Sendrei will have tactical once we're on-site. Our primary mission is recon. Something's up in Kuende Run and we need to know how big of a problem we have. Secondary mission is bug hunting. If it looks like too much, we fall back to here. I don't want us dragging our problems to York."

"*Intrepid* has four operational turrets and can suppress a full three hundred and sixty degrees. If we're pushed back here, she becomes our base," Nick added.

"How have you restored operation?" Ada asked. "Liam burned out all control circuits."

"It's not pretty," Nick said. "I've run cabling along the corridors."

"If there's nothing else, let's get loaded," Marny said.

I helped Tabby out to the Stryker. The interior of the vehicle was clean and straightforward. Against each side were four flip-down seats facing inward. Above these seats were open shelves for gear and rugged vid screens that resembled windows were embedded in the walls. Just below the vid-screens were open shelves for gear. Forward of the seating, against the back of the cockpit, was a built-in shelf that served as a desk; it supported communications equipment and two more vid screens. The seat opposite the desk moved on a track to allow passage into the vehicle's cockpit where there were two seats: one for the driver, the other for a gunner/navigator.

"Looks cozy," I said, helping Tabby into the driver's seat.

"Don't do anything stupid today," she said. "I'm not going to be there to cover your ass."

"Wouldn't think of it."

With Tabby aboard the Stryker, I joined Marny in the workshop where she'd already loaded into her Popeye.

"Any word from York this morning?" I asked, as I fired up my suit's systems.

"Rigdon says it's all quiet."

"Let's hope it stays that way." I punched my arms forward, one after the other, testing the Popeye's function. A quick check showed I had a full load of ammo and fuel. Marny had topped us off. The rest of my systems were running green.

"Sendrei, Cap and I will take lead. I'd like to have you stay back half a click once we're within two clicks of Kuende. If things get dirty, we'll want room to maneuver without worrying about friendly fire. Ada, I'd like you to fly over for a low scan once we're at that two-click mark."

"Copy that, Sergeant," Sendrei replied.

"Read you, Marny," Ada agreed.

A yellow indicator showed in my HUD requesting a 'ready check.' I blinked at the request, which my AI translated correctly to assent. Quickly, the remaining team members, including Bish, updated their statuses.

"We're go," Marny said and loped off down the slight hill in front of Nick's shop and onto the broken road.

As we passed, *Tuuq* lifted slowly from its position next to *Intrepid*. The small ship had become valuable to us as we'd lost *Fleet Afoot*, but I had no love for its anemic engines and cramped spaces. Sadly, *Intrepid* served as more of a reminder of just how much we'd lost recently. Even that thought, however, didn't tamp down the adrenaline rush that accompanied the start of a mission. I was headed back into battle and couldn't deny my excitement.

After only a few minutes we'd run past the last of York's homesteads and were fully in the wilds of Zuri. The road we followed hadn't been maintained since the war and I needed the AI to fill in details so I could figure out where we were going.

"Two clicks out," Marny finally called. It was Ada's cue to fly over and get a snapshot of activity.

"I've got you, Marny," Ada said.

A moment later the sensor data filtered back to my HUD. The Kroerak corpses were right where we'd left them. A single hatchling skittered across the open area next to the mouth of the cave. It stopped, hearing *Tuuq*, and then ran off, disappearing in the heavy undergrowth.

"We're headed in," Marny said.

Chapter 9

BETTER LEFT BURIED

Nervously, I checked my ammo display as Marny and I bounded toward the five-meter wide, mounded entrance. Tension mounted as we passed the Kroerak husks we'd dropped the night before. I didn't think there was a practical limit to the number of hatchlings or even adolescents a Popeye could handle. Warriors, however, were another thing. Unlike Bish, I wasn't willing to ignore the presence of the bugs. Pretending they weren't a threat would only make the problem worse.

With Ada flying a lazy arc overhead and keeping our sensor data fresh, I scanned the HUD's virtual screen, analyzing the entrance. There wasn't much information, the hole dropped twenty meters at a steep angle. At the bottom, two tunnels split off at ninety degrees from each other. Most importantly, the tunnel was large enough to fit our mechanized infantry suits.

"Entrance is clear. We're proceeding to the mouth," Marny said. "Sendrei, surface tactical is yours. We'll drop comm repeaters enroute."

The last comment revealed Marny's concern. Those of us familiar with Popeyes knew they were programmed to eject flea-sized, signal repeating devices whenever the signal dropped below a designed level. She repeated the information to make it clear that if we lost communications, it wouldn't be a mechanical issue.

Side by side we climbed the loose, mounded dirt that surrounded the entrance and peered down the hole.

"Contact, Captain," Sendrei warned.

The tactical HUD showed the Stryker vehicle had closed to four hundred meters, just beyond visual range due to heavy overgrowth. Two red dots were moving away from the vehicle at five meters per second and heading directly at us. A red outline tracked the two through the brush as they approached, even though I still couldn't see them.

"Take incoming, Cap, and try to keep it quiet. Deploying kiss-and-tell," Marny said.

It was SOP during excursions into enemy territory for our squad to drop small pucks that reported any movement in the area. Marny wasn't about to let Kroerak sneak up on us. Without watching, I knew she tossed one of the pucks as far down the hole as she could get it.

I grabbed the multipurpose tool from my calf and flicked it open to a full meter in length. Made from nano-crystalized steel, the tool was good for prying, stabbing, slicing and pounding, depending on which end you held and how far it was extended. I preferred holding the hammer end in my hand with the semi-sharp flattened end extended to a point. In this configuration, the tool resembled a sword. A real sword, however, was much too delicate for someone in a mech-suit to wield — even honed nano-steel would shatter on the first powerful blow. This blade was thick and semi-sharp; it wouldn't cut someone even if they ran an ungloved hand along the edge. It was designed to withstand whatever pain the mechanized infantry might be required to give out.

With heart pounding in my chest, I rushed forward to meet the still obscured, advancing foe. I'd timed it so that both would break from cover just as I closed to within ten meters.

"I got 'em," I said as the two adolescents oriented on me. The young Kroerak were nearly two meters tall, still shy by half a meter of fully grown. Unlike warriors, their carapace segments had yet to fuse together. The two jostled for position as they rushed forward, a behavior I'd only seen occasionally in warriors.

"Thanks, boys." I used both hands to control the blade. Planting my right foot, I used a short down-stroke, swinging through the first bug until the pommel of the weapon came close to my bent left knee. A move I'd worked on with Marny, it allowed me to deflect an opponent's energy to my left side. The impact was devastating to the bug, as the blade traveled cleanly through to its midsection. I allowed the impact to turn my body, raising my left knee as I extracted the sword.

The second Kroerak had been knocked aside when I'd struck its brother. It had dropped down to all fours, its foreclaws digging into the soil, an action I'd never seen — even from a warrior. It was an effective — if suicidal — way of arresting momentum. The idea that it was severely outclassed in this battle clearly hadn't entered this bug's brain. With my left hand, I batted the first bug from my sword. I wouldn't have time for a satisfying, full swing, but I was in go-mode and would take whatever opportunity was provided. I shifted my shoulders hard as I stepped into the bug's low charge and bashed my gloved fist into its head. It clawed at my suit trying to pull me into a deadly embrace, until a satisfying crunch told me I'd hit pay dirt. I flicked the bug off and drove my sword into its back for good measure.

I'd often wondered how people got to the point where hatred of individuals became hatred of an entire group. I'd reached this point with Kroerak. I could honestly say I hated the species for what they'd done to humanity. I'd seen, up close and personal, how the Kroerak mutilated and killed people, treating them just as we treated non-intelligent species — as food sources. My enmity went further than that, though. I'd also seen how Kroerak took sick pleasure in their domination. Still, I took no joy in the kill beyond the visceral feeling that accompanies besting an opponent in mortal combat.

As a kid, I'd read a book about a bug species much like the Kroerak that had been entirely wiped out by the child hero. The hero in the story had been tricked into his actions by his elders and suffered emotionally for his part in the genocide of the species. I can honestly say, at this moment, if I'd had a button that would wipe every Kroerak from the universe, I'd have been happy to push it.

"Cap? You with me?" Marny asked, jogging to where I'd planted my sword into the fallen Kroerak's husk.

"Yeah, let's go." I extracted the sword and flicked it clean.

The slope of the hive entrance was steeper than I liked, but the suit's gyros and arc-jets kept us upright as we quickly covered the twenty meters. We jumped in, landing in the center of a long tunnel.

"Left or right?" Marny asked.

Both directions had seen considerable traffic and the ground was hard-packed. The left branch angled upward slightly, which I liked the idea of.

"I have point." I shortened my multi-purpose tool and flipped it so I had the hammer end available. With a nod from Marny, I started to the left.

She tossed a kiss-and-tell down the right branch, then followed behind me. My AI immediately mapped what it could scan ahead in the dark. The passage was clear for ten more meters, at which point, a branch went off to the left. Together we stalked ahead, as quietly as the suits would allow. When we were two meters from the turn, I tossed a puck across the intersection, imbedding it into the dirt wall ahead. The pucks didn't have video, but their movement sensors included enough data that our AIs could extrapolate the type of enemy, group size, distance, direction and time to intercept — that sort of thing. None of the pucks had yet activated, so we continued.

Our goal was to stay quiet if possible. I didn't expect the calm to last, but there was nothing wrong with surprise, as long as we didn't lock ourselves in too deep. I entered the opening to the left, holding my hammer, ready to strike. My AI registered an oval-shaped room, ten meters long, seven meters wide and four meters high at the largest dimensions. It appeared the room had been dug out, which made me wonder where the material had been taken. The tailings at the entrance weren't enough to account for this room's volume, much less the extensive tunnels we expected were down here.

The room was littered with broken, rigid casings the length and diameter of my forearm, but otherwise empty. I knelt and picked up one of the hollow casings. Something had torn through one side and when I applied pressure, it crumbled in my hand. I stood and dug into the floor with the toe of my armored boot. Instead of exposing clay soil, I shuddered as I pulled up more of the broken case material.

"Creepy, Cap," Marny said. "Has to be eggs."

"Lot of frakking eggs," I agreed.

We exited the room, turning back to the left and continuing down the main passage. Five meters further down, my AI highlighted a section on the wall to my right. I would have missed it, but the AI was nearly perfect at identification.

"I have a bad feeling about this, Cap," Marny said as I inspected the recently hidden opening. The material on the wall was a mixture of broken egg cases and clay. It had been packed and smoothed until the opening was indistinguishable from the rest of the passageway.

I backhanded the hammer into the center of the opening. "I just don't think this is going to get better." The wall crumbled under the impact of the hammer's head and debris cascaded into the hidden chamber. I continued with the hammer, widening the opening sufficiently to allow entry. The entire operation took only a few minutes.

"It's quiet," Marny said, after throwing a puck through the hole.

Stepping in, my sensors read the room. It was a slightly different shape than the first, but roughly the same volume. In this room, there were five, three-meter-high piles of the same cases. In the center sat a two-meter diameter dirt mound.

"Cover me," I growled as I leapt forward and buried my hammer into the mound. As expected, my hammer contacted the harder-than-steel carapace of a warrior. My blind strike hadn't been perfect and the mound exploded with a groggy, albeit really pissed warrior. It quickly turned to orient on me. I flipped my hammer end for end and jammed the handle between the hardened plates that separated its head from its thorax. The warrior crumpled.

"There have to be four-hundred eggs in here," Marny said.

"What's that?" I asked. Along one of the walls, was a pile of rotting native Zuri animals.

"Food sources," Marny said. "My guess is the eggs hatch, they eat through that meat and eventually break out of the egg chamber."

"Frak." My eye landed on a human arm, outlined by my AI. Glad for my suit's internal air system, I rushed over and pushed the disgusting pile back. The arm belonged to a recently killed Pogona male.

"That's a gunshot, Cap," Marny said. A burn on the side of the Pogona's head outlined a familiar-looking hole caused by a blaster pistol.

"No way," I said, not willing to believe any species capable of holding a blaster pistol would supply Kroerak with food.

"We have substantial movement on the surface," Sendrei's voice cut in on the tactical channel, startling me. "Something knows you're down there."

"Copy, Sendrei," Marny replied. "Cap, wrap this up. We might have company soon."

I turned from the rotting pile and dialed a five-minute incendiary grenade into my suit's ordnance manufactory. I jammed two grenades into the center of each egg mound, unwilling to leave behind what my AI counted as four hundred eggs.

"What's the call, Cap?"

"This isn't what we came for," I said. "We keep going."

"Copy."

We continued down the passage to a three-way intersection. Marny kept setting out pucks, but none of them activated. I'd been watching the Stryker team's progress. A veritable horde of hatchlings had erupted from a previously hidden surface opening half a click from where we'd entered. So far, it looked like between *Tuuq* and the Stryker, they were handling it.

I followed the intersection to the left, where my AI highlighted yet another closed chamber. I wasn't sure what I'd been expecting, but non-existent resistance wasn't it. I was starting to question my assessment about the size of the force we'd run into the night before.

On my first strike into the egg chamber, dirt exploded outward. A full-sized Kroerak warrior had been waiting and tackled me to the ground. For a moment, we wrestled, its sharp claws scraping against my suit's armor, searching for a weakness I knew it would have a hard time finding.

The bug went limp and I rolled out from beneath it, jumping back to my feet. Marny retracted her own multipurpose tool and tossed a puck into the egg chamber. Wordlessly, we stepped inside, finding the same scene as before.

"Frak," Marny said, just as three of our kiss-and-tells simultaneously woke up.

"Let's do this. Fire in the hole," I said, launching the same incendiary grenades at the piles, only this time, with no countdown.

Back in the passageway, our shadows danced on the opposite wall as the room was engulfed in fire.

Marny took point and moved back along the path we'd come. "We need an exit plan."

"Back the way we came?" I asked, not loving the idea.

With movement behind us, as well as near where we'd entered the tunnels, we were in danger of being surrounded. It was a devil of a choice. Attacking the horde coming from behind would require us to further commit to unexplored tunnels. At least heading this way, we knew what to expect and where our exit was. Marny made it through the intersection and into the main tunnel.

"Sendrei, what's your sit-rep?" Marny asked.

"Trouble," he replied. "Something stirred a nest. You have a score of warriors incoming. We've engaged, but we're not stopping them. There are too many and the Stryker's guns are taking too long."

"Contact," I said, spinning around and taking a knee. My rear view had caught a line of warriors streaming toward us. "Blowing the ceiling." It was important to share tactical decisions so Marny could react. Ordinarily, I'd let her make the call, but in close-quarters combat, timing was critical.

"Copy," Marny replied as I fired explosive rounds into the ceiling, just past the entrance to the last egg chamber. "Contact right and left." She had returned to the intersection and had my six.

Two warriors caught in the blast rocketed toward me. If I'd been standing, they'd have knocked me over. We were well past silent mode so I opened up on them, firing the armor-piercing rounds every suit manufactured since the Kroerak war carried. I didn't bother to stand, but unloaded automatic fire into the attacking warriors without hesitation.

In my peripheral vision, the tactical target count grew as Marny's sensors recorded bugs in the unexplored section and main tunnel.

The ground shook as great mounds of earth collapsed into the tunnel, burying warriors and cutting us off from the others. For a moment, I was concerned that I might have caused a larger explosion, as the ground continued to shake.

"We gotta move," Marny said.

"Which way?" I asked, joining her at the junction to the main hallway. The obvious choice soon presented itself. By my AI's count, at least three dozen of the skittering horde were closing on our position from the tunnel entrance. In the other direction, there were only a handful of adolescents and hatchlings.

"On my six," she ordered.

The ground continued to shake beneath our feet. Something big was happening and I hoped I hadn't set off a chain reaction by dropping the ceiling. Together, we pushed deeper into the cavern, choosing to engage the smaller bugs first. The basic plan was to gain a defendable position and then take out the encroaching force. At least, that's what I thought the plan was. The hatchlings didn't put up much resistance as we overran them and continued down the long curving passageway.

"Cavern up here," Marny announced.

The tremors in the ground gained strength as we continued forward. Just as we entered the room, she turned and tackled me, throwing me back into the tunnel. While still in mid-flight, she was ripped off me and thrown against the passageway's wall by a three-meter-long Kroerak ship lance.

"Frak!" I yelled, rolling up onto one knee.

The warriors that had been pursuing us from the main tunnel were within five meters. Marny's bios reported that she'd been knocked unconscious and her suit was in the process of applying a stimulant. There were other problems, but she was, at least, alive.

I fired into the crowd and worked to focus on individual bugs. The Popeyes were effective against Kroerak, but one-on-thirty were bad odds. My main weapon would lose effectiveness once the bugs got into hand-to-hand combat range. While I could solo a warrior with just my multi-purpose tool, I couldn't expect to win against more than a few.

I gave ground, firing on full auto as I backed to Marny. One. Two. Three, four, five, six. I was knocking them down in a hurry but for each one I killed, two more jumped over and pushed forward. My only advantage seemed to be the width of the hallway, which allowed only a few abreast. I was thankful for the Kroerak temperament as the warriors slowed, pushing and fighting with each other to get to me.

I reached across my body with my left hand and extracted the multipurpose tool from its position on my leg, not wanting to lose even a second of fire as they pressed in on me.

Finally, they were on me and the fight took on a new dimension. I punched, kicked, and did everything I could to keep them off Marny and from killing me. My suit was taking damage and I wasn't more than halfway through the group, or so my AI said. Personally, I couldn't see much beyond the next punch as I was simply living in the moment.

"We're coming, Liam." Tabby's voice filtered through the sounds of battle.

"Get back in the Stryker," I ordered. I couldn't fathom what would inspire her to exit the armored vehicle. "There are warriors everywhere."

Bright lights illuminated the ceiling of the cavern behind the bugs and the sound of a turret firing filled my ears.

Tabby laughed. "Don't be an idiot."

The three bugs pressing me were unaware of the change in the tempo of the battle, but suddenly I knew there was a glimmer of hope. I buried my hammer into the neck of the closest bug and pulled it across my front. My goal wasn't to kill as much as it was to block the other two who were pressing.

"Cap?" Marny asked, weakly.

"Stay down, Marny. Stryker's in the hallway behind the bugs," I said.

"Cruiser," she corrected.

"No, just the infantry fighting vehicle," I said. She'd evidently taken a pretty good hit to the head.

I felt a clunk on my shoulder as her suit arm came around me. She fired into the bugs at point-blank range, something I hadn't been able to manage. The bug I held on my hammer dropped and I released the hammer with it, swinging my gun arm up and firing into the space Marny had gained. Between the two of us, we pushed the bugs back and I got my first view of the Stryker sitting at an angle in the hallway, firing into the kill box we'd created between us.

"Tabbs, how the frak did you get down here?" I asked, once the bugs had dropped. "That entrance is too steep for a vehicle."

"Cap, we have bigger problems," Marny said as the ground beneath us shook again and great clods of dirt fell from the ceiling.

"What?"

"Take cover." Marny pushed me against the Stryker just as the ceiling fell in on us and everything got very quiet.

"That's messed up," I said after we'd sat for thirty seconds in complete darkness. "Everyone up?"

"Liam, do you see Jonathan and Sendrei?" Tabby asked.

"See them? I don't see anything. I'm surrounded by dirt. They're in the Stryker with you," I said. "We're twenty meters under. I'm not sure we'll be able to dig out." My suit strained as I pushed against the dirt trying to make room.

The ground continued to shake, even more violently than before.

"There was a doorway that opened in the passage filled with lights and technology," Tabby said. "Jonathan saw it and jumped out of the Stryker. Sendrei followed."

"Can you get to that passage?" I asked, hoping it might be a way out of our current predicament.

"I don't know. Bish says the door closed behind Sendrei."

"Frak! What were they thinking?"

The ground shook even more violently and I had to push against the Stryker as it leaned heavily on Marny and me. My HUD showed that we'd somehow changed elevation by five meters. Initially, I assumed we'd somehow sunk further into a cavern below, but I suddenly realized that instead, we'd gained elevation.

"We're lifting. What the frak?" I said and for a moment our comm channels were filled with similar observation.

"Quiet, people!" Marny ordered. "They buried a ship. It's lifting off and we're on it."

"No ship can lift that much dirt," I said.

"We're three meters from the surface," Marny said.

"Shite! Strap in, Bish. This baby isn't designed for non-terrestrial operation," Tabby said.

I chuckled. If Bish hadn't long since strapped in, I'd be surprised.

I strained against the soil, making small headway as I compressed the loose dirt, but the suit just didn't have sufficient power to move the amount of weight that was atop us.

"We're lifting," Marny said.

The power involved in what she was suggesting was mind boggling. First, I'd no idea a Kroerak cruiser could make atmospheric entry, much less bury itself successfully and lie dormant for a hundred fifty standard years. Nick would later explain to me that Kroerak were using gravity fields in a way we still don't understand to achieve this seemingly impossible feat.

The ground around us shifted as the massive ship continued its trajectory toward the surface. It had been lifting the entire time we'd felt the tremors in the ground.

"Liam, what's going on? The entire hillside is heaving," Ada's voice came across the comm.

"Marny, push with me." I reasoned that if Ada's comm signal could make it to us, perhaps enough soil had fallen away that we could free ourselves.

"Hold on to something!" Tabby said as we all started sliding.

We tumbled faster and faster. I got my first view of sky as we separated from the tumbling earth. Clawing against the soil in a swimming motion, I tried to pull myself above it. My AI fired arc-jets the moment I was released, pushing me away from the falling mass.

The Stryker fell, planting itself nose-first in the loose soil on the edge of the massive crater left behind by the climbing cruiser.

Popeyes aren't made to maintain flight and I fell back to the ground, all the while searching the sky for *Tuuq*. "Ada, get out of here!" I yelled, just as I located her.

To her credit, Ada had already turned *Tuuq* and was accelerating away. It was too late, however, as the cruiser fired a wave of lances.

"Ada!" I stepped toward the falling ship.

Chapter 10

NOT A BAD DAY'S WORK

"Get Tabby, Cap," Marny ordered, tearing up the ground as she rushed toward the sinking *Tuuq*.

I raced to the Stryker, two meters of its nose buried in the disturbed earth. An orange warning light directed me left and without thinking, I dove out from beneath a falling mound of dirt the size of our bungalow. As the cruiser continued its climb, it was canting to the side, ridding itself of its extra burdens. Fortunately, it was neither moving toward *Tuuq* nor York.

I jumped up and clung to the wheel of the Stryker while I banged on the rear hatch. "Tabby, are you up?" I asked. "Bish?"

Bish was first to respond. "Aside from hanging like an onion to be dried, I appear to be unharmed."

"I'm attempting to restore systems," Tabby said.

"See if you can get your rear winches powered," I said. "I might be able to get you upright again."

"Copy. Should be up momentarily," she said.

I flipped a mechanical lever next to a gear on both spools. The winch design was nearly identical to what we had back home. I tamped down a desire to consider the implications of aliens and humans coming up with the same design. I dropped to the ground, holding the heavy lead hooks and trailing the thin cables. The stumpy trees of Zuri had deep roots due to the cool dry summers and I chose the biggest two I could find.

"Any luck?" I asked.

"We have power, so you should be able to activate the spools manually," she said. "We're reinitializing the systems. This design has physical memory cores which were unseated in our fall. It'll take another ten minutes before we're going very far."

"Locate Jonathan and Sendrei," I ordered my AI.

"The Sendrei and Jonathan are located within vessel previously referred to as Kroerak cruiser," my AI announced.

"What? Confirm last!"

My AI showed a sequence of videos recorded from different points of view — mainly our suits and vehicle cams. Jonathan, followed by Sendrei, had jumped from the Stryker and run through a briefly opened door just before everything had gone to shite.

"Open comm channel with Jonathan and Sendrei."

My HUD's display of Jonathan's bios drained and disappeared.

"Unable to establish communication channel."

"Marny, we have to get *Tuuq* in the air."

"Tuuq is down hard," she said. "I'm punching out the cockpit glass. I can see movement, but we're pretty shaken up."

"Frak. I think Jonathan and Sendrei are on that cruiser. The Stryker is stuck, but Tabby and Bish are both up," I said.

"Damn. What could they have been thinking?"

I jumped as a sonic boom rolled across the valley. Looking up, I saw that the cruiser was almost out of sight, still climbing.

"Contact Abasi command in Manetra."

"Honorable Hoffen Captain, how might House Gundi be of service to you today?" A neatly trimmed male Felio appeared on my screen.

"I'm reporting a Kroerak vessel making way to escape Zuri gravity," I said. "I'm not sure what sort of response House Gundi desires, but Manetra command should be able to resolve a sensor lock on this vessel. I'm prepared to communicate our data-streams of its current vector."

"Hoffen Captain, this is an official channel. Reporting false information is a serious infraction," he said, scolding me.

I directed my AI to upload the time-coded sensor data of the ship's assent.

"Good. Send that data-stream to your supervisor. You have my ident if you need further information. Hoffen out." I closed the comm channel.

"Send data-streams from 0500 forward to Mshindi Second." If I were more thoughtful, I'd have given her a preamble, but I had more than a few problems to deal with already.

I jumped on top of the Stryker — which, at that moment, happened to be the back hatch — and leaned over to where the manual controls for the winches sat. There was probably a better way to accomplish the task, but I had no idea what that might be, so I pulled in the lines until they were taut and then loaded up tension.

For a moment, nothing happened. Even though the vehicle had landed in soft dirt, it was heavy enough to have buried its nose quite solidly. Pulling against the back of the vehicle meant having to push away the dirt in front of the pointy nose. The winches weren't up to the task.

"Hoffen. Reorient your winch to the side," Bish said, recognizing the problem. "Tip the vehicle over. There's not as much to pull against."

It would have been ideal to pull the vehicle onto its wheels, but getting it out of the dirt was a better objective.

"Going to be a crappy ride for you," I said.

"They say Earthers used to pay for rides like this. Called it a carnival," he said.

Despite my recent dislike of the man, his dry wit made me laugh. I released the tension on one of the lines and jumped off to find a stump perpendicular to the vehicle to tie off to instead. When I loaded tension into the line, the Stryker almost immediately started moving. I jumped off again and quickly relocated the second line so the vehicle wouldn't completely turtle and land on its roof. A few minutes later, I had the vehicle on its side.

"Seriously? After all that, we're lying on our side?" Tabby complained.

"Give me a minute." The mech-suit wasn't quite powerful enough to roll the Stryker over in one push, but by rocking it a few times, I was finally able to right it.

Once upright, I gave the vehicle a quick inspection. Every surface was scraped and big hunks of dirt clung to the sides, but overall, it was in good shape. When I got to the back, the hatch had been sprung but was only open a few centimeters. A broken actuator whined as it tried to lower the heavily armored ramp. Identifying the problem, I reached in and ripped out the broken actuator, allowing the ramp to fall.

"You suck," Tabby said, holding the frame of the vehicle as she hobbled out. "And I never want to get in one of those death traps again."

"Well done, Captain Hoffen," Bish said, smiling as he released the straps that held him in his chair.

"Stay close, Tabbs, Bish," I said. "There are likely Kroerak in the neighborhood."

As I spoke, the interior lights of the Stryker turned on and the vid screens flickered to life.

"There we go," Tabby said.

I jogged back to where I'd tied off the winch cables. One of the cables had buried itself so deeply into the tree trunk that I had to utilize my multipurpose tool to free it.

"*Tuuq*'s in bad shape," Ada said as she and Nick joined us at the back of the Stryker.

Our conversation was cut short by the sound of automatic blaster fire. After converging on the location, we found Bish standing over two hatchlings.

"Damn fine weapon," he said as we approached. "They were running around like chickens with their heads cut off. Didn't seem fair not to put 'em down."

"Nice shooting," I said. "Probably best if you don't get too far from the group, though. A warrior might give you a run for your money."

He pointed into the crater left behind by the cruiser. "Gotta be more than a few of buried down there. Be worth digging them up, a warrior is worth twenty-five thousand."

"You know those warriors are still alive, right?" I said. "And blaster rifles won't penetrate their shell."

It was as if I'd hit the man with a shock stick. He jumped back, turned and ran for the Stryker. As if to punctuate what I'd said, a warrior's claws reached out from the rubble.

"Nice timing." I unstrapped the multipurpose tool, extended it to the sword configuration and leapt into the hole. The ground beneath me boiled. This might have been a terrible decision. A loud thwump announced Marny's arrival and two of us put down seven warriors, as one-by-one they extracted themselves from their dirt graves.

"That's probably not the end of them," Tabby said, once the shooting stopped. She joined us, floating above the crater with the benefit of her grav-suit.

"We're going to need to extend our patrols over here for a while and I'll get Nick to manufacture monitoring equipment. I'd hate to see a warrior or even an adolescent find their way to York," Marny said.

"Do you think they've overcome selich poisoning?" I asked.

"Difficult to know," Nick answered as we climbed out of the crater, dragging dead Kroerak behind us. "There had to be at least one noble to run that cruiser. We've seen before that a noble can override a warrior's survival instinct where it relates to selich."

"They seemed intent on taking you guys in the tunnels," Tabby said. "I didn't see them holding back."

"I'm going to call that a problem for another day," I said. "I hate to be the capitalist right now, but we need to round up the fallen Kroerak. Nick, how bad is *Tuuq*? Scrap or repair?"

"She'll sail again," Nick said. "But we'll wait for Petersburg Station to arrive. We just don't have the capacity to repair the hull damage."

"Frak," I said. "How are we going after Jonathan and Sendrei?"

"We'll get a message off to Munay," Nick said. "It's the best we can do for now."

"This is going to crush Flaer," I said. "I should never have let him come along."

Never one to let me wallow, Marny spoke up. "You're right, Cap. This will be hard on her, but the decision was Sendrei's."

We worked in silence, stacking dead bugs in a giant pile. It was disgusting work, but the necessity of earning credits for our survival pushed us forward.

"That's a crap tonne of bugs," Marny said, tossing a final warrior husk onto the pile.

"By my count, we're looking at a little over four hundred thousand in bounties," I said. "I'd like us to pay off our short-term note and buy us time to get our feet under us again."

"Do you really think Abasi will pay out that much?" Bish asked.

"No question. You know as well as I do, the Abasi are an honorable people. By my count, you're in for six hundred credits. Not a bad day's work, right?" I said.

"Today has been terrifying beyond description," Bish said. "When Tabitha drove into the hole, I thought we were all dead. The slope of the entrance ramp alone should have killed us. How she knew we were too long to flip over, I'll never know. When I realized we'd trapped a gang of warriors, I thought we were dead. And when I realized we were riding on the back of a warship, I thought we were dead. Turns out, you all have a pesky aversion to dying and for that I'm grateful. And no, I don't want my six hundred in bounty, that's all yours, you more than earned it."

"I'll take another bowl of chili," I said, causing the table to erupt in laughter.

I found it difficult to smile. We were down two crew members and there wasn't a thing we could do about it. According to House Mshindi, the Kroerak cruiser had eluded tracking after moving outside of Zuri's anemic tracking systems. Even if we had a ship to give chase with, we had no idea where to go.

Life had slowed significantly in the weeks since the Kroerak ship launched from Zuri and we'd spent the first week patrolling the area between York and Kuende Run, bagging three warriors, a handful of adolescents and even more hatchlings. Unlike those we'd run into in the hive, these bugs seemed uninterested in direct conflict, especially after we'd seen fit to consume copious amounts of the spicy, natural root.

The Abasi — specifically House Gundi — had taken over Kuende Run. Two days after our assault on the hive, they'd dropped in a platoon of heavily armed soldiers. Ever since then, the road past Zuri and our compound had been busy with wave after wave of troop and supply transports. There was even talk of a road improvement project all the way from Manetra, twenty-two hundred kilometers away.

"Patty should pay you a commission on that chili, Hoffen," Hog said, sitting at the chair we always left open for him while eating at Patty's restaurant. "With all this talk of bug warriors running loose, she can't make enough of it."

I gave him a friendly nod and took a seat next to Sempre. She looked away, still uncomfortable with the perceived difference in station between us.

"How are you feeling, Sempre?" I asked, hoping to ease her tension. 'You're looking strong." As far as I could tell, the young Felio had recovered from her injuries. Her pointy ears twitched in response to the positive attention and swiveled back as she looked at me, not quite making eye contact. She didn't smile since it was considered bad manners by Felio to show teeth when communicating, but I'd learned to translate many of her other actions. The ear movements, narrowing of eyes and flick of her tail indicated appreciation.

"She's doing really well," Roby Bishop blurted out from her other side. "Felio have a tremendous healing capacity. I'm not sure how badly she needed the nano-bots. Me, on the other hand, I was toast. Without those bots, I could have died."

"You were brave, Roby." Sempre lowered her eyes and looked at the table as her tail wrapped around her leg.

"I'm glad you're *both* doing better. Any chance you're ready to rejoin the crew?" I asked.

"I'm not sure, Captain," Roby said. "I thought our last trip was going to be it. Sempre and I aren't sure we want to be in the line of fire anymore."

"We have a lot of work ahead to get *Intrepid* going again," I said. "How about you help us with repairs and then make up your mind about crew."

"Sure. We could do that," he said.

"Sempre, is that how you feel too?"

"Yes, Hoffen Captain. Roby is the important one. I am just a cargo handler."

"Fact is, I plan to have a lot of cargo," I said. "The position remains yours if you want it."

"You would take me without Roby?" Sempre asked.

"Oh, dear girl," Ada interjected. "Come sit by me and let me explain how this works."

Sempre looked nervously to Roby who seemed to be both confused and concerned by the exchange. With all eyes on him, he nodded, as if giving permission. I shook my head knowingly. Roby was in for a rough ride.

"Big night coming up, right Mom?" I raised my glass of carbonated red fruit juice to her.

"Are *Tuuq* and *Intrepid* really up for the trip out of the atmosphere?" Mom asked.

Petersburg Station was due to arrive in six hours and the Ophir crew was itching to unpack and get her operational.

"You have another option?" I asked.

"We have shuttles that can easily make the trip," she said.

"Except they're on the station and not here."

"Katherine would be more than willing to send a shuttle down," she said.

"LeGrande is on Petersburg?" I asked. "I thought it was too

dangerous to move with personnel aboard." Katherine LeGrande was an ex-Belirand captain. She had become Mom's business partner after she and her crew had been abandoned in the deep dark.

"Petersburg Station is being moved through TransLoc," Nick said. "I was just being safe by not allowing anyone to ride on it before. When we moved it from Tipperary to Ophir, I didn't have the backup of Mars Protectorate Engineering Core running the calculations."

"I'd like to take both *Intrepid* and *Tuuq* up," I said. "We've made progress on *Intrepid's* repairs, but Petersburg's new dry dock would really get us rolling. I don't think we'll need more than forty-eight hours of work on *Tuuq,* that is, if Petersburg has a decent supply of armor glass and nano-steel."

"How will we bill for that?" Merrie asked.

"Merrie, does not Liam own this company?" Amon, Merrie's ordinarily quiet husband asked.

"She's right, Amon," Nick interjected. "Everyone at this table, except Hog, has a stake in Petersburg Station. The same is not true of *Intrepid*. It would be irresponsible if we were to consume resources without accounting for it. I've created a market projection using Abasi credits for material and finished goods cost. My objective was to create a market to entice York citizens to get interested in asteroid mining, but we should be able to use the same calculations for repairs."

"Am I allowed to set up my own contracts for Petersburg? Or will you be handling this?" Merrie pushed.

"What kind of contracts?" I asked.

"Sheet steel is in high demand in Manetra and I have proposals related to armor glass and nano-steel out to several Zuri manufacturers. If everyone who has replied will sign a contract, I could fill orders for all our sheet stock within a week. The fact is, the Zuri market is under served."

"How much stock do you have?"

"Two thousand square meters in five mil rolls and another thousand in nine mil rolls. We have significantly less nano-steel and armor glass, as we tend to make those products based on orders instead of stocking it," she said.

"Make the deals," Nick said. "I'd like to review anything bigger than fifty thousand credits."

"You've mentioned recruiting miners before," Hog said. "There are several I can think of who might be interested. Are you ready to start talking to them?"

"That's going to be a problem," Ortel said. "A miner needs to have their own equipment, but no one in York would have that. Where's the starting capital going to come from? We could loan out equipment, but that's not fair either. Wear and tear needs to be charged against revenues."

"How much mining equipment do we have available to loan?" I asked.

"Enough for three claims, assuming we keep enough for work at the station," he replied.

"These are all details Katherine and I can work through," Mom said. "Unless you would like to be involved." Her tone of voice warned me that I was stepping into her business.

"Nope. Not at all," I said. "My goal was to put mining behind me and that hasn't changed."

"Good," she said. "I just received a comm from Katherine that Petersburg Station is in place in orbit. If the sky wasn't cloudy, we'd be able to see it with limited magnification."

"She's early," I said. "How is that possible?"

Mom smiled and slightly tipped her head to the side. "Your calculations were made with first run data; there was an update I neglected to pass along. She has been in place for three hours, successfully deployed all station defenses, and if I am to take the message literally, has set a pot of tea on to boil in anticipation of our arrival."

"I'll take that chili to go, then." I stood and walked over to the restaurant's service counter. "Can you have your team ready and on the platform in twenty minutes?"

"We'll be ready," Mom said, smiling like I'd missed something.

"You're ready now, aren't you?"

"For twenty minutes." All she'd give me was a knowing waggle of her eyebrows.

"How are we going to do this?" Ada asked as the five of us piled into the armored patrol vehicle we'd started using as our transportation between York and the compound.

"Ada, would you sail *Tuuq* out to Petersburg after picking up Mom and crew?" I said. "Otherwise, I'd like everyone aboard *Intrepid*. I don't think she's going to appreciate lifting off from Zuri."

"I will and you should have a little faith," Ada said. "The Abasi engineers did a good job of restoring function to the grav lift systems."

"It was a hack," Nick said. "We're only getting forty percent transfer from engines to lift system. A bigger problem is that without our inertial systems, it's going to take us over three hours to get there without pasting everyone."

"Darn it, Liam. Did you really have to burn out every system?" Ada asked. "I get not wanting to turn over technology to an alien government, but you nearly killed my girl."

I wasn't about to answer the question since I already felt bad about my actions. It could be argued that the Abasi wouldn't have returned *Intrepid* to us if we'd left her intact when she was seized by Strix. It was a game of what-if and gotcha that I'd been replaying in my head for months and I was tired of it.

"Oh, don't be glum." Ada said, recognizing my mood and wrapping an arm around my shoulders as we bumped along in the patroller. "I'm sure there's plenty of bilge work that needs doing."

I punched Ada lightly on the shoulder as she climbed out the back of the vehicle. "Be safe, Ada. We'll see you on Petersburg."

"Will do," she said.

We'd worked diligently to get *Intrepid* ready for liftoff for the last two weeks. It was depressing to set foot in the ship, as she'd gone from perfectly maintained to nearly unusable. As it turned out — unknown to Ada — the septic field's gray and black water systems hadn't been targeted by any of the wrath I had Jonathan release. It was one of the very few systems that remained in good working order.

I pushed open the hatch to the bridge and latched it open with a strap I'd improvised. My chair sat dead-center on a slightly elevated platform at the back of the bridge. Cruelly, my imagination reminded me of the once fully operational holo display that had been available. I was reduced to my suit's HUD as I took my place on the chair.

"Let's start systems check," I said as Marny, Tabby and Nick took their stations on the bridge. A single, meter-wide vid screen glowed on the forward bulkhead, which had once been completely covered with an integrated display.

As each of us worked through our assignments, both expected and unexpected failures presented themselves and we worked through them. It wasn't a certainty that *Intrepid*'s gravity systems would generate enough repulsion to put us outside of Zuri's pull.

"*Incoming comm, Ada Chen,*" my AI announced.

"Put it on bridge public address," I replied.

"Hiyas *Intrepid*. We're just lifting off now," Ada said. "See you in a few hours. And Liam, take it easy on my girl."

"Copy that, Ada. Safe travels." I closed comms.

We worked for another hour as Nick and I traveled back and forth to the engine room, manually checking statuses that appeared faulty. Finally, we had exhausted the systems checklist and I sat back in the chair, not feeling particularly great about the exercise.

"Nick, your call. We good to go?" I asked.

"Mechanically, we're good, Liam. She's not going to handle like you want, but we've made good progress. Just take it slow."

"Cap, I have it on good authority that Captain LeGrande has real coffee aboard Petersburg," Marny said.

That perked me up. "You think?"

"According to Ortel, Petersburg has an entire deck dedicated to botanicals and they have twenty mature coffee plants straight from Earth. Play your cards right and I'll bet we can convince Curtis Long to plant an entire hillside of those beans back behind the bungalow. She has cocoa plants, too."

I knew that Marny was trying to take my mind off *Intrepid*'s problems. The fact was, it worked. "Cocoa?"

"Chocolate," Marny answered.

"Let's get this bird in the air," I said. "Nick, give me helm control."

"All yours."

"Cue David Bowie's Space Oddity over public address."

"Seriously?" Tabby asked, groaning.

A man's reedy voice sang forlornly.

Ground control to Major Tom ...

Ground control to Major Tom

Chapter 11

PETERSBURG STATION

"She's rough, Liam," Tabby said as I spooled up *Intrepid's* four massive engines. I was redirecting all the engine power to energize the gravity repulsor system that was reporting sixty percent efficiency. *Intrepid* wasn't that comfortable with planet-side travel to begin with and in her current shape, we were cutting it close to the margins.

There were about a million things wrong on *Intrepid*. Foremost, there was a complete lack of inertial systems, which was causing everything to shake profusely. The engine's roar couldn't quite drown out the distant sounds of unsecured items crashing to the deck as we clawed our way past the first hundred meters.

"Hang on," I said as I worked to keep a level ascent.

There was some good news; after a few minutes, the shaking did start to abate. There had to be a deep, technological reason, but I was just grateful for the reduction.

The climb seemed to take forever, but we finally emerged from atmospheric layers and we switched from a pure repulsive lift to using our engines for their primary function.

"All hands," I started, so that Roby and Sempre who were sitting one room over in the gunner's nest would hear me. "We're switching to primary drive system. Our inertial systems are inoperable so you'll want to face forward. Expect up to 2g in acceleration."

"Nick, bring main engines online," I said.

"In three... two... one...." He counted me down.

On one, I nudged the primary thrust stick forward while watching our altitude and delta-v (change in vector) between Zuri and *Intrepid*. We initially fell back toward the planet, but I'd expected that, as we were no longer lifting. I nudged the stick again and felt the ship push forward as the chair cushion compressed against my back. The sensation reminded me more of driving in the armored patrol vehicle than sailing a space-borne vessel.

We continued to accelerate forward, but were also still falling toward the planet. The latter was disturbing enough that I requested my AI to show a predicted path at current acceleration. The line on my HUD showed we were actually in a pinch if I didn't speed things up. We were at 1.2g, but we could handle more, so I continued to accelerate past 1.4, 1.8, and 2.6.

"Everything okay, Love?" Tabby asked when I passed 3g.

My line was looking better, but my margin of escape was thin.

"I switched from repulsors a little early," I said, my head pinned to the seat behind me. "We'll have a few more minutes of this."

At 4g, I held us there for a full minute before backing to 3g, which

I held for a full five minutes. Finally, I pulled back to 1.5g where I planned to keep us for the ride out to Petersburg Station.

"Incoming hail, Tuuq."

"Go ahead, *Tuuq*," I replied.

"Liam, we have two cutter class ships closing. We're on burn to join up with *Intrepid*," Ada said.

"Copy," I said. "Marny, do you have anything on sensors?"

"Negative, Cap, too much interference," Marny said.

"Linking with *Tuuq*," Nick added.

The forward view screen popped to life with two ships on hard burn for *Tuuq*. My AI predicted they'd overtake the smaller ship just about the same time they came into our maximum weapons range.

"Tabbs, gunnery nest," I said. It was a contingency we'd already discussed. *Intrepid's* ten turrets were not linked and required manual control if there was any hope of shooting an evading ship. Marny would need all the help she could get.

"Roger," Tabby said as she sprinted for the bridge's exit.

"Nick, what do we know about those ships?" I asked.

"Transponders are returning a Genteresk designation," he replied. It was interesting that after being identified as pirates by Abasi, the ships would fly their flag so openly. When they attacked us at the Tamu gate on our way to Abasi Prime, Genteresk ships had chosen to mask their transponders.

"Hail Genteresk ships."

A chime indicated that the comm channel was open, but there was no audible response. If *Intrepid* had been running at fifty percent or better, I would have had no hesitation about engaging the cutters. Heck, I would have run them down because of the flag they were sailing under. Genteresk ships were specifically listed by Abasi as valid privateer prizes. As things stood, I wasn't interested in getting into it with them.

"Genteresk ships, break off pursuit of Loose Nuts cutter *Tuuq* or we'll consider the action hostile," I announced. "I repeat, your actions are hostile and you will be fired upon if you persist."

The comm channel closed without a response, but they continued their pursuit of *Tuuq*.

"Ada, do you have anything else in the tank?" I asked. "It's going to be close."

"No, Liam. We're at emergency burn as it is and *Tuuq* isn't very happy about it."

"Copy, Ada. We'll pick it up on our side," I said. "All hands, prepare for 4g burn in ten seconds."

The good news was both ships were headed in the same direction so we wouldn't need to maneuver much. The bad news was that 4g was annoying. After a full minute of burn, we'd closed enough of the gap that I felt comfortable reducing acceleration to 2g.

"There they go," Marny said. After ten minutes of burn, it became clear we'd rendezvous with *Tuuq* well before the cutters could overtake our position.

"What do you suppose they were doing in the neighborhood?" I asked as I reduced our burn to cruising speed.

"Looking for us; no coincidences in space. I wonder how they knew we were off planet." Nick was repeating a theme we'd come to understand. Space was a vast, wide-open area of nothing. If you got near another object, it was most likely because one of you intended for it happen.

"Someone's watching us," Marny said. "Let's stay in convoy. I wouldn't mind having *Tuuq's* sensor package for the rest of the trip."

"I read you, Marny," Ada replied. "We'll stay close."

Finally, I reversed *Intrepid's* engines on approach to Petersburg Station.

"Petersburg Station, this is Commander Hoffen. I'm requesting positive acknowledgement of Loose Nuts Corporation and wish to register foreign ship, *Tuuq*," Mom's voice came over the comm from *Tuuq*. "And on behalf of the Zuri based crew, welcome to the Santaloo system."

"Commander Hoffen — Silver. So good to see you. It's been a long journey." The voice belonged to Katherine LeGrande. "*Intrepid* and *Tuuq* are reading friendly and you're clear on approach."

"Captain LeGrande, Liam Hoffen. Welcome to our favorite corner of the universe. Do you mind if I request status on your current defensive capabilities? We had a little excitement this evening," I said.

"Greetings, Liam, of course," she replied. "Transmitting now. We're still in the process of deploying to full capacity."

A virtual, translucent sphere extended around Petersburg Station, reaching out ten kilometers. It was considerably less capacity than expected, but before I could ask the question, six additional green spheres illuminated. Long-range defenses would extend out to the expected seventy-five-kilometer reach.

"Once station crew is aboard and settled," LeGrande continued, "we'll deploy our long-range capabilities."

"Katherine, we're bringing *Tuuq* into dry-dock bay one and *Intrepid* into bay two," Mom said.

"We'll meet you there."

"We?" Mom asked.

"Believe it or not, you're not our inaugural visitor, Silver," LeGrande replied. "Code forty-two. Petersburg Station out."

"Code forty-two, Mom?" I asked.

"All clear signal," Mom replied.

The station's familiar short, boot shape was a welcome sight and my HUD indicated a path to what was identified as Bay-2. Unlike Bay-1 which was fully enclosed, I was to moor atop a long platform that was a combination of cleared rock and steel plating. As I zeroed out our delta-v with the station, magnetic cables fired from mooring posts that articulated from recesses in the station's surface and *Intrepid* was tugged into position.

"I didn't see any other ships," I said as we floated down the hallway toward the airlock. "You know anything about this, Nick?"

He shook his head and blinked. "I really don't."

The airlock showed green, meaning there was positive pressure on the other side. In the time it took us to organize and exit the bridge, Petersburg had extended a three-meter-wide, pressurized gang plank to *Intrepid*.

"Someone's rolling out the red carpet," Tabby said as we walked side by side down the spacious umbilical between station and ship.

"Look at that," I said, pointing at the glass that separated us from the station. I'd caught a glimpse of bright yellow and blue.

"What's he doing here?" Tabby asked, jumping to the same conclusion.

I palmed open the station-side airlock.

"Liam Hoffen!" A blue-furred, frog-headed alien who was only a meter tall squirted through the hatch before it could fully open and attached itself to me.

I hugged the childlike creature as it clung to me. "Jester Ripples! What a fantastic surprise."

"I thought you would never arrive." Jester Ripples jumped from me to Tabby and gave her the same unabashed treatment.

A virtual sea of little blue aliens all bobbed up and down excitedly when I looked past Jester Ripples. At the edge of the pack stood a brown-skinned teenager with bright brown eyes, looking at me with a smile.

"Anino?" I asked as I waded into the pile of aliens who apparently considered us all to be family as they climbed on, hugged and generally greeted every member of the crew.

"Hoffen." Anino nodded as I approached.

I pulled the teenager into an embrace. The two of us had our differences, but it was something we could look past. Anino was truly a man in a boy's body. He had survived several centuries thanks to extensive medical treatments, but in the end, he'd been forced to move his consciousness from one body to the next in order to survive. While we disagreed on approach, both of us recognized we were very much on the same side, especially where Jonathan was concerned.

"*Gaylon Brighton* came into contact with the Kroerak cruiser in the Brea Fortul system."

"What about Munay? I have a comm crystal for him," I said.

"Mars Protectorate isn't saying much, but a source reports the crew of *Gaylon Brighton* is assumed captured or dead."

"Damn. Probably shouldn't tell Mom yet."

"Jonathan has been in brief communication — enough to let me know they're alive, but not enough to get a lock on them."

"Sendrei too? Are they looking for extraction?"

"The message is too short to know of your missing friend," Anino said. "Extraction is impossible. We have no idea where the cruiser traveled after encountering *Gaylon Brighton*."

"Why did Jonathan do this? Why would they jump on that ship?"

"They want to see the Kroerak defeated," Anino said.

"Why? Kroerak aren't hunting them. Why do they care so much about humanity?"

"I don't know," Anino said. "All I know is that without them, I'd never have uncovered what Belirand was up to. Without Jonathan, the Kroerak invasion of Sol would have ended much differently."

"I believe that."

Mom, Ada, and Katherine LeGrande appeared from the other end of the hallway. An excited hoot from Jester Ripples warned that he'd caught sight of Ada and suddenly the stream of bouncing Norigans raced toward the women.

"What can you tell me about that cruiser?" Anino changed subjects.

"House Gundi has the site where it was buried locked down tight," I said. "Do you have this?" I flicked him the network of tunnels we'd mapped out.

"No. Abasi aren't releasing details until they've completed their investigation. Understandable. They're embarrassed to discover they've had Kroerak sitting there for so long."

"Liam, there's plenty of time to talk," Mom interrupted. "Katherine has a nice reception waiting for us in the commons."

"Copy that," I said. "Lead the way."

It had been more than a year since I'd seen Petersburg Station, but what I saw now could have been a completely different station. The hallway was standard station build, although it bore a fresh coat of paint and showed a fantastic view of space. In our current orientation, we had a glimpse of Zuri if you stood close enough to the glass that started about chest height and extended into the ceiling.

"How many decks?" I asked as Ortel Licht fell in step next to me.

"Plans are for twenty. We have five functional decks: Command, Engineering, Village-One, Promenade and Bio Recovery."

"Village-one?"

"Living quarters. We were working on opening that up to the promenade so we could have a waterfall all the way down to bio recovery," he said. "We have permanent housing for eighty families and can run temporary for almost a thousand. Of course, coming to Zuri shifted some of our priorities."

"What's on the promenade?" Tabby picked Milenette up. The little girl was having trouble keeping up with her brother, Priloe.

"You'll see soon enough," Ortel said. "That's where this jetway exits."

I'd asked enough questions about the station that my AI had reached out and successfully downloaded a deck layout for the station. The promenade was a recreation level that included a running track, pod-ball court, workout facilities, meeting rooms and a thirty by forty-meter food court. The deck was irregularly shaped, two hundred meters wide and four hundred meters long at its maximum dimensions. While it was by far the largest of the five decks, it also had significant room for expansion.

The promenade was, if anything, more impressive in person than on the layout. The sheer openness of the space was incredible. Bright lights shining from the ceiling offered the same temperature as that of Earth's sun and I blinked in its brilliance. Zuri's sun was yellower and farther away. A stream of water rushed over rocks and pooled into a pond located in the center of the promenade, its humid and brightly lit environment offering a perfect home for plant life.

"Waterfall?" I asked, feeling Ortel's gaze on me as I took it all in. Every space station added bio diversity and it was often cleverly implemented to add artistic interest. Colony-40, where I'd grown up, had been required to import all its bio mass over long distances when it had been founded. As a result, they'd relied on easily reproducible, simple plants that had little aesthetic value. Petersburg Station had been in orbit above a planet where trips to the surface were common and they'd taken good advantage of the opportunity. A wide variety of plants grew all over the lush surfaces.

"Over time, that entire shelf next to the pond will be removed," Ortel said, gesturing to a rocky area. "We have a small capture pond on Village-One that will drain into Bio Recovery. It's dry right now. We still need to remove thirty thousand meters of material."

"How did you get all this cleared?" I asked.

"We worked at it for a long time," Ortel said. "Amon is a machine. He just keeps working."

The sound of splashing caught my attention as the horde of Norigans raced into the promenade's water feature.

"Whoa. Hold on there," I said, caught off-guard. It was considered bad station etiquette to mess with biological matter.

"A most reasonable response, Liam Hoffen," Jester Ripples said, gently grabbing my arm as I moved to intercept the aliens.

I tried to free myself. "I have to stop them."

"If you observe carefully, you will recognize we cause no damage to the station's flora. We nurture the habitat of our home world."

It was hard for me to take my eyes off the Norigans as we continued around the outside of the promenade. The preservation of station resources had been drilled into me so hard. I was sure they were causing trouble, but not once did I see a single, wide, fuzzy foot land on a plant.

"Welcome to Petersburg!" Katherine LeGrande said as we rounded a rocky corner into the main courtyard. Round tables had been set up, each boasting a colorful umbrella to shade the table's occupants from the station's bright lights. The word 'WELCOME' was displayed on the wall above a food-service booth set into the wall.

"What's this floor surface?" I asked as we crossed to the tables.

"Something your mom came up with," Ortel said. "She had Merrie design and create a bot that grinds and polishes the rock so it looks like slate tile. Seems like a lot of work to me, but everyone likes it."

"It really dresses up the space," Ada said, passing us.

Just as Mom said, Katherine had organized a welcome party. An array of baked rolls and pastries awaited our group and, more importantly, just as Marny promised, a carafe sat on one end.

"Is this coffee?" I asked, stepping up next to LeGrande.

She smiled. "You are a spacer at heart, Captain Hoffen. On a table filled with delectable treats, you orient on the coffee. This is my very own roast from seeds I received from Earth."

"Is there enough that I could try some?"

"That's why it is on the table, Captain. I understand you might have a contact on Zuri who could plant a hillside. Is that true?" LeGrande asked.

"I will make it my life's mission," I said.

She smiled conspiratorially at me. "Then I believe we shall be great business partners. We will hook the denizens of this great galaxy on our evil brew and control the spice."

I laughed and gave her an amiable hug, accepting a steaming cup from her. "I like the way you think." I took a sip, closing my eyes as the hot liquid washed over my taste buds. "Oh ... that's delicious." Instead of the synth-coffee's signature bitter aftertaste, Katherine's coffee tasted of pure, quality beans.

"We'll dominate," she said.

"No doubt about it."

"Do you mind if I borrow the captain?" Anino asked, interrupting.

"Of course, Mr. Anino," Katherine said, obviously intimidated by the powerful man, though he wore a teenager's body.

"Mars Protectorate is concerned," Anino said. "The three ships that disappeared were in Nijjar controlled space."

"Pogona?" I asked, recognizing the name of the dominant Pogona government.

"Yes."

"Do you think the Pogona have a relationship with Kroerak?" I asked.

Anino flicked a data-stream at me and my HUD showed the last moments of a Mars Protectorate ship receiving fire from a Kroerak vessel. The stream paused and a ship that was clearly not Kroerak was highlighted. The ship was well within firing range of the Kroerak vessel, but under no obvious duress.

"That ship, *Feskilra,* sails under a Strix flag," Anino said.

"You're saying Strix are in bed with Kroerak?"

"We don't know," Anino said. "And you need to keep that information in confidence."

"Strix being Kroerak puppets would explain some things," I said.

"That is a lot to infer from a single image," Anino said. "Per conversations with Abasi, Strix have multiple factions and it would be dangerous to paint the entire species with such a broad brush."

"Yeah, good point," I said, not interested in getting into it further. "Are all the upgrades to Petersburg your doing?" I asked.

"I like to think that I merely accelerated the work Silver and Katherine were already accomplishing," he said. "I have an excess of capital and simply gave them a nudge."

"Your nudges typically put my crew in danger," I said.

"And yet, you have a remarkable capacity to squeeze out of dangerous spots, my friend," Anino said.

It wasn't lost on me that Nick was quietly listening to the exchange.

"How do we find Jonathan?"

"I think the Kroerak ship is damaged. I also think it's working its way through Nijjar controlled space to the Dark Frontier." Anino placed a small device on the table and a holographic image of a galaxy appeared.

"This is Dwingeloo," he said, cupping his hands and squeezing the galaxy to the size of a person's head. He then pulled at it. As he stretched it out, faint lines appeared, connecting solar systems.

"We're here." He pointed to the Santaloo solar system. "Dark Frontier is considered anything past this system, here — Tanwar."

"So why don't you tell Mars Protectorate or the Abasi? Surely, they're much better equipped to handle this than we are," I said.

"Believe me, Mars Protectorate is ready to go in guns-a-blazing, but that won't work. They don't have a large enough force and there's no way Nijjar government is going to allow a human fleet to traipse through their systems. The fact is, we need a crew that doesn't draw attention and we need that crew near the Dark Frontier so we can act if Jonathan does get a message out."

I shook my head, finally catching up. "Like the crew of a well-armed freighter that just happens to be in the area?" I asked.

"Just like that," Anino agreed.

"We can't take *Tuuq,* it has no teeth. And it'll take months before *Intrepid is* ready to sail."

"Right. If only you had an entire crew of the finest engineers in the galaxy available," Anino said, looking out to the pond where the gaggle of Norigans splashed about playfully.

"Remind me to never play chess with you, Anino."

Chapter 12

CRAPPY MOMENTS

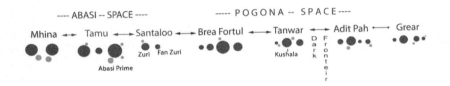

---- ABASI -- SPACE ----   ----- P O G O N A -- S P A C E----

Mhina ← → Tamu ← → Santaloo ← → Brea Fortul ← → Tanwar ← → Adit Pah ← → Grear

Zuri Fan Zuri   Kushala

Abasi Prime   Dark Frontier

"Will you look for him?" Flaer asked, greeting Tabby and me at the entrance to Petersburg Station's medical facilities.

The skin beneath her eyes was red and puffy. I didn't have the heart to tell her that I didn't believe Sendrei to still be alive.

"We received a ping from Jonathan a couple of days ago," I said. "We couldn't get a location, but as long as there's hope, we'll keep trying."

"Sendrei would not want you to risk yourselves for him. The Kroerak will surely have released him to death."

I hugged the small, severe woman. "I know, but that doesn't mean we can't hope."

She drew a shuddering breath and released me. "I will keep my hope. But that is not why you have visited."

I smiled. "True. It's not the only reason."

"This place is huge," Tabby said. She was right, the medical bay was hundreds of square meters, every bit of it fully finished.

"I am not worthy to be given charge of these facilities. We should have a trained physician."

"You are more than qualified," Ada said, joining us.

I took in a quick breath, as Ada was stripped down to her skivvies. On a normal day, it was hard to forget how beautiful she was, but standing there in small, skin-tight shorts and a narrow band around her chest, I had to work to avert my eyes.

"Fight the good fight, precious," Tabby whispered in my ear, placing her hand on my butt and pinching.

"Frak," I said, trying to do anything but look at Ada's flawless, ebony skin.

"Nice to be admired," Ada grinned and turned away.

My heart raced as she removed the black patch that sat atop her empty eye socket. It was a reminder of just how fierce she was and how far we all were willing to go for our team members.

Ada lost her left eye in our last desperate mission to save Earth. She'd been stoic about the horrible disfigurement and had never complained. If asked, she'd tell you it was a small sacrifice for the greater good, but I knew the loss bothered her. For a pilot, vision is critical and Ada had been struggling with the loss of her stereoscopic binocular vision and a reduction of her peripheral field of view. In short, a horrible handicap. I was certain I'd heard her weeping behind closed doors on more than one occasion.

"The procedure is simple," Flaer said. "You just need to step into the tank. I've already placed the eye we grew for you into the machine."

"Be safe," Ada said, embracing Tabby and then me. "When you come back, I should have my vision restored."

Ada wasted no more time and stepped into the tank. With Flaer's help, she donned a breathing mask. We all watched as the fluid filled the tank and Ada was gently put to sleep.

"How many people can you take care of here?" I asked as Flaer lowered the room's lights.

"At capacity, Petersburg Station will host three thousand souls," Flaer said. "This medical facility was designed to care for a population twice that size."

"Nice to have infinite funds," Tabby said.

I shook my head. "I'm not sure if I'm in love with the idea or if I'm terrified Anino thinks we'll need a medical bay this big."

"When will she get out?" I asked.

"Seventy-two hours," Flaer said.

"Hard to see her like this." Tabby placed her hand on the glass. "Get well, girl."

I wrapped an arm around Tabby's waist. Seeing Ada in the tank brought back memories of Tabby's time there. Those were some of my darkest memories and a lump formed in my throat as they were dredged up.

"The medical AI is predicting full recovery with a twenty percent increase in original function," Flaer said.

"Not to complain, but twenty percent seems low," I said as we walked out.

"Any more would cause too much of an imbalance between the right and left sides. She had the choice to replace both eyes but declined," Flaer said. "Tabitha, I have been meaning to follow up with you. How is your leg injury healing? Would you allow for a quick examination before you depart?"

Without hesitation, Tabby unzipped her grav-suit and pulled it off. Flaer ran a med scanner over the leg, which no longer showed any evidence of a scar.

"This synthetic skin tissue is fabulous." Flaer kneaded the calf muscle, causing Tabby to giggle as she brushed the back of her knee. "I see no evidence of your injury. Have you successfully retrained the muscles? It would have been ideal if we'd had the capacity to stimulate them during your recovery."

"Almost one hundred percent," Tabby said, pulling her suit back on. "You'll take good care of Ada?"

"Of course." Flaer stopped at the double wide, sliding doors of the medical bay. "Safe travels."

"Let's roll." We walked through the station's hallways to where the newly repaired *Tuuq* was docked.

The plan was for Tabby and me to take *Tuuq* on a run to Manetra, on the planet below. We'd then sail on to the Tamu gate and Abasi Prime where we'd deliver a bond-less, low value load and pick up Nick's parts from Bakira. Mostly, we were filling time until *Intrepid* was ready to sail again.

"Establish comm, Nick."

Nick and Marny were planet-side at the workshop, having taken the shuttle back from Petersburg Station. He was manufacturing a set of prototype stevedore bots that we'd eventually take with us when we started tracking down the missing Mars Protectorate ships.

"Go ahead, Liam," Nick replied.

"We're about to disembark. Anything you need from the station?"

"We're low on steel sheet. How about twenty meters of three mil?"

"Copy. We'll load it up and be down in thirty," I said.

FOR ALL THE bad I had to say about *Tuuq*, it wasn't an altogether unpleasant ship, especially after the refit. The layout was simple: a two hundred cubic meter, rectangular cargo hold sat behind a three-person bridge, separated by a short hallway with head and galley on port side and single sleeping quarters on the starboard. The ship had lacked for anything resembling exercise equipment so Tabby had installed a running track into the deck of the hallway and resistance bands into the starboard bulkhead.

"Anything on station sensors?" I asked as I worked through the startup sequence.

Petersburg had been tracking several Genteresk ships that had taken interest in our new station, but so far had avoided all attempts at contact. At least two of the vessels had superior speed to *Tuuq* and I wasn't about to set out if they were in the area.

"Negative," Tabby answered.

"Petersburg Station, this is *Tuuq*," I said.

"Go ahead, *Tuuq*," Katherine LeGrande's face appeared on the forward vid-screen.

"Requesting permission to shove off."

"Permission granted, Captain. We're showing clear sailing. Safe travels, Liam."

As I felt the station clamps release, I spooled up the engines and pulled away from the station.

It seemed like forever since I'd sailed in a ship with modern inertial systems and I reveled in the familiar sensations as Zuri quickly grew in the armor glass in front of us. The burn I executed would have turned us to paste on the aft bulk head in seconds without our systems, but all we felt was a growing downward pull.

"Honey, we're hooome," Tabby called as we set down next to Nick's workshop.

"Check this out," Nick said as Tabby and I approached.

"What do you have?" I asked.

Instead of responding, Nick typed at a virtual panel projected onto his left wrist. From the shadows of his shop, a bot arose and sailed over our heads on its way to *Tuuq*. It easily slid two sheets of steel onto extended forks and backed away from the tall stack, returning to the shop behind us.

"That's your prototype?" I asked.

He nodded and grinned at me. "Yup. It's a little rough, but you should take it with you. Maybe you could build interest."

"Are you sure you can give it up?" I asked.

"First one is always the hardest. I'm only missing the steel you brought for the next one. I'll have two more by the time you return. Make sure to capture all operational logs, though. I'm sure it'll need some tweaks."

"Easy enough."

"Did Hog talk to you about an order of supplies for York in Nadira?"

"I haven't had a chance to check comms today."

"I checked your manifest, looks like you have enough room," Nick said.

"No problem."

"You need anything to eat, Cap? We were just getting ready for lunch," Marny asked, walking up from the bungalow where we bunked while planet side.

"I think we'd like to get moving."

"Copy that." Marny handed a heavy bag to Tabby. "Mission supplies," she explained when I gave her a questioning look.

It was a quick flight over to Manetra from York even though it was twenty-two hundred kilometers away.

For most on Zuri, Manetra was on the western edge of civilization. The city nestled against a great mountain range, through which ground vehicles had to pass in order to get to places like Kuende Run, York and Azima. At two million, mostly Felio, the town bustled with activity and I was reminded of the town of Coolidge on Mars.

I'd already transmitted our flight plan to Manetra Air Control. I learned my lesson long ago about giving cities a heads-up before just dropping in. Manetra replied by sending a flight corridor and instructions on what we needed to do if we were to vary from those corridors. The construction company Merrie had located to sell her steel sheet to was located within the industrial section of the city.

"*Hail Gasepi,*" I requested.

"Greetings, Loose Nuts." A male Felio showed on the vid screen. "We've been expecting you. Please proceed to Aisle Twelve."

"Copy that," I replied and followed the geo data provided to the location.

When we arrived next to the warehouse, it became clear it was going to be a tight fit. The receiving yard was clearly set up for narrow land-based vehicles. Even though *Tuuq* was small by my standards, it was still three times as wide as over-ground haulers.

"Gasepi, it looks like we're going to have issues with your instructions. We're three meters wider than the approach to your loading bay." I attached a diagram of the exterior of our ship.

"Wait one," the Felio replied.

I pulled back on the stick and slowly circled the shipping yard.

There was plenty of room for us if we took one of the open spots at the end.

"Loose Nuts, we're going to have you set down on Aisle One," he finally said. "It doesn't look like your vessel is equipped with good mating for our receiving dock. We might have a small delay while we round up labor to unload."

"Copy, Gasepi," I said. "We might have a solution for that, though."

"Negative, Loose Nuts," the Felio said. "Closest you'll get to that gate is forty meters. Our policy forbids manual labor from moving material massing greater than fifty kilograms. Safety inspector would pluck my fur if I allowed that."

"Any chance you could have the inspector meet us at the dock?" I asked.

"Wait one."

I lined *Tuuq* up on the end of the receiving dock and set her down with the aft end of the ship pointed toward the building.

"Hoffen Captain, Mership Inspector will join you in twelve short spans."

"Copy that."

I grabbed my reading tablet and walked out after opening the rear hatch. Tabby would stay behind and man the ship's controls while I oversaw the unloading process.

After a few minutes of standing on the warm pavement, a small knot of shabby Felio slunk out from within the warehouse. They neither made eye contact with us nor did they make any attempt at communication, but simply sat on the edge of the dock, obviously waiting.

After twenty-five minutes, a neatly dressed female Felio drove up in a white, electric vehicle that couldn't hold more than four if you squeezed them in. Felio dress varied significantly based on position. With fur covered bodies, they tended not to have the same conventions as humans and their clothing was often focused on only covering chest and hips. The variety in which they did this was significant. This Felio wore loose tan shorts and a sleeveless tan top.

"Liam Hoffen." I extended my right hand, upside down, which

was the custom when greeting Felio.

"Mership Inspector." She brushed her upside-down paw across the palm of my hand. "I understand my presence was requested. As you see, we have sufficient labor to unload our cargo. Gasepi will find it necessary to adjust payment in future due to increased labor requirements for receiving."

"I requested your presence because of this," I said. "As you know, we are not originally born of Zuri."

"I did not know this. I believe human species has village well to the west of Manetra."

"York," I agreed. "My crew is not originally from York. Where we come from, cargo is unloaded with machinery."

"As it would be if your ship were capable of connection to our dock."

"I would demonstrate our stevedore technology. I asked for your presence so you could observe the safety of our equipment," I said.

"I will not allow my employees to operate next to uncertified equipment."

"Their presence is not required," I said. "Loose Nuts will take responsibility for delivering our product to whatever location within your warehouse you specify."

"This cannot be done. We have procedure," she said.

"What if we delivered it to your automated docking? Wouldn't that be done manually from any vessel?"

The suggestion stopped her and she pulled out a reading pad and started scrolling through it. "I can find no requirement prohibiting this."

"Can you show me where the material is to be delivered?"

"I will need you to sign that you are taking responsibility to deliver your sheet goods to the dock so that I might release the labor that was errantly requested."

I signed on her pad and wasn't surprised that the assembled slouching group didn't immediately disperse.

"That's a lot of mass for a human." I didn't catch which of the gang tossed the comment out, nor did I care.

"The sheet must be loaded onto the blue platform, no more than four hundred kilograms on each stack. The clerk in that booth sees to it that the material is properly bussed upon receipt."

"Begin unloading in stacks not exceeding four hundred kilograms," I instructed my AI.

Nick's stevedore bot glided effortlessly from atop the stack of sheet metal and extended long, nano-steel forks. After peeling off the first stack, it slowly backed away from *Tuuq*, turned and made its way down the narrowing lane to receiving. The inspector took in a sharp breath as the bot allowed the sheet to settle onto the platform, sped back to our ship and started the process over.

"Where did you discover this equipment?" Mership asked.

"It's a product line manufactured by Loose Nuts Corporation," I said, stretching the truth just a little. "I'd be happy to have our sales rep establish a comm with you if you're interested."

The stevedore bot had arrived with a new load and dropped it onto the next platform, the first having already glided into the warehouse.

"What will happen when your machine arrives and there is no bus available?" Mership asked as the bot zipped away and the second platform — apparently called a bus — trundled into the building's dark confines.

"It will wait," I said as the bot returned with its third load. We watched as it pulled up, waiting for one of the busses to return.

"A most impressive display," Mership replied. "I will inform my superior of what I have witnessed."

"Much appreciated," I said as a bus returned and Nick's bot loaded it up again.

Tuuq was only capable of carrying a small load, so twenty minutes later, we'd finished. In that time, we'd drawn a small crowd of warehouse employees who were looking on with interest.

"That went well," I said, sliding into the chair next to Tabby.

"What?"

"Might have gotten Nick a referral for his stevedore bots. Gasepi workers seemed pretty impressed by it."

"Nobody wants to be carrying steel sheets by hand."

"Next stop is only two kilometers," I said, slowly lifting *Tuuq*.

"What kind of load doesn't require bond?" Tabby asked.

"The kind that barely covers the cost of fuel," I said. "I only took the job because I didn't want to dead-head all the way to Abasi Prime."

"What is it, Hoffen?" She sounded suspicious.

"Enriched bio mass."

"What kind of enriched bio mass?"

"Fertilizer."

Tabby flung her hands in the air. "This! *This* is why we make fun of you, Hoffen. You have us hauling shite again?"

"It's dried and in bales. This won't be messy."

Tabby joined me as we exited the empty cargo bay. A familiar rumble in the sky warned of imminent rain as we walked across the dusty lot to a large open building. Upon entering, I received a comm instructing us to pick up the pre-arranged volume of neatly packed bales.

"See, it's a piece of cake." I instructed the stevedore bot to start loading just as rain burst from the sky.

"Okay," Tabby agreed. We glided back to the ship, leaving the bot to work through the heavy rain.

Twenty minutes later *Tuuq* broke free of Zuri's atmosphere and we set our destination for the wormhole that would drop us into the Tamu system.

"Do you smell something bad?" Tabby asked about twenty minutes into hard burn.

"I probably got dirt on my boots," I said.

"The smell is coming through the ventilation system."

I punched up a view of the cargo hold. To my chagrin, the once neatly packed bales of fertilizer were starting to open. The dried material, having been rained on, was swelling and filling the empty spaces of the cargo hold.

Tabby looked at my screen and raised her eyebrows. "You're *never* living this down."

Chapter 13

STANDOFF

"I'm reading two cutter-class vessels at forty thousand kilometers and in close proximity to the Tamu system wormhole," Tabby said.

"I'm not seeing it," I said, looking at my vid screen. My frustration with *Tuuq's* pathetic sensor package was growing.

"They're sailing with low power," she replied. *"AI, show Captain Hoffen the visual spectrum disturbance and project outlines."*

On my vid-screen, the pulsing energies of the wormhole entrance, called the Tamu gate, blinked on and off in a pattern I couldn't discern. However, when the AI outlined two ships, the blinking made more sense.

"How did you do that?"

"Nick's idea," Tabby said. "We kept sensor logs of the light patterns of the energies surrounding the anomaly. While the energies are unpredictable in intensity, hue and many other features, they're consistent in position. We weren't sure it would be useful analysis, but it appears we were wrong."

I adjusted our burn so instead of arriving a hundred kilometers from the wormhole, we fell above the wormhole at two thousand kilometers. We'd been on hard-burn for the better part of seventy-two hours and there was virtually no chance those ships hadn't seen us coming.

"I feel like we've played this game before," I said. What we were looking at by the wormhole was identical to the trap we'd run into with *Fleet Afoot*. I had no doubt if we were allowed to jump through the wormhole, we'd find a welcoming committee on the other side.

"What's the plan, Liam?" Tabby asked, turning to look at me.

"Let's get a feel for their offensive capacities."

"*Tuuq* is out-massed by both ships. A frontal assault is a bad idea." Tabby flattened her lips and rolled her eyes at me. "We could throw big bales of shite at them."

I laughed. "Right, hate to dismiss any idea right out of the box."

We continued to decelerate on our approach to the gate. I'd sure love to have been sailing *Intrepid*; I'd teach these clowns a lesson, but *Tuuq* was outclassed and I was sure we'd find a worse fight on the other side of the wormhole.

"They're powering up and moving to intercept," Tabby said.

"Got it," The two cutters materialized fully on my vid-screen. They weren't much to look at, but neither were we. We had the advantage of speed. Their only move was to anticipate where we'd arrive, given our current deceleration. "Hate to disappoint you boys," I muttered out loud as I brought us out of hard-burn and flipped us over so we faced the incoming ships.

"*Hail ships on intercept course with Tuuq.*" My AI picked up the command and a chime indicated an open channel although there was no response. It was an altogether familiar scenario. "This is Captain Liam Hoffen of Loose Nuts. Desist on your intercept path or we'll consider your actions hostile and reply in kind."

After waiting a minute, I transmitted the electronic version of the Letter of Marque we'd received from House Mshindi.

That brought a response. "Captain Hoffen, our supreme leader Belvakuski sends her regards. You will not trick us this time. You will adjust to our vector, heave-to and prepare to be boarded."

I closed comm. It was unlikely we'd be able to take them on, but we were moving fast enough they'd have difficulty chasing us down. I throttled up and accelerated away at a perpendicular vector.

"Do you suppose they're always sitting here or is someone telling them we're coming?" Tabby asked.

"I'm not sure they knew who we were until I hailed them," I said. "It's not a long shot to wait at the wormhole. According to House Mshindi, several ships pass through daily."

"With these pirates sitting here? How?"

"*Intrepid* wouldn't have any trouble with these jokers."

The cutters had slowed and weren't pursuing us on our new vector. They knew where we needed to go and were counting on us coming to them in the end.

"What kind of long range sensors do we have?"

"Poor," Tabby said.

"Take the helm and keep us away from these clowns, but bring us around so we're not more than five thousand kilometers from the wormhole."

"Copy."

I swiped at the virtual displays and started searching. When we first arrived in the Santaloo system, we'd found it to be too small and undeveloped to be a destination hub. Instead, planets like Zuri enjoyed considerable 'fly-through' traffic, mostly from vessels coming from and going to the Abasi home world — Abasi Prime. Since then, I'd learned there was exactly one other wormhole in this system and it led to the Brea Fortul system. I set our limited long-range sensors to search for ships coming from Zuri, Fan Zuri or from the Brea Fortul wormhole, assuming at least some of them would be headed toward the Tamu gate.

After setting the search, I connected to the ship's data stores on shipping. I'd been so focused on setting up trade that I'd ignored what was sitting right in front of my face. We were weeks from having a first-class, frigate-sized warship. With a pirate threat surrounding the gates, *Intrepid* could provide considerable value. Soon my screen was filled with details of a thriving market for armed trading escorts. In some cases, captains wanted to gang-up with another lightly armed trading ship, and in others, they were looking to simply hire protection. I was galled to discover many of the respondents were Genteresk, who I believed to be the pirate group mostly responsible for the problem.

"How long are we going to do this?" Tabby asked after an hour of circling the Tamu wormhole.

"Right now, our only other choice is to go home."

"I hate this."

I chuckled under my breath. Tabby's lack of patience was epic.

"Get the cards out," I said. "We might be a while."

And so it went. We played cards for several hours as we waited for something to change. I wondered if Mshindi's assessment of the traffic through the gates was reasonable when finally, a chime from my earwig grabbed my attention.

At first, the only hint of change was the two pirate cutters spooling up. My immediate concern was that they were going to make a run on us. They'd certainly had enough time to communicate with Belvakuski and she might have ordered them to chase us down. I dismissed this notion as a frigate-sized ship blinked into existence. A moment after arriving, its large engines fired brightly and started accelerating away from the Tamu wormhole.

"We're receiving a mayday," Tabby said. "*Shetak Blossom* has lost one of its engines and their weapons systems are off-line."

"Frak." I contemplated just how we might be able to help them. "I'm taking the helm."

I nosed over and accelerated toward *Shetak Blossom*.

"What are you doing, Liam?" Tabby asked.

I ignored her as we streaked toward the wounded frigate. "What kind of armor does she have?"

"Moderately armored," she replied. "She'll have a hard time outrunning those cutters, though."

"*Shetak Blossom*, this is Liam Hoffen on *Tuuq*. Do you have any weapons? We're inbound with intent of providing aid."

A male Pogona appeared on my vid screen. "Captain Hoffen, I am Captain Fateh. Your assistance, while appreciated, is unwise. Our assessment of your ship's capacity is that it is insufficient. We left a Genteresk ship disabled in Tamu system. The wormhole is open and you should make your way through."

"Understood, Fateh," I said. "All the same, you'll not make it if we do. Just don't shoot at us."

"My engineer informs me that our primary weapon will be back online in a short span. Your assistance is accepted."

I closed comm and rolled my eyes. It wasn't as if I was giving Captain Fateh a choice. A frigate was likely to have at least a dozen crew. I wasn't about to stand by and watch the pirates take them out.

"Frak, Liam, we can't take out two cutters on our own," Tabby said.

"Just like defending a pod-ball goal when there's a breakaway. We don't need to win, we just need to buy *Shetak Blossom* a little time. Find me a weakness I can exploit."

"Painting them as red and blue," Tabby said. My vid screen updated and the ships took on the colors she'd indicated. "The ships are nearly identical. Blue is the preferred target with slight damage near aft engines."

The cutters wasted no time in attacking the *Shetak Blossom* and seemed to pay us no heed as we approached. It soon became obvious they expected us to jump through the wormhole as opposed to rendering aid. I adjusted course so the Genteresk ships would get very comfortable with that assumption. We were sailing up on the cutters from the opposite side of the wormhole. Captain Fateh quickly recognized our ruse and smartly turned to pull the cutters into our vector.

"Ready?" I asked as we closed the final kilometers.

"I can't wait," Tabby said.

The cutters' guns were small for taking on a frigate, but the damage they were handing out was adding onto damage already done. Fully operational, I don't believe the *Shetak Blossom* would have struggled against the smaller ships. As it was, the frigate would be disabled in several minutes if it couldn't escape the pestering ships.

As we entered the wormhole space, I considered simply activating the wormhole transition engines. We'd be transported to the Tamu system and far away from battle. I shook off the idea and jammed the throttle to full. *Tuuq* didn't really have a combat burn capability, but she wasn't entirely a slug. We were pressed into our seats as the inertial systems started to reach their maximum capacity.

Thut-thut-thut. Tuuq's anemic turret stitched a line of fire into the aft engine of the cutter outlined in blue. Anticipating *Blue's* move, I broke off our acceleration, slapped the stick to the side, rotated one hundred sixty degrees and jammed the throttle back to max. As predicted, *Blue* spun around and accelerated to match our speed. My move had caused *Tuuq* to slide around the aft side of *Blue* in an arc.

Tabby didn't waste time and continued her focus on *Blue's* engines. "Point, Masters!"

The cutter only had two engines and Tabby had knocked out one of them. The last thing I wanted to do was leave the wounded ship, but with half its power gone, it no longer had the capacity to keep up with the fleeing frigate. And we had another problem; our actions had earned us the ire of the cutter highlighted in *Red* on my vid screen. Sure enough, blaster fire erupted on our hull.

"Liam, we can't take much of this," Tabby warned, her voice filled with frustration. At the moment, she was a passenger in the fight — something she was unaccustomed to. *Tuuq* had extremely limited offense when being chased.

"Copy," I said and angled toward *Shetak Blossom*. We'd successfully given the larger ship a break from the constant pounding of the cutters, but had redirected half of that punishment in our direction.

Sailing in a flat line is a bad idea in combat, as predictability will get you killed. My chest ached as I flopped us around while beating my way over to *Shetak Blossom*.

"*Incoming hail, Shetak Blossom.*"

"Hoffen," I grunted.

"My engineer has a single turret online. Move Genteresk cutter into position to bow of *Shetak Blossom*."

"Copy," I replied.

It wasn't as if I had a lot of control over where the battle went. I was mostly responding to *Red's* moves while trying to catch up with my only cover — *Shetak Blossom.* We struggled together in an odd three-way dance where Tabby attempted to find open shots, *Red* attempted to predict our position, and I tried to orbit the larger frigate, dragging *Red* into position.

"Captain Hoffen. On seven count, we request your smooth flight for eight micro spans on attached vector. Our targeting systems are damaged." Captain Fateh transmitted a vector that would have us sailing across his bow.

We'd successfully brought ourselves to the forward section of the frigate and I'd been dismayed at *Shetak Blossom's* hesitance. Eight seconds on a flat line in space combat, would feel like an eternity. *Red* would have clear shooting and there was no guarantee she'd also flatten out her flight to match ours.

"Will comply," I replied.

"Liam!" Tabby voted her opposition at the idea.

"Eight seconds," I said as the countdown displayed on the vid-screen. "We'll make it."

I took my hand off the flight stick and pulled back on the throttle. I might sail in a flat line, but I could at least adjust acceleration so we weren't quite sitting ducks. Blaster fire exploded on the hull of the ship. The power cycled and the bridge was covered in inky blackness.

"Rerouting power," Tabby said, the glow of vid-screens all that illuminated her face. I looked over to her, panic starting to well in my chest.

A burst of light illuminated the bridge just before a cacophony of sounds filled the small space and debris collided with our hull plating.

"Got it," Tabby said and the lights of the bridge came back up.

I flipped *Tuuq* over to get a better view. *Red* cutter was nowhere to be found. I searched the combat display and located *Blue*, burning as hard as it could for Fan Zuri. For a moment, I considered chasing it down, but then thought better of it. We'd taken a beating defending *Shetak Blossom* and I wasn't remotely interested in seeing just how much more we had in us.

"Captain Hoffen. On behalf of Rai Group, I thank you for your brave intervention," Captain Fateh said over our still-open comms. "Is there assistance you require at this moment?"

"Tabby?" I asked.

"We're bruised but we'll be okay if we don't run into more trouble," she said.

"Negative, Captain Fateh," I said. "We'll be on our way to Abasi Prime. Safe travels to you."

"We will accompany you," Fateh said. "The damage we have taken is too great for us to continue our journey, much to the disappointment of our shareholders."

"If you want to continue, you might stop off at Petersburg Station over Zuri," I said. "I imagine they'd be able to get you fixed up. It's not too far out of your way if you're heading to the Brea Fortul system."

Zuri wasn't exactly on the way to Brea Fortul, but he'd save at least eight days travel over heading back to Abasi Prime.

"Petersburg Station is not a familiar destination."

I sent a data burst to him with Petersburg Station's location and services. "Just set up within the last twenty short spans."

"And Petersburg Station is friendly to travelers?"

"Copy that," I said. "Flagged under House Mshindi."

"Rai Group's debt to you grows," Fateh said.

"Be safe, Captain," I said.

It took us twenty minutes to sail back to the wormhole.

"I sure hope he was right about removing the threat in Tamu," Tabby said as I engaged the wormhole engine.

Unlike travel through TransLoc, there was virtually nothing beyond a slight lurch as we transitioned from the Santaloo system to Tamu.

"I'm picking up a small debris cloud," Tabby said. "Whoever *Shetak Blossom* duked it out with has limped away."

"All right then. Abasi Prime, here we come."

Chapter 14

SURVIVAL OF THE FITTEST

"What in Jupiter is all over my bot?" Nick asked as Tabby and I manually unloaded *Tuuq's* cargo hold into Nick's workshop on Zuri.

We'd had an uneventful return trip from Nadira on Abasi Prime, where we'd picked up the anti-grav components rejected by Bakira Corporation. Unfortunately, Nick's stevedore bot had succumbed to the dried animal crap when it expanded to fill the hold. I suspected the bot's damage had something to do with the fact that, when we'd opened the cargo bay door, it had been ejected by the pressure of the expanded crap. Worse yet, it was left to me to dig around in said crap to extricate the beleaguered bot. I wasn't sure if the bot was actually broken, or if it was merely on strike due to poor working conditions.

"Exactly what you think," Tabby said. "Give it a good whiff; I think you'll recognize it."

"Animal waste?" Nick looked at me skeptically.

"Not proud that things got out of control," I confessed. "Apparently, dried bales of Fegoota feces absorb fifteen times their volume in water very quickly."

"But where did the water come from?"

"It was raining when we loaded and I still had the bot running slow due to the demonstration at Gasepi Corporation — which, by the way, went very well."

"True statement on Gasepi," Nick said. "They've ordered two bots and will pick them up next week."

"You should get back to chastising Liam about crapping up your bot," Tabby needled, grinning as Marny joined us in front of Nick's workshop.

"I didn't consider making the bots crap-proof," Nick said, giving me a look. "I'll have to figure out what bricked it."

"Have you stopped in at Petersburg yet, Cap?" Marny asked.

"Not yet."

"They had unexpected visitors, thanks to you. Apparently, you made quite an impression on the captain," she said. "According to Silver, the captain said without your intervention, they might not have made it."

"I'm surprised Abasi won't do something about pirates setting up shop around the wormhole," Tabby said.

"I'm guessing that's what they think a Letter of Marque is all about," Marny pointed out.

"No prizes for us this round," I said. "So, not to change the subject ... Apparently, Gasepi wasn't just impressed with the stevedore bots; they liked the quality of steel Merrie and Amon are making with the zero-g manufactory. We have new orders for forty kilo tonnes."

"All for Gasepi?" Nick asked.

"Gasepi and two other Manetra companies. All word of mouth, too; we never contacted them. Merrie is kicking production into high gear, but she's going to run into supply problems with the ore. Do you think you could push Hog on identifying miners? Merrie has been talking with House Gundi about getting her ore orders onto their commodities exchange, but that's a long play."

"No grass growing under that woman's feet," Marny said with a laugh.

"She lives on a space station," I said. "How would grass grow under her feet?"

"Earth idiom, Cap," Marny said.

"Any chance you can get that bot fixed before we take off?" I asked. "We have a stop in Azima before heading back to Petersburg."

"No need," Nick said. "I'll exchange it with one of the Gasepi prototypes. They're not due for another week and I'm sure I can fix whatever you broke."

"How is our cash flow?" I asked.

"Tight," Nick said. "Paying off that note was helpful, but between *Intrepid's* repairs, Petersburg startup and manufacturing, we're burning through credits. Selling steel helps, but we need a lot more income than what that's generating. I had to take out another short-term note."

"How much?" I asked.

"Two hundred forty thousand," he said. "Our share of the steel sales will keep us afloat, but we need to keep that rolling. Tell me you have an idea on how to use *Intrepid* to bring in cash while you're hunting for Jonathan. I'd like to keep *Tuuq* close to home for running deliveries."

"Sure, but I assume you know that Anino isn't here just to be nice. He's going to ask for something and I bet it won't generate cash," I said.

"Anino is getting antsy to leave, Cap," Marny said. "He said he's been holding TransLoc open so he can return home."

"Word is that *Intrepid* is ready to sail. They repaired all essential systems and started on the less important ones," Nick said. "Better yet, Anino is offering forty thousand in platinum fingers to give the Norigans a ride back to Chitundu."

The mention of the space station we'd once visited above Abasi Prime's moon Rehema made me smile as I recalled Jester Ripples accidentally discovering a group of Norigans who were headed home. His joy in finding family he hadn't seen for a decade was one of my fondest memories.

"That fits in with an idea I have to make money and get us over to the Tanwar system," I said. "What did we end up doing with my proposal for switching out *Intrepid's* crew-country deck for an expanded cargo hold?"

Intrepid was originally designed for a crew complement of eighty sailors. In that we rarely exceeded twenty crew, I'd proposed a substantial reorganization — primarily, taking the lower deck of the forward section and converting from quarters to a twelve-hundred cubic meter hold. Between our new hold and the existing three-hundred-meter hold, we'd be able to carry two and a half times as much material as *Hotspur*.

"Just like you requested," Nick said. "We even have enough power to run a pressure barrier when the hold is open. Speaking of *Intrepid*, I have a load for you to take back with you."

"Do I have enough room with the supplies I'm picking up in Manetra?"

"Just," Nick said. "I've programmed both loads into your new stevedore."

I took in a sharp breath. "You programmed the new stevedore while we were standing here talking?"

"I might have had some warning on your cargo problems," Nick said, his eyes flitting for a moment over to Tabby.

"You guys suck," I said as a stevedore flew out of Nick's workshop and started loading crates onto *Tuuq*. "What's in the crates?"

"Vid screens and holo projector parts," Nick said. "Petersburg could have made them, but I have better access to the specialized materials."

"I hate to rush off, but I'd like to get back to Petersburg and check out *Intrepid*," I said.

"I'll be coming along, Cap," Marny said. "Give me a second and I'll grab my go-bag."

"You sure?" I asked. "We're going to be out for a while."

"Roger that, Cap. Nick and I are squared away."

I glanced at Nick, who didn't look quite as certain as Marny. I remembered the feeling very well when I'd watched Tabby leave me to go off to the academy. It wasn't quite the same, but I certainly understood.

"Take as long as you need," I said. "We'll be aboard."

I opened *Tuuq's* hatch and followed Tabby through the starboard airlock. As a group, we weren't interested in traipsing through the hold. It was mostly cleaned out, but still transferred odors to anything that entered.

"Permission to be about the bridge," Marny called from the short hallway.

"Granted," I held my fist out to her and she bumped it with her own. "Glad to have you aboard, Marny. Tabbs, you have the helm. Could you take us to Azima?"

"Copy that, Liam. I have the helm," Tabby said.

I'd been working on an idea for making money as we traveled through Pogona space to Tanwar. While I wasn't about to ignore Anino's warning about attracting undo attention, it occurred to me that the right kind of attention might be just what Loose Nuts needed.

The idea had to do with the trouble we were constantly running into at the Tamu/Santaloo gate. I'd queried several shipping companies about providing armed escorts from Tamu through to Tanwar. The issue was that we had no reputation, and what company was going to pay an unknown, heavily armed ship to escort them into dangerous territory? For all anyone knew, maybe we were the pirates. Our brush with Rai Group was helping to build our reputation, but we needed something even splashier — and I had just the right idea.

The second issue was that not a single person on *Intrepid* knew a thing about Pogona, the Nijjar government, or Genteresk pirates. I couldn't imagine sailing into potentially hostile alien territory without help. The best guide I could come up with lived in Azima and as luck would have it, I was feeling like grabbing a spicy lunch wrap.

"Azima ground control, this is *Tuuq*. We're on approach to Blue Zone. Please advise," I called as we closed in on the small city. I'd already cleared our plans for taking on supplies, mostly because I wasn't sure if anyone might be holding a grudge, given our last visit.

"*Tuuq* this is Azima ground control. Welcome back and you're clear for landing in Blue Zone."

I chuckled as I closed the comms. We'd paid mightily during our last visit and I suspected our warm welcome was related to some freshly lined pockets.

"It's going to be tight on the way back to Petersburg Station," I said as Tabby landed. "I'm hoping to take on new crew."

"What kind of crew, Cap?" Marny asked.

"Pogona," I said. "Figure if that's the direction we're headed, we'll be better off having someone on our side who can speak the language. Tabbs, would you mind supervising loading while Marny and I go talk to our potential new crew?"

"I think I can handle it," Tabby said.

I followed Marny off the bridge and strapped a heavy flechette to my waist. With our grav-suits, I wasn't concerned about trouble from locals, although I suspected our reputation for dealing with trouble would be a sufficient deterrent.

"Cap, you're thinking Koosha will come along? What about his business?" Marny asked as we made our way down the narrow streets through the shopping bazaar. I was once again struck with how poor Azima felt in comparison to Puskar Stellar of Mars.

"It was his idea. I'm not even sure how Koosha knew where we were going. He said he had a proposal, but wouldn't talk about it through electronic communications."

"He's an unusual bird," Marny said. "But I get a good feeling from him."

"Liam Hoffen, Marny Bertrand." The sound of Koosha's solicitous voice caught me before I saw him. "I have been ever so anticipating a chance to speak with you. Please sit and share tea with my family. Jala, bring tea and the boys. We will sit and drink with our friends."

Surreptitiously, I raised my eyebrows at Marny. Koosha always laid it on thick, but he was making an extra effort and I wondered what I'd gotten myself into.

The glint of sunshine glancing off armor caught my attention as my HUD displayed a red flashing indicator. We had incoming hostiles and they were close. I slipped from my chair, took a knee and grabbed for my flechette as Marny spun and extended her bo staff. In the blink of an eye she snapped the bo staff out and caught an armed Pogona beneath the chin, laying him out onto the ground.

"Nooo!" Koosha wailed. His concern was too late as I zeroed in on the second armored Pogona who was extracting a holstered blaster pistol. I fired five flechette darts into his center mass. Three of the darts deflected harmlessly off the armor, but two found their home.

"Stay down," Marny growled as I leapt across the space that separated me from my adversary. I brought the butt of my pistol down on the wrist that had grabbed the pistol and several rounds were fired into my leg. I can't say it didn't sting like crazy as my grav-suit absorbed the energy, but I was fortunate that the alien had an inexpensive weapon. I scooped the blaster from the ground as it clattered away harmlessly.

"Why have you attacked my boys?" Koosha exclaimed, as if I'd mortally wounded him. I couldn't blame him entirely for his concern. One of my darts had creased the skin of the lanky youth's loose wattle and pale orange blood streamed to the ground.

The Pogona youth looked at me with contempt and tried to sit up.

I lowered my weapon at him menacingly. "Keep moving and you'll be wearing the rest of my clip," I said, pushing him back with my foot.

"Gunjeet," Jala said, dropping to her knees near the boy's head. "What has happened?" She looked up at me, confused. "Why would you attack my children?"

My AI recognized my need to understand why it had flagged the two Pogona as imminent threats. My HUD replayed the scene from Goboble's attack at the green landing zone. The two Pogona boys were unmistakably highlighted. I heard a grunt of understanding from Marny. She'd seen the same accounting.

"Your boys are lucky to be alive this day," I said. "They were part of Goboble's team when we were attacked."

"No," Koosha said. "This must not be so. They are good boys."

"Get off," Gunjeet said, pushing at my foot. He was strong enough that I started to lose balance. Wearing my grav-suit gave me options he couldn't understand. I lifted up from the ground and pushed my foot harder into his neck, letting it slide to his still-bleeding wattle.

"Arijeet? Speak the truth." Jala looked to the boy still lying beneath the tip of Marny's bo staff. I had to give it to the woman, she was not easily flapped. Sure, she was concerned for her boys, but her voice had hardly risen during the entire encounter.

"We have no bad intent — today," Arijeet said. "We wore our armor to make an impression."

"Arijeet, this is no answer," Jala said. "Gunjeet, do you deny what Liam Hoffen shares with us? Have you joined with the gangs?"

"My life is my own," he said. "Have your best shot, human."

I pulled my foot up as I floated back and set his confiscated blaster pistol on the table. "Out of respect for your parents, I will hold my hand."

Jala helped Gunjeet to a chair while Koosha retrieved a clean towel and dabbed at his son's bleeding chin.

"Humiliation upon my head. I beg of your forgiveness, Liam Hoffen," Koosha said.

"Stop it, old man," Gunjeet said. "You grovel like a sickly sewer rodent."

"Gunjeet, you will leave us," Jala said. "You have no place."

The words were spoken quietly, but the impact to Gunjeet was great. I had to replay the last few seconds in my head. It was as if Jala had reached across the distance between them and struck him with a club.

"You are lost and you take Arijeet with you," Jala continued.

"No, mother," Gunjeet pleaded.

"Koosha," Jala spoke wistfully, as if we weren't there. "Arijeet and I can still travel with Liam Hoffen. Tell him."

Gunjeet got up from his chair and reached for his blaster. I placed my hand on it and shook my head in the negative.

"How could he ever trust my family?" Koosha asked.

"Convince him, Koosha. Save Arijeet," Jala said.

"What is it you want from us, Jala?" I asked.

"Take my wife and my son," Koosha answered instead. "I give them to you."

From the corner of my eye, I caught Marny's raised eyebrow. I would never live this conversation down. If not for the lizard chin, Jala was about as attractive a woman as I could imagine and now Koosha was intimating that she was property. Somehow, I knew this was going to turn around on me in the worst possible way.

"Uh. That's not how we do things," I said. "You can't give your family away."

"Jala is strong, as is Arijeet. They will work tirelessly," he said. "You have said you need understanding of our people. I ask that you allow me to entrust my heart with you."

"Marny?" I asked, looking for help.

"We will take both boys in addition to Jala. They will report to me. Do you understand?" Marny asked.

"A man does not answer to a woman," Gunjeet said, having stopped several meters from where we were talking.

"Oh, by all means. I'm in, Cap," Marny said, smiling.

"PETERSBURG STATION, this is *Tuuq*. We're requesting bay assignment," I said.

"Greetings, Liam," Katherine LeGrande answered. "I believe the Norigans anxiously await your arrival. You're cleared to raft up next to *Intrepid's* Cargo Bay Two."

"Copy that, Katherine. *Tuuq* out," I said. "How about that? Cargo Bay Two. I'm gone for a couple weeks and suddenly we have another cargo bay."

"What, you didn't believe Nick?" Tabby asked.

"I wasn't expecting it to be fully functional."

I rolled *Tuuq* as we passed alongside *Intrepid*. Something was up with her armor — it was splotchy-looking in a way I didn't much appreciate. It was confusing since there had been nothing wrong with the armor. The idea that someone was messing with it irked me.

"What do you think, Cap?" Marny asked as we slid around to the new forward, starboard cargo bay. It was open and large enough that we could fit *Tuuq's* nose inside.

"Now that's a cargo bay," I said, trying to tamp down my ire.

From our vantage point, the armor on the round forward section was uniformly black. It was then that my brain caught up with what I was looking at. "Is that *Hotspur's* stealth armor?"

"Caught that, did you?" Marny asked.

I frowned at her. "But it's only on part of the ship."

"Anino is waving us in," Tabby said.

Indeed, Anino, Roby, Sempre and the entire gaggle of Norigans were looking out at us through the transparent pressure barrier.

"I'd hate to ruin their presentation." Marny nodded toward the assembled group. "Ask 'em about it."

I couldn't imagine what unevenly applied stealth armor would do for us, but the revelation had put my mind at ease. Perhaps they hadn't had time to skin the entire ship and would get to the rest shortly.

"Copy that," I swung the aft end of *Tuuq* around and slid its hatch through the barrier. As soon as the ships made contact, a light on my console showed a strong magnetic connection had been established, joining us.

It took some climbing to get over the supplies we'd ferried from Azima. The smell of fresh station air greeted us as I dropped the ramp. Sempre's whiskers twitched as our atmo comingled with theirs. It had to be from the scent of the residual bovine crap.

"Welcome back, Hoffen," Anino said, stepping forward. "What do you think?"

"Thanks. If the rest of the ship looks anything like this cargo bay, we're in for a pleasant surprise," I said.

"No shortage of upgrades on this old girl," Anino said.

"Liam Hoffen!" Jester Ripples clambered up onto me and gave me a hug that I hadn't realized I'd missed. I'd never considered myself a touchy-feely person, but I did miss the Norigan's daily presence. Just as quickly as he arrived, Jester jumped down and made the rounds with the rest of the new arrivals.

"Cargo bay looks really nice," I said.

"What do you think of the armor?" Roby blurted out, grinning wildly.

"I'm not sure I understand it."

"Did you bring the screens and holo gear Nick was manufacturing?" he asked without explaining further. His question caused a wave of tittering through the already excited Norigans.

"It's at the front of the hold. We'll have to unload the station supplies first," I said.

I'd barely gotten the words out when a Norigan I'd met only once, Big Cabbage, stepped forward, powered up the stevedore bot, and started offloading *Tuuq's* cargo onto grav pallets.

"The Norigans would like you to wait until they have a chance to install the last of the equipment onto the bridge before you see it," Sempre said. "Is that acceptable?"

"Sure, I can help take supplies to the station," I said.

"Liam Hoffen, please do not go. We have only a short duration required to finish with *Intrepid's* bridge."

"We could drop our things into our quarters and get a shower," Tabby said. "*Tuuq* wasn't equipped with a real head and I've been looking forward to cleaning my suit."

"Marny, why don't you show Jala, Arijeet and Gunjeet to their quarters."

"Copy that, Cap," Marny agreed.

"Please utilize the port passageway," Jester Ripples said. "We will take care to unload supplies."

My HUD highlighted the passageway that exited the cargo bay on the port side. With a little imagination, I could still see the crew bunks that had been removed to make way for the bay. It was the same place a Kroerak had broken through the ship's armor, attacked Nick, and nearly taken me out. I felt guilty leaving the cargo to the Norigans to unload, but I understood their enthusiasm. I was also with Tabby; a shower sounded amazing.

I breathed a sigh of relief as we entered our quarters. It was a sight I thought I'd never see again and it felt like home. A fresh coat of paint, new bedding, and a suit cleaner had been installed. My desk and chair were still missing, but that was something I could find at a future date.

Twenty minutes later, we'd both showered and cleaned our grav-suits. Tabby had just fallen asleep, resting against my chest with one leg tossed over mine when I heard a light knock at the door.

"That's us, Love," I said. Tabby sighed and pushed away from me. We'd been pushing hard and were both running short of sleep, but I was excited to see what the Norigans had to show us.

I opened the door to find Sempre holding Jester Ripples on her hip. I smiled, enjoying for a moment their new friendship.

"Big Cabbage has asked that you join us on the bridge so that he might officially return control to Hoffen Captain," Sempre said.

"After you."

Tabby and I fell into step behind Jester Ripples, who'd dropped from Sempre and was now pulling her along. I'd never heard the Felio giggle before. It was infectious, as was the excitement I felt as we passed the Norigans. They had lined up in the hallway and were saluting us as we walked through. It would have been comical if the stubby, frog-headed sentients hadn't looked so serious.

"It is I, Sempre, who request entry to the bridge. I am honored to escort Hoffen Captain and Masters First," Sempre said, sounding official.

"Permission granted," Ada answered.

The bridge was one of several technologically dense sections of the ship. The destruction I'd initiated had left the room completely burned out and devoid of any usable systems. The change from that burned-out husk was dramatic. Instead of a single captain's chair sitting fully aft, there was now a trio of chairs, two forward and one slightly elevated behind them. It was the layout we'd had on *Hotspur* and fit our style.

"Captain on the bridge," Marny announced and stood stiffly, just short of attention.

The bridge had been narrowed, but since the cubicle-style stations had been removed, there was more space available. Aft of the captain's chair was a u-shaped configuration of stations: one against the port side, two along the aft bulkhead and another single station against the starboard. Further, the entire forward bulkhead was covered in vid-screen glass that curved when it reached the corners and wrapped around on the sides, coming back a meter.

"As you were," I said, reciting the words Marny had taught me to release bridge crew from observing discipline when I entered.

"What do you think, Liam?" Ada asked.

"It's beautiful," I said. "I have so many questions. Is it all working?"

"Big Cabbage," Ada said, turning to the Norigan standing between the pilot's chairs and the forward vid-screen. "I believe the captain has requested a forward view."

"Oh, Ada Chen, it is my excitement to demonstrate this delightful view." Big Cabbage seemed to vibrate as he bounded back to the starboard workstation. His powerful tri-digit fingers flew across an embedded keyboard and suddenly the vid-screen glass disappeared and a full view of Petersburg Station showed, as if *Intrepid* simply ceased to exist.

"Wow," Tabby said, grabbing my arm and clamping on. "Wait! Your eye!"

I did a double take as I looked back to a smiling Ada. The brown skin of her face was just as I remembered down to the freckles along her cheek bones. Perfectly matched, her two bright eyes looked back at us where, before, the left had been covered by a patch. Tabby jumped across the space separating them, pulled her into a hug and swung her around, joyfully. When they stopped moving, I wrapped my arms around them both.

"Seriously, guys," Ada finally said, opening her arms and gesturing around the bridge. "What do you think?"

"It's so clean," I said, wishing I had a better description. "Is it all working?"

"Liam Hoffen, I programmed your holo display just like you used to have it," Jester Ripples said. "You should see that all primary and critical secondary systems are functioning at high levels of perfection."

I moved to the captain's chair and used a familiar gesture to bring up the holo-projector, which cycled through system statuses. Jester Ripples was right, there were several non-functional systems, but those were very much in the minority.

"How was it possible to affect this much repair?" I asked. "Was the damage to *Intrepid* not as bad as I believed?"

"I brought the critical components with me," Anino said. "It's funny, you know. I always believed Jonathan's fate would rest in your hands."

"How do you know he and Sendrei are still alive?"

"Jonathan and I have always communicated using embedded quantum crystals. They are literally a part of both of us," Anino said.

"You really went out of your way on *Intrepid*," I said. "You must have spent millions."

"We left millions behind quite a while ago," Anino said.

"Then why not just bring a new ship?" Tabby asked. "With a load of platinum bars instead of making us work so hard to survive?"

"Successful crews all have one thing in common," Anino said. "Would you care to guess what that is, Tabby?"

"Alcohol consumption?" she shot back with a wide grin.

Anino paused and looked to the side for a moment. When he looked back to Tabby, he smiled. "Alcohol poisoning to interrupt cognitive function is indeed common, Tabbs."

"That's Tabitha to you, Tommy," Tabby shot back. For some reason, she found Anino abrasive. I suspected it had something to do with how she interacted with her own wealthy family who refused to come to her aid when she'd been injured and needed medical treatment.

"Struggle for survival, Tabbs," I said. "He's saying he only wants to get us back on our feet. We have to work for the rest."

"You have proven the value of this time and time again, Hoffen," Anino said. "It is only when your survival is threatened that you truly meet your potential."

Chapter 15

BACK IN BLACK

"Captain Fateh of the *Shetak Blossom* asked me to communicate his regards," Mom said. "You've made a friend for life in that one. I believe his words were: 'courage in the face of adversity.'"

We were enjoying an evening meal together on the promenade deck in advance of our upcoming trip to Rehema, a moon over Abasi Prime, to drop off the boisterous Norigans.

"Anyone would have done the same. Those cutters would have ripped him to shreds if we hadn't helped."

"Well, he was quite impressed." She gave me a warm smile. "Big Pete would have been proud."

I'll be honest. I enjoyed hearing the pride in her voice.

"We cleared twenty thousand on ship repairs, refueling and the like," Merrie said. "Rai Group is a huge Pogona corporation. I think there's a good chance we'll get additional business through Petersburg, especially when Zuri's orbit lines up between Brea Fortul and Tamu wormholes."

I smiled. I'd also done research on Rai Group. Captain Fateh sailed for their shipping division. Ordinarily, their frigates sailed in convoys of three or four, which would have eliminated the issues they'd run into. I suspect *Shetak Blossom* had been under time pressure. Under duress, previously hidden mechanical failures made the ship vulnerable at the worst possible time.

"Okay, now someone needs to tell me what's up with *Intrepid's* patchwork of stealth armor," I said.

"Liam Hoffen loves *Intrepid* too much to see everything clearly," Jester Ripples said, having taken a place on Sempre's lap. I found it interesting, although not surprising, that the young Felio and the Norigan had bonded so quickly.

"You aren't overly observant," Anino said.

"What are you guys talking about?" I asked.

Jester Ripples jumped from Sempre and placed a small holo projector onto the table where Tabby and I sat. *Intrepid* sprang to life, showing a starboard view.

"Your ship is beautiful." I jumped as Jala, who'd been quiet during dinner, had come up behind me and placed her hand on my shoulder. I chanced a glance at Tabby, whose pupils had grown about a centimeter.

I sighed and focused on Jester Ripple's projection of *Intrepid*. "It is, Jala," I said and removed her hand from my shoulder. "There's stealth armor buildup on the back and around the engine cowls, but it stops on the forward edge. It's all over the back of the habitation dish, but it stops about halfway."

Jester Ripples waved his hand and the image of *Intrepid* slowly turned on its vertical axis. As the ship oriented so the engines were pointed directly at me, the purpose became clear.

"I'm not sure if I should be offended or not," I said. From directly behind, the purpose of the armor's placement became clear. If *Intrepid* was pointed directly away from another ship, they would see nothing but the stealth armor. In essence, if we were running away, we'd be well hidden.

"Liam Hoffen has no reason to be offended," Jester Ripples said. "The stealth armor had to be layered and the additional mass to cover the entire ship would have been too burdensome. We chose to change the aesthetic and add considerable function." He spun

Intrepid around and I discovered that from the front, she was also covered in *Hotspur's* stealth armor.

"How many degrees off can we sail before we're detectable?" I asked.

"No more than five degrees," Anino said. "Even so, my modifications to the engines will make up for the additional mass."

"Tell me again how to get to Dark Frontier? I can't find any reference to it."

"You should not go to the Dark Frontier, Liam," Jala said. "Even with your *Intrepid* you would find great danger. Only three systems separate Adit Pah from Santaloo. Our lore tells about many ships that have attempted passage through this Dark Frontier, but few have returned, is not just a story told by parents to settle wayward children."

"Oooh," Tabby said. "Sounds scary. Those M-Pro sloops would have had crystals, though. What about that?"

"They did," Anino said. "There have been no further transmissions since we learned of their being attacked."

"Well, since you're not opening your checkbook further, I've found a way to pick up the bill for travel to Tanwar." I said. "Jala, how do we get to Adit Pah from Tanwar? I found nothing in public archives."

"The location of the wormhole to Adit Pah is not well known and there is no law beyond a ship's might," Jala said.

"It's not too late for you to turn back, Jala," I said. "We'd be happy to return you to Azima."

Jala placed a hand on my chest. "Liam, Koosha has entrusted me to you. I will follow wherever you lead."

"For the record," I said, removing her hand a second time. "Humans are uncomfortable with too much touching. It sends a message of desired intimacy."

"My apologies," she said. "There is no shame in our attraction. I have no desire to stand between you and your mate."

"Because his *mate* is the jealous type," Tabby said, glowering at me. "Let's get this back on track. How is this Dark Frontier any different than Zuri? Genteresk pirates have free reign here in the back waters of Santaloo," I said.

"Don't be naive," Anino said. "Not all of Santaloo is frontier status, only parts of Zuri. The Abasi have laws governing space travel. Adit Pah has no law."

"Abasi seems to let pirates roam freely."

"The corsair menace in Santaloo is substantially less than what you'll find in Adit Pah," Anino said. "Pirates in this system aren't any different from Red Houzi in Sol. The patrol area is too large to make safety for all practical."

"Have any of you thought about what we're supposed to do if we actually find that Kroerak cruiser, or worse yet, a fleet of them?" Tabby was annoyed and it carried through in her voice. "Pirates I can understand. *Intrepid* hardly stands a chance against a cruiser, though."

"We're being set up," Tabby accused. "You're putting our asses on the line, once again. I wish we'd never met you."

"Believe it or not, Ms. Masters," Anino replied. "I wish none of this was necessary. Thing is, last time your asses were on the line, you saved humanity. I believe that soon Jonathan will need saving. You wouldn't turn away from this if you could."

There wasn't much more to say, as we'd hashed out this line of conversation so many times that all points were well known. Anino had used us, knowing a Kroerak invasion was imminent. He'd strongly believed we would be the catalyst that would bring about a successful outcome for humanity, despite overwhelming odds. The fact that we'd proven him right bothered me still. It was as if he knew something we didn't.

I stood and shook his hand. "It's time to get loaded. Anino, good luck to you."

"Safe travels, Hoffen," he said and walked away.

"Jester Ripples, would you ask your family to make way to *Intrepid*? Roby, Sempre, it's time to make your decision. Are you crew or not?"

"Sempre and I will stay behind," Roby said. "I talked with Silver and Merrie about sailing *Tuuq* to deliver steel and setting up a mining colony in the Kafida cluster."

"That is all important work. I'm sorry we won't have you as part of the crew, Roby. I'm sure Mom and Merrie will be glad to have you," I said and turned to Sempre. "Are you linking your fate with Roby's? You have a crew position on *Intrepid* if you'd like."

"She's staying with me," Roby interrupted.

I smiled tightly and nodded in Roby's direction, not making eye contact. "Roby, be quiet. Sempre has the right to make up her own mind on these things and I would like to hear what she wants."

"You would take me without Roby?" Sempre asked. "I have no value and I am not brave."

Roby started to speak but quieted when Tabby's hand came to rest on his shoulder.

"We have discussed this, Sempre. We can train anything except loyalty and bravery; both of which you possess in abundance. What would you like to learn to do?"

"Could I learn to be a warrior and fire ship weapons?"

"Sempre," Roby said through clenched teeth. "You can learn to fire weapons on *Tuuq*. I promised to teach you."

"And I could teach Sempre about overbearing men," Ada said.

"That's not fair," Roby complained.

"Keep talking, pal," Ada said.

I dared a glance at her. She had a fire in her eyes that I'd seen on a few occasions.

"Please, do not fight," Sempre said, looking at the ground. "I am sorry, Roby. I will travel with Liam Captain and learn from the great warriors of Loose Nuts."

"Then I'm coming too," Roby said. "That is, if the offer is still on the table."

Ada harrumphed. I knew I'd be causing trouble, but the fact was, Roby was an excellent engineer and could be counted on in a pinch. The fact that he had antiquated ideas about how to treat women, or at least Felio women, was something I felt could be worked out. That is, if he survived.

"Welcome to the crew, Roby Bishop, Engineer Second Class, and Sempre Neema, Gunner's Mate Third class?" I looked to Marny, questioning Sempre's assignment. She returned my glance with a quick nod. "This trip, you'll be joined by Jala and her sons Arijeet and Gunjeet."

"Gunjeet is a gangster. He'll betray you the first chance he gets," Roby said, not daring to look at Jala.

"The three of them are crew. Jala will be helping with negotiations and handling the mess. Arijeet and Gunjeet will start as third-class cargo handlers. We will treat all crew with respect."

"You should have asked me before you agreed to this," Roby said.

"Please escort Jala back to the ship and report to Marny at 2130," I said. When he didn't move, I pushed harder. "You have your orders, Mr. Bishop."

"Be safe, Liam," Mom said hugging me. "I didn't come out here to lose you too."

"I love you, Mom."

Moving Norigans and rounding up our cat, Filbert, turned out to be very similar tasks. Every Norigan wanted to say goodbye to every member of Petersburg station personally. It eventually dissolved into the ridiculous when I started noticing the fuzzy, little, blue frogs were actually making the round of goodbyes multiple times.

"Jester Ripples, will you communicate that *Intrepid* will be departing in forty-five minutes and anyone not aboard will be left on station and responsible for their own transportation to Rehema?"

"Of course, Liam Hoffen. Please do not be frustrated with my family. We find it difficult to part with friends," he said.

"For a species that makes friends so easily, I suspect this causes problems."

"I am unaware of problems."

"Forty-four minutes, Jester Ripples."

"Very well, Liam Hoffen. We will expedite our farewells."

"They're so cute," Ada said as we worked our way through Petersburg Station's main concourse and onto the pressurized catwalk that joined to *Intrepid's* primary, starboard airlock.

"Where are we sticking them all and what do they eat?" Tabby asked.

"We still have quarters for ten in the old crew country on Deck-2," Ada said. "But if I understood Big Cabbage correctly, they'll take over the crew mess area."

"I'll schedule crew to use the wardroom for mess," Marny said.

I found it difficult to focus on the minutiae of planning as we walked down the hallway from *Intrepid's* foyer. The air inside ships and stations all have subtly different smells. More than anything it was *Intrepid's* unique mix that my subconscious instantly recognized and accepted as home.

The hallway to the airlock was only a few meters. At the end, if we turned right, we'd head forward into crew country which consisted of crew bunks, crew mess, observation lounge, gymnasium, a new meeting room and the new forward cargo bay. We chose to turn left toward the bridge and officer's country. Just aft of the entry hallway was a down ramp, where the medical bay and brig were located, as well as a secondary entrance to the new forward cargo bay.

"Tabbs, Ada, Marny, could we spend twenty minutes and work out shifts and watches? We'll be talking about our navigation plan as well," I said. "I'd like to get underway in half an hour."

"I think you gave the Norigans forty-five, Cap," Marny said. "And that might be pushing it."

"And that is why I need you so badly," I said, palming the security lock on the bridge. A yellow warning flashed on my HUD. Someone had attempted access to the bridge without authorization. "I assume you've seen the access warning?"

"Copy that, Cap. I'll be working with crew on access procedures," Marny said. "Tomorrow morning at 0600, I'd like to have you and Tabby present for crew training. We'll be going over daily exercise requirements. I believe Arijeet and Gunjeet would benefit from the standard Loose Nuts demonstrations."

The entrance to the ready room was through a hatch in the bridge's port bulkhead, opposite the entry hatch. The three of us sat at the spartan, polished steel table. We'd originally had a wood topped table, but that had burned in the fire.

Ada flicked a scheduling grid onto the wall's display. She showed a four-hour watch schedule that rotated herself, Tabby, Roby, and me through the days. Marny's absence wasn't unexpected due to her responsibilities with the new crew.

"What's the mission, Liam?" Ada asked. "I get that we're looking for Jonathan, but how are we going to actually find him?"

While I hadn't used it yet, Jester Ripples had bragged about the high resolution holo projectors he'd installed on both the bridge and in the ready room. I brought up a map of the systems between us and the Dark Frontier.

"First, we're not looking for Jonathan. Anino thinks he has an idea where that Kroerak cruiser was headed. We're going to work ourselves into Nijjar space and hope we're close enough to respond when the time comes," I said.

"If we know where Jonathan and Sendrei are, we should go looking for them," Ada said.

"Mars Protectorate has been banging around out there and lost nearly half their fleet. We can't do the same. We'll establish a good cover and work our way into Nijjar space like the good capitalists we are," I said.

"So then, what are we going to be doing?" Ada asked.

"Convoy protection detail. We'll sail to Tamu system and meet up with a convoy on Chitundu. After that, we'll escort the convoy back to Santaloo, through to Brea Fortul, and then on to Tanwar system. In total, we'll be out forty-two days with three stops before reaching Kushala Station on Tanwar. Pay is good — we should clear sixty thousand after fuel and supplies."

"How did you find this job?" Ada asked.

"There's a marketplace," I responded. "House Mshindi did us a huge favor with the privateer status. Without it, we wouldn't have had enough reputation to compete. Apparently, Pogona captains aren't impressed with low bids as much as they are with actual experience. I'll give them credit for that."

"I suspect an armored frigate has a certain cachet as well," Tabby said. "We need to pick up some missiles."

"Not in the budget," I said. "Loose Nuts will clear sixty thousand for the trip to Tanwar after fuel, atmo, supplies and crew payments. That number moves to eighty-five if we end up engaging with hostiles. Current market on the only missiles I can find is running at forty-five thousand and they're not nearly as advanced as what we're used to. We just don't have the credits."

"I suppose with just turrets, *Intrepid* should be able to hold her own."

"Cap, where are you expecting the most trouble?" Marny asked.

"Well, Master Chief, the two wormholes out of Santaloo — Tamu and Brea Fortul — are the most dangerous," I said. "Once we get through Brea Fortul, we should be in the clear. I'm expecting a dustup on the way out, though. I'll need you on your toes in five days. We've yet to clear Tamu wormhole without a challenge and I'd like to send the Genteresk a message."

"Let's go with Gunny. That whole Master Chief thing drives me nuts. And we'll be ready," Marny said. "If you don't mind, I'd like to keep my appointment with our new crew."

"Aye, go ahead," I said.

"Big Cabbage is requesting permission to board," Ada said, switching the displayed schedule to video showing the airlock umbilical full of wiggling Norigans.

"Granted," I said. "If you'll get us ready to go, I'll see to the Norigans."

"Are you sure?" Ada asked.

I smiled and gave her a quick nod as I stood. "*Intrepid* wouldn't be in the shape she is without their help. I owe them a personal greeting at the minimum."

"I think I'll help Ada with the checklists," Tabby said.

"Coward."

By the time I made it forward to the airlock, a steady stream of Norigans was pouring into the ship.

"This way," I said, ushering a smaller Norigan, whose name I couldn't remember but my AI showed as Wet Nuzzle. I wondered how Norigan's earned their names. So far, the names had always made sense. I suspected there was a story available, if I was willing to request it. I'd most likely ask at some point on our trip to the Chitundu station over the watery moon, Rehema.

"Liam Hoffen, we are within the forty-five minutes you request-ed," Jester Ripples said, climbing onto me as we greeted.

"Thank you, Jester Ripples," I said. "Your family did an amazing job on *Intrepid*. I don't know how to thank you for all of your work."

"You must thank Thomas Anino for providing transportation and materials," Jester Ripples said. "Norigans do not find it a burden to help family."

If there was a single, important fact about being in the presence of a gaggle of Norigans, it was that you needed to be comfortable with physical intimacy. I'm not talking about the type of intimacy between consenting adults, but rather the type caused by constant hand hold-ing, hugs and clambering up and down one's body. Physically, I found it tiring as the little beasts were in constant motion.

"Hoffen Captain, Marny Gunny asked me to assist with our Norigan guests," Sempre said as she approached from the port-side passageway where apparently two Norigans had already escaped.

"That would be most helpful," I said. Between the two of us we successfully herded the blue horde into the crew mess.

Directly forward of the crew mess was an observation deck which had a wide pane of armored glass providing occupants an unob-structed view into space. The hatch between forward observation and crew mess was heavily armored, just as the bulkhead that separated them. It was expected that in combat this viewing deck might be compromised. The Norigans had opened the hatch and were streaming between the two spaces. For now, it would be okay to leave open, especially since all the Norigans wore vac-suits. If we got in a pinch, however, we'd need to close the hatch or risk vacuum expo-sure to the otherwise heavily protected mess.

"Most Felio find Norigans beneath their dignity," Sempre said. "After spending weeks with them, I do not understand the sentiment.

They are so intelligent and friendly. I do not understand the attitude."

"Perhaps it is because Norigans are pacifists to the point they won't even eat animal proteins," I said.

"*Verify all Norigans are aboard*," I instructed my AI. A green check-mark showed positive response.

"You should return to your duties, Hoffen Captain," Sempre said. "I will tend to our guests."

"Thank you, Sempre."

I breathed a sigh of relief as I made my way back into the now empty passageway. I decided to take the portside passage back to the bridge. It was the long way around, but I didn't mind. As I passed the downward ramp to the much smaller crew quarters and cargo hold, an exchange between Marny and Gunjeet wafted up and I paused out of curiosity.

"I am a warrior and do not acknowledge your position," Gunjeet said defiantly.

"Per your family's contract with Loose Nuts, it is within my purview to restrict your movements aboard ship and place you off *Intrepid* due to insubordination."

"I will leave now," Gunjeet said.

"We are no longer at dock with Petersburg Station," Marny said.

"Of course we are. We have not moved."

"This is a true statement. The Captain has locked exterior hatches and therefore we are no longer considered at rest. You will need to determine if you remain as crew or complete the trip to Chitundu in our brig," Marny said.

"Gunjeet, you will show Gunnery Sergeant Bertrand respect. You bring shame to your family," Jala's voice cut in.

"Mother, you will humble yourself. I am of age and you well know that you have no standing in this conversation," Gunjeet said. He was so sincere in his delivery; it occurred to me he had no idea how ridiculous his words were.

"Please consider your father's instructions."

"Decide, Gunjeet," Marny said. "You will follow the orders of your superiors of which I am one, or I will escort you to the brig."

"You are my superior only in words, but I will respect these requirements," he said and then added, "for now."

"You are not allowed passage off this deck. At 0545, you will meet me at this location to begin your training. Jala, if you would accompany me, I'll show you to the wardroom where we'll be taking our meals. I believe you have volunteered for meal preparations."

Marny's voice grew louder as she walked up the ramp. I hurried down the passage so I didn't get busted for listening in.

"*Intrepid's* tradition is to make sure coffee is available at all times. The beverage has a mild stimulant which is useful for our crew standing watch," Marny said as I rounded the corner that would take me past the wardroom, captain's quarters, and to the opposite side of the ship where I could enter the bridge.

"Captain on the bridge," Roby said as I palmed my way in. I found Ada and Tabby comfortably seated in the pilot's chairs working through pre-flight check lists. Roby was at one of the two engineering stations typing furiously.

"As you were," I said. "Everything checking out, Roby?"

"Yes. All systems are green." I caught sight of Gunjeet kicking a hatch in the crew quarters just before the image blinked off.

"Electronic eavesdropping is against our policy," I said. "Please refrain, Roby."

"What a jackass," Roby said. "I can't believe Marny is so patient with him."

I bit my tongue and didn't respond with the easy comparison between Roby and Gunjeet. Tabby, on the other hand wasn't as circumspect.

"Right, because the way you treat Sempre is so different," Tabby said. Ada held her fist out so Tabby could bump it on top in agreement.

"That's not fair."

"And it's not a conversation we're having right now. Marny, are we covered on weapons?"

"Copy that, Cap. Turrets are linked currently, but Tabby would very likely join me in the gunnery nest if push came to shove," she said.

"Establish link to Petersburg Station public address and Intrepid's public address. Cue AC/DC 'Back in Black.'"

"Petersburg?" Tabby asked as Ada shook her head, smiling.

A rock guitar started playing in rhythm to a heavy drum beat. I raised my left eyebrow to Tabby's questioning look as the raspy rock legend started singing.

> Back in Black
> ...
> I've been too long I'm glad to be back

A vid popped up on my HUD showing Mom's face with a big smile. She said something that I'd have to listen to later since the music was too loud. My breath caught in my chest as the bridge's forward vid screen showed *Intrepid* pulling away from the station. Frak, but it really did feel good to be back.

Chapter 16

BEST LESSONS ARE HARDEST

As we sailed away, I reviewed the sensor data from Petersburg and *Intrepid*. Petersburg's sensors were considerably stronger than *Intrepid's*, although it had to contend with interference from Zuri. At any given time, a few hundred ships were in orbit around Zuri. Most of those were 'in-system' ships, ferrying material and people between Zuri and Fan Zuri.

The problem I was working on, however, was that every time we sailed to the Tamu wormhole, a hostile reception awaited us. Had we run up against a permanent welcoming party that was set up to prey on any smaller, undefended ships that came near? Or were we somehow being targeted by Belvakuski and her Genteresk thugs?

I instructed the AI to track patterns of the ships within sensor range. If the AI found a correlation with our movements, it would bring those ships to my attention. I pulled out the comm crystal Munay had provided. The crystal pairs communicated through quantum resonance which, in short, meant that when one half vibrated within a frequency range, its twin vibrated at the same rate. The primary function was communication, although a useful secondary feature with whole crystal pairs was position location. If you had one half of the crystal, you could easily locate the second half. It was something of a risk to carry the crystal with us, but even if Munay no longer had the crystal, the person who found it would have to understand how to use it.

I opened a panel on the arm of my seat and set the crystal into an empty receptacle. I had room for six crystals and currently had three already mounted: one for Nick's workshop, another for Petersburg Station and a third for Anino. The Strix had confiscated our collection of past Belirand mission crystals. I'd recently heard from Parl, a Cetacar friend, who believed those crystals would be returned in short order. The only problem with Parl's assurance was that 'short order' for a Cetacar could mean years.

As expected, the missing sloop's crystal showed no activity.

Ada looked over her shoulder at me. "Liam, you have a shift in four hours, perhaps you should get some rest. I'll raise you if we run into anything."

"Right. That shift's going to be rough, but I'm hoping Tabby and I can catch some sleep soon. First, how does she feel to you?" I asked.

"*Intrepid* has always danced like a ballerina," Ada said. "The new armor has given her a little extra mass on her fore and aft but she's more than made up for it with added power."

"Do they let ballerinas have extra on their bottoms?" Tabby quipped, turning in her chair to Ada.

"Don't judge," Ada said playfully. "She's still beautiful."

"Nothing wrong with curves," I said, carefully walking the line I knew Tabby was waiting for me to cross. "Maybe she's more salsa dancer than ballerina now."

Ada laughed in response. "Okay you two. Now get out of here. I'm not going to put up with you missing your shift."

I stood and looked over to Tabby, who was working on something at the master gunnery station. "Tabbs, you going to get some rest?"

Tabby stood and led me from the bridge into the hallway. When the door closed behind us she pushed me up against the starboard bulkhead and leaned into me, her hands running along my suit as she kissed me roughly. "Now what was all that talk of curves?"

"Only one set of curves I'm interested in." I rested my hands on her hips and pulled her closer.

"By the way, I saw the way you looked at Jala when Koosha gave her to you," Tabby said, rocking against me suggestively. "For the record, that would be a bad idea for both of you."

I grinned. Tabby was getting heated up and as she pushed against me, I found I was unable to concentrate on anything else. I slipped out of her embrace, pulling her aft. With her free hand, she grabbed at me. I laughed as I let go and ran for the aft passage that joined the port and starboard main hallways. We were the second hatch on the aft side, just before the wardroom.

Movement further down the passage caught my attention as I placed my palm on our quarter's security panel. Jala's long, platinum blonde hair disappeared through the normally open wardroom door. I suspected she'd been listening to our conversation in the hallway. The idea of people as property wasn't new to me and Koosha had been clear about how he felt about the woman. I'd have to deal with Jala soon and clear up her position.

"Don't get confused." Tabby pushed me through the door.

I used the momentum to propel me to the bed, where I turned onto my back, expecting her to follow. Instead she stopped and ran a finger down the side of her grav-suit causing it to peel away from her skin. I fluffed a pillow under my head and waited with anticipation as she dropped her suit on the ground, exposing a lacy bralette and panties.

Let's be clear, I needed absolutely no enticement from Tabby to become excited. I'd been in love with this woman for as long as I could remember and the fact that she'd chosen me was still something of a mystery. That said, the black lacy material covered her just enough that I needed to see more.

"Like them?" Tabby asked, crawling onto the bed with sultry exaggeration, her voice low.

"Where did you get them?" I asked, lightly cupping the material.

Tabby placed a finger on my lips to quiet me then ran her hand down the side of my suit, releasing it. It took a moment to wriggle out.

Once free, she pushed me back onto the bed and sat atop me, not bothering to remove her skimpies.

"You are mine, Liam Hoffen," she said. The forcefulness of her words surprised me, but I wasn't about to argue. I'd given myself to her long ago and her claim over me as we shared in each other's bodies was neither new nor upsetting.

"Always," I answered, tucking her coppery hair over her ear.

I rolled the two of us over so she was on her back. It didn't escape me that she could have resisted if she wanted. It wasn't the nature of our relationship, however. She would always give what I asked, as I would give to her.

"When can we get married?" I asked.

"I think in some cultures, this would probably have done it," Tabby said, smiling and pulling my face to her own so our lips met.

I pushed away. "I mean it, Tabbs. I'm in this for the long haul."

She rolled out from under me and sat up on the edge of the bed with her back to me. I knew her better than I knew anyone in the universe. She was afraid of getting married, because not a single relationship in her family had survived it. I scooted over and placed my legs on either side of her wrapping my arms around her bare midriff.

"We can't let the past decide our future, Tabbs." I moved her hair out of the way and kissed her neck.

"How do you always know what to say?" When she turned, there were tears in her eyes.

"Just trying to figure out how to get those panties off." I waggled my eyebrows.

"You're such a dumbass." She swiveled and pushed me onto the bed.

AN ALARM CHIMED in my ear. I'd been dreaming of battling bugs in our Popeyes while trying desperately to find Jonathan, who was trapped in a Kroerak hibernation egg. I blew out a sigh of relief, my conscious mind slowly separating the dream state from reality.

I smiled as I looked at Tabby, sleeping and sprawled mostly naked. A sheet just barely covered her bottom, which was still wrapped in her latest lacy addition, of which I was a big fan. I didn't want to wake her so I slid out of bed, jumped into the head and took a quick shower.

It was 0200 and I was working on less sleep than I liked, but such was the nature of watch schedules. When I got to the door leading out of our quarters, I noticed that one of the arms of Tabby's grav-suit had inadvertently fallen in the path of the door so that it hadn't fully closed. My mind jumped back to what I might have said while we'd been at it the night before. It wasn't as if I had anything to hide, but someone listening could have heard things I wouldn't ordinarily say in public.

I picked up her suit and dropped it into the cleaner. The grav-suit, like most smart fabrics, had the capacity to clean itself, but it was a good practice to occasionally send it through a freshener, as it would unload the grime collectors and leave it neatly folded.

I had a few minutes before my watch started, so I walked down to the wardroom and was surprised to find Jala sitting quietly, her back to the door. I didn't know the beautiful, pale-skinned Pogona very well. She'd always been nice enough when we'd visited Koosha's, but she was also an alien and I wasn't sure of her motivations.

When I stepped around, I noticed her eyes were closed and her breathing was very light. As quietly as I could, I pulled a cup from the cupboard. As a send-off gift, Nick had manufactured twenty of the mini gravity-controlled cups that would keep liquid from sloshing out, even in the most ridiculous space battles. I set the five-hundred-milliliter cup under the coffee dispenser and reveled in the smell. We were still working with synth-coffee, but since I was running on low sleep, it smelled like liquid gold to me.

It was then I sensed a presence behind me and a light hand came to rest on my shoulder. "I have waited for you, Liam Hoffen. Will you take me to your bed, now?" Jala's voice was as soft as ever.

I'll admit to a moment of confusion as I turned and considered the woman. A small part of me was thrilled at the offer. It was a part

of me that I knew would be lost — both figuratively and literally —
once Tabby discovered my indiscretion.

"Good morning, Jala," I said, pulling her hand from my shoulder.
"I'm afraid I haven't done a good job explaining how this works.
You're crew on *Intrepid*. While I'm the captain, it doesn't give me the
right to physical relationships with the crew."

"But Koosha..."

"Hold on," I said. "I'm not finished. You are a beautiful woman,
but I'm in a relationship with someone I love deeply. For humans,
this is a one-and-done thing. This doesn't mean you and I can't be
friends; it does mean we won't exchange physical intimacy."

"Why would you allow me on your ship? Passage to Tanwar is
expensive. Koosha has no other means in which to pay you."

"You are crew, Jala," I said. "You will perform duties as assigned to
you by Marny. For this you will receive a small share of the earnings
of the ship, including free passage to wherever we go. The same is
true for Arijeet and Gunjeet."

"Gunjeet is a strong man."

"I'll be honest, this conversation is confusing. The most powerful
Pogona I know is Belvakuski, a female. How can you devalue yourself
like this?" The conversation was driving me nuts. I'd run into a
similar issue with Roby with respect to Sempre.

"I am nothing like Belvakuski."

"I'm glad to hear that," I said. "Let me be clear. While on *Intrepid*,
you are a free person and can make decisions for yourself. You only
owe me the respect due an officer. At 0600, Marny will be working
through all this as part of crew indoctrination."

"You are an unusual man, Liam Hoffen," Jala said.

"So I've been told," I said. "Do you need help finding your
quarters?"

"No, and you may tell Tabitha Masters her message was well
delivered. I will make no further overtures."

I gave her a quizzical look and it crossed my mind that Tabby
might have seen Jala, as I did before we entered our quarters the

night before. It was possible her suit blocking open the door had not been the accident it appeared.

"I'll pass it along," I said, working my way around her and heading toward the bridge.

I found Ada on bridge watch by herself. "Anything to report?"

"One of the atmo scrubbers is reporting buildup, so I shut it down and put it on Roby's list for this morning," she said. "Otherwise, we're one hundred thirty-four hours from the Tamu wormhole and there are no ships within a hundred thousand kilometers."

"You are relieved." I repeated the ritual we'd established for watch changes.

"I stand relieved."

I sat in the captain's chair directly behind the two pilot's chairs. Ada had the forward vid screens showing an unobstructed view of space in front of *Intrepid* with system statuses scrolling on the starboard side.

"Get some rest, Ada."

"Will do, Liam."

After settling in and assuring myself everything was as Ada had reported, I turned my attention to my comm queue. Several items required my attention and I worked through them. Perhaps the most important was a request for further information from the convoy organizer, Aantal Tutt. In addition to requesting confirmation that we'd arrive on time in fourteen days, Aantal also asked for *Intrepid's* weapon systems, how they were laid out, and how many actual gunner's mates we employed. I was careful in my response. I didn't want to lose the contract, but I wasn't about to compromise our security. I was pretty sure other, better-known companies didn't have to answer questions like these from nervous captains. For this first run, I'd sold our services at a bargain since we had virtually no reputation. That was something we could change quickly.

For most of the remaining watch, I sifted through Pogona message boards and communication portals, looking for a job that would take us into the Adit Pah system. There were several available and I shot them each an offer, but I wasn't hopeful. The subtext of the job offers made me believe the shippers were looking for ships with local experience. It couldn't hurt to apply, however.

My watch passed quickly as I had a lot to do, and at 0545 Tabby entered the bridge with a lopsided grin, two cups of coffee, and meal bars.

"Good morning, Love," I said. "You're early. Did you sleep okay?"

"Marny's asking for you in the gymnasium," Tabby said. "And, yes, last night was wonderful. Do you have anything to report?"

I transitioned bridge watch and gratefully accepted the meal bar and fresh coffee. "Jala asked me to pass on that she received your message last night."

"Perfect," Tabby said, settling into a pilot's chair. "I was afraid that I was going to need to be less subtle."

I kissed her on the forehead and took the long way around to the gymnasium, first stopping at the wardroom to drop off my cups for cleaning.

There are two entrances to the gymnasium, located forward on the portside of *Intrepid's* oval crew section. The entrance I typically used would take me through the crew mess, where the Norigans were settled. I wasn't about to get bogged down by the friendly little critters, so I took the long way around through the forward cargo hold. I was pleased to discover this lesser-known back entrance hadn't been removed.

The gymnasium had been built for use by a crew of a hundred. Of course, that meant it was designed to accommodate twenty or thirty people at any given time. It was spacious by spacer standards, especially for the seven of us: Marny, Roby, Sempre, Jala, Arijeet, Gunjeet, and me.

When I arrived, I found the crew lined up in familiar formation with Marny giving instructions as she had so many times before. I stood by and listened as she continued describing the function of the ship and the various duties for each of the different crew stations.

"Any questions?" Marny asked, finally.

"Why do you care that we exercise?" Gunjeet asked. "It is not your business."

"It is in your contract, Mr. Gunjeet. And from this moment forward you will recognize me as Gunny or Gunnery Sergeant Bertrand when addressing me. Is that clear? You may respond with either 'No, Gunny,' 'No, Gunnery Sergeant Bertrand,' or 'Yes, Gunny.' I think you get the idea."

"You can't make me say that."

I smiled. There was always one in the crowd who wanted a demonstration. I had no doubt Tabby was watching from the bridge. We all enjoyed this particular ah-ha moment for new crew. Even Roby had the good sense to wince as Gunjeet expressed his distaste for discipline.

"Gunjeet, you will show respect," Jala said, quietly.

"Ms. Jala, you will not address the other crew when standing at attention," Marny said. "Mr. Gunjeet's discipline is my responsibility."

"Yes, Gunny Bertrand."

"Fantastic. So, we've just learned Gunjeet's problem is not hereditary, as Ms. Jala is most respectful."

Jala nodded while her son sneered at her.

"Mr. Gunjeet. Currently, you will do what I say because I am your superior and responsible for your wellbeing. If you prefer to ride in the brig, this remains your option. What will it be? Would you like to continue as crew?"

Marny had worked her way over to Gunjeet and now stood with her face only inches from his. She stared into his eyes provocatively, obviously preferring to provoke a test of wills early instead of drawing it out.

Gunjeet was fast. He drew a hidden knife from his vac-suit and brought it up. As expected, Marny's response was similarly quick as she disarmed the lanky Pogona youth and twisted his arm brutally. A familiar cracking sound could be heard as bone broke and he howled in pain. Arijeet jumped from his position in line to aid his brother and was immediately dropped to the floor by Marny's leg sweep. She followed the move with a quick punch to his chest, which left him gasping for air.

"My boys," Jala said, crumpling next to the fallen brothers. Technically, Marny could have insisted she stay in line, but it was an understandable reaction.

"Captain, would you bring a med-kit? I believe Gunjeet is in need of medical attention," Marny asked, standing and straightening her suit.

I located the kit and extracted a break cuff that could be slipped over Gunjeet's broken arm. The arm would take a couple of days to heal, but I believed the lesson would likely stick for a longer period of time. If it didn't, there wouldn't be much hope left for the youth.

Chapter 17

WORTHY OPPONENT

"That was not your target, Captain," Marny scolded lightly.

"But I fragged it." I raised my eyebrows, hoping that was sufficient defense. Marny had been drilling the entire crew on gunnery operation and discipline for days. Leave it to the Navy to have so many rules regarding weapons fire.

"Simulation hold. If I could have the class's attention on the center screen," Marny said. The gunner's nest was a narrow, long room forward of the bridge and had six stations that controlled *Intrepid's* eight turrets. This go-round, I was controlling one of two aft blasters.

In response to Marny's request, our screens froze and our controls stopped responding. I looked down. I was about to be made an example of — again. We'd all discovered that Marny was no-nonsense when it came to ship's weapons. There was a right way and anything less was to be dissected so the right way could be exposed.

"Mr. Arijeet, could you describe the primary characteristics of our aft blasters?"

"There are two; both have the designation sixty millimeters. They are the second heaviest weapons aboard the ship and have the largest field of view, with the ability to cover the entire aft field of view and up to twenty degrees forward. When engines are at full burn, the gunner's responsibility is to pick up aft..."

"Thank you, Mr. Arijeet. Mr. Gunjeet, in reviewing Mr. Hoffen's last attack could you offer any positive criticism?"

"No." Gunjeet responded sullenly. His attitude wasn't new, although he seemed to enjoy working the gunner's station.

"Ms. Sempre?"

"I don't know if I can," Sempre replied. While she had quick reflexes, Sempre's skill on the guns wasn't great, although she showed improvement. So far, the Pogona boys both showed considerable raw skill.

"It is permitted, Sempre," I said. "We learn more quickly with examples." It didn't seem fair that I should have to encourage someone to pick on me, and I'd already seen what Marny was going to hang me on.

"Many apologies, Liam Captain, but by following your target into a covered zone, you exposed our flank and provided an unobstructed shot for these two ships. Had we been in combat with a single or even multiple ships that were concentrated forward of the meridian, your actions would have been reasonable."

"Very good, Sempre. Your analysis is spot on." Marny highlighted a ship that had just cleared the corona of the engine's burn. "Captain Hoffen very likely experienced what is commonly referred to as tunnel vision. Once locked on, the predator that lives within us all filters out extraneous information and utilizes all senses to defeat its single objective. This instinct can be overridden with training."

"This is dumb," Gunjeet muttered. "He killed that ship."

I wasn't naive enough to believe he was defending me, but I had to admit it felt good that someone understood what I was doing.

"AI, please show simulation of the top three likely outcomes if Captain Hoffen had returned to his own firing lane."

On each of our vid-screens, the small portion of battle played out three different times, with slightly varying results. In each case, instead of following the ship, I released it when it crossed out of my firing lane. Two of those times, Sempre picked it up with a mid-ship blaster and finished the job. The third time she missed and it peeled away.

"She missed. That's proof enough for me," Gunjeet said, smugly.

"Tell me, Mr. Gunjeet. Which is better, a strong offense or a strong defense?"

"Easy. Offense."

"The correct answer is that it depends," Marny said. "In a battle of attrition, however, the opponent with the strongest defenses will prevail. By leaving our flank open, *Intrepid* received considerable damage to a starboard engine. In the simulations, however, the aft gun provided a successful deterrent and the damage was limited."

"Gunjway," Gunjeet muttered. The term was a Felio derogatory term, referring to a neutered male.

"Mr. Gunjeet, if you ever wish a seat in my nest, you will keep a civil tongue," Marny said.

Gunjeet turned away, not saying anything, focusing instead on the gun controls, obviously surprised we'd heard the term before.

"Again," Marny said and restarted the battle simulation.

"Which of the crew are ready for combat?" I asked.

As was our practice, available officers sat for lunch at 1200. We'd been sailing for six days and were a few hours from the Tamu gate. Marny gave us daily updates on the crew's effectiveness on weapons, just as Roby had kept us up to date on the continuing repairs by the otherwise bored Norigans.

"We would not be ready against a professional Naval ship," Marny said. "We lack discipline of fire. Gunjeet has by far the best shoot-down record with accuracy in the low teens. Sempre's accuracy is in the low twenties but she is conservative in her shot selection. Arijeet is somewhere between the two."

Jala carefully placed a basket of steaming rolls on the table and smiled as she heard her son's name used positively.

Tabby and I both consistently scored in the mid to high twenties, which was the percent of shots taken to recorded hit. The number was skewed as hits were recorded for any shot within forty meters of a fast-moving target. Harassing a ship was nearly as valuable as hitting it outright.

"We'll likely have a test coming up at the Tamu gate," I said, "although the gate squatters might give us a pass, given our size."

"I'll have Sempre, Gunjeet and Arijeet seated on approach. The crew will be on simulated turrets, but they won't know this. I need to see how they each respond to combat. Tabby, I have an open chair if you'd be willing to join us."

"Aye. Count me in, Gunny," Tabby answered.

"Red berry juice, Captain?" Jala asked, quietly sliding between Tabby and me.

"Yes, thank you. What are these rolls? They're delicious," I said. The puffy yeast rolls had been filled with a creamy mix of vegetables and crispy protein cubes. I didn't recognize the seasoning, but found it pleasant enough.

"A recipe Gunnery Sergeant Bertrand shared with me. I believe the flavor you are experiencing is rosemary. I found a package of dried needles. I hope they weren't too far aged."

"It is delicious, thank you," I said. "This evening, we will be arriving at Tamu gate. I would like you on the bridge."

"Yes, Captain," she replied demurely, bowing her head.

"On an entirely different front, we might have an issue with our escort contract," I said. "My contact has requested a meeting and walkthrough of *Intrepid*. He's talking about canceling our contract as we're too much of an unknown."

"Can they do that?" Tabby asked. "Shouldn't we have a penalty built in?"

"Yes, they can and no on the penalty. We're competing against established escort services."

"You make it sound so tawdry," Marny quipped and I had to replay the words in my head before I rolled my eyes at her.

"It's sordid business. That's for sure," I said. "I'm hopeful I can be convincing when we meet. Otherwise, we'll be looking for a cargo run to Tanwar. Although, that's not ideal."

"Why's that?"

"We blew our bond," I said. "That's a black mark on our record. Shippers aren't willing to consider unbonded cargo with us. They're afraid we'll dump and run like we did with the shipment for Goboble."

To say I was nervous about our approach to Tamu gate was an overstatement. I had nervous energy, but I was confident in *Intrepid's* capabilities. What we couldn't shoot down, I felt reasonably certain we could outrun. Such was the design of a General Astral Frigate.

"I'm admitting Jala to the bridge," Ada said. There had been considerable activity on the bridge as we closed the final hundred thousand kilometers to the gate. In the end, however, only three of us remained: Ada, Marny, and me — Jala making a fourth. Roby and Jester Ripples were in the engine room, and the gunnery crew in the gunner's nest. We'd closed the armored hatch between the remaining Norigans in the crew mess and the forward observation lounge, just in case we took fire forward. It felt like we were being overly cautious, but as Marny drilled into me time and time again, there's no time for preparation after things get dicey.

I gestured to the port side bulkhead where there were two open spots. "Jala, please take a seat at one of the empty stations."

"Your view is beautiful," Jala said as she sat, straight-backed in the chair, crossing one leg over the other.

"Agreed."

"Cap, I have two ship signatures at thirty thousand kilometers," Marny said. "Both cutter class. Single turret."

"Standard Genteresk chasers," I said. "Care to guess if Belvakuski's cruiser is on the other side?"

"Unlikely. It would put her at risk of detection by Abasi. I'd expect her to stay in Santaloo. Although, if she's expecting us, that would change my answer."

Marny was repeating what we'd talked through several times in the past few days. The most likely scenario was playing out. The two smaller ships would give way due to our size and we'd go through unhindered.

"Ada, slow to stop at ten thousand kilometers."

"Aye, aye, Liam," Ada replied and gave a bit more juice to the engines to slow us.

"Do you think they've seen us?"

"Aye, Cap, they know something's out here. Those cutters would have sensors similar to *Tuuq's*. I'd imagine they're not getting a strong read beyond our location. What's your plan here?"

"I'd like to heave-to and observe. Tell folks to get comfortable, we might be here for a couple of hours," I said.

"Aye, Cap. SOP. Hurry up and wait. Good lesson for us all."

As Marny and Ada communicated my change in plans to the crew, I turned to Jala. "Thanks for joining us on the bridge. There's some possibility we'll need to communicate with the crew of those ships. Our translators do a fine job, but I'd like your take on things if they're Genteresk, as I suspect they are."

"Why do you wait?" Jala asked. "*Intrepid* is a much larger ship; can you not simply ignore them? They would be foolish to attack."

"We have flexibility in our plan," I said. "And I have experience with these particular gate campers. They're waiting for a weaker ship to come through the wormhole so they can attack and board. According to our agreement with Abasi, we have the authority to intervene on behalf of a ship in distress."

"And you would like to intervene?"

"Cap, we have ships coming through from Tamu," Marny said. "Heavy freighters with armed escorts. Tweedle Dee and Tweedle Dum are backing off."

My holo projector displayed a convoy of eight, three of which were fast attack craft deployed moments after transition from wormhole space. The ships accelerated on line with Fan Zuri and took no interest in either the pirate cutters or *Intrepid*. Although it wasn't clear to me if they could resolve *Intrepid* now that we'd slowed to a zero delta-v with the wormhole anomalous space.

Minutes turned into an hour as *Dee* and *Dum* returned to their positions.

"Marny, when did those ships move in relationship to that last convoy's arrival?" I asked. "Did they have advance warning?"

After a moment, Marny replied. "That's affirmative, Cap. They started moving fifteen seconds before the convoy transitioned."

"Let's take the crew to a relaxed posture. I'd like to wait this out a bit longer."

"Copy that, Cap. We'll go to a three-minute standby." Three-minute standby would keep people at their posts, but the crew could shift out to stretch their legs or visit the head as long as they could return within three minutes. Only half the crew could be out at any time.

Forty minutes later, the two pirate ships moved away from the Tamu wormhole again. Just as before, a grouping of freighters arrived. In the lead were two beefy freighters that appeared reasonably armored and armed.

"How long will we stay out here, Liam?" Ada asked when we reached the three-hour mark.

"Let's give it two more hours," I said.

"Do you really think any reasonable captain would bring a convoy through the wormhole without protection?" Ada asked.

"I don't, Ada," I said. "Last time, those cutters attacked a much bigger ship that had been damaged while fighting on the other side of the wormhole."

"Copy that," Ada said. "I'm not sure why I'm impatient sitting here. It is not much different than sailing, but it just feels like we're not going anywhere."

Marny chuckled. "Maybe because we aren't."

Two hours passed without another group moving through the gate. Ada was right, it was a long shot, but we'd had some time to burn. We could afford to hang out for another twenty hours, but I was also anxious to resolve the issues with our convoy contract.

"All hands, this is the Captain," I said. "I'd like everyone to return to their stations. We'll be setting sail shortly. All stations check in for immediate departure."

I had a short delay from engineering, but didn't push it. Finally, all stations checked in.

"Ada, take us in, but keep us on silent running," I said, standing. "I'll be back in five minutes."

"Aye, aye, Liam," Ada said, giving me a concerned look.

Briskly, I walked off the bridge and headed aft. Instead of turning toward our quarters at the first intersection, I continued to the upper engine room where Roby and Jester Ripples were.

"What's up, Captain?" Roby had difficulty talking around the last bite of one of Jala's stuffed biscuits he'd jammed into his mouth. He looked at me guiltily.

"Liam Hoffen, aren't you sailing the ship?" Jester Ripples asked, bounding up to me and climbing into my arms.

"Headed back to the bridge in a second, Jester Ripples," I said. "I was hoping I could get help from my brain trust back here."

Roby slugged down a drink of water and swallowed hard. A flash of annoyance coursed through me as I noticed how the surfaces were covered with several days' worth of crumbs and debris. I pushed the problem aside.

"Sure," Roby said, brightening at the compliment. "What can we do?"

"I need it to look like *Intrepid* is having engine troubles right before we go through the wormhole," I said.

"How big of a problem do you want?"

"Just to be clear; I don't want any real problems," I said.

"No, I got you, Cap," Roby said, getting more comfortable in the conversation. "Are we talking catastrophic collapse or imminent explosion? Or are you thinking something subtler?"

"More like we're limping back to civilization and are easy pickings," I said.

"Liam Hoffen, wouldn't this be dangerous? If those ships are indeed brigands, they might find your actions enticing," Jester Ripples said.

"I've sure missed you, little buddy," I said, scrubbing behind his ears affectionately. "And, that's exactly what I'm hoping for. If we don't get these cutters to stop parking here, it remains too dangerous for those who sail through without a ship like *Intrepid*."

Jester Ripples nodded his head, thoughtfully considering my words. The pacifist in him did not appreciate the idea of a conflict, but he also didn't like the fact that others were being put in danger by the pirates. Of course, the general Norigan answer was to give aggressors what they wanted. I had a hard time imagining how their species had survived with that approach, but I was nonetheless glad they had.

"I got it, Cap," Roby said. "When do you want this to happen?"

"Hit it at five hundred kilometers from the wormhole and then again at two. If there are ships on the other side, give me one more display once we're through plus five seconds," I said.

"Roger that."

I set Jester Ripples down and jogged back to the bridge. *Intrepid* had covered half the distance to the wormhole by the time I entered. It was clear neither ship had seen us yet.

"Ada, things are going to get interesting. Roby is going to..."

Before I could finish my statement, three ships transitioned from Tamu into Santaloo.

"Marny?" I asked.

"That's the Genteresk ship, *Sangilak*," Marny replied. "Two attack craft flanking her."

"Ada, spin it up and take evasive," I said. "Roby, belay previous order."

"Frak, copy that, Cap," Roby replied.

"Jala, pull those straps on," I said. "This is likely to get dicey."

"*Incoming hail,*" my AI warned.

"*Don't show bridge crew other than myself and accept hail,*" I instructed.

The thickset Belvakuski appeared on the forward vid-screen, transmitting a vid of herself from the waist up. I pinched my fingers, shrunk her image and pushed it to the side so we continued to have a wide-angled view of space.

"Captain Hoffen, once again we meet as adversaries," she said. I was momentarily distracted by her flabby jowls and how her jewelry musically echoed in response to her movement. "I find I am intrigued by one who escapes my grasp a second time. I do appreciate you awaiting my arrival, however."

"Zone defense, alpha," Marny ordered, as she grasped the gunnery station controls. "Stay tight, kids, these guys mean business."

We'd drilled on only four scenarios — or packages as Marny referred to them: Alpha and Beta for both offense and defense. The zone defense was designed for multiple, fast targets. The goal was to keep ships from breaching a five-hundred-meter perimeter and thereby reducing potential damage to *Intrepid*.

"Belvakuski, why am I not surprised to find you here?" I asked. "I take it you're sore about Goboble?"

Belvakuski smiled. Surprisingly, it was a winning smile. To be a truly effective pirate leader, you would have to have equal parts carrot and stick in your personality. I knew for a fact she had plenty of stick.

"I don't suppose you would save us all the effort and turn over your ship before I pound it into dust? It is such a pretty thing," she said.

"And what? You'd let my crew go?"

"No, I'm afraid that wouldn't be possible. But I would certainly consider placing a fine man such as yourself in my harem. I haven't enjoyed a shapely human such as yourself before."

"What is it with you Pogona?" I asked, disgusted. "You're either misogynists or extreme feminists."

"Feminist you say? This is a word I will cherish."

"All hands, combat burn in three, two, one," Ada announced.

Intrepid's engines fired and I was pinned back into my chair as the four massive engines fired and the inertial systems attempted to bleed off the excessive g-forces. The fast-attack craft still closed on us, but *Tweedle Dee, Tweedle Dum,* and *Sangilak* dropped quickly behind us.

"Where are you going, Hoffen?" Belvakuski said. "Your ship is most impressive. I really must have it."

"*Cut comm.* Marny are you ready for a flip?" I asked.

To keep up with us, the small attack craft had fallen in line with *Intrepid* and were now directly behind us.

"All gunners, prepare for Aggressive Offense Beta," Marny instructed.

"Ada, once they're in firing range, I want a flip and reverse burn so we stay with the attack craft as long as possible," I said.

"Copy, Liam," Ada said. "On your mark."

Whoever was flying the smaller ships had no trouble staying out of the way of *Intrepid's* aft-facing sixty-mil cannons. The cannons were designed for larger ships, so while it was disappointing, it wasn't completely unexpected.

"We're taking fire, Cap," Marny said.

The attack-craft blasters plunked away at our haunches, but it was mostly ineffective; the two most heavily armored sections on the ship were fore and aft. Add to that the stealth armor layer and I was willing to take a few hits as they closed in.

"Copy that, Marny. All hands prepare for combat flip, in ten seconds," I said. I punched the synchronized counter so everyone received the same countdown.

"Focus fire on *Larry,*" Marny said, quietly. It was unnecessary, but reassuring, nonetheless. *Larry* was a reference to the first-priority ship and *Bob* was priority number two. In the Aggressive Beta plan, all gunners were to shoot at the top priority if they had any line on it. We'd risk some damage from *Bob,* but the goal was to burn down one ship quickly.

My stomach flopped as Ada smartly spun us over. Streams of fire erupted from five of our eight turrets, four of which focused on a very surprised *Larry.*

"*Larry* is down. Concentrate on *Bob,*" Marny said as *Larry's* engines blinked out and the ship dropped its pursuit.

"Second fleet entering Santaloo," Ada said.

"Give *Sangilak* a wide berth, Ada," I said. "Put her in the hole if you can."

"Copy, Liam," Ada said, her voice tight.

The 'hole' referred to a maneuver designed for escape, usually from a larger and more powerful ship. Because of our flip, *Intrepid* was now headed into the path of the incoming *Sangilak*. Ada would attempt to keep the ships apart, but on opposite trajectories. If all went well, *Intrepid* would shoot past *Sangilak* while increasing acceleration. If *Sangilak* wanted to find us, she'd have to work against her own acceleration, turn, and then burn hard to match the acceleration Intrepid had gained. It would work well, as long as we could stay away from Sangilak's guns on the way by. While dangerous, Ada knew our sensor image was the most difficult to read if she pointed us directly at the incoming ship.

"*Bob* is down. Disengage," Marny ordered and then two seconds later she reiterated. "Disengage!" The fast-attack craft exploded beside us.

I wondered what was going on, but we were in the thick of things and there would be plenty of time for arm-chair analysis later.

"I'm taking a close pass on *Tweedle Dum*," Ada said. We'd made up names for every ship other than *Sangilak,* primarily because they weren't transmitting transponder codes.

Ada's line on our pursuers made sense. They hadn't yet adjusted to the fact that we were accelerating directly at them and as a result, our delta-v was ratcheting up at twice the expected rate.

"Marny, any read on the new fleet?" I asked.

"Looks like a merchant convoy, Cap."

"*Incoming hail, Abasi flagged ship, Flaking Bark.*"

"On screen," I said. "Captain Hoffen."

A female Felio wearing a traditional officer's uniform appeared on the forward vid screen.

"This is Imara Captain. Is assistance requested?"

"I believe we have this, Captain," I said. "Thank you for the offer. I recommend staying clear of Genteresk ship, *Sangilak.*"

"Yes. *Flaking Bark* desists."

"Gunners, Zone Defense Alpha," Marny instructed.

"*Incoming comm, Sangilak.*"

"*On tight screen,*" I answered.

"I will not underestimate you again, Captain Hoffen," Belvakuski said and touched her fist just beneath her chin.

"*Sangilak* is pulling off. Should I adjust?" Ada asked.

"No. Keep our original line. We don't need to mix it up with a destroyer if we can avoid it." Belvakuski had made the right decision. Her fast-attack craft had been woefully under-armored for facing off with a frigate and she no longer had ships capable of catching us if we decided to run.

"All hands, stand down," I said.

"Permission to leave bridge," Marny said. She was fuming about something.

"Granted," I said.

"What was that about?" Ada asked.

"I'll let her cool off before asking."

Ada chuckled in agreement.

"Jala, any thoughts you'd like to share regarding Belvakuski?"

"Does Belvakuski know my face now?" Jala asked. Her expression was stoic as always, but I was learning how to read her and saw fear.

"She does not, Jala. I kept the camera tight to my own," I said.

Jala sighed almost inaudibly, but I caught it. "Belvakuski is a legend among our people. I had not anticipated how intimidating she would be. You are wise to treat her respectfully and as an equal. When captured, she will make your death quick and painless."

"Let's hope it doesn't come to that," I said.

"Yes," Jala agreed.

"What did her gesture mean when she rested her fist beneath her chin?" I asked.

"She did this?" Jala asked.

"It was on screen; did you not see her?"

"I turned away. I was afraid, Captain Liam Hoffen."

"*Send video data-streams of all communication between me and*

Belvakuski to Jala. Replay final minute of conversation." The AI immediately started replaying Belvakuski's conversation which ended with the odd fist-beneath-her-chin gesture.

"Respect, Captain Liam Hoffen. Belvakuski considers you a worthy opponent."

"Great. I'd settle for her considering me invisible."

"Yes. That would be best," Jala agreed.

"Ada, do you have a line on *Larry?* Seems like we should collect *Intrepid's* first official privateer prize."

"We're burning toward her now," Ada said.

Chapter 18

PRIZE

"Careful of the turret, Cap," Marny warned as Tabby and I stepped off the edge of the forward cargo bay's deck, through the pressure barrier, and into the space that separated *Intrepid* and the fast-attack craft Jester Ripples labeled *Larry*. According to Ada, Jester Ripples had been reading old Earth history and had taken to naming the otherwise unnamed ships for characters he'd discovered in his reading.

Larry's eighteen-meter-long, ten-meter-wide design was simple and obvious; it was made for speed and maneuverability. A single, fat engine sat behind gracefully swept-back wings that attested to its ability to function well even in atmospheric operations. The cockpit that could accommodate four passengers sat atop the wings. Just behind it was a turret with a limited range of motion.

"Why do you suppose Belvakuski abandoned these guys?" I asked. "Couldn't she have just picked them up on her way?"

"*Intrepid's* superior speed would have put *Sangilak* at risk of strafing runs," Marny said. "The fact she sent two minimally armored ships after *Intrepid* suggests she underestimated our capabilities. If you look at it from her side, she had to be wondering why *Intrepid* didn't engage the cutters at the wormhole. Belvakuski might have thought your actions were designed to call her out," she added. "Too many unknowns for her to risk coming back for this ship."

"What happened to *Bob*? Was it Gunjeet who blew it up?" I asked.

"Stay in the moment, Cap. *Larry* is rotating," Marny warned. She'd remained behind on *Intrepid's* cargo deck specifically to watch for hostile actions by *Larry's* crew.

I'd seen the same blast from *Larry's* directional jets. The pirates were attempting to line up on either *Intrepid* or us, no doubt concerned we'd space them once we gained control of their ship.

Before I could react, *Intrepid* nudged forward, her cargo bay swallowing Tabby and me like a giant fish might swallow its prey. We fell to the floor in the artificial gravity at about the same time *Intrepid's* hull contacted *Larry* and sent it slowly tumbling away.

"Jala, see if you can contact that crew and explain that we'll keep 'em alive if they settle down. Ada, can you help her get a comm contact?"

"Sure thing, Liam," Ada answered.

I picked myself off the cargo bay floor and looked on as *Larry's* pilot attempted to right the ship. *Larry* would just fit into our forward hold if we depressurized and left the nose sticking out. Our plan had been to do just that. We would bring it with us to space station Chitundu, where we'd file a prize claim with House Mshindi.

"To answer your question about who blew up *Bob*; that was on me, Cap," Marny said. "I'd given the rookies control over turrets for a period. We were in no real danger from those attack craft once *Larry* was down. I assumed the gunnery crew would understand that and would be disciplined enough to stop firing."

"I can review the logs, Marny."

"It was Sempre."

"Really?" I asked. If anything, Sempre was generally too timid.

"She didn't understand the idea of privateer prize and believed *Bob* still posed a threat."

I nodded. Marny had her hands full with our current crew. "Did you ever figure out what the security issues were when we boarded *Intrepid* from Petersburg?"

"Gunjeet attempted access to every hatch on the main deck. He also took a bag full of med patches and stored them in an unused footlocker in the crew bunks."

"What's he going to do with those?" I asked.

"Sell them," Marny said. "Our med-patches are considerably more potent than anything Pogona manufacture."

"That's horrible. We should transmit the pattern universally," I said. "There's no reason for people to have poor medical treatment."

"Wouldn't help," Marny said. "Replicator technology is highly controlled by Confederation of Planets. Only the powerful would benefit."

"Captain Liam, I have the information you requested," Jala's soft voice interrupted our conversation.

"Go ahead, Jala," I answered.

"Pilot Jaspati agrees to acquiesce," Jala said. "He requests an honorable death for he and his co-pilot at the hands of his victor."

"I take it punting them into space without a suit is not considered an honorable death?"

"You speak with truth, Captain Liam."

"Inform them that we have no intent to kill them, either honorably or dishonorably. Also, tell them to release atmosphere from their cockpit and exit their ship," I said.

"I will transmit this information," Jala said.

"How will you discipline Sempre?" I asked, turning to Marny.

"I won't, Cap," Marny said. "I put her into a position she wasn't ready for and the fault is mine. I cost us that ship, not Sempre."

"And Gunjeet?"

"Same issue. I placed him on the ship and failed to lock down the medical bay. He had been given no expectations."

"Sounds like you're getting soft on your recruits," I said, immediately wishing I hadn't.

"Sounds like you're second guessing me."

"Hold on, you two," Tabby said. "Let's focus on the task at hand. Everyone's always a little jumpy when boarding an enemy ship, no reason to be stirring up trouble."

As *Intrepid* closed on *Larry,* a puff of atmo billowed from around vents surrounding the cockpit. A moment later, two figures appeared at a hatch on the ship's keel.

"Captain Liam. Pilot Jaspati requests a safety line and would convey that their external ship suits have no capacity for movement once detached from ship."

"We'll retrieve them," I said and jumped away from *Intrepid,* easily covering the two hundred meters that separated the two ships.

"Tabby, Sempre, would you join us in the forward hold?" Marny asked over tactical. "I'll need you to place these two into the brig while Cap and I clear *Larry.*"

"Copy," Tabby replied.

"I have point," I said.

"Roger that, Cap," Marny replied as the two of us slowly made our way back to *Larry.* "Toss a disc in before you enter."

"Copy," I agreed.

When I arrived at *Larry,* I twisted so that I sailed slowly underneath and lined up for an angled toss into the ship. Upon entering the hatch, the coin-sized sensor disc attached itself magnetically to the first surface it contacted.

"Negative on movement, you're a go," Marny said. While I maneuvered to toss in the disc, she'd been orienting herself to back me up on insertion.

"Copy." I ducked around and wriggled through the hatch with blaster pistol held in front. "We're clear."

There was seating for four, with two narrow rows. It didn't take a lot of imagination to realize the ship had the dual purposes of ferrying passengers planet-side as well as combat missions.

Marny worked her way through the open hatches of the simplified air-lock and surveyed the interior. "Think you can get her backed into *Intrepid?*"

"We'll let Roby and Jester Ripples pull it back with come-alongs," I said. "Hey, sorry for giving you the business back there. I didn't mean to overstep." Marny and I had always been tight and I had difficulty leaving tension between us.

"Appreciate it, Cap, but not your fault. I'm pissed about letting things get out of hand like I did."

By the time we made it back to *Intrepid*, Roby, Jester Ripples and what looked like the entire gaggle of Norigans awaited, looking excitedly out at the broken ship.

"Liam Hoffen, please attach these cables to my specifications," Jester Ripples said, handing me magnetic heads at the ends of cables that had been spooled out. A schematic of *Larry* showed precisely where Jester Ripples wanted me to connect.

A low-volume cheer bubbled through a small group of Norigans standing next to the industrial replicator built into the aft bulkhead of the cargo hold. A long part was spooling out into the confident hands of those assembled.

"We're already making parts?" I asked.

"The design of the ship designated *Larry* is well known," Jester Ripples said. "*Larry's* failure is easy to diagnose, but we have limited time before arriving at Chitundu."

I knew better than to question the Norigan's resolve. They hadn't stopped working on *Intrepid* since we'd been under sail and were running out of meaningful fixes to make. I'd even suspected that a few minor system failures had been caused, simply to give them something to pass the time.

I flitted out and attached the cable ends, returning to the deck as the ship was winched back onto the deck. Twenty minutes later, *Larry* was magnetically clamped inside the hold with five meters of its nose sticking through the pressure barrier.

"Roby, we'll want to be underway in a few minutes. Please make sure *Larry* is secure enough for combat," I said.

"You're expecting combat?"

"Negative, but it's not what I expect that worries me," I said as Marny and I exited the cargo hold.

Marny gave me a quick look of approval and unexpectedly swatted me playfully on the butt. "You see, Cap, it's all about training. When we first met, you'd have asked the same question as Mr. Bishop there. But here you are, all grown up."

It seemed like all the women in my life worked hard to keep things confusing. There was no way I'd ever stray from Tabby, but it didn't change the fact that I found Marny's thick, muscular figure attractive and playful contact just brought that idea to mind.

"You're naughty," I said.

"Copy that, Cap." Marny winked. "I'll check in on our prisoners."

I shook my head ruefully as I trudged up the incline to the main deck.

"Hiyas, Liam," Ada said as I entered the bridge. "How bad a shape is *Larry* in?"

"I'm not sure it matters," I said. "The Norigans are swarming it. Apparently, they're bored."

"Has Jester Ripples talked to you yet?"

"I've talked to him a few times. Anything specific?"

"He wants to stay on *Intrepid*. He's concerned you might not want him to stay, though."

"What? Why in Jupiter would he think that?"

"He's afraid you feel like you might feel betrayed because he left before," she said. "You need to reassure him."

"I'll talk to him," I said, turning around and heading back to the hold. "Take us in to the Tamu gate. I'll grab Jester Ripples and get the hold cleared just in case we run into trouble on the other side."

"Fifteen minutes, Liam," Ada called as I stepped out into the passageway, almost running into Marny and Tabby. I had limited time, so I smiled and moved past them.

"Where are you headed?" Tabby asked, jogging to catch up with me.

"We need to get the Norigans out of the hold until we've cleared the wormhole. The cargo bay is open to space. Not a good situation if there are enemies on the other side."

"Copy that," Tabby said, falling in beside me.

The scene in the forward cargo hold was even more chaotic than when I'd left it only fifteen minutes previous. It seemed like the Norigans had removed *Larry's* every panel, cowl and cover, including the heavily mullioned glass of the cockpit. *Jester Ripples* was deep in it, with his thin blue arms fully embedded into control circuitry on the starboard side of the engine.

"Liam Hoffen, it is delightful to see you again. What a wonderful challenge you have presented us with." Jester Ripples' comical face beamed with excitement. "Are you here to help with our project?"

"Not directly. We're going to transition through the Tamu wormhole and we need to clear the cargo bay until we know it is safe to be in here."

"I will pass the word," Jester Ripples said, not showing any sign of releasing his current project.

"I need this done in the next ten minutes. We're headed toward the wormhole right now," I said.

"Yes, this is clear, Liam Hoffen. I can see the beautiful wormhole growing larger upon approach. We will abide by your wishes."

"There's something else. I haven't wanted to talk to you about this because I don't like to pressure my friends."

"There is no reason for friends to withhold conversation, Liam Hoffen. I trust you to be kind."

"It's just that ... well ..." I shook my head. I couldn't believe the little blue alien amphibian had me so flummoxed. I cleared my throat and started over. "Jester Ripples. I'd like you to be part of Loose Nuts and stay on *Intrepid*. I totally understand if you want to be with your family, but you should know how the crew feels."

This got Jester Ripple's attention and he pulled his arms from the guts of the machinery and gripped my shoulder with powerful fingers. It was a familiar move and I adjusted so he could easily transfer. With his free hand, he pulled Tabby in closer. He had a surprising amount of strength in his thin arms.

"You are my family, Liam Hoffen and Tabitha Masters. I *will* stay with you."

CHITUNDU STATION WAS a welcome sight as we pulled into orbit above Abasi Prime's moon, Rehema. I had mixed feelings about Chitundu, as this was where Strix had seized *Intrepid,* ostensibly to force repayment for the mess we'd made when entering Tamu so many months ago. It had also been where we'd met new friends. It helped that I now knew Strix had virtually no relationship to the station or even the star system.

"Liam, we're being hailed by Abasi command," Ada said.

"Hoffen," I answered.

"Ah, Captain Hoffen. Koman is pleased to greet our esteemed visitors." An older Felio male showed on the screen. Unlike the warrior males I'd met, Koman's fur around his shoulders and up his neck had been trimmed short.

"Pleasure to meet you as well, Koman."

"I received your claim of privateer prize. I must say this is a most unusual circumstance and one that Koman has very little experience with."

"I see. I believe the data-streams showing our adherence to the dictates of our Letter of Marque were included. Is there a problem with our petition?" I asked.

"I have cleared *Intrepid* for docking at A-Four. I humbly request a meeting with Captain Hoffen to resolve satisfactorily, the issues I have little experience with," Koman said. My experience with Felio hadn't prepared me for this small, nervous man.

"Copy that, Koman. We'll be docked in twenty minutes." I nodded to Ada, who was watching to make sure I was serious about moving forward.

"I await your arrival," Koman said and I closed comms.

"That felt weird," Ada said before I could say anything.

"Like he was afraid to talk to us, right?" I asked.

"Like he was peeing himself," Tabby agreed.

I chuckled. "I might not have said it that way."

Ada slid *Intrepid* into place next to the large, circular space station.

"I'll come with you," Tabby said. "Think we need to be strapped?"

"I wouldn't," Marny said. "The 'A' level is a reserved, governmental level. They might not appreciate weapons."

"Ada, Marny, could you work on shore leave while we're out?" I asked.

"How long will we be docked?" Ada asked.

"Sixty hours," I said. "Our current arrangements are to meet the convoy in seventy-two. I haven't received coordinates, but the contract specifies they won't be more than two hours on a Schedule-C burn."

"We'll get on it, Cap."

"What do you suppose this is all about?" Tabby asked as we worked our way through *Intrepid's* airlock and started crossing the catwalk joining us with Chitundu station.

"Mshindi Second gave us an expectation that we'd have to meet with a prize court to claim our prizes," I said. "I think they've just never done it."

Tabby palmed the security panel that would give us entry to the station. The hatch opened to a passageway that was appointed very much like the interior of an Abasi warship: spotless short dark-green carpeting with slightly squishy padding, light brown evenly-spaced raised ridges every meter along the wall and light blue carpeting on the ceiling. The design served two purposes. First, it reminded the Abasi of a forest. I didn't see it, but then it wasn't made for me. Second, in the case of gravity loss, Felio claws would have something to grab onto regardless of orientation.

"Captain Hoffen. First Mate Masters. On behalf of Mshindi First, the Abasi High Command and the Felio people, I welcome you to Chitundu Station."

"A beautiful greeting, Koman," I said. "I applaud you on your recall of our names and titles."

"I would be eternally shamed if I were to embarrass friends of House Mshindi. Please, we will address the issues of importance in a more comfortable setting."

We followed Koman around and through a series of passageways, finally arriving at the impressive entrance to Abasi High Command — or at least that's what my AI translated the script over the wood-paneled entrance to say.

The room we entered was already teeming with Felio. Our pres-

ence quieted the group and while I recognized several House
Mshindi representatives, they were Felio I had only a passing
acquaintance with.

"You are invited to speak to our assembly," Koman said, leading
us to an ornate table that was too tall to sit behind, but comfortable
for someone standing. Two worn bags sat on top of the table and
when I peered in, they were both empty. The table was separated
from a gallery of seats by a wooden railing. The assembled guests
came forward to fill the chairs. The gathering reminded me of
another time when Mshindi Prime had attempted to move several
Abasi houses to intervene against the Kroerak and come to humanity's aid.

Koman bowed and backed away from Tabby and me, leaving us
in the middle of the room.

"What do you wish to know?" I asked, looking boldly out to the
group, not singling anyone out, but also not dropping my eyes if I
happened to make eye contact. It was rude to stare down a Felio and
you were likely to be challenged if you did so. On the other hand, to
look down was a sign of weakness. It was an uncomfortable dance,
but I'd been briefed more than once on the importance of posture
when addressing Felio.

"You have made claim of a ship to which you have provided the
name *Larry*. There are many who feel House Mshindi's actions were
not warranted."

With hands clasped behind my back, I looked to the male Felio
who asked the question, focusing on his furry ears and not his eyes.
He hadn't asked a question, so I waited him out. Finally, he growled.
"What do you say?"

"I agree. I claim the ship, *Larry*," I said. "The pirate Belvakuski
engaged in an unlawful attack on my ship. My crew destroyed *Bob*
and we captured *Larry*." I struggled not to smile at the stupid names
Jester Ripples had picked. "Per our agreement with House Mshindi
and Abasi High Command, we ask for remuneration for the full
value of *Larry* or unhindered possession of same."

"Why did you wait in Santaloo system after you approached Tamu wormhole?"

"There were two cutter ships sitting in ambush," I said. "I didn't believe they would attack *Intrepid*, as we are substantially larger. We waited so that *Intrepid* could take action once they provoked other ships."

"You admit to proactively waiting to engage in hostilities?"

"As is encouraged by our Letter of Marque. We have been attacked every time we have transitioned from Santaloo to Tamu by Pogona pirates, specifically Genteresk. You will note that we neither took first shot, nor did we actively pursue any of the Genteresk ships. It was not until we were pursued and fired upon that we took action."

"Your actions of waiting were provocative."

"Do you speak for Abasi High Command?" I asked. "Do the Felio people really believe that watching known pirates is provocative? It seems like you don't like the agreement, which it appears you haven't read."

"I speak for many and I have read much of this agreement and dislike it greatly."

An angry murmur flitted through the crowd. I caught the eye of one from House Mshindi, who stepped forward. As she did, the room quieted.

"Badru, House Mshindi is within its right to extend agreement with Loose Nuts," she said. "This agreement was presented to the council and approved. Our discussion is to determine if Captain Hoffen followed the agreement and how we might award a prize to he and his crew. Do you have objection beyond dislike of the agreement?"

"I lodge a complaint that Loose Nuts was the aggressor by awaiting silently. What do you say to this, Captain Hoffen?"

"I say you should read the agreement in its entirety. If you had, you would discover that the provocative action of not transmitting a transponder signal was enough for me to engage *Intrepid* with the cutters. The agreement is clear; we're in trouble if we shoot first and Abasi High

Command determines that the ship we attacked was about a noble purpose. If we are shot at, then we are absolved of responsibility. What I don't understand is why you oppose this agreement. There are pirates sitting at your gates, preying on innocents. This can't be good for anyone."

"Perhaps Badru is annoyed because Loose Nuts is on the tongues of the merchants of Abasi Prime." The voice belonged to a male whose uniform I didn't recognize. "No captain has stared into Belvakuski's eyes and caused her to look away. I offer that Loose Nuts be awarded the ship *Larry*. I ask for the confirmation of this assembly."

For a moment, the room erupted in chaos and all that could be heard was shouting and yowling. I knew better than to do anything but stay put. Felio were impassioned people and we didn't need a full-out riot.

It wasn't until a very old Felio padded to the center of the room that everyone quieted. The male seemed to smile as he bowed slightly to Tabby and me. Wordlessly, he dropped a pebble the size of my thumb into one of two bags in front of us and walked out of the room.

It was as if a dam had broken and a steady stream of Felio followed suit, dropping pebbles of different sizes into the bags. Most of the stones ended up in the bag the older Felio had used, although there were plenty in the other bag.

Finally, the room was empty with the exception of Koman, Tabby and me.

"That was strange," Tabby said. "Who was that old guy?"

"Council Member Simba," Koman said. "He was once a very strong warrior. It is said that when he was young, no five could stand against him."

"I give. What's with the bags?" I asked.

"See how deeply this bag sits in the table?" Koman asked. He was right, as pebbles had been added, it had sunk about two centimeters into the grooves in the top of the table. "Your petition was upheld. Your words against Badru have set you as his enemy."

"I have a way with people."

Chapter 19

OVERCONFIDENT

"What's the word, Liam? Are we keeping *Larry*?" Ada asked as we re-entered the bridge.

"Don't ever say humans are the only asshats in the universe," Tabby spat before I could say anything.

"We lost the ship?" Marny asked.

"No, but Liam got grilled by a self-important jackass. He saved us by doing his normal talk-nice-but-point-out-the-facts thing. People just piss me off."

I nodded. "There was a competitor in the protection gig. He was upset that we were getting so much attention after taking it to Genteresk. Apparently, word got back that we made Belvakuski stand down in addition to taking out two of her ships."

"Frosty," Tabby grinned. "You knew a conflict would raise our reputation."

"Calculated risk," I said. "Genteresk has been putting it to us regularly and we've had several close calls. I needed to send them a message that we're off the menu. Bullies always choose the easy marks and now we're no longer in that category. The fact that we've increased our value proposition at the same time seems like having cupcakes *with* frosting." I finished my last statement by looking point-edly at Marny.

"Haha, okay, Cap. Message received. We haven't had cupcakes for a long time. Maybe I can show Jala how they're made."

"Mostly kidding, Marny," I said. "Although chocolate is my favorite."

"About shore leave," Ada said. "When can we start releasing crew?"

"We'll need to re-dock. Can you find us something on C-Level? Also, I'm approving a prize payout based on our schedule. Would you see to moving that money?"

"Can do, Liam."

"Are we keeping the fast-attack craft?" Tabby asked.

"That's a discussion we should have. Market for that specific ship in good shape is one hundred ninety thousand credits. The Norigans kindly restored functionality and I think we could get just about that. On the other hand, we lack a decent atmospheric entry vehicle and *Larry* could fill that role."

"Would you strap it belly-side like we did *Hotspur*?" Marny asked.

"Plenty of room for that," I agreed. "An alternative is to buy a palette of rockets I have my eye on." I flicked the specifications in an arc from my HUD to each of the bridge crew.

"Not exactly state-of-the-art," Marny observed. "That's a hell-of-a yield. Can that be right?"

"I queried the manufacturer," I said. The stated explosive power was double that of missiles we'd previously carried. "They suggested that ever since the Kroerak war, the focus has been on punch at the expense of sophisticated guidance. The price is good, too. They're ten thousand a piece or a palette of twelve is a hundred thousand even."

Marny whistled. "That's a tenth the cost of missiles back home."

"Like you said, they're not exactly state of the art. They have limited range, guidance and their agility ratings are deplorable."

"There's a reason we don't have any missiles left, Cap," Marny said.

"Sure, because Strix stole them," Tabby added quickly. "*Larry* gives us a second attack vector. We might need that if our convoy is attacked by a large group of small ships."

"If you recall, we were down to four missiles when Strix commandeered *Intrepid*. My point is, in a pinch, they give us options. Those options have often been the difference between destruction and success. The fast-attack craft gives a slow ship the option to engage smaller, nimbler opponents. *Intrepid* doesn't suffer from range issues like this. The design of a frigate is to engage the small ship. *Larry* is a glass cannon, with lots of firepower and virtually no armor. The ship is designed as a pawn. It's expendable and you're not, Tabby."

"How many rockets can we get?" Tabby asked, ceding the point.

Blowing out a breath, I looked around the bridge. There was so much left to do. "I have two interested buyers for *Larry*. I say we buy as many rockets as we can after paying out prizes. I think I can get a palette and a half if I work on it," I said. "Ada, am I on first watch? I have a couple of meetings I need to schedule."

"No watch for the captain. We're doing two hour watches with someone on the bridge and someone at the airlock at all times," Ada said. "And for the record, we're under station control. We'll start the transfer of waste and consumables momentarily."

"Time to say farewell to our Norigan friends, in that case," I said.

"TO A SAFE AND SUCCESSFUL TRIP." Aantal Tutt placed long nailed fingers beneath his jaw in a gesture I'd seen other Pogona's make. The narrow-framed Pogona had a generous paunch that pushed his simple woven tunic as he sat. He was at a beautifully carved wooden table in one of the station's many restaurants.

"Last we communicated, you called into question our contract," I said, not sitting. Jala, who'd already taken a seat at the table, noticed my position. She slid off her chair and joined Tabby and Marny, next to me.

"Oh come, let us dine together," Tutt said, solicitously. "This was surely a miscommunication. Our translation devices have made a mistake. There are details to consider, but we remain steadfast in our desire to contract with Loose Nuts Corporation. Why, just this morning, before traveling to Chitundu, I transmitted full payment for fuel and consumables, per our contract."

"I have seen no such payment," I said.

"Please verify this once again," Tutt said, smiling. "Perhaps there is growth within the pipes."

I accepted my AI's prompt to check for a deposit of funds and then looked at Jala. "Growth in pipes?"

"Yes, Captain Liam Hoffen. It is a common idiom for blockage of sewer pipes. Captain Aantal Tutt conveys that something may have interfered with the transfer of credits."

"A lovely description by an even more lovely woman," Tutt said. "You must have paid dearly for her."

Even as I heard Tabby sucking air through her teeth, I knew I couldn't let the comment stand. "Captain Tutt, Jala is a free woman and a valued member of my crew. You will refrain from addressing her without the respect you would show me."

"I had not heard that humanity was a matriarchy as are the Felio," Tutt replied, evenly. "I mean no offense."

On my HUD a notification blinked, showing payment had been received twenty minutes ago. "Payment was received. Let's talk," I said, sitting across from the man.

"Ah, yes, there is a simple matter of a final revision my shipping group desires. It is unusual that you would exclude from safety, ships that fail to respond to your directives. There is also a matter of expended ordnance reimbursement."

"I'm willing to concede that your ships can do whatever they want while we are under hostile circumstances," I said, "as long as you remove payment penalties. If your captains endanger themselves by their actions, we can't be held responsible. As to ordnance, we're considering taking on a load of rockets. They are as effective as they are expensive."

"In combat situation, you will follow my orders. As will the members of the convoy," Tutt said. "We cannot be responsible for expensive ordnance. These are not negotiable terms."

"Captain Tutt, would you share your military combat experience?" Marny asked.

"I have none, nor have I need of it." Tutt refused to look at Marny. "I have been leading and arranging runs through the Dark Corridor for a multitude of long spans."

"You should not have signed our agreement, in that case," I said. "I have a crew full of highly trained, professional ex-military. Not only have they seen significant combat but we have, as a crew, been highly successful. I will not negotiate on this. As to the use of ordnance, that's your call. *Intrepid* is a deterrent. If we run into a sufficiently large force, you may come to regret your decision as we have limited capacity and ship-to-ship combat is often decided in seconds."

"You sincerely believe I will turn over convoy command if we come under attack?" Tutt asked as a Felio waiter slid a delicious smelling, albeit unrecognizable dish into the center of the table. "And please, eat."

"It is a requirement, Captain Aantal," I said as Jala pulled a generous portion of what looked like a pie filled with gravy and meat, and set it on the wooden platter in front of me. The move earned her a glare from Tabby, who fortunately left the subject alone and grabbed some for herself.

"I provide to you an opportunity that someone with your unknown status would not ordinarily have," Tutt said. "You must learn how we operate in the Dark Corridor, if you wish to be a serious vendor of protection services."

"I do appreciate the opportunity," I said. "We both know that failure in this mission would be the ruin of my crew's reputation. It is therefore imperative that I not concede this point."

Tutt sighed. "You have me in a disadvantaged position, Captain Liam Hoffen. There are few hours that remain before our departure. I am dissatisfied with your intractable stance, but will abide by the contract."

"Are you certain?" I asked. "I have inquiries from other trading companies. I would refund your fuel deposit fully if you prefer to be released from our contract. It seems a poor way to start a partnership — with one side as dissatisfied as you appear."

Tutt pursed his lips and his chest shook, which had the effect of causing his jowls to jiggle. A moment later, he couldn't contain himself and he laughed out loud. "Are you sure you are not of the trader's guild?"

"CAPTAIN TUTT, please hold the convoy back until we've had ten minutes to clear the Santaloo system," I said.

The convoy was comprised of heavily laden freighters that seemed to crawl through space as we made our way to the gate that joined Tamu with Santaloo. We'd successfully sold *Larry* for a hundred forty thousand credits and taken on fuel and supplies. With the proceeds from the sale, we'd paid out the crew, purchased a pathetic atmospheric shuttle, and loaded six rockets. Given sufficient time, I felt certain I could have gotten a better price for *Larry*, but I wasn't about to sail away without rockets if it was within my power to do so.

"Is this entirely necessary?" Tutt replied.

"Ten minutes, Tutt." I closed comm. He'd either agree or he wouldn't.

"On your mark, Liam," Ada said.

We were well prepared, but I'd yet to transfer between these two systems without running into a significant force. I had no reason to expect this trip would be any different. "Go ahead."

"We have contact," Marny said the moment after we transitioned.

"*On holo,*" I said. Two moderately sized cutters appeared in tight formation two hundred kilometers from the gate.

"They're moving in on an intercept," Marny said.

It was unnecessary information, as I could see their engines firing up and virtual indicators showed their relative acceleration vectors in relation to *Intrepid*.

"Hail approaching ships."

A smug Pogona showed on screen. "Greetings, Captain of Abasi flagged ship, *Intrepid*. You'll need to cut engines and await inspection."

"Negative," I replied. "Maintain a fifty-kilometer standoff. We're accompanying a trading company and will take aggressive action for noncompliance."

I nodded so my AI muted the comm. "Ada, full burn directly at the cutter communicating with us. Marny, would you give them a quick captain's call?" I'd adopted the term Marny had used when describing various sabre rattling techniques we'd rehearsed. In response, the four forward-most blasters each lit off a five second stream of moderate fire.

Turning the comms back on with a head-tip, I responded. "Your choice, lizard neck, but we're also privateers and you're not transmitting transponders. I have to admit, I find that quite intriguing."

The response from both ships was instantaneous. A clear Nijjar transponder signal started transmitting and they both turned, beating hard in an opposite direction.

"My apologies, Captain. It appears we had a technical malfunction with our transponders. We request you stand down from hostile action."

"Fifty kilometers," I said and closed comms.

"Would you like me to pull back?" Ada asked. "We're still closing on them."

"Tempting targets," I said. "But I'm not sure the prize court would consider their actions as provocative enough, even though it's within the letter of our agreement. Let 'em go."

"Copy, Liam." Ada flipped *Intrepid* and we retreated to the wormhole entrance.

A few minutes later, the first freighter of Aantal Tutt's convoy appeared and was followed soon by the remaining eight.

"Captain Hoffen, I don't appreciate the delay while transitioning between systems," Tutt said, not even bothering with normal pleas-antries.

"Call me old-fashioned," I said. "I prefer ensuring your safety."

"There is risk in everything, Captain."

"Copy that." I closed comms. "Ada, keep us between the convoy and those cutters."

The would-be pirates had backed off to two hundred kilometers and were fading away as the convoy slowly accelerated toward Fan Zuri. It would take us twelve full days of travel through Santaloo to reach the planet.

"KEEP YOUR HANDS UP," I instructed Gunjeet, having just sent him reeling from a kick which caught him on the side of the head. Gunjeet was fast but lacked discipline, which made it easy for me to pick shots when we sparred. He had a tendency to lower his defenses when I wasn't within arm's reach.

"You do not fight real," he complained. "Who would fight without weapons?"

"I agree. Most fights I've been in end almost before they start because, as you know, they're rarely evenly matched. That's why pirates and thugs like to gang up on smaller, weaker prey; because they can't fight back. That's not why we spar, though."

He opened and closed his mouth in rapid succession, making a slight popping sound and jiggling his wattle — the Pogona equivalent of a teenager rolling their eyes.

"That is why I would join Genteresk if I could," he said.

"You're one crazy kid," I said. "Genteresk are my enemies. I should toss you in the brig for saying that and you could join the other pirates we have down there."

"There is no wrong in admitting this," he said, swinging his elbow around, trying to catch me off guard while we chatted. "Genteresk are heroes."

Unlike Gunjeet, I wasn't about to lower my guard while fighting. I caught the back of his elbow with my forearm and used his momentum to throw him to the ground. I held my fist above his face in the classic I-could-have-punched-but-I-held-back pose.

"If you move against my crew, I will treat you as Genteresk," I said. "I have honor."

I released him and stood up, extending my hand to help him up.

"We will be to Fan Zuri in five days," I said. "Will you disembark and join Genteresk then?"

He slapped my hand away and rolled to his feet. "It is not that easy. A warrior must prove himself and be asked to join Genteresk."

"Genteresk steal from others," I said. "I don't see the honor in taking what you have not earned."

"They protect their people. I will not discuss this with a *human*." He raised his arms, showing he was once again ready to fight.

The disdain in which he said human surprised me.

"What do you have against humans?"

"You are the black slugs that live in water and suck blood from the living."

"Leaches?" I asked, landing a nice combo to his mid-section. I was hitting about three quarters and I could tell it hurt. "Why do you think humans are leaches?"

"Show me this thing where you use your leg," Gunjeet said.

"It takes practice and flexibility."

I stepped back and swiveled my hips as I brought a side kick past his face. In that I didn't make contact, my leg's momentum brought me around. I felt a knife enter just beneath my ribs as Gunjeet rode me to the ground. I rolled away, separating. The pain was excruciating.

"No, Gunjeet," I said, holding up my hand.

He'd gained his feet and grinned. "You trust so easily. No wonder the Felio keep you in that pathetic pen you call York. You are weak. Like children."

Rolling up to my feet, I felt blood running down my back beneath my suit liner. The ship had already warned the crew and help was on the way. Gunjeet must have sensed he had limited time because he rushed me, his thin blade dripping with my blood.

From the corner of my eye, I saw a streak of orange fur as I met Gunjeet's charge and threw him over my back. The world greyed as I landed on my wound and struggled to face my attacker.

"Yoowl," Sempre screamed as she launched herself at the larger Pogona. Gunjeet was fast. His blade slashed the young Felio, a spray of blood following the arc of his swing. Sempre turned into the swing, ignoring the slice and stepped into the Pogona, bringing her paw up in a quick jab. Gunjeet's head snapped back on impact.

"Sempre, down!" It was Marny's voice that commanded her.

For a moment, I imagined that Sempre would continue. She had the advantage and her blood had to be boiling with the rush of the fight. It surprised me when she twisted away and flattened to the floor.

A blaster bolt caught Gunjeet in the chest, knocking him back several meters.

"Hoffen Captain, help is on the way." Sempre's face appeared in front of my own. I must have lost track of time because the last I could remember, she was flattened out on the deck.

"Your arm." I fumbled, trying to inspect her arm, but I couldn't get a grasp on it and my vision blurred.

"Stay with us, Cap." Marny's strong arm helped me up. "We're going to take you to the medical bay."

The movement caused fresh pain and a surge of adrenaline. "Gunjeet."

"Alive."

"That was stupid. Why are your bios so low? Frak, Hoffen!" Tabby spat, joining us in the passageway that led down to the medical bay.

"Knife," I grunted. Marny had applied a patch that staunched the bleeding on my back, but it was obvious more damage had been done.

"He's bleeding internally," Marny warned.

"Where's Gunjeet?" Tabby demanded.

"Take Liam," Marny answered, shifting me painfully to Tabby's strong arms. "I left Sempre guarding him."

"I'll kill him."

"My fault." I stumbled into the medical bay and flopped face-first over the stainless-steel table. It felt glorious to stop moving, although my back throbbed in unison with my heartbeat.

"You'll get yours. Don't worry." Tabby placed a med-scanner on my back. I tried to focus on the details scrolling across my HUD but found it impossible. "Don't move. I've got to prep the tank."

"Shite," I complained as my legs gave out and I crumpled. I hadn't realized Tabby had been keeping me pinned to the table as my legs had lost feeling.

"Hold on," Jala said from behind, guiding me to the deck, having arrived too late to stop my descent.

"Liam, if you can hear me, you're going to take a short bath in the tank. Gunjeet's blade clipped your kidney," Tabby instructed. The only thing clear to me was that a pain-management patch had been applied and I smiled dopily.

I must have passed out as it was a full twelve hours later when I started to wake. Tabby smiled through the glass as fluid drained from around me. It felt like no time had elapsed and I struggled to remove the mask once my arms were free.

"You're the worst patient of them all," Tabby complained, slapping my hands away.

"How are Sempre and Gunjeet?" I asked.

"Sempre had a pretty good slash on her left arm, but it's already healing. Gunjeet is in the brig, just like you planned. Was it worth it?"

I wasn't surprised Tabby had figured out my ruse, but I was a little embarrassed that it had gone so terribly wrong. I'd known about Gunjeet's knife, having felt it in his clothing when we sparred. What I hadn't counted on was the fact that he'd be so quick to slip it between my ribs.

"I don't know. Was it?" I asked.

"So far they haven't talked much." She was referring to the Pogona prisoners we already held captive in our brig. I'd overheard

Gunjeet say on many occasions he'd do just about anything to get accepted to Genteresk. He'd avoided temptation when there had been other people around, but he'd taken the bait once we were alone.

"How is Jala taking it?"

"She's embarrassed and sad, both. I suspect her and Koosha have had their share of trouble with that one," Tabby said.

Chapter 20

SLIPPERY WHEN WET

"Liam, we're receiving a hail from Aantal Tutt."

"Go ahead, Tutt," I said.

"Captain Hoffen, we're within the protective confines of Nijjar control over Fan Zuri. We'll once again join you in forty short-spans at our pre-arranged coordinates," Tutt said. "I recommend getting rest, the next portion of our journey is unlikely to be as uneventful as our first."

We were a million kilometers from Fan Zuri, which had grown to the size of a marble when viewed with the naked eye. I always got a thrill when approaching a planet. I could imagine what it must have felt like for ancient mariners who sailed the barren oceans of Earth, when they first sighted land on a long journey.

"Copy that, Tutt. Hoffen out."

"Difficult to understand their logic," Ada said. "It's Genteresk who threatens the convoy when they're out in the deep dark, but put them within a million kilometers of Fan Zuri and they feel safe as can be."

"I'd like to take on fuel at Jhutti Station. Can you work up shore leave?"

By space station standards, Jhutti Station wasn't large. According to the information we could gather, it was home to eight hundred permanent residents and another fourteen hundred transients. It was about as unimaginative a layout as a person could come up with. Rectangular boxes of steel had been welded in haphazard layers, no doubt as centuries of expansion projects had been completed. The construction method wasn't unfamiliar, as it was the least expensive way to build something in orbit.

"We're not here long, so leave will be short," Ada said.

"We're lucky to get any time at all. Tutt wanted the convoy to take right off and we would have, if not for a last-minute addition," I said. "I need to work in a trip to the surface with Tabby, Jala and Marny. Nick has a couple of stevedore bots he wants me to drop off in Jhutti." I flicked her the meeting schedule I'd set with the two large manufacturing companies.

"Not sure that's going to work," Ada said. "Marny scheduled crew training at that time."

"During shore leave?" I looked at Marny, questioningly.

"Aye, Cap. We'll be taking a walk-about on Jhutti Station. I'd like to drill the crew on the do's and don'ts of visiting space stations in possible hostile territory."

"No problem. Tabby, Jala and I can handle it," I said.

"Marny, would you excuse Jala from training?" Ada asked, joining Marny through comms.

"That works," Marny answered. "Cap, you want me to put out feelers and see if we can offload prisoners?"

"Wouldn't the Pogona just let them go?" Tabby asked.

"Nijjar law is specific about piracy, although it's hard to tell how serious they are about it."

"Sure. Put out some feelers," I said. "I could meet with someone if it comes to that. The data-streams are compelling. I was surprised Abasi wouldn't take 'em."

"Will you hand over Gunjeet, too?" Tabby asked. I appreciated that she hadn't needled me on the fact that my stunt didn't yield any information.

"I'm not sure what to do with him. I guess I'd prefer to keep him until I do," I said.

"Looks like we have company," Ada said.

Two bright white frigates had slipped into view and hailed us.

"I've got it, Ada," I said. "This is Captain Hoffen of *Intrepid*, go ahead."

There was something about active military folk that didn't change from one species to the next. Well, I suppose Kroerak were an exception. The Pogona man, wearing a tidy uniform complete with ribbons that appeared to be military honors, appeared rigidly on the bridge's forward vid-screen.

"Lieutenant Commander Meel of Tulvar. Welcome to Fan Zuri, *Intrepid*. I'm requesting a heave-to for a brief inspection. Do you have any locked-down cargo to declare?"

"Affirmative. List is being transmitted and we'll comply," I replied. I wasn't overly concerned by his request, especially since we were flying under an Abasi flag and had never been seen in these parts before. "We're currently flying escort and have limited cargo, all of which is destined for Jhutti."

"Protocol allows for holstered weapons only when greeting a Pogona patrol," Tulvar said.

"Copy that. Hoffen out." I closed comms.

"Trouble?" Tabby asked.

"Hope not."

With Marny and Tabby close behind, I made my way forward to the airlock and waited for Commander Tulvar to arrive. He was shorter than I'd expected, but no less military in his bearing.

"Bill of lading?" he asked, after a momentary exchange of pleasantries. He'd brought four armed, heavily muscled marines along with him, although they looked more bored than anything, especially since neither Marny nor Tabby were obviously armed.

I handed Tulvar a reading pad that showed two stevedore bots, a stack of steel sheet and several squares of armor glass.

He looked up from the short list. "Most captains would fill their holds when traveling as far as you are."

"New to the system," I said. "We're looking to establish trading partners."

"We'll need to inspect your holds, engine room and brig." He turned to the crew he'd brought along. "You two, take a post here at the airlock. The rest are with me."

"Tabbs, you got this?"

"Aye," she replied tersely.

"We had difficulty reconciling your ship signature with the data from your transponder," Tulvar said. "Your armor has unusual qualities. We have seen this on other human ships. Is this common on your home world?"

I wasn't sure how to answer his question. If I let him know just how uncommon it was, he might become overly interested. If I suggested it was common, he might expect us to share information about it. I chose to play it straight.

"It is uncommon," I said. "We first ran into the armor in a scrapyard back near the fourth planet from our sun. The intellectual property for producing it is very expensive and not directly within our control." The last was a lie. We had the ability to manufacture as much of the armor as was necessary to outfit *Intrepid*. What we couldn't do was hand over the formula to anyone. Especially not an alien government.

"A sensible precaution. It hints that human sensor technology is similar to that of Pogona."

"I believe that to be true," I said. "I might as well get the sticky part out of the way first."

Tulvar raised an eyebrow in anticipation. "Sticky? As in you are nervous about my reaction?"

"I think that's a fair representation," I said.

"What problem do you have on this lower deck that causes you concern?" Tulvar asked as we approached the brig.

"Them," I said as I ordered the glass panels to change from opaque to transparent, showing Gunjeet and two other prisoners.

"Why are they locked in that enclosure. Is that your brig?"

"It is."

"I would say that looks more like a spa than a brig. How must the rest of your crew live that this is how you provide for prisoners?"

"It's not a lot different, except that the doors open for crew."

"Why do you detain only my brethren?"

"Each of these have shown themselves to be too dangerous to allow free reign on my ship," I said. "Gunjeet, that one," I pointed to Gunjeet, "he pulled a knife on me while we were training. The other two were aboard a Genteresk fast-attack craft that we disabled."

"Why did you engage with a fast-attack craft. Was it your intent to take the ship from them?"

"I didn't say we took the ship," I said.

"News of your engagement with Belvakuski has reached Fan Zuri, Captain Hoffen. It is the reason I have boarded your ship today. My superiors wish to know if it is possible that there is truth in the reported occurrence."

"I have no idea what was reported. However, Belvakuski sent two fast-attack craft and didn't provide adequate defensive support for them. A frigate such as *Intrepid* or either of the ships you command has little trouble combating a vessel that small."

"Have you proof of your accomplishment?"

"Would a data-stream suffice?" I asked.

"You are not compelled to share this with me," Tulvar said. "It would most likely make your visit to Nijjar space more pleasant, though."

I flicked the data-stream of our dust-up with Belvakuski to Tulvar and waited for a moment as he pulled out a reading pad of his own. He fast forwarded through the action and located the moment when we'd destroyed our first ship.

"Your weapons are formidable," he said.

I wasn't sure how to take the comment, so I remained quiet as he continued to watch the video.

"Please show me your holds," he said, after a few minutes of watching the video.

"This way." I led him aft to the smaller of our two holds.

"There are only supplies in this hold," I said. My eyes lit on the large crates that held our Popeyes.

Tulvar followed my gaze. "What is in those crates?"

"Ship equipment. It is on the declared list of items not for trade."

"Funny." Tulvar agreed, looking at me slyly. "A more suspicious man might think you were trying to bring contraband into the Nijjar Commonwealth of Planets."

"Not at all."

"Of course. Tell me, what do you plan to do with your prisoners? Will you sell them in Jhutti?"

"Not sure. Humans generally take issue with selling people, though."

"How then does your Navy fill its ships during times of war?"

"If you'll pardon my interruption, Cap. I think he's referring to the practice of press gangs," Marny said. "It's not as foreign of a concept as you might believe."

"Seriously? We do that?"

"North Americans and Mars not so much. Russians, Chinese, Indians, Persians ... absolutely."

Tulvar smiled slightly, as if he were being patient with a slow student. "It would be a waste to release them to space. Our Navy would find much better use for them. Would this not be more benevolent?"

"Wait," I turned to him. "You want my prisoners?"

"I believe it would allow me to provide a positive report on Nijjar's first meeting with the ship *Intrepid*. Otherwise, I will have to insist on opening those crates."

My stomach churned as I realized that I was being leveraged. It was then I made my decision. I wasn't about to lose my ship to yet another government.

"I'd keep Gunjeet, the one who attacked me," I said. "I am not convinced he is unredeemable."

Tulvar grinned, showing a mouth full of jagged teeth, or whatever Pogona had. "You are truly a kind individual. I believe I've seen enough for today. We'll pick up our new crew members and see our way from your ship."

"You'll leave us alone while we're on Fan Zuri?" I asked.

"Absolutely." His smile and reassuring nod of his head did nothing to convince me.

Intrepid's brig had four individual cells: two next to the starboard hull and two more separated by a hallway. Each cell would comfortably hold two, but in a pinch, could hold up to eight for short periods of time. I'd separated Gunjeet from the two Genteresk pirates.

I wasn't sure if it was the uniform or if the two pirates recognized Tulvar. While they didn't say anything, the look of defeat in their body posture was clear as I approached.

"Prisoners. Commander Tulvar has accepted responsibility for your sentences," I said. "You will accompany the Nijjar guard."

"Captain Hoffen, it occurs to me I haven't correctly inspected your munitions," Tulvar said with a genuine look of remorse.

"Oh?"

"It would be remiss of me to allow a warship such as *Intrepid* into Nijjar space without completing this part of the inspection."

"Marny, give us a minute," I said and led Tulvar into the hallway.

"What's this about, Commander? We already reached a deal," I said. "What's with this new inspection? Please speak plainly."

"Recorded conversations are difficult, Captain."

"Cease all recordings by Captain's order."

A positive chime sounded in my ear and I nodded to the smaller Pogona.

"Gunjeet of Koosha is known to Nijjar government," he said. "We will take him by whatever means necessary. We will also search your ship for other Koosha family members. You should be grateful I don't bring you to a magistrate for carrying one so dangerous."

"He is in my brig," I said, quickly, trying to figure out what I'd gotten myself into.

"This is why I believe we may still have an amenable relationship."

"Liam, another Nijjar frigate has arrived. They're requiring we submit to a turret lockdown," Ada said. Tulvar crossed his arms behind his back and smiled smugly.

"Copy that, Ada. We'll comply."

"An appropriate response, Captain Hoffen. I do not seek to make this more painful than necessary. Instruct your crew to stand down and we will take no more than sixty of your tiny spans to complete our inspection."

"And you'll restrict your search to finding these people?" I asked.

He smiled tightly. "I do not wish a poor relationship to be established. I will do as I promised."

"All hands. Please stand by for a Nijjar inspection team that will briefly look through the ship. This is a standard procedure. Please be courteous," I said and nodded to Tulvar. "Our doors are open, Commander Tulvar."

"Bring the prisoners," Tulvar commanded as we walked back into the brig where Marny and Tabby stood, looking questioningly at me.

"Apparently, Gunjeet has unfinished business with Nijjar," I said. "We'll be turning him over to Commander Tulvar."

"Doesn't smell right," Tabby said. The comment earned her an appraising look from Tulvar, but he ignored it and led his guard out of the brig with the three prisoners in tow.

I nodded and followed Tulvar back to the airlock where we ran into a column of armed soldiers waiting patiently.

"What's going on, Cap?" Marny asked.

"Gunjeet or at least Gunjeet's family is known to Nijjar," I said. "We're fortunate he was in the brig."

Tabby's mouth narrowed as she considered my words. "Frak."

"Cap, you should be on the bridge," Marny said. "I'll oversee this."

"Copy that, Marny. Keep me up to date," I said.

Thirty minutes later my comm chimed just before Marny started talking. "Cap, Nijjar boarding party has departed and is retracting the companionway."

"Copy that, Marny. Tabbs, would you work with Jester Ripples to sweep the ship for bugs? I definitely saw a few get planted."

"Good plan," she said.

"Incoming hail, Commander Tulvar," Ada said.

"On bridge," I said. "This is Captain Hoffen. Go ahead, Commander Tulvar."

"You're free to go about your business, *Intrepid*. On behalf of Nijjar and the Pogona people, welcome to Fan Zuri." Without further warning, Tulvar closed comms and the three Nijjar frigates slid away, each in a different direction.

"You handed over Gunjeet?" Ada asked, her voice hot with accusation.

I looked to Marny, who was running our bug scanner over the surfaces of the bridge, guided by an AI that had monitored the boarding party's actions. "Bridge is clear, Cap," Marny said, grinding two tiny devices together with her fingers. "Not overly sophisticated as bugs go."

"My choice was to turn him over or turn over the ship," I said. "Do we know where Jala and Arijeet are? I believe she has some explaining to do."

"They wanted her?" Ada asked.

"Tulvar referenced the Koosha family," I said. "I believe he would have taken Jala if they'd found her. My question is where could she have hidden?"

"Found her," Marny said. "You're going to want to see this."

On the forward vid screen, Marny projected an image with a time code of about forty minutes previous. The video showed Jala and Arijeet crawling into an access panel that led to the bilge. From there they crawled over pipes and worked themselves to our gray water processing facility, where she opened a long panel, exposing a thousand liter well of cloudy water.

Unexpectedly, Jala removed her outer layer of clothing. Her long white hair hung over the chalky white skin of her slender back, which showed numerous long-healed wounds. I winced as I considered the abuse required to cause that much damage. Wordlessly, she nodded to Arijeet who also removed his outer clothing. She quickly placed the bundle of clothing into a bag, sliding it into a fifteen-millimeter section of spare pipe. From the same pipe, she removed two small masks and handed one to Arijeet. With calm deliberation, she slipped over the edge and into the well of gray water, holding the mask to her face. Arijeet followed his mother's example with significantly more trepidation than she'd shown.

"Crazy," I said as I watched the lid of the well close, sealing them in.

"I'll go," Marny said.

"Tabby." I wasn't about to send Marny into the bowels of the ship without backup. She was no doubt plenty capable, but I refused to further underestimate Jala.

"On it," Tabby agreed.

Twenty minutes later, Jala was led into a small room just aft of the brig on the lower deck. It was both convenient to where she'd entered the bilge and the brig, where I currently expected she'd continue the rest of the journey.

"Tell me why I shouldn't put you off on Jhutti Station?" I asked.

Jala's already ashen face drained of all color as water dripped down from wet hair and onto her face. Shivering, she held her arms protectively across her chest, which was only covered by the wet undergarment. I sighed. While I was angry, I wasn't about to interrogate her while she was half naked. Fortunately, Marny arrived a moment later with a thick towel.

"Please do not hand us to Tulvar," she answered.

I looked to Marny who must have had the same thought I did. "How did you know it was Tulvar who boarded our ship?"

"What has happened to Gunjeet?"

"Explain your link to Tulvar, first."

"I had hoped he would not take interest in such an unimportant convoy. Meel Tulvar is an enemy of my family," she said.

"What are you leaving out? Why would you risk my crew if you knew Tulvar was on Fan Zuri?"

"Much time has passed. There was no reason for me to believe he would still be stationed on Fan Zuri," she said. "Please. My son, Gunjeet."

"Tulvar took him," I said. "There was nothing we could do. I believe if he had found you, he would have done more than take Gunjeet. You have endangered my crew, Jala."

"I am so very sorry." Jala looked at the deck as tears streamed down her cheeks. As a younger man, I would have had more difficulty with the tears of a beautiful woman. Even now, I felt the pull of compassion. Fortunately, I'd been played the fool before and wasn't about to be drawn in again.

"Liam." Ada cut in.

"Go ahead, Ada."

"We're docking at the station," she said. "We have thirty-eight hours before we meet up with Aantal."

"Go ahead and take on fuel and supplies. Remove Arijeet and Jala from shore leave. I'm on my way up."

"Will you hand us to Tulvar?" Jala asked.

"The two of you will spend time in the brig," I said. "We'll sort this out once we're underway."

The relief in Jala's face was evident. "Thank you, Captain."

"What if we're boarded by station personnel?" Marny asked, following me out.

"Seems Jala has a reasonable hiding place," I said. "If it comes to that, we'll let her return."

Chapter 21

TRIBES

"Captain on the bridge," Sempre announced as I entered.

"What did they think of Nick's stevedore bots?" Roby asked, rising gingerly from my chair, all the while looking guilty.

Jester Ripples crawled down from where he'd been sitting with Sempre and raised his arms so I'd bring him onto me. I hadn't spent much time with him recently and welcomed his company.

"Pogona love to haggle," I said. "They were trying to get me to negotiate price on the demo units before they'd even seen them operate."

"Is Jhutti beautiful?" Sempre asked. "I have heard the Pogona of Jhutti are well known for their flowering gardens."

"I think you mentioned that before we went down," I said. "The industrial area where we dropped off the bots and steel samples wasn't particularly nice. But one of the companies took us to a social gathering on the shore of the large lake east of Jhutti. It reminded me of planet Curie in the Tipperary system back home — tropical and lush with exotic plants. How was shore leave?"

"Insightful," Roby said, obviously not interested in talking about it further.

"Jhutti Station is in poor repair, Liam Hoffen," Jester Ripples said, taking Roby's terse answer as a prompt. "Roby Bishop is very likely not feeling well as he consumed a considerable volume of something that translates as pork chop mead. I find this translation to be confusing as it references meat from a porcine animal, but it was clearly a beverage distilled from fermenting grain."

"That was just the brewer's brand," Roby said, annoyed.

"Did you get a hangover patch?" I asked.

"Yeah. I'll be fine."

"No fights in the bar?" I asked.

"Gunny wouldn't let us talk to anyone after our third round," Roby said. "There was this dumb-ass Pogona who was ogling Sempre the whole time."

"You wanted to set him straight?"

"I guess," Roby shrugged his shoulders and winced.

"So, you *did* get into a fight!"

"Wasn't much of a fight."

"Roby was very brave," Sempre added. "The alcohol he consumed slowed his reflexes. The Pogona had not been drinking as much."

"Marny break it up?" I asked.

"I was near and defused the tension. It was the lesson Marny Gunny had been training us on earlier," Sempre said.

"Yeah. After the guy dumped me on the ground."

Sempre nodded her head in agreement, but otherwise said nothing.

"It's a story as old as ships and taverns, Roby. Crew always wants to blow off steam. Locals like to put them in their place."

"Were you successful in demonstrating the armored glass and rolled steel from Petersburg Station, Liam Hoffen?" Jester Ripples asked. "I have been in communication with Merrie. She is quite anxious to know of your success."

"The Pogona were interested in the specifications of the armored glass," I said. "They are determined to do their own testing because they didn't believe the specification sheet I provided."

"Why would they not believe Liam Hoffen?" Jester Ripples asked.

"I took it as a compliment," I said. "The glass used in this sector has limited armor characteristics. Our armor glass would be a significant improvement for just about any commercial application."

"That is indeed good news. Will you allow Jester Ripples to share this with Merrie? I will preface with an expectation that Liam Hoffen will provide additional information."

"Sure, Jester Ripples," I said. "Roby, do you have anything to report?"

Roby looked at me with surprise at my invocation of formal watch change language.

I raised my eyebrows and returned his glazed look.

"Uh. No. All personnel have returned to *Intrepid* apart from Ada Chen and Tabby, both due back in forty-two minutes. All systems are showing satisfactory status, although there appears to be something that might need attention in our gray water system beneath Deck-2, starboard side."

"Roby Bishop, you are relieved," I said taking my chair. "I order you to report to medical bay for a thorough check. After that, you can re-seal the gray water well on the starboard bilge."

"How? Oh, never mind," Roby said and left the bridge.

"I was just thinking of getting rest, Jester Ripples," Sempre said. "Do you feel like a nap?"

"Yes, Sempre Neema. Liam Hoffen, it is unfortunate that you must occupy bridge watch. I miss napping with you."

I smiled. While I didn't mind resting with Jester Ripples, it wasn't high on my list. "A captain's life is filled with tasks. Maybe another time."

After re-checking all of our systems and verifying we'd taken on both fuel and supplies, I turned to writing up the status of our meetings with the Pogona businessmen. I tried not to leave anything out and after an hour, sent all the details I could recall to Nick, Merrie and Mom.

"What are you doing on watch?" Ada asked two hours later, joining me on the bridge. She carried a small bag, obviously having picked something up on Jhutti Station.

"Roby wasn't feeling well. I think he got into some trouble while on leave," I said.

"Marny mentioned a minor dust-up in the bar," Ada said. "I'm surprised he brought it up."

"I don't believe anyone would accuse Roby of being stoic," I said. "What's in the bag?"

"Bulbs of a beautiful red flower," Ada said, pulling a drying flower from the bag. It was indeed a brilliant red. "The petals are both edible and contain significant quantities of capsaicin. I believe Flaer would enjoy potting these and utilizing them for her fledgling restaurant on Petersburg Station."

"Just make sure to plug them into the bio equation for the station, but I doubt bulbs will cause any problems," I said. "And make sure you wash your hands after handling that flower."

"Do you think the flower is a contaminant? My AI shows it as harmless."

"Some plants have adverse impact on others. Petersburg Station is a closed biome. Everyone has to play nice — even plants. As for capsaicin; if you get it in your eyes, you'll regret it."

She furrowed her brow and carefully placed the flower back into the bag. "Are we ready to get underway?"

"I am. All crew is accounted for and systems are in good working order. If you'll pull back from Jhutti Station, I'll get crew to general quarters."

She nodded.

"All hands, this the captain, please report to general quarters."

For most ships, it wasn't required that all hands report to general quarters stations when leaving port. *Intrepid,* however sailed light-handed and I wanted everyone in place when we changed the ship's attitude. I didn't expect problems, but as Marny had constantly impressed on me it was rarely what we were expecting that caused problems.

The ship boiled with activity as crew hastily made their way to stations and checked in with their team leaders. Each leader, in turn, reported readiness until we were fully staffed and ready to go.

"And we're off," Ada said, expertly guiding *Intrepid* back from Jhutti Station and smoothly transitioning to forward acceleration.

"Feeling better, Mr. Bishop?" I asked once we'd been under sail for ten minutes and the station had dropped from view.

"Aye, Captain," he replied.

As we cut through the blackness of open space, I got my first view of the moon Cenaki, the well-known base of Genteresk pirates. The white surface of the moon gleamed a hundred thousand kilometers port and forward of our position. Idly, I wondered how many eyes on the moon were tracking our progress and hoped it was none.

After traveling less than a hundred thousand kilometers, we ran up on the stern of a heavily laden freighter that was laboring to accelerate. My AI identified the ship as the *Singh*. It was a new ship joining our caravan and would be with us through the next system, Brea Fortul, and then on to Tanwar.

"*Hail Singh,*" I said. "Greetings, Captain Boparai. Captain Liam Hoffen of *Intrepid*. I think we're part of the same convoy, would you care for an escort to our rendezvous?"

A chubby Pogona appeared on the forward vid screen. Beside him sat a slightly smaller version of himself.

"Greetings, Captain Hoffen." The man had extremely thick jowls. It took a minute to understand he was chuckling as he spoke, the movement in his chin more demonstrative than I'd previously thought possible. "I don't believe we could stop you if I did. You're more than welcome to join with me and my boy. I'm afraid we're cutting it rather close on time, though. I'm sure Aantal Tutt will make sure to leave us behind because of it."

I checked his current acceleration vector. He would be fifteen minutes late to the rendezvous. My contract required us to meet all time deadlines within thirty minutes or receive a penalty.

"I'll send word that we're accompanying *Singh*. I suspect he'll wait for *us*," I said.

"Mighty kind of you," he said. "There'd be a bottle of fine spirits in it for you."

"Not necessary," I said.

"I insist. Boparai out."

"Could this guy go any slower?" Tabby complained, pacing.

"It would appear *Singh* is expending considerable effort to maintain its current acceleration," Jester Ripples said. "This ship appears to be leaking critical coolant and this might be why Captain Boparai is slowed."

"I'm not sure I'm the right woman for escort missions," Tabby said.

An hour later, Ada turned slightly. "Incoming hail, *Dullo*. Putting it on main screen."

"You are behind schedule, Captain Hoffen," Tutt said. "There is no provision for you to take up with *Singh*. If Boparai can't keep up, that is his problem."

"I believe we're within the agreed time."

"Prepare for course correction," Tutt said, ignoring me. "We're seventy-eight hours to Brea Fortul wormhole. Just make sure to keep up." Tutt closed comm after transmitting a new navigation plan.

"Is there some sort of rule that he has to be an asshat?" Tabby asked.

I laughed. "All hands, we're back to standard watch schedule. The helm is yours, Tabbs."

"Same rules? I don't get to shoot or ram him?"

"Copy that. Marny, would you mind accompanying me to the brig? Now that we're out of Fan Zuri control, I'd like to get to the bottom of the intrigue surrounding Jala of Koosha."

"Aye, Cap," she agreed and followed me from the bridge.

Ada caught up to us. "Would you mind if I tagged along?"

"Not at all," I said. "I'm not sure how much she'll tell us or if we have any reason to keep her locked up."

"I expect she'll say anything to get out," Ada said.

"Jala has had a hard life. There are wounds on her back consistent with torture," Marny said. "And she has made no overt actions against *Intrepid* or our crew. I think we need to keep an open mind."

I knocked on the glass wall that separated each brig cell from the corridor. Marny had thoughtfully allowed the cell glass to be mostly obscured, so that only a narrow line of viewing was possible from the outside. We had the capacity to change the opacity level in the glass in virtually any pattern. High-risk detainees required that we allow full visibility at all times. For Jala, I preferred to give more of the impression of locked quarters.

Jala was seated on the lower bunk, reading something on a pad. Her back was to the wall with her legs were stretched out in front of her. At the sound of my knocking she deliberately set the reading pad down and gestured for Arijeet to join her. She stood with the same undisturbed confidence she always seemed to exude.

"Please enter," she said, smoothing her dress.

"Can we talk?" I asked.

Arijeet shook his head in disbelief. "You give away my brother and lock us in a cell. What is there to talk about?"

"Stay quiet, Arijeet. This is to be a conversation between Jala of Koosha and Liam Hoffen. Arijeet has no voice today. Liam, of course we may speak. I owe you and your crew an apology," she said.

"I am sorry for the loss of your son, Jala," I said. "I saw no option but to turn him over to Lieutenant Commander Tulvar."

"Lieutenant Commander," she said, mostly to herself. "Meel Tulvar has done well for himself. I do not find surprise in this. You are not at fault. It was I who should have anticipated the danger we would experience in visiting Fan Zuri. I had hoped that the Tulvar had moved from Jhutti, but it is not so."

"Are you saying your argument is with Tulvar and not Nijjar?"

"Oh, by the sands of Fernox, of course not. Nijjar accepts all its children. Meel Tulvar is a petty worm who has grown in power. We come from Tanwar, where our families found conflict," she said.

"How did you know to hide?" Ada asked. "You admit you had no idea Meel Tulvar was aboard the Fan Zuri frigate."

"I understand your confusion, Ada Chen," Jala said, turning calmly. "Nijjar ships proudly display faction flags. Arijeet and I watched for the approach of the Nijjar patrol and recognized the Tulvar flag. We knew this put us in danger and so we hid."

"What are you doing aboard *Intrepid*, Jala?" I asked. "Why would

Koosha put you in danger? You knew enough to watch for the faction flags. What aren't you telling us?"

Jala nodded. "We owe you this truth."

"No Mother. You give them leverage. You saw that they gave Gunjeet away to save themselves, they will do the same with us," Arijeet argued.

"I don't need her explanation to do that," I said, cutting off Jala's response. "You've endangered my ship and crew. Why shouldn't I contact Meel Tulvar and tell him to come pick the both of you up?"

"I can get you through Adit Pah, Liam Hoffen," Jala said.

"What do you know about Adit Pah?" Marny asked.

"Adit Pah is on the edge of the Dark Frontier and is dangerous beyond anything you have experienced in Santaloo. You should not go there."

"How did you hear this?" Marny asked.

"Some of the crew are not careful with their words, Gunny Bertrand," Jala said. "The reason your human ships have failed is that they cannot pass through Adit Pah."

I frowned. "We don't know what happened to those ships."

"I can find this out for you," she said. "Deliver us to my home on Tanwar and we will talk with my brother. He will know what has happened to the human ships."

"How did you find out about our mission? Is this why Koosha offered to send you with us?"

Jala gently laid her hand on my forearm. "We are not enemies, Liam Hoffen. I will help you and tell you as much truth as you request. I need your assurance that you will not turn over my family to Tulvar."

"You are too late, Mother," Arijeet said. "Gunjeet is lost."

"Gunjeet has been lost for many spans, but you are of age, Arijeet. Koosha will accept you into our people. You will wear our flag and you will hold your head proudly."

"I hate to agree with Arijeet, but Tulvar is behind us. There's no way Koosha will be coming through the Brea Fortul wormhole," I said.

"Cap, I believe Koosha isn't a familial name," Ada said. "I think Tulvar and Koosha are faction names."

"We belong to the Koosha tribe," Jala said.

I shook my head. "But, that's your husband's name."

"Ameek of Koosha is my husband," Jala said. "The people of Azima call him Koosha. It is a name we are proud to bear."

"What's the play, Cap?" Marny asked.

"Jala, you and Arijeet are restored to duty. You will restrict your movements to your duty station or the mess. I will receive a report if you venture beyond those areas."

"I have no right to ask, but would you allow the forward observation also?" Jala asked. "I miss the stars."

I looked to Marny, who shrugged.

"And the forward observation room. Please, do not give me a reason to revoke this freedom."

Chapter 22

CHOOSE YOUR FIGHTS

"Hail, Dullo," I requested. I'd separated *Intrepid* from the convoy and arrived at the Brea Fortul wormhole gate in advance of the remainder of the convoy. There were no ships near the gate, which was finally in our favor.

"Go ahead, Captain Hoffen," Aantal Tutt replied, only allowing an audio connection.

"We're going to pop through the Brea Fortul wormhole. I want you to give us twenty minutes before coming through. It will give us time to clear any enemy ships."

"That is ridiculous. It is not the protector's role to dictate our schedule. Because of *Singh* and your late arrival, some of us risk penalty," he said.

"Twenty minutes, Tutt," I said. "I don't believe that your contracts are at any risk. No good freighter captain would schedule arrival times without a buffer. Do not risk your ships."

"Do your job, Captain Hoffen," he said. "Tutt, out."

"All hands, we're at General Stations," I announced. The announcement was anticipated and all sections checked in immediately. "Ada, take us through."

There was always a short period of time after transitioning

through the wormhole where we all fought to get our bearings. Ada was by far the quickest and I knew something was up when *Intrepid* turned sharply and her overpowered engines thrummed as we accelerated.

"Contact. Four unmarked ships," Marny said. "On holo."

The holo field just in front of my seat and to my left jumped to life. Four cutter-sized ships were spread out in the twenty-kilometer zone, just outside the area of uncertainty where a ship traveling between systems might arrive. To sit within this radius was dangerous as a ship might arrive on top of you.

"They're giving chase," Ada said. It wasn't specifically necessary as the holo field clearly showed the four ships orienting on us and accelerating.

"*Transmit message to unflagged ship,*" I ordered my AI. "You will create a stand-off of one hundred kilometers from the wormhole or we will consider your actions hostile. You have ten seconds to acknowledge."

"Ada, combat burn on that first cutter," I said.

"Ah, the infamous Captain Liam Hoffen. Perhaps you do not recognize that you are well outnumbered. We are quite aware of the company that follows."

"Cap, we'll have trouble controlling four of them once the convoy is through," Marny said. And, just as if she'd called them in, *Dullo* transitioned, nineteen minutes early. Tutt's ship was followed by the remainder of the freighter convoy.

"Tutt is trying to raise you on comm," Ada said as the three non-targeted cutters spread out, our current target was beating hard on retreat, leading us away from the wormhole and the convoy.

"Ada, protect the convoy," I said. "Tutt, you're early. What do you want?"

"Those are pirates, Captain Hoffen. It is your duty to protect us."

"Copy that, Tutt and cut the chatter," I said. "I want you and your group to make all possible haste to planet Bargoti. Stay tightly packed. I won't be able to protect you if you're spread out."

"There are too many. It will be better if we let the faster ships make a run for it."

"That's not what you're paying for. Stay together. We'll get through this." I cut comms.

"Enemy has closed to ten kilometers," Ada warned.

I was grateful Tutt had at least listened to me about grouping up. I was not happy that our little group would now accelerate on pace with the slowest freighter. To make matters worse, only Tutt's ship had any armor.

"Marny, if you have a missile lock, I want you to take it," I said.

"Roger that, Cap. Be warned though, these rockets don't work like you're used to. We'll need to be lined up and within a kilometer. Cutters are too wily and the rockets have little in the way of intelligence."

"Copy that. Ada, coordinate with Marny. Priority is keeping the jackals at bay," I said. "If you can get lined up, I'd be all about increasing our odds."

For twenty minutes, I sat back and watched as Ada methodically intercepted feints and lunges by the enemy fleet. With four enemy craft, we were unable to find an advantage and I could only imagine the stress the freighter captains felt as a few blaster bolts impacted their hulls. So far, the reports of damage were minimal, but tension was growing.

"Tutt, freighter *Singh* is having trouble keeping up. You need to slow down the convoy," I said.

"I'm talking with Captain Boparai," Tutt replied. "He is experiencing mechanical problems. You need to dispatch these ships, now."

"Not possible," I said. "We're at a stalemate. We can keep them off, but there are too many for us to effectively engage. Once we did, the remainder would have a clear path to the fleet. Stay together. We can wait them out."

"Liam," Ada said, drawing my attention. Apparently, the enemy fleet had discovered *Singh's* weakness. Two of the cutters broke from their harassing pattern and sailed directly at the wounded ship's bow, clearly looking to split off the weak member of the herd.

Without warning, the remaining members of our fleet put on a burst of acceleration. It was a clear move, meant to sacrifice the wounded ship.

"Tutt, what are you doing? You need to stay together," I said.

"*Singh* has broken contract with the trading company," Tutt said. "It is required that all ships be in good working order. Captain Boparai's failure to maintain his ship has put the entire fleet in danger. As such, I have formally terminated our contact."

"You can't do that," I argued. "They'll tear him apart!"

"It is your failure, Captain Hoffen. You were not capable of defending our company and it is Boparai who will pay the price of your ineptness."

"You are required to follow my instructions during combat," I said. "You will slow and allow *Singh* to catch up. I will not be intimidated by your accusations. We do not need to lose this ship."

"There is no cause for slowing. *Singh* is no longer part of our company and as such Boparai's fate is not my concern, nor is it yours."

"You're a piece of shite, Tutt," I said.

The cutters slowed with *Singh* and allowed the fleets to separate. Not unexpectedly, they refrained from attacking the substantially outnumbered ship as it cut engines.

"Do your duty, Captain Hoffen. This does not need to be a negative report on your services," Tutt said.

"What's your call, Liam?" Ada asked as the separation between the fleets became more pronounced.

"*Hail Captain Boparai, private channel,*" I order the AI.

"You have doomed me and my son," Boparai answered, not bothering with pleasantries.

"I want you to burn as hard as you can for the gate," I said.

"It matters not. My engines are frail; we cannot make it."

"Would you give up when your son is aboard? Show courage, man. You have a chance," I said.

"The enemy will cut me down."

"They will space you," I said. "Make your last act one of defiance."

Boparai cut comm.

"Hold back, Ada. Make it look like we're providing a buffer," I said.

"What are you thinking, Liam?"

"*Singh* could give us an opportunity. Marny, you have those rocks ready?"

"Aye, Captain, that we do."

"Ada, any read on if we can outrun these cutters?"

"We lack agility, but on a dead run, we have three of them," she answered.

"Then target the fast one," I said, just as *Singh's* engines lit.

"*All hands. Combat burn imminent,*" Ada announced. A moment later my body was slammed into the seat as *Intrepid* flipped and burned with everything she had at one of the cutters.

"How's it feel to be singled out?" I spat through gritted teeth as we jumped forward.

It must have taken the enemy a moment to realize we had re-engaged, something I've come to attribute to our fancy stealth armor. That moment was sufficient to give us the time we needed to cover the distance.

"Rockets off," Marny said.

My AI enhanced the contrails of twin rockets as they sped forward, making contact with the main cutter. A brilliant flash announced its destruction. Unexpectedly, the remaining three turned on *Singh* and opened fire, which seconds later followed suit and exploded.

"Frak! Jupiter piss!" I exclaimed. "Line up on number two." We followed the three ships as they all turned back toward the convoy, which was fleeing at best possible speed. I highlighted the closest cutter.

"Rockets, Cap?" Marny asked.

"Yes! Burn 'em down," I said.

"*Transmit to remaining enemy ships,*" I ordered my AI. "This is Captain Liam Hoffen. Heave to or be destroyed."

The three ships peeled off in different directions, but we were close enough that running down the ship I'd targeted was still possible. As a group, they stood a chance, but separated, we'd chew them up like the roaches they were.

"Cap, one of them is going for the convoy," Marny said.

"Stay on target. Those bastards left Boparai to rot. They can take a little heat," I said.

There's not much a ship can do to put distance between itself and an enemy, unless it's a much faster ship. When more evenly matched, as we were with the cutter, any turn or evasive maneuver they tried would only eat into much needed acceleration. The cutter was now down to a mere four-kilometer lead.

"If we burn a rocket, he'll have to turn," Marny said. "It's expensive, but it'll speed things up."

"Do it," I said. "*Hail, Aantal Tutt.*"

"Captain Hoffen, there's a cutter on intercept. Your responsibility is to my fleet. Defend us!"

Marny launched a rocket which streaked toward the cutter and caused it to veer off. Ada adjusted and we gained on our prey.

"Pirates are spineless worms," I said. "Only one way to end this."

"Captain! I order you to break off and defend us!"

"Copy that," I said. "Now shut up."

"Ten seconds to rocket range," Ada said.

The bridge was eerily quiet as we covered the final distance to our prey.

"Rockets away," Marny announced.

Ada wasted no time and turned back to the fleet as our rockets finished the cutter.

"*Transmit to enemy fleet,*" I said. "Two down, asshats. Heave to or you're next. I'm done playing. If you so much as fire a shot at those freighters, I won't spare a one of you."

"We're sixty seconds from the fleet," Ada said.

"That's enough time for them to take out at least two freighters," Marny added.

"*Transmit to Tutt.* Tutt, turn the fleet back to *Intrepid*," I said. "You can't outrun them and you'll reduce the amount of contact time."

"You've failed, Hoffen," Tutt screeched. "I can't follow the orders of a madman."

"You haven't followed my orders one time," I said. "If you had, I could have run those cutters off before you even arrived in-system. Do what I say or I swear I'll run you down myself."

I cut the comm, sweat dripping down the side of my face. I hadn't been so angry in a very long time. The greedy jackass had guaranteed the death of Boparai and his son.

The fleet abruptly turned and made a beeline toward *Intrepid*.

"*Transmit to enemy fleet.* Feel free to run, little ones. I'll happily chase you down," I said.

It wasn't an unexpected move when the cutters turned away in opposite directions from each other. It was the move I'd have made under similar circumstances.

"Ada, take the starboard ship," I said.

"Won't his mate just turn back?"

"We'll keep an eye on him," I said. "I'm betting he won't. Tutt, stay on my tail. I'm going to run this one down."

"Negative, Captain Hoffen. The ship poses us no threat. Leave it alone."

"Probably not," I said. "And if you know what's good for you, you'll come along, just as I've requested."

THE FIRST CHASE took twenty minutes. As expected, the second cutter turned, trying to disable one of the fleet ships while we were busy.

"What are you doing, Captain Hoffen?" Tutt asked, annoyed.

It seemed obvious to me. *Intrepid* had forced the first cutter to heave-to. Tabby and I were armored up and prepared to board the ship.

"We're taking the ship," I answered. "What does it look like?"

"We have a trade mission," Tutt said. "We have no time for petty vendettas."

"Check the contract, Tutt. We still have enemy ships in range. I have control over the fleet. Stand down and we'll have this resolved as quickly as possible," I said.

"You will unnecessarily anger Genteresk."

"Don't worry, Belvakuski already has my number." I closed comm and followed Tabby across into the already opened air-lock. Idly, while jetting between the ships, I wondered what silly names Jester Ripples had given the unnamed cutters.

"Liam. The second cutter is closing in on the convoy. Should we give chase?" Ada asked.

"Absolutely," I said, cycling the airlock. "Tabbs and I have this."

The second cutter was coming up behind the slowest ship in the convoy, hoping to do just enough damage to get the freighter left behind. That move turned out to be a critical mistake, which they soon realized after Ada flipped and ran down the attacking cutter, turning the hunter into the hunted.

"Keep your head on, Cap," Marny warned as *Intrepid* turned and accelerated hard away from the fleet.

"Copy that," I said and opened the lock so we looked into a passageway amidships of the pirate cutter.

"I'm on point," Tabby pushed past and tossed a Flash-Bang-Disc (FBD) down the hallway before us. The discs were a non-lethal combination of disabling noise and brilliant flashes of light. Our suits were programmed to filter out both disruptions: setting up a noise canceling wave, blacking out our faceplates on each cycle and projecting an image on our retinas of the unaffected scene. The manipulation was noticeable; anything that moved appeared to stutter instead of moving fluidly.

The cutter was sixteen meters long, which was smaller than our first ship, *Sterra's Gift,* but larger than *Tuuq.* The airlock placed us midship and I followed Tabby forward, toward the bridge. Locked doors on either side of the passageway made me nervous, so I kept my back to the starboard bulkhead and continued to sweep behind me. We arrived at the door where we believed the crew was holed up.

We had temporarily given up the immediate threat of *Intrepid* and it didn't take much imagination to believe we'd receive more resistance now that she was gone. We had, however, achieved the most difficult part of breaching a ship, which was gaining entry.

"This is Liam Hoffen," I announced over the comm we'd previously established. "Open bridge door. Provide no resistance and you'll get a free — meals included — vacation to Fan Zuri in my brig. Otherwise, we'll blow the door and come in hard."

"Turn off your noise weapon and we'll surrender." The voice belonged to a male Pogona who was shouting so as to be heard above the sound of the FBDs. I found it interesting that he was having difficulty with the devices on the other side of the bridge hatch. Sure, it'd be noisy, but not as bad as if he was in the hallway with us.

Tabby switched off the FBDs and lowered her blaster rifle as the bridge door unlatched but didn't slide open.

"Contact aft." I fired at a figure that had popped out from one of the locked doors we'd passed. The figure popped back and my thigh stung like the dickens where the pirate's bolt impacted my armor.

"You up?" Tabby asked. Her HUD would have warned her I'd been shot and that it wasn't a lethal hit. The chances of a seriously damaging wound were low, given our armored grav-suits. The gulf of experience between 'not dead' and 'didn't hurt' was wide and I counted myself lucky the pirate's weapon wasn't more powerful.

"Good," I answered.

"Go," Tabby replied.

We had two choices: take the bridge or clear the shooter. This was a scenario we'd drilled on many times and I let training take over. I hustled down the hallway and posted up on the doorframe. Tabby turned the FBDs back on and came around behind me. Together, we'd swivel through the open door; Tabby would take high and aft and I would swing around, taking low and forward.

As we swung around the opening, my HUD showed enemy contact and I squeezed off two triple-shot rounds into the center mass of our opponent. While I couldn't hear it, Tabby did the same thing. I almost felt sorry for the pirate, who only got off a single wild shot in response.

"Contact, forward." Tabby spun, taking a knee. I rolled into the room as Tabby fired down the short hallway. I winced as Tabby grunted in response to two bolts striking her in the abdomen. She returned fire and worked her way back through the hatch to my side. As soon as she entered, the door slid shut, locking.

My priority was to verify that the pirate, with whom we now shared a room, was incapacitated. It was a necessary precaution, but he was dead. I'd been smug earlier about how easy it had been to breach the ship. That was the sort of thing that always seemed to come back to haunt me.

"We'll have to blow the door," Tabby said, unwinding the sticky, breaching cord we carried as part of our standard assault pack. I pulled a heavily soiled mattress from the bed and kicked debris out of the way next to the exterior bulkhead. Tabby slid in beside me and we ducked low.

"Fire in the hole," she whispered.

Smoke filled the room as the breaching cord ignited and burned through the hatch.

"There are two on the bridge," I said as I ducked out and got a quick view. Tabby's FBDs were still chirping away and the pirates were nowhere to be seen.

"Frag 'em?" Tabby asked.

"Nah, if they had an answer for your FBDs they'd be down here already."

I dove through the hole Tabby had made, careful not to scrape against the slag on the door. When I came back up, I noticed the bridge door remained closed. I reopened the comm channel we'd used to talk with the pirates.

"Surrender. You have nowhere to go," I said.

"Belvakuski will kill us."

"Sounds like a problem for tomorrow. Turn over the controls and I'll drop you on Pooni station in a week." Our convoy was headed to the orbital station above the planet Bargoti.

"You should murder us now," the Pogona said. "The Genteresk will kill us for losing their ship."

"How about Azima?" I asked, as a plan started forming in my mind.

"Why would you do that?"

"Let's say I don't enjoy killing people, even if they are Genteresk," I said.

My AI chimed as the ship's controls were turned over to me.

"Lie on the deck, face down. If you move when we enter, we'll shoot," Tabby instructed as we worked our way through the bridge door.

Two Pogona lay on the deck with hands behind their backs. I mag-cuffed them both and pulled them to their feet.

"*Intrepid*, we're secure on … what'd we call this ship?"

"*Fred*," Marny answered. "*George* got a good jump on us. We'll have to burn hard to catch him. Ada estimates ninety minutes."

"Copy that," I said. "Hoffen out."

With prisoners in front, we worked our way aft, opening the remaining two doors within the passageway. The scene reminded me of my first time aboard *Sterra's Gift*. The rooms were littered with trash and there was a high concentration of methane and biological particulates in the air. It wasn't toxic, but I knew from previous experience with those air quality signatures that it must stink badly of waste.

"Are there any more crew?" I asked. "Only one chance to get this right. I'll space the lot of you if I get another jack-in-the-box."

The two prisoners looked at each other, confused. No doubt my jack-in-the-box reference wasn't something our translation circuits would do well with, but I suspected they could figure it out, even so.

"Three of us. What has happened to our companion?" the smaller of the two asked as I pushed them into the room where the third lay dead.

I ignored the question and moved the mag-cuffs around to the front and loaded a baby sitter program onto them.

"The cuffs are programmed to painfully disable prisoners who take provocative actions. I recommend not testing them. We'll be notified if you do. To be clear, you're a pain in my ass right now and I wouldn't mind tossing you out the airlock."

I left the room and headed forward.

"I'll clear the rest of the ship," Tabby said.

"Copy that."

It would have been safer if I'd joined her, but this was still an enemy ship and I needed to make sure we were secure.

The bridge of the small cutter was as cluttered as the rest of the ship. I kicked debris out of my way and sat in one of the cracked-hide chairs.

Fred's controls were like *Tuuq's* and I did a quick survey of system statuses. To the extent I could get status on a system, it was generally not good. The ship was in poor shape, although fully loaded with fuel. As I searched the systems, I discovered I didn't have full access. Worse, a distress message had been sent on a tight beam.

"Jester Ripples, do you read?" I called over our comms. I wasn't surprised that I couldn't raise him as *Intrepid* was on hard burn, chasing the second cutter — and would be for the next ninety minutes.

"Calculate round trip message from nearest destination. Show as count-down timer." Six minutes showed on my HUD and continued counting backward.

I jumped from my seat and headed back to where the two prisoners sat with their backs against the forward bulkhead.

"What happens when your bosses get that message you sent?" I asked.

Tabby joined me in the room.

"What message?" the larger of the two asked.

"One of you sent a message after we boarded the ship," I said. "We have about six minutes before any response makes it back here. I'm guessing we'll either be locked out of the ship by then, or worse."

My translator had a difficult time keeping up with a rapid-fire exchange between our prisoners. The gist of it, however, was clear; the larger of the two was angry about the message that had been sent.

"You will die with us," the smaller said with contempt. "You sent your ship away, but Belvakuski will remotely destroy this ship and we will all die. My name will be spoken as hero. You are not so clever."

"Get these guys to the airlock, Tabbs," I said and sprinted from the room. Once back in the pilot's chair, I turned the cutter away from the fleet that was sitting hove-to near our position.

"Tutt, this is Hoffen," I called. My AI established a channel.

"Are you done playing pirate yet?" Tutt asked.

"No. We have about five minutes before this ship will be remotely destroyed. Don't follow us."

I cut the comm and programmed the ship to accelerate toward Bargoti at ten meters per second or roughly 1g. I ran back to the airlock. Tabby was looking down at the smaller prisoner as he lay unmoving on the ground.

"What's going on?"

"Tried to jump me and the cuffs demonstrated baby-sitter discipline," Tabby answered. "The airlocks aren't responding."

It made sense. The pirates wouldn't want us getting off the ship, but if they'd locked out flight controls, it would have tipped us off sooner.

"Back to the bridge," I said, roughly pulling on the Pogona who lay on the floor. He resisted. "Your choice, dumbass." I let go and ran back to the bridge.

Four minutes. I couldn't believe how long every small action seemed to take.

Back on the bridge, I pulled a breaching cord from my pack. I wasn't sure if it would break through the glass and thick steel mullions, but we didn't have a lot of choice.

"Fire in the hole," I said, pushing the larger prisoner back through the hatch and into the first room. It occurred to me that I wasn't giving clear instructions, but I was way down the path of improvising. My HUD showed four minutes as I ignited the breaching cord.

"Frak," Tabby exclaimed. The fact that we hadn't violently depressurized was a good clue the cord had been ineffective.

Three minutes thirty seconds.

"I'm setting a charge," I said. "Go to the back of the room and hunker down."

Tabby brusquely pushed the prisoner out of my way. I glanced down the passageway to where the smaller prisoner spasmed on the deck. Apparently, he continued having difficulty accepting the baby-sitter's lessons.

The char on the windows showed that the cord had burned through a considerable depth. The glass, however, was an excellent insulator. I'd have to remember that for next time. I placed a charge into the center of the glass panel I'd tried to burn through with the cord. My reasoning was that I'd likely weakened the area and my charge would be that much more effective.

Three minutes.

I set the timer for ten precious seconds I didn't feel I had and sprinted for the back room where Tabby had pulled up the same soiled mattress to crouch behind. On the way past, I grabbed the smaller Pogona and dragged him through the hatch. He resisted and I gave up, diving for cover next to Tabby.

Debris pelted the interior walls of the ship as the charge exploded. Almost instantaneously, the flow reversed as the pressurized atmosphere rushed to fill the void of space, dragging crap along with it.

"Go!" Tabby said, pushing the Pogona prisoner.

Two minutes thirty seconds.

As we passed, the smaller pirate grabbed at our legs, causing us to pile up at the doorway. Once again, he spasmed as the cuffs jolted him unkindly into passivity. Tabby pulled the larger Pogona from the pile and stumbled forward.

"We won't escape the ship's gravity," the Pogona complained as Tabby pushed him toward the hole.

Tabby jabbed him with the end of her blaster rifle. "Stop arguing or we're leaving you."

The pirate climbed through the hole and onto the outside of the ship. As he'd predicted, the ship's artificial gravity held him to the hull.

The effect extended several meters beyond the ship and a suited crew member would have difficulty escaping. Generally, this was considered advantageous, as most crew wouldn't want to be separated from their ship. Currently, however, this feature was *not* to our advantage.

Two minutes.

I followed Tabby through the jagged hole. Our course of action was obvious and we grabbed the prisoner under each arm and pushed our grav-suits to separate us from the ship. We were in deep space, with little in the way of gravitational fields to work with; it was where our grav-suits were at their weakest. Even so, we slowly floated away from the cutter, accelerating with every second.

At zero, we'd gained a hundred meters of separation, but were still being pulled along in the wake of the ship. At that range, we were in considerable danger of being struck by shrapnel.

"Are you sure they're going to blow it?" Tabby asked.

"Depends on how quickly someone responds to the message," I said.

Minus thirty seconds.

The ship was two kilometers from our position when it brilliantly exploded, sending shrapnel in all directions. I counted ten and then checked our bios on the HUD. No issues. We'd survived and had picked up a new friend.

"*Incoming comm request, Aantal Tutt.*" My AI chimed.

"Go ahead, Tutt," I said.

"You live." Tutt stated the obvious.

"Ship was compromised. We had to take an alternate course of action," I said.

"Tell your ship to turn around," Tutt said. "You can see this is not a profitable venture. The Genteresk would prefer to destroy their ship rather than allow you to take control. I demand that we get underway immediately."

"*Intrepid* is under hard burn and won't be available for comm for another hour," I said. "That said, we could start burning for planet Bargoti. The area is clear."

Ten minutes later, Tutt's freighter, *Dullo,* lumbered toward our position and matched our velocity.

Once we cycled through the locks, we were met by Tutt and three armed crew. "Captain Hoffen, you will relinquish your weapons while aboard *Dullo.*"

I nodded my head in agreement. When I put myself into his shoes, it wasn't hard to understand. Tabby and I had just forcibly boarded an armed warship and it had been blown up. Precaution was reasonable.

An hour later, we finally received our first communication from *Intrepid.*

"Liam, I'm not showing *Fred* on sensor," Ada said.

"Small problem with a remote destruct."

"Copy that. Jester Ripples defeated a similar problem on *George.* We're burning to the fleet and expect to arrive in sixty-five minutes."

"Copy. We're hanging out on *Dullo.* Captain Tutt is quite the host. Who's sailing *George?*" I asked as I eyed the guard who was posted at the door to the small room we'd been placed in. According to Tutt, the guard was to prevent the Pogona pirate from escaping. I suspected he also appreciated showing me who was boss.

"Sempre and Roby," Ada said.

"Roby and Sempre were on a boarding party?"

"Sempre, yes. Roby no," Ada said. "Marny and Sempre boarded. We sent Roby over once it was clear."

"How did you know to stop *George* from being destroyed?

"That was Jester Ripples," Ada said. "He intercepted the command override from Genteresk. *George's* systems are now fully within our control."

"Copy that," I said.

"You received a comm from Anino. Do you want me to forward it while you wait?"

"Of course."

"What does it say?" Tabby asked, having overheard Ada's offer to send along the message from Anino.

"It's not much. He's had more contact with Jonathan and thinks they might be in Adit Pah. Munay's crew is alive and they're hot on the trail."

"Any word on Sendrei?"

"Nothing. According to Anino, he's received less than thirty-two bits of data in total, so he's actually guessing on everything he's telling us."

"Thirty bits? That's ridiculous. No one can communicate anything useful with that little data," Tabby said after a moment's pause. I suspected she'd used a few seconds to identify what the data measurement referred to.

"Maybe Munay will uncover something."

"Maybe," Tabby agreed.

Chapter 23

POONI

"That was amusing," I said, joining Ada, Marny, Jala, Arijeet and Jester Ripples in the wardroom. With Roby and Sempre aboard *George*, we were starting to feel the pinch of being short-handed and there was no reason to separate crew from officers for meals.

"Amusing — right," Ada said, pursing her lips. "I believe Tutt would argue over the color of bathroom tissue."

I'd listened to the exchange between Tutt and Ada as she worked to convince the surly trader to stop his acceleration long enough for Tabby and me to transfer back to *Intrepid*. In the end, she'd placed *Intrepid* nose-to-nose with *Dullo* and dared him to ram her. It was an uneven match as *Intrepid's* nose was heavily armored. While *Dullo* had a small sheath of armor, it was nothing in comparison.

"Cap, what did you learn from Anino?" Marny asked.

"Not much more than we're headed in the right direction," I said. "Anino believes the Kroerak ship is headed for the Adit Pah system — if it isn't there already."

"And, there's no word on Sendrei," Tabby added.

"What happened to Munay? I thought he was taken out," Marny said.

"There weren't a lot of details. Jala, what can you tell us about planet Bargoti?"

Jala smiled demurely at the attention. "It is cold, but with substantial water resources," she said. "Most people gather around the middle band of the planet where it is warmest. It is the third planet inhabited by Pogona and most known for the great, furred beasts that inhabit the icy wastelands. They are called Svelti. The most common tribe on Bargoti is named for these creatures who serve as companions."

Ada flicked a short video she'd found showing a Pogona wrapped in furs, walking across a frigid, barren landscape. Behind the Pogona, two extremely wide-shouldered humanoids covered entirely in thick, dirty white fur pulled a sled through the snow. The Svelti's pitch-black faces were devoid of fur and bore peaceful expressions, even though their massive hands sported long, sharp-looking black claws.

"Are Svelti friendly?" I asked. "Those claws are terrifying."

Jala smiled. "Svelti are simple creatures who have adapted to living in an extremely cold climate. They are adept at clawing through ice to find sustenance. They are passive and have a simple language. Occasionally, one will turn back to its wild ways and have to be put down."

"Looks like slavery to me," Tabby snapped.

"I make no judgment about this," Jala said. "The Pogona of the Svelti tribe are, however, very protective of their lesser companions."

"I'm not sure we'll have a chance to visit the surface," I said. "We weren't able to find any manufacturing or shipping operations interested in our stevedore bots."

"You're looking at the stevedores, right there," Tabby said, still annoyed.

"Tabitha is correct," Jala said. "The tribe protects all manual labor for the Svelti. It is their contribution, which they enjoy. I have seen this firsthand, if only briefly."

"Five days," Ada said. "Fortunately, planet Bargoti's orbit is close to the wormhole locations."

"I imagine that's all part of Tutt's master plan," I said.

POONI STATION BUSTLED with activity as we arrived. Each ship in the convoy was given a docking bay along the outside of a great ring that was connected at four points to an interior, tube-shaped station that had capacity for twenty thousand souls. According to Jala, long ago both ring and station had rotated to generate gravity, but had been converted a few centuries back. Orientation of the artificial gravity on the ring was outward, with our feet pointed to space and our heads toward the station.

The arrival of our nine-ship convoy caused quite a commotion. A herd of squat, furry Svelti flooded out from the spokes of the station and onto the decks of the ring to greet each ship.

"Glub, glub."

Two ivory-furred Svelti approached *Intrepid's* forward cargo bay, pulling a heavy, rustic, wheeled cart. Their front paws gripped the thick neck yoke, which sat at the end of a long wooden falling tongue attached to the wagon.

The offered Svelti greeting had a musical quality to it.

"I'm sorry, my translation isn't working," I said, looking for help from the fur-covered, young Pogona that sat high on a bench, at the front of the cart.

"She is greeting you," the Pogona said, jumping down gracefully. "Her name is Glub Glub."

I nodded. "Liam Hoffen." I smiled, careful not to show teeth as I did. I'd yet to run into any species beyond human who thought showing teeth was a friendly gesture. "It is nice to meet you Glub Glub."

Glub Glub's black face bore a peaceful, childish expression, but I wasn't about to offer my hand for shaking. She had thick, long claws that grew along the backs of her fingers instead of protruding like nails. A malodor hit me as she and the other Svelti stood, bobbing their heads as if listening to music.

"I understand you have a load of sheet steel and armored glass?"

The Pogona pronounced the last with an up inflection, making armored glass sound like a question.

"Yes," I said. "We've a new orbital steel mill in Santaloo system and are delivering samples. Skanti Manufacturing?"

At the mention of Skanti, the two Svelti started bobbing more quickly. "Anti, anti," Glub Glub sing-songed, making me wonder if her name was actually just Glub.

The Pogona nodded. "That's what I have. Looks like a small load. We'll get right to it."

Tabby and Marny stood further back in the forward hold. We'd agreed that it would be best if we didn't approach the Svelti as a large group, just in case they were skittish — which didn't seem to be the case.

"Glub, bring the cart inside. No hurt." The Pogona stepped into the translucent energy barrier that stretched across our forward hold.

Docking at Pooni had presented Ada a significant challenge and we weren't confident in the seal between ship and station. We had decided, therefore, to leave the barrier in place.

Glub Glub lowered her head. She and her smaller twin pushed the cart into our hold as I indicated the stack of steel and glass to be offloaded.

The Svelti weren't particularly fast in their task, but were more than strong enough to lift a hundred kilograms of sheet on each load. With little help from the Pogona, they completed the task in thirty minutes.

"Thank you, Glub," I called, after signing the Pogona's offered pad.

"Glub Glub," she called back, looking over her shoulder for a moment.

A chime sounded, notifying me that payment from the convoy had been transferred from Tutt and in turn, I sent payment to the crew.

"We're clear, Ada," I called over tactical.

A moment later, *Intrepid's* magnetically attached glad-hands released and retracted. The station's locking clamps also released, setting *Intrepid* adrift.

"What was your impression of Svelti, Captain Hoffen?" Jala met us as we exited the cargo hold and walked up the ramp to *Intrepid's* main deck.

"They seem friendly enough," I said. "Do they keep all of Pooni Station as cold as the docking bay? It was minus ten on the deck; I thought my cheeks were going to freeze."

Before Jala could answer, Tabby jumped in. "Best hope they do, big man. Glub Glub had quite a smell to her and I'd hate to be around if that fur of hers thawed out."

Uncharacteristically, Jala chuckled. "Pooni tribe prefers the cold. It is rumored they do this to discourage emigration. The station is not as cold, however, and is kept at ten degrees."

"Did you want something?" Jala's presence was welcome, but it was unusual that she would meet us after unloading cargo.

"I would speak with you privately if First Mate Masters would allow." Jala looked at Tabby and lowered her eyes, demurely.

"He's all yours," Tabby said. "And by that, I mean look but don't touch."

Jala gave Tabby a quizzical look, obviously trying to parse the human idiom. Tabby and Marny left Jala and me in the passageway.

"What's up?" I asked.

"I have friends on Pooni," she said. "They whisper of a mysterious ship that passed in the dark space near planet Bargoti."

"Mysterious ship? Where did they see it?"

"My friend would not say. They are careful not to speak of things when they are transmitted."

"That's pretty oblique. A mysterious ship with no location is hard to do anything about," I said.

"You are invited to speak with them, but it can be only you and one other, with Arijeet and me. You will need to be disguised as Koosha and the other as Gunjeet."

"I'm not sure how to do that," I said.

"I have replicated traditional Koosha clothing and you will be covered with furs. It is not difficult," she said. "If we were to take the ship, *George*, we would raise no suspicion."

"Bring the disguises to the wardroom," I said and transmitted the conversation to Marny, Ada and Tabby.

"Liam Hoffen is pleased?" Jala asked.

"Yes, thank you, Jala. This might be important," I said.

"What the frak is that all about?" Tabby asked as I entered the bridge.

"I take it you've listened to the conversation?" I asked, looking at the three women I trusted with everything I had.

"Liam, I don't know if we can trust Jala. This could be a trap, but none of us believe you'll listen to warnings just now," Ada said.

"How can I turn away from this? What if this will help us find Jonathan and Sendrei?" I asked.

"Sendrei is dead, Cap," Marny said. "Even if he somehow avoided the bugs on their own ship, he's had no access to food or water for over a month."

"Doesn't change anything," I said defiantly.

"I'm coming with you," Tabby said.

As promised, Jala's disguise was convincing. There was little of either Tabby or myself that could be seen beneath the heavy replicated skins and furs we were wrapped in. And, even when those were removed, we wore beige linen robes with colorful scarfs that covered our heads and masked our necks.

George was in typical shape for a pirate-run cutter. Trash and debris were piled in every corner and kicked out of the main walking paths. I was grateful to discover the critical components of the head worked, though we wouldn't be taking any showers.

The small bridge was in better shape than *Fred's*. The seats bore only a few cracks in the fabric and the flight sticks, while worn, appeared to have been regularly maintained. There was seating for the four of us and Tabby and I took the two forward chairs.

"Captain, would you allow for a suggestion?" Jala asked.

"Of course."

"If I am to be your mate and Tabitha your son, it would be more appropriate for me to be seated next to you," she said and then hastily added, "I mean you no disrespect, Tabitha Masters."

"Oh, for frak's sake." Tabby stood and gestured overtly to the co-pilot's chair. "Take the seat already."

"Ada, we're disembarking," I said as I peeled away from the underside of *Intrepid*, where *George* had rafted up.

"We copy, Liam. Be safe."

"Copy that, Ada. Hoffen out." I closed comms. "Where are we headed, Jala?"

I slowly arced away from Pooni Station toward Bargoti. Unlike other planets we'd visited, Bargoti was covered with whites, grays and light blues, with just a band of green around the equator.

Jala pinched at her vision and flicked instructions. My AI traced a path on my HUD to the planet's surface and illuminated a golden circle within a wide gray and white area.

"Looks hospitable," Tabby said, sarcastically.

"Koosha tribe has a tentative friendship with Pooni," Jala said. "Our enclave here is small and has not earned a place within the warmth. We are fortunate to be accepted."

"Just how big is Koosha?" I asked.

"There are perhaps five thousand on Pooni," Jala said. "You should not ask questions like this of my people. Pogona tribes hide their strength unless they are strong."

"Like Genteresk?"

"Yes. Like Genteresk."

George shook as we entered Pooni's thin atmosphere and I turned my attention to the task of keeping us on track. "Do we need to hail anyone as we approach?"

"It is not necessary."

Slowing our descent, we approached from a few kilometers north of the position Jala had given. The sky was crystal clear and a gusty wind picked up snow and lifted it hundreds of meters into the air.

Brea Fortul's star glittered through the sparkling ice crystals in a pretty display of colors. Like sand, the snow drifted across wide open plains.

The first signs of habitation were a trio of creatures. Two golden Svelti romped through the snow, a small Pogona sitting in a pack, nestled against one of the furry beast's backs. Amidst the swirling snow, I finally made out the low, rounded building they headed toward. We sailed across dozens of similar structures, finding only a handful of hardy souls braving the blowing snow that now obscured direct line of sight.

Lights blinked atop the frost-covered landing pad where I set *George* down.

"What is that?" I asked. With the engines quiet, I'd become aware of an eerie howling.

"The wind, Captain Hoffen," Jala said. "It is time. You must raise your cowl. We should not let on that Ameek and Gunjeet have not made this trip."

"And then what?" Tabby asked, pulling the fur-lined parka hood over her head.

"Thuga of Koosha will learn of our arrival and come to escort us," Jala said. "I believe it is he who approaches."

I would not have been able to pick Thuga out if my AI hadn't outlined the approaching figures in what turned out to be a blizzard on the surface.

"It is customary for a visitor to present a gift to the host for their hospitality," Jala said. "When we enter Thuga's home, you will present this to him." Jala handed me a simple, rectangular wooden box a little shorter than my arm.

"What is it?" I asked.

"It is meant to look like spirits from our home of Tanwar," Jala said. "It holds five hand weapons that we purchased on Azima."

"Our gift is guns?" Tabby asked.

Jala smiled wanly. "For tribesman, it is a most revered gift for it communicates concern for Thuga's wellbeing. They are also powerful enough to diminish your weapons stock."

I tucked the box beneath my furs and punched the security panel on the rear cargo bay door. The wind blasted into the bay and debris swirled around us.

A thickset Pogona peered at me through large, round goggles. Apparently, not finding what he was looking for he moved over to Jala and embraced her.

"Follow," Jala instructed as the two Pogona turned back into the gale and trudged away.

I was almost knocked down as I stepped from the back of *George*. Fortunately, my grav-suit allowed me a semblance of control against the random buffeting of wind.

The hold door refused to seal completely from ice crystals that had found their way into the gaps. I'd have to deal with it later.

"You must lead," Jala prompted as I fell in at the back of the pack. I found it difficult to make my way through the snow that came up to mid-calf. I realized the native Pogona was walking on a well-packed path. I gently lifted with my suit, just enough that my weight barely broke through the crusted snow. With this modification, I caught up to Thuga.

We had walked for only a hundred meters, when Thuga turned toward one of the low, round-topped buildings. We followed him down a stairwell and beneath an awning that provided a break from the blowing snow. Another fur-covered Pogona stood in the doorway and ushered us inside.

"Ameek of Koosha speaks well of these humans," Thuga stated to Jala as he helped his companion pull a drape over the door we entered. The windows were all covered, though it would be impossible for anyone to see us through the blizzard outside.

"You honor our family bond," Jala replied. "To you I present Arijeet son of Ameek. I also present friends of Ameek— Liam Hoffen and mate, Tabitha Masters."

"Son of Ameek." Thuga turned his attention to Arijeet. "You are of age, Arijeet of Koosha. It is time that you separate from Ameek and join with the tribe. Is this why you travel on to Tanwar?"

"I am no Koosha," Arijeet spit on the floor. "And these are no friends of Ameek. This one gave Gunjeet to Tulvar."

"Arijeet," Jala whispered harshly. "You embarrass your family."

"What would you be if not Koosha?" Thuga asked. "Would you live in the street?"

"I would be Genteresk." Arijeet stuck his chest forward and forced air into his chin, blowing out his jowls.

"Is this so? What say you of Arijeet's claim, Jala of Koosha?" Thuga asked.

"Liam Hoffen provided refuge after Gunjeet attacked him. When Tulvar searched his ship, he did not give away our deception. It is as I say, Liam Hoffen acts with honor," Jala said and cut her eyes to the box she'd given me.

I handed the box to Thuga, who'd shrugged off his outer furs and hung them on thick pegs near the door. The sunken building was a simple design — a broad central room, with only three doorways. Thuga's companion also shrugged off her fur coverings. The woman was a dead ringer for Jala, if not a little younger. She caught my glance and returned Jala's patented demure smile.

"They are a beautiful pair, are they not?" Thuga asked, setting the box on the table without opening it. "I tell you the truth, their mother is even more beautiful. And please, your identity is safe here, you may remove your cloaks."

Tabby and I pulled the cloaks off and hung them on open pegs. "It is a burden to always be in the presence of beautiful women," I said. "One never knows where to look without offending."

Thuga choked out a laugh of surprise as he turned, his eyes coming to rest on Tabby. "I see what you mean, Liam Hoffen. Burden would not have been the first word that came to mind, however," he said as he reached out to pat Tabby's butt.

Tabby's hand shot out in a blur and grabbed Thuga's wrist. The man's instincts must have misled him, as he reached for a knife. Tabby twisted his arm, turning him as she did and wrenching the knife from his hand.

The whine of a blaster's capacitor charging caught my attention as Jala's sister raised a pistol, holding it only centimeters from Tabby's head.

"No, Phael," Jala said, trying to step between Tabby and her sister. "It is a simple misunderstanding. Human women are not accustomed to playful men."

Tabby released Thuga's wrist and handed him the knife. As quick as I could imagine, he accepted the knife and slashed downward, attempting to strike her across the forearm. "To lay hands on a man in his house is punishable..."

In a blur, Tabby smacked the back of Thuga's wrist, dislodging the knife, while disarming Jala's sister at the same time. Phael took a surprised, involuntary step backward.

"Whoa there," I said, holding my hands up defensively. "We don't need a problem here, but touching without permission doesn't fly."

The grimace on Thuga's face shifted to a broad smile and he laughed. "You are like Abasi. It is strange; you look so normal. Like Pogona."

"Are we okay, here?" I looked from Thuga to Jala.

"As you say, Jala. A misunderstanding. I must say, Liam Hoffen. To have such a woman," he held his hands out as if holding Tabby from a distance. "What a treat that would be."

I breathed a sigh of relief and hoped Tabby would be able to set aside the misguided misogynistic behavior.

"A treat you might not survive," Tabby growled, setting the blaster pistol onto a small table near the front door.

"But what an adventure," Thuga's eyes twinkled with mischief. "We drink! Phael, bring out spirits. We are in good company tonight."

We joined the Pogona on soft fur-lined cushions on a semi-circular couch that overlooked a bubbling pool of clear water set into the far wall. Steam rose from the water, but dissipated quickly into the air.

"Why do you heat the water?" I finally asked after tasting the warm sweet, brown liquor provided by Phael.

"The water is from springs deep within Pooni," Thuga said. "Delicious, no?"

"Really heats you up," I said, still feeling the fire in my throat.

Thuga must have liked the answer because he smiled. "Jala says you have interest in the ship my people found in the dark spaces."

"We might be," I said. "Can you describe it?"

"Do not think us simple because of our lifestyle," Thuga said.

"Of course not," I said. "Your home is very comfortable."

Thuga smiled and then pinched off a still picture of a Kroerak cruiser. Something in the picture was off. And then I realized there were no stars behind the ship.

"When was this taken?"

"Not long ago, Liam Hoffen." Thuga motioned for Phael to refill his glass. My heart thumped in my ears as I waited for him to take another drink.

I finally broke the silence. "Do you know where it is now?"

"Perhaps."

Chapter 24

FOURTH DAUGHTER

"Anything worth eating on Pooni Station?" I asked.

Marny and Jester Ripples were keeping me company on the bridge. I'd volunteered for the final watch so the crew could take full advantage of our short stay.

"Virtually no grains," Marny replied, "although they have a dark berry that grows in abundance. I think you'd like their sweet purple beer. I loaded the wardroom refer with it." She sighed. "I'd kill for a decent synth burger and fried potato strips about now."

"The veck berries are delicious and provide carbohydrate, protein and citric acid," Jester Ripples added. "I would also add that I have further refined the image provided by Thuga of Koosha."

A grainy image of stars behind the Kroerak cruiser appeared.

"Were you able to match these stars?"

"I have, Liam Hoffen," Jester Ripples said. "The stars are Adit Pah, as Thuga of Koosha reported."

"Do we have enough data to tie down a time?"

"I will continue to work with it," Jester Ripples said.

Just then Tabby and Ada stumbled onto the bridge, arms around each other's waists, laughing. In Tabby's hand was a clear, nearly empty bottle of something dark and fizzy. The nearly empty part was fortunate, given how precariously she held it. Tabby separated from Ada and launched herself at me, the smell of alcohol reaching me well before she did.

"Tell her, Hoffen. Tell her how Thuga tried to lay his hand on my ass and I nearly broke it off." Tabby's voice slurred as she planted a sloppy kiss on my face, only partially covering my mouth.

I'd never seen Tabby or Ada quite so wasted before. I held on, preventing Tabby from turning around, and watched over her shoulder as Marny deftly applied a sober med-patch onto her neck.

"Killjoy," Tabby said, unsuccessfully reaching for the patch.

Ada smiled and accepted a patch from Marny, choosing to apply it on her own.

"How about we get you to bed," I said. "You've been up for twenty-four hours."

"Nope." Tabby released me and slumped into the port-side pilot's chair. "I'm going to sit right here while these little buggers drain all the fun out of life."

"Cap, since we're all here," Marny said. "You want to give us a rundown on what you talked about with Jala's friend?"

"Brother-in-law. Not sure why she kept *that* secret." I flicked the still image Thuga had provided. "The star field was removed so we couldn't figure its location, but he did say the Koosha tribe tracked this Kroerak ship not more than five days ago in the Adit Pah system. They lost track of it, but for a price he thinks they could locate it."

"What price?" Marny said.

"This is rich," Tabby said. "Did you know that to give a gun to a Pogona is a nice housewarming present? Yeah, it shows that you care about their safety and that you don't need the gun because you're strong. Messed up, right? Give you one guess what Hoffen offered."

Marny and Ada looked from Tabby back to me. Apparently, Ada hadn't been drinking nearly as much as Tabby, because she seemed to be sobering quickly. "What did you offer, Liam?" Ada asked.

"No, really, guess," Tabby pushed and then couldn't hold back. "*George.* He said if they could get eyes on that cruiser long enough for us to catch up, he'd give them *George* on the spot."

"What'd Thuga say to that, Cap?" Marny asked.

"He'll send word to the tribal leaders of Tanwar," I said. "I kind of got the feeling he'd been exiled and this might be his way back in."

"These drunk patches are a complete buzz kill," Tabby complained. Her eyes were drooping, but her speech had cleared up.

"Ada, would you mind putting our girl here to bed?"

"Copy that, Liam," Ada answered. "I wouldn't mind a bit of shuteye myself. Are you still okay to take us out?"

I chuckled. "Go."

Tabby wrapped her arms around Ada's neck as she pulled Tabby from the pilot's chair. Marny, Jester Ripples, and I watched as they left more quietly than they'd arrived.

"Roby, did you get *George* lashed down? We're twenty minutes out."

"Just putting final touches on the mooring plates," Roby said. "AI says we're good for twelve hundred newtons. I'd like to do better. Amon can forge nano-crystal steel parts to withstand that kind of force."

"Let me know when you're aboard," I said.

"Copy," Roby replied and closed the comm.

"I feel like we're over our heads with these Pogona," Marny said. "Jala is more of a player than she's let on. There's no way she didn't know that Tulvar was stationed at Fan Zuri. It took preparation to have those breathing masks ready. I searched the replication logs, she manufactured them the day after she came aboard."

"Do you think she's trying to hurt us?"

"That's the problem, Cap. I have no idea. Why is she on our ship? How did you hear she was willing to accompany us to Tanwar?"

"Who initiated the conversation, you mean?" I asked.

"Right."

"I remember telling Hog we were looking for someone who knew Nijjar space," I said. "I assumed he reached out to Koosha, since I received a message from Ameek shortly after that."

"Did you follow up with Hog?"

I shook my head. "How would Koosha and Jala have known about our trip otherwise?"

"Not sure. Maybe I'm just being paranoid," Marny said. "We need to be careful."

I wasn't sure what to do with Marny's concern and allowed myself to be dragged back into the mundane tasks of readying *Intrepid* for the next and final leg of our trip. I'd spoken briefly with Tutt. The final leg through the Tanwar gate and on to the orbital platform of Mannat would be the least dangerous of our trip. Both endpoints of the wormhole were patrolled and tribal conflicts were highly discouraged.

"CAN YOU BELIEVE THIS?" I asked, looking at the report Tutt had posted to the escort service feed. "Frakking Tutt is hanging the destruction of *Singh* and deaths of Captain Boparai and his son on us."

"Asshat," Tabby said, not paying a lot of attention.

"Seriously, if he'd paid attention to what I told him, we had a chance."

"Can't you respond?" Tabby asked.

"And say what?"

Tabby shrugged. "Tag it with a data-stream of Tutt refusing to follow your direction and what he said about Boparai not being part of the convoy and how we should leave him behind."

"Cap, there's no arguing with people like this. If you wrestle with a pig, you both end up muddy and only the pig is happy," Marny said. "Take the high road and respond with how the convoy had broken apart due to mechanical failure during combat and that you regret we were unable to save *Singh* before it fell prey to an aggressive attack."

Tabby sighed. "At least mention we took out the ships that attacked."

The last leg of our trip through the Tanwar system was every bit as uneventful as Tutt had predicted. Just out of the gate, there'd been tension when we'd picked up a Nijjar patrol's attention and been followed. The ships were reminiscent of Mars Protectorate, gleaming white and bristling with radio antennae and weaponry. Fortunately, they decided we weren't interesting and after three tense hours, returned to their duties.

When we were finally on approach to planet Kushala, I'd reached the limit of my patience in hearing nothing from Anino and reached out, using the quantum crystal he provided. "Anino, this is *Intrepid*. Over."

I waited a few minutes as was customary, and called a second time. Before I could call a third time, Anino responded. "Go ahead, Hoffen."

"We're on approach to Tanwar. I need a sit-rep," I said. "Tell me you're holding back information about Jonathan."

"There's been no word from Jonathan or Munay. I fear the worst." His voice was tired. "Admiral Sterra called off the other ships. It's a stupid move, but things are chaotic in-system here. She's worried that it's bad optics to be focused on problems in another galaxy."

"What do you mean, chaotic?"

"Earth's governments are failing. The Kroerak planted eggs every-where and we're having trouble with Kroerak spawn. It's a mess."

"What about the selich root? That should keep the spawn away," I said.

"There are too many factions; they're causing trouble with distrib-ution and there's a rumor about selich resistance. Look, is this what you want to talk about?" Anino asked, growing impatient.

"I'm transmitting a still image of the Kroerak vessel," I said. "It appears the picture was recorded in the Adit Pah system. Jester Ripples is trying to pin down an exact location and date."

"Give me the entire file," Anino said, perking up. "I don't care if it takes ten hours to transmit. And Hoffen ..."

"Yeah?" I asked.

"You have to find Jonathan," he said. "If reports of selich resistance in some of the bugs here are real, Earth may still be lost. If Earth falls, it's just a matter of time for the rest of the worlds they've infected. They have to be stopped."

"ROBY AND JESTER Ripples request permission to enter the bridge," Ada said.

"Granted," I replied mechanically, still reeling from Anino's dire warning.

Predictably, activity on the bridge intensified as we'd passed to within half a million kilometers of Kushala, the capital planet of Nijjar government. With a population exceeding thirty billion, Kushala was nearly as dense as Earth had been before the Kroerak attack and five times more populated than the much smaller Mars. Even at long distance, the number of ships in the area grew more quickly than I expected, until I realized that Tutt had us lined up to pass within fifty thousand kilometers of Kushala's only moon.

"All hands. We'll need everyone at general stations," I announced and turned over the helm to Ada.

"Incoming hail, Aantal Tutt," Ada announced a few minutes later as I gazed out at ships of every possible shape and size buzzing around the heavily populated moon.

"Hoffen," I snapped. I'd run out of the capacity to be anything beyond civil.

Tutt's face appeared on the screen where, uncharacteristically, he was smiling. "No need to be so glum, Captain Hoffen. I'd say for your first trip through the Dark Corridor, you performed admirably. Our losses were low and our profits will be high. It's a good day to be alive."

I studied the Pogona's face, just to make sure I was actually talking with the same annoying grub I'd been forced to live with for the last forty days.

"I see you were willing to blame *Intrepid* for the loss of *Singh* and Captain Boparai," I said.

"You should not dwell on your failures, Captain," Tutt said.

"Boparai knew the risks of traveling in dangerous territory with a ship that was poorly maintained. It was unfortunate, if not predictable. I'm transferring the final credits now, although I wondered if perhaps you would take a ten percent reduction. With this consideration, I imagine I could modify my report if you find it so distressing."

I gestured so the conversation was private and routed through my earwig. "Tutt, that's a new low. You're negotiating on how you'll report on our reputation? How can traders trust what's said if you're willing to manipulate it?"

"Every good trader knows how to read between the lines, Captain. I'm surprised you don't know this."

"Seems like if everyone can read between the lines, I probably don't need your help," I said.

"Come now, you know as well as I do you'll lose possible contracts if you have a poor rating. Five thousand credits. It's as low as I'll go."

"Don't you dare," Tabby said, looking over her shoulder. She couldn't hear Tutt's side of the conversation, but must have read my body language as I considered what he was saying.

"Seems that our aggressive counter-attack cost the convoy at least three hours," I said. "I'd be willing to forgo twenty-five hundred credits to put aside any hard feelings."

Tutt smiled more broadly and nodded his head. I hated giving in to the man, but he was right. Reputation was critical at this point and rolling around in the slop with him wasn't going to do us any good.

"Thirty-five hundred and I believe we will have reached an under-standing."

"Three thousand," I said.

"Done."

My AI chimed. An updated contract had been transmitted, along with a copy of a new posting to the services portal showing a glowing review. Without giving myself further time to wallow, I signed the contract, sending it back.

"A pleasure working with you, Captain Hoffen. If you'll be in the area for a few days, I'll be putting together a return trip. I'd love to have you along."

"Safe travels, Tutt." I closed comms.

"You gave him three thousand," Tabby said. "What kind of shite is that?"

"I can live with it," I said. "Ada, do you want to find us a slip?"

"How long are we staying?"

"No idea," I said. "Let's get refueled and take a thirty-six-hour leave. Warn people not to be out of comm range or more than thirty minutes away. I want to be able to take off if we get word on that Kroerak ship."

She turned to begin handling my orders.

"Marny, can you get Jala and Arijeet fully checked out? Jala informed me this is terminus for the two of them."

"What happened to going back to Zuri and her husband, Cap?"

"After we visited Thuga on Pooni, she indicated they would be staying on planet Kushala. She seemed happy about it."

For a few minutes after passing the moon, traffic seemed to abate and the bustle of ships slowed. As we approached one of three public space stations orbiting Mannat, however, the pace and volume of the ships increased dramatically, reminding me of my first visit to Puskar Stellar.

"You good, Ada?" I asked, standing.

"We're a hundred twenty meters long and as narrow as a teenage boy," Ada said. "This is nothing compared to pushing a barge over Mars."

"Teenage boy?" Tabby asked, tilting her head and raising an eyebrow. "Why Ms. Chen, what bilge water has entered your mouth? How long has it been?"

"Stop it, you fiend," Ada said. "It's not like there are lovely men at every station in these parts."

"I hear Pogona men are quite compatible," Tabby said.

I shook my head and worked my way to the bridge door, opening it and stepping through.

"How would you even know that?" Ada asked, adopting a scandal-ized tone.

Tabby grabbed my elbow to propel me off the bridge and turned back with a grin. "I'll send you the lowdown."

"Is that a real thing?" I asked as we turned the corner to the wardroom where we found Arijeet and Jala standing next to the bags they'd brought along. "Ready to go?" I was more than willing to change the subject.

"We are, Captain Liam," Jala said.

"Marny get you checked out?" Tabby asked. My AI brought up a display in response to her question. Marny had indeed signed off on their bags and departure.

"She was very efficient," Jala answered. "Will we utilize station services to visit Mannat?" My best translation of her question was whether we would utilize the shuttle services between the surface and the station we'd docked at.

"What's your recommendation?" I asked. "I had thought to take *George*."

"This is a reasonable course of action," she said. "I hate to ask such a question, but do you have clothing that is not skin tight? You will draw attention to yourselves on the surface in those suits."

Tabby and I exchanged a look. We'd picked up festive clothing a while back on one of the cloud cities, Nuage Gros. The clothing was colorful and loose fitting. It was a simple matter to grab the bag that held our civvies (as we called them) and bring them along.

"Good call," I said. "*Intrepid* will be docked shortly; we should get going."

The four of us walked aft and down the ramp that led into the secondary cargo hold. A few minutes later I felt *Intrepid's* magnetic mooring lines deploy. The sound was subtle, but if you were expecting it, identifiable.

"That's our cue," Tabby said, nodding to the hatch in the hold's deck.

With reduced gravity, it was an easy transition from *Intrepid* into *George*. Arijeet stumbled in the changing gravity and had to rely on

Jala to keep him steady. I wasn't particularly surprised to find she was comfortable outside of a ship.

"Someone's been cleaning up in here," Tabby said as we worked our way through the airlocks. She was right, not only was the trash gone, it looked like one of *Intrepid's* cleaning bots had been set loose and gotten several layers of grime removed.

George was a twenty-meter long cutter, making it smaller than our first, *Sterra's Gift*. It was capable of hauling a hundred fifty cubic meters of cargo and after a trip to the chandler, could sleep four comfortably - more if hot-bunking. Perhaps the biggest limitation was the ship's lack of strong inertial systems. I'd been at *Intrepid's* helm when we chased down *Fred* and I couldn't imagine what the pirates had suffered while trying to evade us. *George's* single, forward-facing turret mounted above the ship had significant freedom of movement, but virtually no visibility beneath. These ships had not been designed to be sailed alone, at least anywhere hostilities might be likely.

"Liam," Ada broke through my thoughts.

Tabby and I were working through a pre-sail checklist that Roby had built and Ada had approved.

"Go ahead, Ada," I said.

"*Intrepid* is at rest. You are clear for separation," she said. "Stay out of trouble, okay?"

"We'll do our best," I said. "Can you pull the clamps?"

There's always tension between two objects that are joined artificially in zero-g. Without friction to hold against the force caused by these objects, they drift apart almost immediately when freed. I watched through *George's* cockpit as *Intrepid* appeared to fall away from us.

At twenty meters, the traffic was quite a bit easier to consider. I'd spent most of my youth dodging asteroids and making as much trouble as possible with mining sleds. I lit *George's* engines, shoved the throttle stick forward and gently rolled away from the station toward Kushala.

"We're receiving a turret lockdown request from Mannat," Tabby said, accepting the lockdown.

"Copy."

"Jala, any recommendations on how to get to Koosha Central?"

"You should not make such characterizations once we arrive," Jala said, stiffening. "Pogona find centralized government to be offensive."

"Wouldn't that make Nijjar offensive?"

"Nijjar is necessary so that we have bargaining power with other species," Jala said. "It has no capacity to rule tribes. Nijjar itself is a collection of tribal leaders who agree, principally, on how to interact with others."

"My mistake," I said, not particularly interested in getting into why I felt her argument basically defined centralized government. "Do you have a preferred navigation path and do we need to let anyone know we're coming?"

Jala flicked a route to me and I plugged it in. The Koosha tribal region was roughly a hundred thousand square kilometers of mountainous, desert terrain. A small sliver of the territory joined with the massive city, Mannat.

"I would see to the task of announcing our arrival, if this is acceptable," Jala said.

"I think that's best."

As expected, *George* complained raucously upon entry into Kushala's atmosphere. Fortunately, the shaking and bouncing stopped after a few minutes and I leveled out our flight, synchronizing with Jala's navigation plan.

It was hard to miss the city of Mannat, even though we had to land two hundred kilometers northeast of the main population. It was a modern city and packed with millions of people. Skyscrapers reached high into the city and small craft buzzed like swarms of angry insects as they moved from one location to the next.

"What are those?" Tabby asked as two atmospheric vessels approached. We'd just crossed into Koosha territory when they appeared on our sensors. "Get a load of that." She hadn't paused to hear an explanation and instead zoomed in on one of the two.

The vessels that approached were open-air, with minimal air-foils and a single, medium-sized turret mounted on its top deck. A smoking power plant sat dead center on the twelve by four-meter rectangular deck. Waist-high wooden sides with gunnels along the top looked to be the only safety for crew and I shuddered to think what would happen if the ship canted to the side. A crew complement of six hardy sailors all manned different stations.

"We're being hailed, Liam," Tabby said.

"Go ahead," I answered.

"You have entered Koosha tribal district." The voice belonged to a young male. "Turn back or you will be fired upon."

"Would you allow me?" Jala asked.

I looked to Tabby who shrugged. "Sure, all yours."

"Glider rats, you will escort this great ship *George* to the tents of Anghad of Koosha. Our great one knows of my arrival and will place your chests beneath the skeg and drive your drift boards into the cliffs if you do not."

"You should not speak this way," the young male voice replied. Even I could tell he'd lost most of his bluster. "Who is it that would speak for Anghad of Koosha?"

"It is I, Jala, fourth daughter of Anghad, who brings glory and riches to Koosha today."

Chapter 25

EFREET

"Thuga warned that my fourth daughter, who was given to Liam Hoffen by Ameek of Koosha, traveled to me with an angry warrior princess," Anghad said. "Am I to believe this wisp cowed the mighty Thuga?"

The Koosha settlement was like nothing I'd previously experienced. Thousands of wide cloth tents sat beneath bright blue skies that spread across the red sands of a valley resting between two mountains. We were at an elevation several thousand meters above Kushala's seas and the crisp air smelled faintly of pines that grew defiantly in the harsh environment.

The three of us had been escorted from a rocky landing pad by a group of ten beige-robed male Pogona. We'd left Arijeet aboard *George*, not sure what we were getting into. The leader of the group had not greeted us as much as he'd placed an ornately inscribed, curved sword over his heart, bowed and then turned, walking away from the ship. On Jala's urging, we followed, only to be flanked on both sides by his similarly armed men.

Anghad was a lean Pogona with scarred, ruddy brown skin and a chin full of sparkly stones, connected by gold and silver loops. Like his guard, he wore a highly polished, inscribed sword that I had no difficulty believing he knew how to use.

He was more interested in Tabby's exchange with Thuga than he was in meeting a daughter he hadn't seen for a long time and that concerned me.

"A misunderstanding we're willing to chalk up to differences between species." I took a half step in front of Tabby, attempting to deflect unwanted attention.

Anghad refused to look at me and held Tabby's gaze. I dared a glance. Tabby had a closed mouth and a half smile I recognized as anything but friendly. She cocked her head slightly as Anghad pushed a hand in my direction.

"What is she? Warrior or property?" The menace in Anghad's voice was clear and quiet fell across the welcoming party within his tent.

"Frak," I breathed as Anghad's hand came into contact with my shoulder.

"Mate," Tabby said, pulling a bo staff from beneath her robes and bringing it to within a centimeter of Anghad's wrist, without striking. A collective gasp reverberated as the once jovial crowed pulled back in expectation of violence.

It was more than Anghad's guard could take and three of them pulled swords. Rough hands grabbed me, forcing me backwards. A startled squeak warned that Jala had also been grabbed.

Instinctively, I grabbed the hand that had reached over my shoulder and dropped to a knee, rolling forward, throwing the Pogona over my back. A second pair of hands reached for me and I brought my elbow back into the owner's crotch, dropping him to the ground. I rolled away from the chaos toward Jala and flicked my nano-blade to full length, punching the one who held her, but careful not to strike either with the blade. With my free hand, I grabbed Jala's robes, pulled her to me and waved my nano-blade threateningly in a circle, creating a buffer around us.

"Tabbs?" I called, not immediately finding her.

"Just a minute," she replied over tactical comm, trying to sound unconcerned.

A body flew backward from a few meters away. I swished my blade, clearing a path in the direction of the chaos. A clear path opened to Tabby, who was fending off a group of robed guards, her staff a blur of action. She was mostly defending her flank, but occasionally landed a crushing blow, dropping a combatant who was quickly replaced. The main pole of the large tent at her back provided her a small amount of cover.

"Jala, why is he attacking?" I asked, backing her into the circle Tabby had established.

"He is angry at my return," Jala said. "You should not have brought me; I have endangered you. Ameek was wrong. Anghad has no room for forgiveness."

"I can work with that," I grunted, swinging around to meet a large swordsman who charged the two of us. I gave a silent prayer and fended off his sword strike with my forearm and plunged the point of my nano blade into the left side of his hip. My attacker's eyes widened in surprise at my choice of defense. It must have looked suicidal to him, but while he easily sliced through the dress robes from Nuage, my grav-suit hardened, deflecting the blade. I winced as the nano-blade exited, plowing its way free.

"I'm trying not to kill 'em," Tabby said. "There are too many."

"Frak this." I turned and sailed up, driving my blade through the narrowing center post, three meters beneath where it met the thick, tent material. "Lights out, Tabbs."

Where there had been chaos before, there was now pandemonium as the tent's inhabitants realized we were bringing the house down. Struck from behind by a heavy cable, I flailed, trying to adjust my flight. I struck the ground hard, knocking over a few unlucky bodies.

The center post had fallen to the side, but was caught in cabling and material. Above the fray, Tabby lifted off, surprisingly carrying Jala in one arm and blasting her way through the top of the tent with a heavy pistol. That way out was good enough for me and I squirted up behind her. I grunted as I took a stinger in my side from small arms fire. A moment later, we were free of the tent, making all possible haste for *George.*

Seconds are often the difference between success and failure in battle and today was no different. Unfortunately, this time we ended up on the short end of the stick.

When we got close to the ship, we were greeted by several drift-board crafts. The crude vehicles had caused me little concern while inside *George,* since their single guns were no match for our larger vehicle. Grav-suits, however, lacked speed, making us easier targets and I doubted very much we'd live through a lucky turret strike. Three boards raced to our position and fired over our heads, forcing us to the sand.

"Kneel." The command came from a particularly surly Pogona who saw fit to jam the stock of a rifle into my back once he'd pushed us onto the deck of his drift board. A second Pogona clamped mana-cles to our wrists and ankles, effectively holding us in the kneeling position as he sailed back to the tent city.

The drift board came to rest in front of Anghad and a small group of his armed guard.

"Mate, you say," Anghad said. "Are you truly the same species as the humans of Zuri? No human has ever been known to cause such a … I cannot think of a word."

"Ruckus," Tabby offered defiantly, straining against the chains that held us in supplication. The deck buckled where her chains were attached, but didn't break.

Anghad tossed his head back and guffawed, hand on hips. "Such a wonderful word from a spirit of war. Is there a cell that could hold this one? Does she mate like she fights? One such as this cannot be bound. She must be killed or released, to do otherwise would bring ruin."

"We came to you offering a trade," I said. "There is no reason for hostility."

"You destroy my tent and yet talk of trade. You are either clever or stupid. Why would I trade with the one accompanied by my daughter, the thief? Did you think my head would be turned by the efreet in your presence and I would forget of the trespasses of my own blood?"

"I bring you a grandson, Father," Jala said quietly, her head bowed. "Arijeet is of age."

"Do not speak in my presence!" Anghad's hand struck more quickly than I'd have thought possible. His knuckles contacted Jala's chin and snapped her head to the side. She collapsed on the deck in front of him.

A loud crack startled the chieftain causing him to jump back as Tabby pulled one chain free from the deck. Her action was met by the shuffling of weapons by a nervous guard.

"Hold spirit!" Anghad said, regaining his composure. "Weapons down."

Tabby spat at the closet guard, whose gun barrel shook ever so slightly.

"We can work together and profit, Anghad," I said. "Or we can fight each other and both lose great blood. My crew will not leave us on this planet and they will certainly rain down hell on your people if we are hurt."

"Thuga said there was a boy. Is this true?" Anghad asked.

"There are two. Arijeet is on my ship. Meel of Tulvar took the other, Gunjeet."

"You will return the thief to your vessel. Bring my grandson to a feast. We will speak of the ship you seek."

After being released from the shackles, Tabby and I picked the still unconscious Jala up from the deck and carried her back to *George* where we treated her wounds. Arijeet was aloof, seemingly unconcerned for his mother's condition. We ignored him as we worked.

"That was messed up," Tabby said. "He could have killed her."

Jala's eyes fluttered and she murmured. "I am surprised to live."

"He is lucky to be alive," Tabby said. "I thought about ending him when he sicced his goons on us."

"Arijeet, we have a date with your grandfather. Apparently, this trip was all about trading you so your mother could get back into his good graces," I said, standing and walking from the bunk room where Jala lay. "We're throwing fifties."

Tabby choked down a laugh at my pod-ball reference. We'd be giving the kid to Anghad, but there would be no forgiveness.

"I do not fear Koosha."

"Perfect," Tabby said, locking Jala into the bunk room.

I pulled off my Nuage clothing and left it in a pile in the hallway. I was done playing dress up. We were here to trade. I mounted my quick-draw chest holster and lined up a strip of grenade marbles and FBDs along my belt.

"Ready?" I turned to Tabby, ignoring Arijeet.

"You're sexy when you get all riled up," she said. "We should do this more often."

I shook my head. I wouldn't give us fifties at surviving the next two hours yet somehow I was turning her on. In retrospect, her confidence made me feel invincible, if only for the moment.

A single guard stood outside *George* when we disembarked. He pointed down the sandy hill we'd already traveled. In the short time we'd been aboard, a larger cutter had landed next to *George* — no doubt insurance against us leaving early.

The people of Koosha were curious and peeked out to catch a glimpse of the people who'd caused so much trouble. As we came even with them, they would disappear, only to reappear behind us.

"Captain Hoffen and his efreet. You've brought the boy who would be my grandson." Anghad's voice boomed as he welcomed us with a wide smile. He waved at an old woman who rushed up to Arijeet and grabbed his arm. Arijeet pulled it back only to have her roughly grab it again. "Do not resist, boy. If you have my blood, you will have nothing of which to worry."

Arijeet allowed the woman to jab him with a device that she had kept hidden in the folds of her clothing.

"He is born of Anghad."

"Is he of age?"

"He is, Master Koosha," the old woman replied.

"Come to me, my boy. Take your place by my side. You are the first in my line to come of age." Arijeet smiled. It wasn't a surprised smile, but rather more of a conniving smile. "Tell me. I hear that your older brother, Gunjeet was given to Meel of Tulvar by these humans. What would you have me do with them?"

My heart sank. Arijeet was no friend and he'd already ratted us out to Thuga on Pooni.

"My brother died many years ago. So says my mother. So says my father," Arijeet said. He wasn't quite able to wipe the shite-eating grin from his face as he said it. "Captain Hoffen has treated us well and acted with honor. He will confirm the statement of my father, Ameek of Koosha."

The look the boy gave me was clear. He wouldn't throw me to the wolves if I backed up his claim. I still remembered the feel of Gunjeet's knife as it entered my side. I owed him no loyalty.

"What the boy says is true, Anghad," I said. "I witnessed Ameek of Koosha say to the one I believed to be Gunjeet that he was not his son."

"Why did you say otherwise when we met?"

"My tongue stumbles on Pogona names," I said, twisting the truth. "Meel of Tulvar was quite insistent that the one I thought to be Gunjeet belonged to him."

"Let it be settled. Young Arijeet, what would you have us do with your mother, The Thief?"

"Would that you find some capacity for her to earn a humble place at your fire as even a servant," Arijeet said. "She has confided in me that she regrets deeply her trespass."

I looked at Anghad. Surely, he had to know that everything Arijeet had said was rehearsed. It was too well said for a boy of his age.

"Five lashes and it will be as if she had never left. I will not abide my favorite daughter to live in rags any longer. Fetch your mother, The Thief. Redemption will be our entertainment tonight," he said. "Now, let us eat!"

He clapped his hands and dozens of people sprung to life, moving tables, chairs and musical instruments.

I dared a glance at the post I'd cut through with my nano-blade. A temporary cable had been wrapped around timber splints. The fabric sagged, but it looked like a reasonable, temporary fix.

"Your clothing leaves little to the imagination," Anghad turned to Tabby and me as we were seated next to him. "It is a remarkable material that would stop my swordsman's blade so easily."

"I'll tell you a secret, my suit didn't stop the blade entirely." I pulled the sleeve back where a long cut was healing on my arm. "How is your man? We have technology that would aid in repairing his hip."

"I do not believe any Koosha were wounded."

I raised my eyebrows at his obvious lie and was grateful that Tabby either missed or ignored it.

"I understand it is customary for a visitor to bring a gift that shows his respect for those he visits," I said, standing.

"You have brought nothing but Arijeet. I would otherwise see it on your person. But, I accept this gift with gratitude," he replied.

I placed my hand on my chest over my pistol. Guards who had tried to remain inconspicuous, raised their weapons threateningly. Anghad motioned them to back away.

"This gun is made in my home galaxy, which is called Milky Way. The manufacturer of this weapon has been crafting these guns for fifteen centuries." I ejected the clip and pulled the slide, releasing the bullet from the chamber, catching it. "I used this very weapon to kill an adult Kroerak warrior. I have fought with it in a war defending my homeland and against pirates who have attempted to take what is mine. I present this gift to you, Anghad, so that you know how much I would value our friendship."

I seated the clip back into the Ruger pistol and slid it over to the man. Apparently, I'd gotten his attention with the grand gesture and he nodded his head in appreciation. He picked up the weapon and inspected the slide. "Pull this back?" he asked, intuiting its function.

"That's right," I said. "I'll warn you. It's loud and has a kick."

He scrunched his eyes, questioningly. I hadn't seen chemically propelled weapons with Pogona, so I wasn't sure they'd taken the gun powder path in their development. He took aim at the tent's center post and pulled the trigger. There were more than a few surprised screeches at the blast and his arm flew back, as he'd been unprepared for the kick. A sizeable chunk of wood splintered from the post where the bullet struck.

Anghad looked back at me. "A most thoughtful gift, Captain Liam Hoffen. Please accept my apologies for your earlier treatment. There is more to you than I might have expected, traveling in The Thief's company."

"ADA, CALL EVERYONE BACK," I said, lifting off from planet Kushala's surface. "Are we resupplied?"

"Locked and loaded, Liam. I'm placing the recall now. What's going on? Is everything okay?"

"We have intel on that Kroerak ship. Koosha tribe has a ship following at distance. They reported in ten hours ago," I said. "We've got to go!"

"Where is it?"

"I'm transmitting the data now," I said.

Chapter 26

SPRUNG

"Lashes?" Marny asked.

"He called it entertainment," Tabby said. "I'll give it to Jala, she didn't cry out until the third one broke open her skin. It was horrible. I'm saving a bullet for Anghad of Koosha."

"You don't mean that," I said. "Jala asked for the lashing. She wanted to come home."

"You're an idiot," Tabby retorted. "Jala is his daughter and he whipped her so hard we could see muscle. Nobody wants that, even if she agreed to it. He's a monster."

"Ada, can you get any more speed out of *Intrepid?*" I asked. We'd argued about this too many times already.

"No. Dragging *George* on our belly isn't helping, either," she said.

"Cut it loose," I said. "We can come back for it. If Koosha tribe comes through, we'll be handing it over anyway. Might as well leave it in the Tanwar system."

"If we cut acceleration, I could put it on a vector no one would ever guess," Roby said. "We're far enough away from Kushala no sensor could pick it out of the dark."

"Do it," I said. "This might be our only chance to find Jonathan."

"And Sendrei," Tabby said.

At the mention of Sendrei's name, a shot of adrenaline soured my stomach.

Twenty minutes later, Ada cut the engines. Roby and Sempre scrambled to release *George* and give her a nudge in the right direction after shutting down all systems. She was nothing more than one more tiny piece of junk in a vast sea of black.

Without *George*, *Intrepid* accelerated even more quickly and in four days we arrived at the wormhole leading to Adit Pah.

"Three ships, Cap," Marny said. "Ten thousand kilometers. I don't think they've seen us yet."

I'd already called for general quarters, although with the dwindling crew it wasn't necessary - everyone knew the drill.

On my holo display, three larger sloops sailing in formation arced gently around the wormhole at fifty kilometers. It was a good distance. If something too big came through, they could easily run off. Anything smaller wouldn't have a chance to spool up and run before the pirates would be on them.

I ran the different options through my mind. They hadn't seen us, or if they had, they weren't letting on. We'd dropped hard burn at fifty thousand kilometers and still needed to burn off speed to zero out with the gate, but we'd had enough problems that I wasn't about to give away both our approach and the advantage of speed.

"How many seconds of burn do we need to enter the gate?" I asked.

"Twenty-three," Ada answered.

"Marny, can you predict when they'll have visibility on the unmasked portions of the hull?"

"Aye, Cap, eight degrees, should put us right about there." She flicked a ghost image of *Intrepid* onto the forward holo.

"Ada, what's that do to your twenty-three seconds if we start burn at that point?"

"We'll overshoot two hundred kilometers," she said. The AI picked up on the conversation and showed a third *Intrepid* overshooting the gate.

"*Run simulations, show best point to reengage burn,*" I ordered. A moment later, the ghost versions were cleared and a single, ghostly *Intrepid's* engines kicked on, stopping just past the wormhole.

"Got it, Liam," Ada said.

We watched the three sloops lazily patrol as we continued gliding toward the wormhole in silence.

"I don't understand why Nijjar government doesn't do something about these pirates," Ada said. "Or Abasi, for that matter. They'd have more trade. There's no benefit to society in allowing them to continue to operate."

"There's only one recognized population in Adit Pah," Marny said, "and none past it. According to everything I can find, we're on our own out here. There is no law."

"Nijjar isn't a government," I added. "It's a loose collective. If you think about it, that's what the Confederation of Planets is — just trade agreements and treaties. Members share information, but don't have centralized enforcement."

"Other than Strix," Tabby said. "Don't forget those asshats."

"Strix involvement seems erratic," I said. "They just take advantage of the chaos."

"All hands, hard burn in ten," Ada announced, cutting through our nervous chatter.

For almost five seconds after *Intrepid's* engines fired, the unidentified sloops continued their lazy flight, seemingly unperturbed. It made sense, they'd be expecting sensors to catch incoming ships much further out or emerging from the wormhole, not arriving at speed almost on top of them.

"It's going to be tight," Ada said.

The three ships streaked toward our future position, knowing full well our destination.

"We're taking fire," Marny said, mostly unnecessarily as we could all see a stream of blaster fire stitching through the space between us. "Armor is holding, Cap. Return fire?"

"Negative," I said. "We're not going to be here that long."

I glanced nervously at the countdown timer. We were a long fifteen seconds from entering the wormhole.

A red indicator blinked on the starboard hull. A lucky shot had peeled back an armor plate and ruptured the skin. The familiar sound of instant decompression rattled through the ship. Quicker than I could respond, Jester Ripples closed off the affected section.

"Five seconds," Ada said.

Our speed was such that we were becoming an easier target for the sloops.

"Cap, returning fire," Marny said. *Intrepid's* guns burst to life, catching one of the sloops that had been emboldened by our lack of fire by surprise. The damage, while not fatal, caused an explosion, followed by a significant plume of gasses that dissipated almost immediately. "We holed her!"

"All hands, transitioning now," Ada reported.

My stomach lurched and for a moment, I fought for clarity as the star field on the forward display shifted to our new position.

"Multiple contacts," Marny warned.

"All hands, combat burn," Ada announced.

We all twisted to the side as *Intrepid's* engines whined with exertion, trying to dig us out of the hole we'd entered by coming to a complete stop at the wormhole. While it's true that speed is relative and there's no such thing as truly being stopped. It's mostly an academic conversation when you find yourself with zero difference in acceleration, sitting in the midst of twenty hostile ships.

"It's Genteresk," Tabby announced. "That's Belvakuski's light cruiser, *Sangilak.*"

"Marny, find us a hole," I said.

Belvakuski's ship was long and narrow, much like *Intrepid,* though its mass was easily seven or eight times greater. Her design was all warship. Heavy triple barrel turrets looked like they belonged on old battleships from Earth's ancient oceanic navy. *Sangilak* was well out of *Intrepid's* league and it occurred to me she could fight up a weight class or two. No wonder Belvakuski was so revered.

"Brace, brace, brace," Marny repeated. A moment later, *Intrepid* shook as something struck forward and port. A klaxon warned of a depressurization. We were still good, so I pushed it from my mind.

"That was *Sangilak's* main gun," Marny said. "Ada, we can't take too many of those."

I strained to make out the battlefield as Ada turned hard twenty degrees and accelerated directly toward a thirty-meter cutter. Rockets streaked from *Intrepid* just as a second explosion rocked our aft section.

"Roby, how's that armor holding?"

"Those are heavy hits," he said. "We're holding, but engine three has taken damage. I need to shut it down."

"Not a good time for that," Ada said, tension evident in her voice. She tipped her control yolk down and the shoulder straps bit into my skin.

"Oofa," Roby transmitted. "Frak, I'm not tied in very well down here. We're burning through the plating. We have to shut her down."

"Hold tight. We're in a bit of a pickle," I said.

Intrepid's guns found no shortage of targets and I watched in awe as *Ada* wove her way through the confused fleet. There was method in her mad flight as she was deftly keeping ships between *Sangilak* and *Intrepid*.

"Making a break," Ada said. "I need everything you have, Roby."

An explosion rocked *Intrepid* and once again I felt the telltale thump of atmosphere venting and hatches slamming down, sealing us off.

"Forward hold breached," Tabby announced.

"You're going to blow that engine," Roby complained. "She's about to blow the mid-coupling. It'll be like a bomb if she does."

"Get out of there, Roby," I said. "Do it, Ada."

I watched the holo as Ada took her opportunity, freeing *Intrepid* from the Genteresk swarm. A few smaller ships gave chase, lighting up our aft armor, but after several shots from our heavy tail cannons, they gave up the chase.

Ada rode the engines hard for several minutes and finally, we were rocked by a final explosion as engine three's status changed from red to black. Inoperable.

"Roby? Can you get her back online?" I asked.

JAMIE MCFARLANE

"There's a fire," he said. "I'm trying to staunch fuel flow, but it broke the line."

I pulled up the systems displays and my heart sank. Engine three's explosion had ruptured the main fuel line. We were hemorrhaging fuel. "Go dark, Ada." I jumped from my seat and raced off the bridge.

"Liam, are you crazy?" Ada asked. "They have a line on us. We're not far enough away."

"Get creative." I leaned over and careened through the hallway with my grav-suit keeping me aloft. "We're dumping fuel like it's on sale."

I slammed into the aft bulkhead as *Intrepid*'s engines cut off. Only slightly dazed, I recovered and pulled open the hatch to the upper engine room which joined engines three and four. The walls were black with soot and I found Roby crumpled at the bottom of a ramp. He'd stayed too long and gotten caught in the explosion. I checked bio signs. He was up, but unconscious.

It was a hard decision. He desperately needed medical attention, but if I didn't staunch the fuel loss, we'd all soon need more than that. I pulled him so he lay straight on the deck and raced up to the main portion of the room.

My ears popped as I cleared a pressure barrier at the top of the ramp. My heart nearly stopped. The engine room was open to space. Worse yet, engine three wasn't just irreparable, it was gone, only the thick strut that held it to the ship and two meters of housing remained.

"*Locate fuel line*," I instructed my AI.

A blinking outline drew my attention.

"Liam, they're catching up," Ada warned. "I need engines."

"Buy me some time." I rummaged through a cabinet, grabbing an armor repair kit and a cutting/welding rig.

"You have thirty seconds before the first ship is here," she said.

I rolled my eyes. It would take me half that time just to get to the problem area. "Do what you have to, but no engines until you get word."

Any movement from the ship would drop me into space. My grav-suit was good, but I couldn't come close to staying up with even an injured ship.

I wasn't looking for a great patch; I just needed to stop our precious fuel from dumping into space. The hole was ragged and the patch material I'd brought along was too small. I stitched the panel in place and rushed back to the engine bay to search for more patch material. The explosion had caused chaos, but my AI was more than capable of keeping up with my needs and outlined the dislodged items.

"Taking fire," Ada said. "We're a sitting duck, Liam."

"Copy," I grunted.

Bright flashes were all I could make out as one or more of the faster Genteresk fleet arrived on our position. I pushed it out of my head and tacked more pieces over the breach, weighing my need to do a solid job against the amount of time we were giving the pursuing fleet.

"Atmosphere lost in main hallway," Ada announced. "They're making strafing runs."

I dropped the welding rig and leaned back toward the ship. "Ada, go in three seconds."

I was tossed into the aft bulkhead of the engine room as *Intrepid* roared to life. The inertial system wasn't operating well and I slid toward the rent in *Intrepid's* hull. Scrabbling around, I grabbed for any handhold I could find. Engine three's explosion had caused the hull plating to be forced into the engine room and I was fortunate to catch myself on the jagged remains. For some reason, however, fortunate wasn't the first word that popped to mind.

Ada leveled out flight and I strained to move, knowing that at any moment, she could juke and I'd be dropped into space if I wasn't careful. I took a gamble and jumped across the opening, finding good handholds forward. The risk was rewarded in that I now found myself within *Intrepid's* functional gravity field.

I looked up and to the right, my eyes dwelled momentarily on an amber medical status display for Roby. I blinked, activating the display. He was still unconscious and bleeding internally. The explosion had concussed his body and his brain was swelling. He needed medical attention immediately.

I glanced at the hatch that would bring me into the hallway leading down to *Intrepid's* main deck. My HUD overlaid the hatch with a pressure warning. Roby sat within a well of atmosphere created by the pressure barrier above and the hatch at the bottom of the short ramp.

I looked up to the right again. Combat status was also amber. I dwelled and blinked. The AI showed that we were two kilometers from our nearest enemy and were separating at thirty meters per second.

Roby's helmet had not deployed correctly as he'd neglected to raise it when we entered combat. I'd have a talk later with him about that. He was lucky to have found one of the few, pressurized locations within *Intrepid*. I worked his helmet back on and watched in satisfaction as it sealed over his face. The kid could be a pain in the ass, but despite his often goofy social behavior, he was good in a pinch and had a heart the size of Mars beating inside that chest.

I half carried, half dragged him to our medical bay, which was the second best armored section of the ship after the bridge. I struggled to lift Roby's body onto a table after I depressurized and repressurized the entryway. While under combat burn, the gravity in the ship was turned up to 2.0g to help balance the inertial systems. Lifting Roby was like lifting a hundred-fifty-kilogram man onto the table. After securing him with straps, I placed a med scanner on his forehead and started applying appropriate patches.

Getting back to the bridge wasn't going to be possible as we'd lost pressure in the main hallway. We'd been holed in three places: the engine room which couldn't be fixed immediately, the bilge compartment that Jester Ripples had sealed off and a third, port side. It was this third that rendered *Intrepid* unable to hold atmo, so I loped around, happy to be free of Roby's additional weight.

The scoring on the inside bulkhead of the port passageway was immediately obvious. Opposite the scoring, a head sized, oval tear was open to space. *Intrepid* was equipped with vac-stop canisters in both hallways and with the AI's help, I located the nearest one, aimed the nozzle at the edge of the opening and depressed the trigger. Foam that expanded in vacuum and would stick to anything shot out and adhered to the edge. It set almost instantly, was as hard as cement, and required a special chemical agent to remove it once a more permanent patch was in place.

With atmosphere building back in the passageway, I checked the inside bulkhead. In the center of the carbonized finish, I found a second hole, very similar to the first. It was the wall into Ada's bunk. I overrode security and slid her hatch open. It was as if a bomb had gone off. The forward and aft bulkheads had been blown out by shrapnel. A sphere twice the size of my fist was embedded in the interior wall, which I knew to be the bridge.

I breathed out and placed my hands on my knees. Somehow the armor around the bridge had stopped what the armor around the ship had not. I could not imagine what damage might have been done if the projectile had also made it through the bridge armor.

"Liam, you're being hailed," Ada called.

"*Accept,*" I said. "Calling to gloat, Belvakuski? That's not really your style, is it?"

"Greetings, my old friend," Belvakuski said. "You are wily, like the furry peraflop from my home world. How did you like your first taste of my iron?"

"Nothing a little foam and some imaginative welding won't fix up," I said.

"It truly would be a shame to destroy such a fine specimen as yourself. Your witty lies alone are worth five of my best," Belvakuski chortled. "I find your ability to evade me both maddening and stimulating. You should give up this madness and join my fleet. I would make room for you as my number two."

"I'm going to have to say no, just now," I said. "Better luck next time?"

"Until next time, dear boy. I suspect it will be sooner than you expect."

"THAT WAS TOO EASY," Marny said. We'd successfully separated from Belvakuski's fleet and had restored pressure to most of the ship. I glanced over to see Marny reviewing the combat data-streams from our last encounter. "Twenty ships? Even accounting for Ada's skills and *Intrepid's* agility, she let us go."

"Are you sure?"

"Look at these." Marny highlighted four sloop class vessels, each of which had clear shots on *Intrepid* as we worked our way free of Belvakuski's fleet.

"She's softening us up," Tabby said. "Extending the hunt."

"I'll take whatever we can get," I said. "I'm just glad Roby made it." Roby was recovering in the medical bay and we'd repaired much of the damage to *Intrepid* - if only temporarily.

"Time to make the call," I said.

We were forty hours into a class-D burn that would take us to the position Jester Ripples had uncovered in the picture I'd obtained from Thuga. I'd agreed to wait until this appointed time to attempt contact with the Koosha scout ship I hoped was still in Adit Pah.

"You are understood, *Intrepid*." A slender, hard-faced Pogona appeared on the vid screen.

"Are you still tracking the Kroerak vessel?"

"I am transmitting our location to you now," he said. "Provide time estimate on your arrival."

"Ada?"

"Thirty-six hours."

I relayed the information.

"We look forward to taking possession of the ship you refer to as *George*."

THIRTY-SIX HOURS WAS NOT enough time with the amount of damage *Intrepid* had taken, but with staggered shifts, we kept up a constant repair effort. Roby had spent the minimum time in the tank - twelve hours – before we had him up and assisting with the repairs.

We were as ready as we were ever going to get.

"Have you given any thought to what we're going to do once we find the Kroerak? I think it's a safe bet the Kroerak have destroyed every ship that's approached it," Tabby said.

"You mean, other than this Koosha scout," Ada said.

The coordinates provided were in orbit above Deshi, a solo moon above Kameldeep, one of Adit Pah's uninhabited worlds. The moon was a barren rock and the planet a mix of beautiful browns, oranges and reds along with a murky green ocean that covered over half the surface. According to the latest surveys, Kameldeep's surface, while a reasonable mix of oxygen and nitrogen, was unstable and given to frequent volcanic eruptions.

"Cap, something feels off," Marny said.

"I know. I feel it too," I said.

The Koosha scout ship was puttering along, holding tight to the moon.

"*Intrepid* to Koosha scout ship," I kicked up communications again.

"You are understood, *Intrepid*." It was the same Pogona who'd answered my previous call.

"This is when you show me where the Kroerak ship is," I said.

Almost immediately a location on the planet's surface was transmitted. *Intrepid's* sensors weren't sufficient to penetrate most atmospheres, but Kameldeep's was thin enough that we had no trouble locating the Kroerak ship's signature.

"What's it doing down there?" I asked.

"Uninteresting," the Pogona replied. "You will transmit codes and location for ship named *George*."

I transmitted the codes.

"What is that?" Tabby asked, pointing at the moon's horizon.

"Liam, we have multiple contacts," Ada said.

"It's Belvakuski's fleet," Marny added. "Koosha sold us out."

Chapter 27

ENEMY OF MY ENEMY

Koosha's scout ship fired its engines and zipped away from our location as if someone had lit its tail on fire.

"Put that ship down," I ordered.

"Aye, aye, Cap."

Three turrets locked on the small cutter and it exploded moments later. I might regret the decision later, but I wasn't about to have that ship join Belvakuski's fleet in the chaos that was headed our way.

"We're being hailed," Ada announced.

"Ada, give us some distance," I said.

Belvakuski's fleet had been waiting on the opposite side of the moon, hidden from our sensors as we approached.

We couldn't hope to outrun the entire fleet with only three engines, but we could use the moon to cut down on the number of ships we had to engage at any one time. One thing I knew for sure was *Intrepid* couldn't stand toe-to-toe with *Sangilak* for more than a few moments.

"We're taking fire," Marny said, her voice tight.

"What? Where?" We were two thousand kilometers from the main fleet.

The outline of three stealthed ships popped into view on the holo projector. Explosions rocked *Intrepid* as together they loosed a fusillade of blaster fire and missiles.

"That's Munay's sloop, *Gaylon Brighton!*" Tabby exclaimed just as the AI flagged it.

"Return fire!"

My order wasn't particularly necessary as Marny, Tabby and Sempre were already firing *Intrepid's* blasters. Our fire was defensive — Marny was trying to give Ada time to put distance between *Intrepid* and the three stealth ships.

I forced my mind away from the momentary details of the fight. We wouldn't survive on short-term, tactical decisions. We needed a strategy that would work for more than the moment. Belvakuski had split her fleet and approached from two sides. The sloops were positioned to prevent us from escaping into the deep dark, something our stealth armor would certainly allow if we could put enough distance between us and our enemies. Her plan was solid, but no plan was foolproof.

"They're targeting engines," Marny said. "Rockets away."

The rockets forced the Navy sloops to break off their attack and a seam opened in the battlefield. I'd have preferred that it led out to safety. All the same, it was an opportunity of which we had to take advantage. There was no possibility of us standing against this fleet.

"Burn for Kameldeep!" I said.

Ada guided *Intrepid* into the gap created by Marny's rockets, even though she questioned the sanity of the decision. "Liam, they'll trap us against the planet."

"Engine two is offline," Roby called from the engine room, the sounds of explosions carrying through his comm channel. "We can't take much more of this!"

Intrepid turned hard as we returned fire on the sloops that still had the drop on us.

"Bitch!" Tabby exclaimed from the gunner's nest just as one of the ships accompanying *Gaylon Brighton* exploded.

"*Accept hail.*"

"Stop firing and you'll live," Belvakuski said. "You're outnumbered and you will not outrun my shiny new human Navy ships."

"Marny, cease fire," I said.

"Don't do it, Liam," Tabby said. "She'll never let us live."

I felt the weight of the universe on my shoulders once again. We might survive the Navy sloops, but Belvakuski would eventually run us down. The pounding we were taking ceased as we stopped firing.

"What have you done with Munay and the crews of those ships?" I asked.

"Always the hero," Belvakuski said. "Are you not worried about your immediate future?"

"Tell me, Belvakuski," I said.

"The human soldiers were a most resistant lot," she answered. "We found they were not suitable for lives as slaves."

"You killed them?"

"To be honest, I'm not sure as to their fates. Turn over your ship and we will negotiate. I could perhaps find those that remain. It will be expensive, however," she said. "As will the lives of those aboard *Intrepid*."

The two remaining Mars Protectorate sloops moved to flank us.

I muted comms. "Marny, can you take both those ships out?"

"Tough call, Cap."

"On my word, put everything we have into it," I said.

"What do we have to trade if we give up *Intrepid*?" I asked, unmuting.

"There is no *if*, Liam Hoffen," Belvakuski said. "You have been surprisingly adept at escaping my net, but your single-minded pursuit of the wounded Kroerak ship exposed a weakness."

"You've gone to a lot of trouble to chase me down, Belvakuski. Is *Intrepid* really worth all this?" I asked.

"You peck at me like a Farmogan worm on a Begod. My very reputation is at stake," she answered. "Without reputation, we are nothing."

"You will come out of this with less than you started, Belvakuski," I said. "Marny, do it!"

Rockets streamed from *Intrepid's* launch tubes and her turrets sprang to life. I watched as the weapons batteries drained and rocket inventory bottomed out. The first rockets missed their targets, as the ship captains had been wise enough to anticipate our actions. Marny however, was smarter, anticipating their evasions and poured fire into their paths. *Gaylon Brighton* was sent broken and tumbling through space just as the third Naval sloop peeled off, running hard for safety beyond our guns.

"Spunky to the last," Belvakuski said. "I will have you and your ship, Liam Hoffen. Your fighting against me only makes you more desirable."

I cut comms between us.

"That's not creepy," Tabby said.

"Roby, do we have enough power to land on the surface of Kameldeep?"

"Landing is one thing, Captain," Roby answered. "Taking off again might be something entirely different. I don't think we should do it."

"What are you thinking, Cap?" Marny asked. "We'll be trapped on the surface. From a fleet that size, we can only expect to hide for a matter of hours, at best."

"I'm taking *Intrepid* off the table and giving us some breathing room. She can't take what she can't reach."

"Liam Hoffen, the average surface temperature of Kameldeep is seventy-one degrees. It is also geologically unstable," Jester Ripples said. "Long term survival is unlikely."

"Sounds like a bargain," I said. "We won't survive more than an hour if we stay up here. Ada, take us down, fast as you can."

"Won't they just come get us?" Tabby asked.

"I'd be more concerned with them knocking us down before we land," Ada said. "Everybody strap in. This isn't going to be pretty."

A blinking light on my HUD showed that Belvakuski was trying to re-establish comms. I ignored her and gestured at the virtual display of Kameldeep on the holo, pulling it to me for inspection. The planet was twice the size of Mars and not suitable for habitation, even though it had a mostly breathable atmosphere.

"Give me a location to shoot at Liam," Ada said.

"Working on it."

Intrepid shook and I looked up, hoping a fourth stealthed ship hadn't appeared. Instead, I realized we'd already entered Kameldeep's upper atmosphere.

"Put down there."

The location I tossed to Ada was three kilometers from where the Kroerak cruiser had set down. I hoped we were outside the range of the cruiser's devastating weapons.

"That will put us right on top of the bugs," Ada said, "Don't we have enough problems?"

"That cruiser will provide cover," I said. "Any of Belvakuski's ships that fly over will get a quick lesson in Kroerak etiquette."

"Cap, there are limits to that 'enemy of my enemy' saying. I like where your head's at, but I'd like a bit more room between us and those bugs," Marny said.

I pulled the terrain map closer and expanded my search to a twenty-five-kilometer radius around the Kroerak ship. The next best location was on the opposite side of a mountain ridge. We'd be fifteen kilometers away and lose some of the cover the Kroerak ship would provide. The slope, however, would allow Ada to orient our heavy aft cannons skyward and provide some amount of protection.

"Check that," I said, my voice quavering due to our descent through Kameldeep's thin atmosphere.

"Got it, Liam," Ada said.

I pulled out Anino's crystal and plugged it into the transmitter. If this was to be our last moments, I would at least share what we knew about the Kroerak, not to mention, Genteresk and Koosha tribes.

"Anino, come in," I called, once I had it plugged in.

"Did you find the ship?" Anino replied immediately. He must have been waiting for my call.

"It's on the surface of a planet called Kameldeep. Genteresk set a trap for us and *Intrepid* is badly damaged. *Gaylon Brighton* is here. Belvakuski has taken it and two other Navy stealth sloops. We destroyed one of them," I said.

"That's a lot to take in. Where are you now? Are you secure?"

"Safe for the moment," I said. "We've been forced to set down on Kameldeep. They've taken out two of our engines."

"How? That ship can outrun anything," Anino said.

"It appears Koosha ratted us out," I said. "They were waiting for us at the Adit Pah gate. Sangilak landed an eighty-millimeter cannon hit and took out engine one. We escaped, only to have the Navy stealth ships jump us. They took out a second engine. We're not in good shape."

"You can't escape Kameldeep gravity, can you?" he asked.

"Not without repairs."

"Surface of that planet is unstable. You need to get out of there as quickly as possible."

"Got it, Anino," I said, annoyed. "Why would the Kroerak set down on Kameldeep?"

"Energy. Magma is loaded with it. They probably set down over a vent," he said. "Those Kroerak were probably left behind after the war because they were damaged. You flushed them out. My guess is they won't stay long. Not with all this activity."

"I'll have Jester Ripples send as much data as we can," I said.

"Be safe, Hoffen."

"That ship sailed a long time ago, Anino," I said. "In no small part due to you."

"I'll apologize if it'll make you feel better."

I pulled the crystal from the cradle handed it to Jester Ripples. "Would you work with Anino and send him whatever he wants?"

"Yes, Liam Hoffen," Jester Ripples said. The colorful lids around his eyes were pulled back — the furry, little alien was terrified. For a moment, I wondered if all this was worthwhile. If we'd just left things alone, how much more peace could we have had?

"Thanks." I rubbed between his eyes, smoothing his fur. The effect was immediate as his brow eased.

I sat back in the captain's chair and looked out through the forward video display. The surface of Kameldeep rushed up to greet us as we dropped into a steamy cloud nestled against the mountains. I'd seen the pocket of vapor when I'd chosen a landing spot half a kilometer north. At the last moment, however, Ada adjusted and set us into the middle of the cloudy gas.

"Vapor won't provide much block against their sensors," Ada said. "But it's at least something."

"You're brilliant, Ada. Shut down all non-essential systems," I said. "Belvakuski wasn't close enough to track us all the way to the surface. Between the vapor and our stealth armor, she'll have to look long and hard."

We were all jostled as *Intrepid* came to rest against the mountain-side at a thirty-five-degree angle. Without the gravity system, we wouldn't have been able to stand. As it was, the incline felt perfectly natural.

"Roby, can you fix that engine?" I asked.

"I need to get outside," he said. "It's really buggered up."

"We need to secure the LZ, Cap," Marny said.

"We might be here a while, Roby," I said. "Do what you can from inside."

"What's LZ?" he asked.

"Landing zone," I said. "We'll get you a trip outside soon enough. Jester Ripples could you head aft and help Roby?"

"I do not like Kameldeep." Jester Ripples jumped from his seat and bounded through the bridge hatch, nearly colliding with Tabby.

She was focused on our position. "We're blind. We need to drop a sensor package on the ridge. Time to break out the Popeyes."

"Ada, the ship is yours," I said, jogging after Tabby's retreating form.

"Never a doubt in my mind." Ada's voice drifted through as the bridge door closed behind me.

"Marny sent a pattern up to the replicator," Tabby said. "It'll take twenty minutes to complete, though."

"That's about how much time we have before the Genteresk will arrive if they're coming," I said.

"You think they tracked us?"

"Hope not."

I hinged open the crate's lid and placed my hand on the Popeye's chest cavity, causing it to open. It reminded me of the first time we'd uncovered a mech suit in the warehouse on the Red Houzi base, only this time, the suit was as familiar to me as an ore sled. I sat in the suit, shimmying my legs into position. Lying back, it closed around me, holding me firmly in place.

Running a quick systems check, I verified the multipurpose tool was strapped on my shin and thrust my hands down. With just the right amount of force, this maneuver would pop an experienced operator into a standing position. I'd failed enough times in the past that I was careful not to over rotate.

Tabby was only a moment behind so I punched in the code that would open the hold. At three and a half meters tall, the Popeye was too big to fit in most places within *Intrepid,* including the airlock. The size of the cargo hold door, however, was more than sufficient. We were on low power use, so couldn't fire up the pressure barrier. As a result, clean ship air exited and steamy, nitrogen-rich Kameldeep air quickly swirled through the hold. I felt wasteful, but there wasn't much to be done about it.

My suit read the external temperature at seventy-nine degrees. Twenty degrees warmer and liquid water would turn to gas. The Popeye didn't seem to mind, although I wasn't sure if the sweat on my brow was due to nerves or if the suit's air chiller wasn't keeping up. One thing was clear, normal vac-suits would struggle with the Kameldeep environment.

I jumped onto the rocky soil. The planet's gravity was .6g and I felt right at home as my boot sank four centimeters into the powdery ground. I kicked up a small cloud as I moved.

"Ash from the volcanos," Tabby said, watching the cloud settle.

"Should show tracks if anything's been through here," I said.

"Look there." Tabby pointed at a ten-centimeter track crossing beneath where *Intrepid* had landed. The track was a series of thin, crossing lines.

I pointed to where a six-legged bug resembling a spider skittered across the surface of the ash. "Wouldn't have expected any life at all."

"Spiders," Tabby said. "Frak. Why is it always spiders?"

As we climbed along the slope of the ridge, the ash lessened. We were careful not to step too far from the gas cloud, preferring instead to patrol the edges, popping out for a few moments at a time to gather sensory data and step back in. Aside from spiders, Kameldeep was spooky in its silence. Most notably, even after forty minutes, we caught no sign of a Genteresk ship.

"You think we're clear?" Tabby asked.

"For as long as we want to stay holed up, I imagine," I said. "Belvakuski doesn't have to run us down, she just has to wait. That's something those pirates have to be good at. Can you imagine how much time they burn sitting at wormhole gates, waiting for hapless ships that can't defend themselves? I think waiting is part of being Genteresk."

"Seems a waste to me," Tabby said, knocking on the airlock door that sat next to the forward hold.

Marny opened the door and looked out at us.

"Heya kids, anything interesting?" she asked, just making conversation. She'd had access to our feeds the entire time we'd been patrolling.

"Frakking spiders," Tabby said.

Marny nodded sagely. "Remind me to tell you the story of the green wooly dingo spiders we ran into in the Amazon. Venom would numb you. If they got you when you were sleeping, they'd have you wrapped up in silk, unable to move by morning."

"Not helping," Tabby complained.

"Put these at least two kilometers apart." Marny handed me three cylindrical devices, each two meters tall and four centimeters in diameter. "Plunger on top activates them. They need line of sight on *Intrepid*. I've marked locations, but anywhere near my spots will work."

"Tell Roby he's clear to work outside," I said. "You'll need to watch his bios though. His vac-suit won't hold up long in this heat. I'll help when I come back."

"Aye, Cap," Marny said.

Tabby and I set off down the mountain. We'd plant the easiest sensor first. Outside of the gas cloud, it would provide a good view of the sky. We exited the cloud and trudged across the planet's surface, kicking up small plumes of dust as we moved. I didn't like being exposed, although I knew we were just tiny specs moving across a vast planet.

We paused, waiting for confirmation of the sensor's contact with *Intrepid*. A dull green throb of light pulsed in acknowledgement. Still I waited. I wanted to know if we'd been followed into the atmosphere and if a fast-attack craft or cutter waited just out of my suit's passive-sensor range, waiting to pounce on us.

As so often occurs, there was no immediate feedback beyond a higher resolution map of the surrounding area. The sensor had no difficulty penetrating the vapor cloud at eight hundred meters and suddenly, *Intrepid* sprang to life with an overlay on the HUD.

"Next?" Tabby asked, spurring me onward.

We placed the second sensor on the opposite side of the ridge. It would give us visibility of the valley where the Kroerak ship sat. Tabby and I stood stock still on the Kroerak side of the ridge but below the top of the hill, so we wouldn't stand out as we waited for the sensor to activate. I didn't need the sensor to tell me there was movement in the valley below. Initially, I thought the bugs were congregating, my mind jumping to thoughts of a coordinated attack.

"What are they doing?" I quietly asked over comms."

"Looks like they've been mining," Tabby said. "That's a tailings pile." She roughly drew a circle around a feature I hadn't yet noticed.

The sensor came online and the details of terrain around the Kroerak ship snapped into focus.

"Jupiter piss, that's a hatchery," Long furrows had been dug out of the ground and hundreds of meter-tall eggs sat proudly atop perfectly constructed pedestals.

"It's not the only one," Tabby said, pointing to a second hatchery, identical to the first in all but one important detail: the shells were empty, their walls cracked, lying on the ground. "What's the incubation period?"

"One month," I said. "Someone's building an army."

Chapter 28

OUT OF THE FRYING PAN

"Down, down!" Tabby leaned against a jagged, volcanic rock formation, where she stood in shadow.

I was wide open, having just placed the final sensor high on the mountain's ridge. If something was looking for us, there were two things that would give us away: a silhouette standing above everything else and movement. I was too far away to join Tabby so I jumped off the ridge onto what I thought was a hard-packed slope. I was wrong. As soon as my boots touched the first rock, I started a chain reaction that ended in a landslide. Dust billowed up as I slid with the scree and scrabbled for purchase. Unable to arrest my movement, I lit my arc-jets and moved to the side, down the slope, finally finding cover.

"Subtle," Tabby quipped, once the majority of the landslide had stilled.

"What'd you see?" I asked, zooming out my sensor display.

Fifty kilometers to the southwest, a small ship approached at three hundred meters per second. It could be no coincidence that it was headed directly at us.

"Ada, we might have company soon," I called over the tactical channel.

"Copy, Liam. We're tracking it," Ada replied. With the final passive sensor in place, *Intrepid* had a better view than we did. "It appears they caught your tumble and adjusted their original course. There's a second ship breaking orbit. You need to hurry."

"Negative, Ada," I said. "*Intrepid* isn't exposed. It's just me. I'm going to lead them off."

"Cap," Marny cut in. "Don't do it. First ship will be on you in three minutes. You need to get back here to cover."

I jumped from my hiding place and landed on the scree slope that led into the valley where the Kroerak ship sat some ten kilometers away. At max speed, I could reach the cruiser in a little over six minutes.

"Tabby, stay put," I said. "I'm going to lead them to the Kroerak. Once we're clear, you head back to the ship."

"Frak that," she said.

Running down a scree slope in .6g with a Popeye turns out to be not that big of a deal. The Popeye's AI adjusts to all types of terrain and takes most of the work out of staying upright. On my tactical display, I chinned up a visual of the approaching craft. Fifteen meters long with swept-back wings, it looked like a big steel bird, hungry to snatch me up in its talons.

"Tabbs, what happened to running the play?" I asked. She'd broken cover and was slowly catching up with me.

"Isn't a game, Love," she said. "And you're crazy. What part of running at the giant ship filled with angry, people-eating bugs makes sense to you?"

"We need time to repair *Intrepid*," I said. "What's another option?"

"Company," Tabby announced.

A stream of adolescent and hatchling Kroerak poured from beneath the grounded cruiser and made their way directly at us. Any other time, I might not be that concerned, but with two enemy ships coming our way, we couldn't afford to be slowed down.

"First ship will be on us in sixty seconds," Tabby said.

I slid to a stop and switched my weapon to fully automatic. "Defensive position, Tabbs," Taking a knee for stability, I lined up on the vessel's path and started firing. In the thin atmosphere of Kameldeep, our weapons easily had the necessary range to reach it. Unfortunately, what was good for us, was also good for our enemy. We fired for no more than five seconds when a tell-tale on my HUD warned of an incoming missile.

"Incoming!" Tabby exclaimed before I could.

The two of us leapt from our positions, fueled by adrenaline, gravity and arc-jets. We made it roughly ten meters before the explosive blast of whatever ordnance had been shot at us sent us tumbling ass-over-teakettle to the bottom of the hill.

Tabby recovered more quickly than I did and fired a few rounds at the ship as it banked hard, obviously looking for a second run at us.

"How many rocks you think that guy has?" I asked.

"Carrying three more, Cap." Marny's answer surprised me. It was easy to believe we were on our own out here, but as long as we were within line-of-sight of the sensors, *Intrepid's* crew had a front-row seat.

"Can you get a damage report?"

"On the ship? Negative, Cap. We're not tracking any damage to the enemy," she said.

The tactical AI predicted the arrival of the first wave of hatchlings and adolescents in forty-five seconds. Belvakuski's scout would be around on us in half that.

"Stand and deliver," I ordered in a desperate move. Once the wave of bugs crested on us, we'd lose most of our mobility and the flying vessel would have no difficulty taking us out.

"Copy," Tabby said.

We both turned and locked in on the ship as it flew at us. It had slowed, obviously preferring to spend more time with guns in range than to keep making passes. Blaster rounds exploded on the ground around us and were deflected by my suit's armor. I switched my weapon to explosive rounds and laid into the bird with full auto.

"Rocks away!" Marny warned.

Tabby leapt but I held tight and prayed my suit could take the near miss my AI predicted. It would hurt at an epic level, but our backs were pinned to the wall. The extra seconds of fire paid off and a contrail of smoke spewed from the back of the ship just before I was blown back up the mountain. I struggled to remain conscious.

The ship diverted, making a low pass in my direction. Pinpricks along my back alerted me to the injection of combat stimulants and pain killers. I refused to look at my bios, knowing that something bad must have happened for the suit to respond that way.

Like my plan to stand-and-deliver, the pilot's decision to follow his kill was equally poor. I raised my weapon to fire and realized I no longer held a weapon. This was bad, as the weapons are integrated with the suit's armor. Tabby, however, bore no injury and with the benefit of easier targeting, stitched a line of explosive rounds through the plane's starboard wing. I felt an odd sense of symmetry watching the wing detach and fall away. Bemused, I followed the plane's progress as it augured into the side of the mountain and exploded brilliantly.

"Cap, your bios are showing trauma to your left arm," Marny said.

"Copy that. We're going to pretend that didn't happen for the moment. I'm on go-go juice, I'll deal with it later," I said and chinned the painkillers and stimulants a few more times.

I plucked the multipurpose tool from my suit. Frak guns. I didn't need that shite for bugs. Somewhere in the back of my mind, I knew the imperious, devil-may-care feeling caused by combat drugs was a bad thing - but *seriously*, that was the point of having them! If the shite's hit the fan, what's wrong with a little bravado?

"Liam!" Tabby said. "We gotta get back to *Intrepid*."

"Marny, how far out is that second ship?"

"Ten minutes."

"Any chance they're not tracking us?"

"None at all. Our sensors are showing that Belvakuski is moving her fleet into position in geosync. They can easily track movement on the ground."

"Plan hasn't changed, Tabbs," I said, bounding back down the hill. I wasn't sure why these combat drugs were illegal in most markets. I felt like a billion credits.

I braced as the first of the bugs finally made it past Tabby's onslaught. I couldn't fathom how the little bugs couldn't see their brothers and sisters having the life sucked out of them by her armor piercing bullets. They just kept coming. Compelled to skitter over the corpses of their – family? Brood? Clutch?

My multipurpose tool sang as it sliced through the air, bashing in one crunchy little proboscis or thorax after another. I reveled in the mess I was making as I flung bug guts across the rocky plane. I must have been ignoring the tactical channel or screaming into the microphone because suddenly, a heavy, armored glove appeared and stopped my swinging.

Tabby's face appeared in front of my faceplate. I could make out the words she was saying, but I kind of didn't care.

"Medical override. Counteract stimulants and painkillers. Hoffen is tripping out, you daffy AI."

She was such a warrior. Always so serious. I wasn't sure what she was so worked up about.

She pulled me along, not letting go of my right hand, which still held my multipurpose tool. After a minute, reality set in — my left-hand was on fire.

"What the frak?" I exclaimed. My stomach felt like I'd eaten too many sweets and I might throw up.

"You back with me?" Tabby asked.

"Yeah, sorry. Might have overdone things."

"Look forward to replaying the data-stream," Tabby said. "You have some dark shite in that head of yours, Hoffen."

I still had fleeting images of me spinning through a pile of bugs, cutting them apart.

"How's your ammo?" I asked.

"Ten percent."

"I'm at forty-two," I said. "We'll need to transfer some, I won't be needing any more this trip."

"Your arm is messed up."

"Yeah, let's put a pin in that for now."

The ground shook as we closed in on the Kroerak ship and eight, fully grown warriors jumped down and raced to our position, three of them dropping as Tabby drew down on them and sprayed armor piercing rounds.

"I'm almost out," Tabby said.

The Kroerak cruiser started to lift and a new problem presented itself. My entire plan had been to take cover in the shadow of a ship no Pogona would ever get near. Now, that ship - and our cover - was trying to leave. If it did, we'd be left in the open. Knocking down a small, atmospheric scout ship had been one thing. An armored ship at the end of the valley would be another thing entirely.

Killing a hatchling or adolescent with a hammer isn't really that hard. Sure, they have a crusty exterior, but the Popeye's power is sufficient to crack that like an egg. Warriors were doable, but it required more finesse and several more tries.

I met the first warrior in the group head-on. My hammer dazed it, but couldn't break through. I cursed the lack of a functional second hand. I needed to wield the tool as a long sword, but that required two hands to both extend and brace it.

A second warrior rushed past its stunned brood mate and attacked, clamping pincers onto my suit. I'd had plenty of experience with bugs in tight quarters and knew the bug wouldn't immediately break through. What I hadn't counted on was the bug taking an interest in my wounded hand.

I screamed as a pincer grabbed hold and crushed whatever flesh had been exposed and later covered with nothing quite so hard as armor. A small prick in my back warned me of additional combat meds being injected and a wave of relief coursed through my body. I would not, however, ask for more. I needed a clear head.

Over the warrior's shoulder, the Kroerak cruiser continued its ascent. The broad irregular disc shape shook as the portion of hull buried under Kameldeep's surface was pulled from the earth.

Frantically, I punched the bug away from me and smashed the hammer into the side of its head, just above the thorax. Still no good. That is until the point of Tabby's multipurpose tool skewered it.

"We gotta go!" I screamed, racing toward the only portion of the huge vessel that was relatively close to the ground.

With arc-jet assist, I leapt and buried the pick side of the hammer into the surface of the hull. Tabby landed next to me. It was there we remained, attached like barnacles on an old wooden schooner, while the Kroerak cruiser lifted into space.

"Cap, get off! We can't come after you," Marny called.

"Do your repairs, Marny," I said. "Then get *Intrepid* out of here. Tabby and I are dead if we stay in that valley."

"You can't survive on the outside of that ship, Cap. We'll bring *Intrepid* over and provide protection," she said, pleading.

"That was an order, Marny," I said. "You and Ada have to take care of the crew."

"Damn it, Cap."

A million ideas, each one worse than the last floated through my head as we slowly lifted out of the atmosphere. I wasn't in the best position, but apparently, I'd buried the hammer deeply enough that I would stay attached. That and a small gravitational pull toward the ship helped hold us on.

One option would be to halo drop from the ship. If Belvakuski weren't looking for us and wasn't tracking the Kroerak ship, it would work. Of course, she was doing both of those things. We finally caught a break when we freed from Kameldeep's gravitational pull and were able to walk upright on the cruiser's crusty surface.

I'd never been this close to a Kroerak ship and found its armor to be unlike anything we'd previously seen. The skin was rough, almost like cement that had been poured. I knew from experience that rockets could chip away at the hard surface, but they never seemed to fully break through, as the layers just got harder.

The next idea to present itself was an attempt at entering through myriad rows of weapons ports. While some of the ports were indeed empty, the lances they launched were five to ten centimeters across, not allowing for any type of entry. Tabby, having vamped ordnance from my pack, tossed a grenade down a couple of the open shafts without significant results.

"Hoffen, is that you crawling on the skin of that bug ship?"

Belvakuski asked. I'd ignored the hail, but she'd transmitted anyway. "What are you up to?"

It was just then a hatch, previously hidden in the rocky skin swiveled open. It could be a trap, but then, there was nothing to be gained by staying outside.

Chapter 29

WE WILL ROCK YOU

The passage we entered was ten meters long — too narrow for us to turn easily and too short for us to stand completely upright in the mech suits. The AI, recognizing our predicament, activated what I can best describe as hunch-mode, which further limited our mobility but allowed us to move forward.

"Are you crazy, Hoffen?" Tabby asked. "This is a trap! It's frakked up on so many levels."

Tabby still stood outside the ship, peering in. She wasn't particularly fond of enclosed spaces.

"Stay out there. I'll see if there's another door."

"Frak that. I'm not getting stuck out here." I smiled. Like I said, she wasn't overly fond of enclosed spaces, but it turns out she's a lot less fond of being cut off.

Tabby had no sooner hunched and waddled into the hallway when the outside door slid back into place. Turning in alarm, she fired what seemed like a hundred rounds into the hatch — to no avail. While she fired, the atmospheric pressure in the small passage rose until it was fifty-six kPA or about half what most air-breathers needed. The makeup of the gas that filled the chamber was a Freon 12, oxygen mixture and entirely consumable by humans.

"Hoffen." Tabby's voice held warning. She didn't like our predicament.

"This is an airlock. Lower the gun, I'm taking ricochets," I said.

"This is frakked up beyond your normal, Hoffen," she said.

I turned and worked my way back to her, placing my helmet's face shield against her own so she could see me. "We're alive, Tabbs. It's been touch-and-go, but we survived like we always do. Hold it together."

"But your arm," she said. Her eyes showed fear. I wasn't used to seeing that from her. Something about my injury and being trapped must have dredged up memories of her own brush with death when the Naval ship she'd been assigned to was destroyed.

"Not the first injury for either of us. We'll get through this if we keep our heads. You with me?"

"I'm trying."

"Good," I said. The pressure in the room changed and I turned back to find that a new door had opened. "I need you to trust me. Turn off your lamps. We're drawing too much attention."

"We'll be blind. I'm not going in there blind, Hoffen." Her voice sounded like it belonged to a much younger version of herself — higher and less confident than I was used to.

"Trust me one more time."

She held her breath and closed her eyes. A moment later her suit lamps dimmed and then went out. Together we stood, face to face, unmoving. I wondered how much attention the racket she'd made while firing in the small chamber had garnered.

A bright green glow flooded the chamber. I pulled away from Tabby and worked my way to the end of the passage. Whatever I'd been expecting, the sight I beheld wasn't even close. I stood at the edge of a precipice on a three-meter-wide shelf at the end of the airlock. Ahead was a giant spherical cavity that took up sixty percent of the volume of the ship. Dead in the center, a twenty-meter-wide, sixty-meter-tall column joined the ceiling to the floor.

Bright bioluminescent veins wrapped the entirety of the massive cavity, their shape resembling a vascular pattern more than something engineered. Kneeling at the edge of the platform, I brushed my armored hand across plant growth that filled in the spaces between the glowing lines. A broad yellow-petaled flower closed hastily when it came in contact with the metal of my suit. When I turned my glove over to inspect it, moisture beaded before dripping off.

"Freeze, Hoffen," Tabby warned.

I checked my HUD. She'd tagged a massive, two-meter-tall spider crawling down the wall five meters above us, its thorax gently brushing over the plant life. My AI picked up on my interest and highlighted several hundred more spiders crawling all over the interior.

"Back," I said, slowly moving away from the opening.

We held our breath as the spider ambled its way over the lip of the platform and approached. I couldn't blame Tabby when she fired, although I wasn't as sure as she was that it meant to harm us. Apparently, multiple beady eyes scattered across its head and a snapping beak the size of my gloved hand was enough for her. She fired sixty rounds into its swollen abdomen, breaking it open and spilling life juices onto the platform.

"Incoming," I said. My AI highlighted twenty nearby spiders that responded to the gunfire. I pulled out my multipurpose tool and prepared for the worst. Predictably, Tabby fired again, splattering one spider after another, effectively halting their charge.

"Stop firing!" I finally said, recognizing that the fallen spiders were being picked up by other nearby spiders and torn apart. Their remains were broken, crushed and even julienned before being spread onto the nearby plants.

I hooked the pry bar end of my tool into the spider in front of us and flung it from the precipice. The skittering horde turned away, giving chase before finally obliterating their dead companion.

"What now?" Tabby asked.

"We go."

"Where?"

I pointed to the center of the ship where the tall column joined the top of the ship to the bottom. I jumped from the edge of the precipice and landed hard on the sloped side of the cavern's concave surface. Instead of fighting the fall, I continued moving my legs as if I'd been running and allowed the suit to absorb the fall's impact.

"I hate spiders," Tabby complained as she caught up with me.

Popeyes and fields of bioluminescent plant life are essentially incompatible. I felt almost guilty as we plowed a furrow through the previously pristine fauna.

"Looks like the feeling is mutual."

A swarm of angry spiders rushed toward us as we tore through the field. Initially, we didn't find it difficult to swat them aside or jump over them, but the closer we got to the center, the more organized they became.

Tabby fired into what had become a sea of furry bulbous-bellied spiders, while I hacked at them with my hammer. The spider's secondary attack - after trying their hardest to bite us - was a sticky spray. The material was acidic, but the suits were capable of withstanding it. That is, except for the portion of my suit that had been torn off. The back of my left arm, down to my hand, burned afresh as we fought through the bugs.

We finally arrived at the center column, and with our backs to the rocky material, fought the spiders off. Since we were no longer defiling their fields, we didn't draw new spiders into the battle. This alone gave me hope. The fight of attrition was exhausting, but finally ended when no new spiders attacked.

"Hold fire," I said, wearily placing my good arm atop Tabby's gun. She lowered it reluctantly. The spiders that approached now were only there to distribute their deceased cohort's crushed remains out into the fields.

"That's completely messed up, Liam," Tabby said.

"Let's find a way in," I said.

Careful to stay away from the plants, we worked our way around the column. We found a wide entrance on the opposite side, but the ceiling was too low for the Popeyes to fit in without crawling. Inside the column, a narrow, curved ramp hugged the outside wall and disappeared above us. The space wasn't large enough for a Kroerak warrior.

"You're not thinking of going in there, are you?" Tabby asked. "Seriously, Liam, what are we doing here?"

"What's the choice? You heard Marny, it's only a matter of time before Belvakuski finds *Intrepid*. Stay here."

I chinned the eject and blinked acknowledgement at the requisite prompts. It was the first time I'd had a chance to see the back of my hand. Nanobots had formed a translucent film of skin over what remained. Melted skin, crushed bone and a portion of my index finger were all that remained below mid-forearm. It wasn't a good look. Gingerly, I pulled at the grav-suit's material, causing it to flow over the damage, knit around the end, and seal the injury in.

"I thought you gave your Ruger to Anghad." Tabby ejected from her suit and unclipped a new laser pistol from her waist holster.

"I might have exaggerated the provenance of the pistol I handed to Anghad," I said, sheepishly.

"You ... That's ..." Tabby looked at me bemused. "It was a lovely speech."

"You should have stayed suited," I said. "What if we run into warriors?"

"No warrior can make it up this ramp and I'd be willing to bet those spiders are designed to keep warriors off the grass," she said. "That, and you're down a paw. Not sure why you can't get it through your head — we're in this together. The good and the bad."

Before stepping onto the ramp, we gave the lowest level a cursory look. I wasn't sure what I hoped to find above us, but I knew we had to keep pushing forward. Our odds of survival had been on a steady decline from the moment the Genteresk fleet had peeked over the horizon and *Intrepid* lost its second engine. We needed a break.

With pistols held in front, we walked up the ramp. Technically, I floated, using the grav-suit's capabilities to lessen the effort. It was tight quarters and we had to move in single file. I took point with Tabby right on my tail.

After a complete revolution, we'd gained twenty meters of elevation, but had run into a translucent barrier. I reached forward and tentatively pushed on the veil. With sufficient force, the material stretched and pushed in a few millimeters. I wasn't able to break through, but discovered a band of slightly thicker material down the center that gapped slightly upon contact. On instinct, I holstered my pistol and ran my good fingers across the material, inserting them in the invisible seam at the center. The right side of the membrane gave way and pushed easily to the side. Gingerly, I thrust my left arm into the opening and elbowed that half of the membrane out of the way, creating an opening big enough to slide through.

"Careful," Tabby warned.

I nodded and released the opening. It snapped back into position. I drew my pistol and, once again, pushed open the orifice, this time using the barrel of my gun and thrusting my shoulders through. The material caught on my body, but with the help of the grav-suit I wiggled through, landing on the opposite side. A moment later, Tabby followed, albeit more gracefully.

We'd arrived at a second level in the tower. Unlike the barren first level, this deck had several initially undistinguishable piles. My AI outlined the remains of a human form and I rushed over, expecting the worst. Tabby followed just as quickly.

"Frak," she said, laying a hand on my shoulder.

"Jupiter piss," I said. It was Jonathan's body. His chest had been torn open and hollowed out.

"His crystal," Tabby pointed at something I hadn't seen.

She was right. A quantum comm crystal was poking up out of the viscera that remained. Instinctively, I reached in and pulled the crystal out, placing it into a belt pouch.

"They couldn't have survived," I said, referring to the collection of sentients that had resided within the sticky mess. "There was no host." I felt like a thousand kilograms of steel sat on my chest and I had a hard time breathing. They'd given their lives so willingly in hopes the Kroerak could be stopped.

"Sendrei's sword and his vac-suit," Tabby said, lifting a limp suit and extracting a sword from another pile of indistinguishable material.

"What happened here?" I asked. "Sendrei wouldn't have gone down without a fight."

"You are correct, Liam Hoffen and Tabitha Masters."

I spun and fired my pistol in a single move. Tabby — faster and stronger — leapt across, turning in midair, swinging her bo staff.

There were three of them. Two were the size of adolescents, but with significantly different physical attributes. The third was twenty centimeters taller. All three glistened, emitting yellow light that reflected off glossy, multifaceted golden armor carapaces.

Kroerak warriors were fast, but their primary skillset was to attack ferociously and in a straight line. Mostly, warriors didn't run into things that could easily harm them. The stand-and-deliver method of combat really worked for them. By the time you chipped into their armor, they were ripping out your innards. Point was, there was nothing subtle about them.

Oddly, the two slightly smaller bugs were anything but direct. While I had turned and fired as quickly as I could, one of the two had anticipated my shots and already extended a wing from its back, deflecting the bolts harmlessly into the floor. The second fluttered up to meet Tabby, catching her bo staff in a thick pincer and wrenching it from her grip.

I drew my nano-blade and pushed my grav-suit forward. There was no doubt in my mind. This was the group that had killed Sendrei and Jonathan. We might very well die here, but we wouldn't go down without a fight.

Tabby responded to the loss of her bo staff by producing Sendrei's sword, flicking it open and slicing at the bug's extended pincer. I wanted to cheer as the pincer and bo staff clattered onto the deck. Everything was happening so quickly that I had to look away as I sliced my own blade through the air. We were in this thing. It was time to deal with these asshats.

My elation was short lived. I failed to land a strike on the bug I'd engaged. It moved so quickly I had difficulty tracking it. Where I had failed to make contact, the bug did not. I sailed backward, dropping the nano blade when I made violent contact with the opposite wall.

Through blurred vision, I watched Tabby engage the small golden warrior. I pushed off the wall and stumbled forward, looking around for anything I could use as a weapon. Tabby was making progress, up to the point when the second gold bug joined in.

"Tell your mate to desist, Liam Hoffen. We have limited patience for poor behavior." The voice sounded in my head, but didn't register with my AI. As if to emphasize the statement, Tabby flew across the room. She arrested her flight by planting her feet against the back wall and pushing off. She'd been disarmed, but pulled out a short blade and raced back into combat.

I knew I had to back her up. One-on-one, Tabby was faster, but against two, she would lose. I rushed forward, leaning into my grav-suit for acceleration. I barreled into one of the gold bugs and wrapped my arms around it, pushing as hard as I could to separate it from Tabby.

"Hoffen!" In her voice was concern. I'd chosen to attack the stronger of the two bugs. She'd already clipped a pincer from her bug and I'd let her continue to deal with that one. We might just make it out of this yet.

Fire in my side alerted me to a new problem. Something had sliced into me just before the bug and I slammed into the wall. I thought it was possible I heard cracking, but I wasn't sure if it was the wall, the bug or me.

"You will submit!" My mind bent to the will of the voice and I fell to the ground, no longer able to control my grav-suit.

I turned to Tabby who screamed in agony, thrusting her blade into the open maw of her opponent. Together they fell as one to the ground.

"Violence is not called for," the voice that compelled me to my knees continued. "You have fought with skill and honor." I felt a swell of pride at what we'd accomplished. It had been truly spectacular and we'd done it in a way to make all of mankind proud.

"Don't give in, Hoffen," Tabby said, through gritted teeth. "It's frakking with our heads."

A seed of doubt sprouted in my mind.

I looked at the third bug, which had done no fighting. I'd seen a Kroerak noble before. It had talked to me through a solid wall. Nobles were more colorful than the guards, their wings delicate and thorax less armored and narrower. My mind wandered and I wondered if this noble was the equivalent of the ship's captain. It was certainly beautiful and needed our respect; it was a wondrous and powerful creature.

"I *am* considered beautiful by my peers, Captain Hoffen. You should not seek to compare your station with my own. I am responsible for this vessel, but unlike human captains it is I that controls its every function."

She or it, was terrifying in its power. I was nothing next to it.

"You are correct. I am neither male nor female. I am Noble and you are my guests. And no, Tabitha Masters, we do not seek to eat you. Not while you both stink of the technology of humanity. To defile your bodies in such a way shows little understanding for the purity of your species. You are a good breeding pair and we will sow you as crops on a beautiful new world. Your children will be delicacies worth more than any. The mighty usurper, Liam Hoffen, brought to bended knee."

The noble turned and walked up the ramp, its wings fluttering to help it balance, the remaining golden warrior falling in behind.

"Come," it said.

I found I was unable to resist the force of will exerted by the bug.

"How do you know about me?" I asked. "You've been on Zuri for a hundred eighty stans."

"The communications device you covet from your null friend. I watched you placed it in your pocket. Do you find it so difficult to believe my species would have devised something superior? My kind was colonizing solar systems when yours still rooted around in the mud."

"You don't colonize. You destroy peaceful civilizations," Tabby spat.

"It's always the warriors that come to understanding first," the noble said. "I would know of this Jonathan you keep considering. Think more about this person. You believe it inhabited the null body. We found nothing."

"Ohhhh, Johnny boy ... the pipes, the pipes are calling. From glen to glen and down the mountain side." I wasn't much of a singer, but for some reason, I remembered hearing a crusty old miner singing the song when working on one of my dad's claims. The bug was reading my mind and singing was the only thing I could think of to push the noble from my head.

"Danny boy," Tabby corrected.

"What are you doing?" The noble asked.

"You were asking about Johnny boy. I was remembering a song about him," I said.

"You are trying to hide something. It won't work. Human brains are open to me."

We'd been led into a control room and were sixty meters up. The walls thinned and were translucent, showing a three-hundred-sixty-degree view of the spiders as they worked the fields.

"You had no choice, Tabitha Masters." The noble answered a question that hadn't been asked aloud. "I discovered your presence when you destroyed the tenders. Spiders, I believe you call them. I suggested to you that the only way out was to explore my lair. Your minds were weak and you came straightaway. Can you not see why humanity should serve us? Is this not what humanity has done to every other species it has discovered?"

"Humanity does not enslave other sentient species," I argued.

"A moral line drawn to most easily suit your needs. The Kroerak Empire has drawn its line ever so close to humanity's."

"If you are so powerful, why didn't you stop us from killing your guard?"

"It amused me and taught my children a valuable lesson. We should be wary of non-domesticated stock."

I glanced around the room. I'd never seen Kroerak technology close-up and was somewhat surprised to see video displays, levers, dials, buttons and the like.

"Do you run this entire ship yourself?" I asked.

"The important parts. I find it difficult to manufacture the lances your human ships are so easily defeated with. I need workers and for workers I need a steady supply of food. It is of no consequence. I have been recalled. My honor will be restored due to the great cunning which caused you to be captured."

"You're a windbag," Tabby said, offended. "You twist everything to sound like you're some big, important bug queen. You're just a slug. An overgrown worm."

Tabby screamed in agony, clutching her head. I tried to get to her but found myself rooted in place.

"Stop!" I yelled.

The noble turned to me and Tabby's screaming lessened. "She must be broken, Liam Hoffen. She must be docile. Her training will be painful, but the trip home is long."

The screen flickered for a moment behind the noble. Words appeared — *But come ye back when summer's in the meadow.* I'd forgotten them, but they were the start of the second verse of 'Oh Danny Boy.' It made no sense.

Tabby screamed again as the noble turned her attention back.

A second screen flashed with more words. *Buddy, you're a boy make a big noise, playin' in the street, gonna be a big man someday.* The words were familiar, like something I'd forgotten and just needed the right context for.

Tears streamed down Tabby's face as she stared defiantly at the noble and screamed in agony. "We ... will, we ... will rock you!"

Suddenly, the words on the screen made sense. It was from my ancient music collection. I didn't recognize the verse, but the chorus I absolutely recognized. I joined in with her. "We ... will, we ... will ... rock you."

The screen flickered — *again.*

Instead of singing the whole verse, I simply repeated. "We ... will, we ... will ... rock you."

"Stop this!" The noble's voice blasted in my mind and I reeled from the blow.

Tabby refused to stop and continued belting out the chorus. She actually had a pretty decent voice, if not a little hoarse from the screaming. The golden warrior rushed forward as Tabby found her feet. Without warning, it stabbed a pincer deep into her shoulder.

"No!" I'd felt the noble's grip loosening while we sang, but as I started for Tabby, my knees crumpled.

Blood sprayed from Tabby's mouth as she coughed.

"That wasn't necessary. Bind her wound," the noble instructed.

Tabby drew breath. "We ... will ... rock you," she wheezed between coughs.

In a pure act of defiance, I joined with her and helped carry the tune.

The noble spun on me, its evil intent clear as malice crashed through my senses like a wave breaking on the beach.

Movement caught my eye and a dark figure streaked toward us. The golden warrior turned and headed for the noble. Tabby launched herself at the golden warrior, wrapping her one good arm around its head.

Tabby's move was pretty ineffective, but it was enough to slow the warrior's progress. The bug had to pause in order to toss Tabby aside. Seemingly in slow motion, my eyes — and those of the noble — tracked a naked, sword-wielding Sendrei flying through the air. I could finally see what Tabby must have already understood; the warrior would successfully intersect Sendrei's attack.

"We ... will, we ... will rock you!" I sang out, throwing my body into the path of the golden warrior, jamming my good arm into its pincers as I did. My voice squeaked as the claw closed on my suit and the pressure instantly became unbearable.

Time reverted back to normal and Sendrei's sword sliced through the noble's shell. For a moment, it was as if nothing had changed — I was spinning out of control, away from the golden warrior and Sendrei's sword was arcing away from the noble.

I caught myself against the control surface that looked out over the interior of the ship. Wordlessly, the noble tipped forward just as its head rolled down the glimmering carapace. And with the noble, the golden warrior also fell.

Shakily, I pulled my Ruger from its holster. My mind was suddenly clear enough to realize it was still at my side. I turned wildly, looking for further danger, but only found Sendrei. He was standing with his sword in hand, looking at me in disbelief.

"You came for us," he said, dumbfounded. His body had lost much of its muscular mass and he suffered from many poorly healed cuts, welts, bruises and contusions, but it was absolutely him.

I pushed off the console and wrapped my arms around him, hugging him tightly. His whole body shook as he dropped his sword and sobbed. I could only imagine the hell he had been through in order to survive. Tabby joined us, leaning against my side, holding my hand in her own.

EPILOGUE

"Do you have water?" Sendrei asked.

"Come with us," I said, making my way to the partition that would lead us back down.

My mind was clear of the Noble's influence. We'd abandoned the Popeyes, something I could not fathom, given that we were in the heart of a Kroerak ship. A single warrior could have ended us in seconds. Frak, given the shape both Tabby or I were in, a couple of adolescents would do us in.

Sendrei followed us downward. On the second level, he picked up his tattered vacsuit and then threw it back to the ground.

"How did you survive?" I asked.

"It was Jonathan's doing."

"I hope they didn't suffer," I said. Sendrei's suit was only meters from Jonathan's ruined shell.

"They're a wily group," Sendrei said. "They've been hiding in the ship's systems."

"He's not dead?" I asked, knowing better than to singularize them, but feeling so elated at the news that I didn't care.

"We are doing quite well, Liam. Thank you for your concern." Jonathan's voice came across my suit's tactical channel. "I apologize for breaking in, but we have urgent issues to attend. The Genteresk fleet has discovered *Intrepid*. There is a firefight and it is going poorly for our crew. *Sangilak* has started shelling the surface with their cannons."

Hastily, I pulled my vac-suit off and tossed it at Sendrei. "Suit can leach water from the ground." I sprinted down the spiral ramp and clawed my way back into the Popeye and closed it. "Jonathan, how much control of this ship do you have?"

"Without the Kroerak noble blocking us, we have complete control, Liam."

"Can you transfer ship control onto my HUD and set a navigation path directly at *Sangilak*. I need all possible speed," I said.

"Yes. The controls will, necessarily, be virtual," Jonathan replied.

The Popeye's high-resolution view-screen displayed a passable three-dimensional rendering of normal ship controls. I grabbed the virtual yoke with my hands, not caring that my left had been numbed to the point of no feeling. I'd been flying ships my entire life. Between my AI and Jonathan's 1,438 sentients, I had ultimate confidence they'd find a way to translate. I wasn't to be proven wrong.

"And hail that frakking lizard-chin!"

The Popeye involuntarily stepped back, responding to a shift in the Kroerak cruiser's attitude.

"This is *Sangilak*, Your Eminence. Please convey to me how I might be of service," Belvakuski groveled.

"You will die!" I said. "Jonathan, do we have any lance weapons left?" I left the comms with Belvakuski open as I spoke.

"Aye, Captain. There are sufficient lances for a single, formidable strike," Jonathan replied.

"Are you opposed to aiding in targeting?"

"We would prefer violence only when there is no other option," Jonathan replied.

"They're killing our crew," I said. "We have to act now."

A three-dimensional view of the Kroerak vessel and the Genteresk fleet appeared in front of me. Translucent yellow streaks appeared in the space between us. It took a moment to realize it was the predicted damage paths from the lance weapons. It was terrifying in its potential. I found I could adjust the wave of lances by shaping it with my hand. Of course, I had to let go of the flight controls, but we could safely fly straight at the fleet for the several minutes of separation we had between us.

"Hoffen?" Belvakuski asked in disbelief.

"You should have left us alone, Belvakuski," I responded.

Sangilak's huge turrets turned in our direction and great puffs of fire erupted from the ends of the barrels. Inside the Kroerak vessel it sounded like thunder when the great steel shot impacted the rocky hull.

I held my fire and continued toward the Genteresk fleet. *Sangilak's* guns were terrifying at just how great their range was. Of course, in space, there was no drag to slow the shot that had been hurled at us. Over the few minutes we approached, Belvakuski continued to fire as smaller ships lifted from the atmosphere, joining in defense of their leader.

"Fire!" I finally called when we'd closed sufficiently.

In an instant, the Genteresk fleet lost eight ships to complete and utter destruction. Another four, including the heavily armored, light cruiser *Sangilak*, were heavily damaged.

Belvakuski cut comms just after I launched the wave of lances. Until then, she might have held out hope that I was bluffing. Beyond surrendering, I wasn't sure of her options. The Kroerak cruiser was nearly as quick as *Intrepid* and I would have run her down in less than an hour.

"Anything left, Jonathan?" I asked.

"There are no more lances."

"See if you can raise Belvakuski," I said.

"Stop, Hoffen," Belvakuski said, this time allowing video comms. Her bridge was filled with smoke and her face was covered in black soot.

"Do you surrender?"

"Surely, we can work something out," she wheedled. "Do you really want to take eight hundred hostages?"

"You will turn over *Sangilak* and *Gaylon Brighton* to me immediately. You will then inform your fleet to gather what they can from the wreckage and leave the vicinity within ninety minutes."

"And *Fleet Afoot*," Tabby added hastily.

I looked at her quizzically. "Really?" My AI recognized my confusion and zoomed in on the awkwardly beautiful little racer we'd had stolen from us.

"And *Fleet Afoot*. It's only fair."

"What special joy do you have planned for me?" Belvakuski asked. "A disemboweling?"

"You will escort all remaining human personnel to Kameldeep's surface where you will be transferred to *Intrepid's* brig," I said. "If you comply, you will come to no harm by my hand or that of my crew."

Belvakuski narrowed her eyes at me. "You would leave me alive? That is madness."

"I am not asking. I am demanding," I said.

She placed a fist beneath her chin and held it firmly. "You have my word of honor. I have been bested today. I will comply."

"Did you get that, Marny?" I asked, noticing that Jonathan had patched in *Intrepid* to my conversation.

"Damn skippy I did, Cap," she answered jubilantly. "And don't you ever do that to me again. We thought you were dead!"

"Your starboard main is smoking again, Liam," Ada called over the comms.

"We're working on it," I said. "And for the record, this bucket is a piece of crap."

We'd taken command of *Sangilak* and discovered that it's only redeeming qualities were its armor, which was as thick as most asteroids I'd mined, and its guns that could knock down anything standing in its way. Otherwise, every system was antiquated beyond comprehension.

Intrepid had taken quite a beating and it had taken us three days of work to get her lofted back into space, but she was mobile, albeit with only three engines.

We'd recovered a very grateful Commander Munay and eight of the hardest working, gung-ho, hooyah Naval officers I'd ever come into contact with. If any of them got more than three hours of sleep at night, I'd have been surprised. That said, the aged warship was every bit a match for their zeal.

"I might have judged you a bit too harshly, Mr. Hoffen," Munay said, standing next to me, staring off into the deep dark.

Sangilak had more than enough fuel to get the entire fleet all the way back to Petersburg Station as long as we traveled at the one speed she had — medium slow.

"Appreciate you saying that. Perhaps I'll tell Mom you're not the asshat I thought you were." I must have caught Munay off guard because he grunted out a laugh.

"You going to get that looked at?" He gestured to my left arm which was still missing most of its fingers.

"Probably not until we're home," I said. "Your boys and girls were pretty beat up. Between Sendrei and them, *Intrepid's* tank has been working overtime."

"What will you do with the Kroerak ship?" Munay asked.

The question took me aback. "I guess I thought you'd be working out something with Mars Protectorate. Weren't you the guy ready to take *Intrepid* if I didn't do what you wanted?"

"Maybe you haven't figured it out yet, Hoffen. Not a man or woman working on this ship would lift a finger against you after what you did for us," he said.

"What about you?"

Over Munay's shoulder I saw the entire surviving crew of Naval officers walk somberly onto the bridge and stood in a neat line.

Munay, sensing their arrival, stiffened, clicked his heels together, and drew back a salute that was echoed by the entire squad standing at attention.

"Commodore Hoffen. Respect is earned, we pledge our loyalty to you, in service to our homeland of Mars."

I looked from Tabby and over to the ragtag line of proud men and women, many of whom were my senior and certainly all of them capable and accomplished. I met each set of eyes and saw a fierce determination. This was a group that had given much and would give even more. I felt wholly inadequate in that moment.

"I'm not sure what to say," I said.

"I generally go with 'dismissed,'" Munay said, with a rare grin.

But of course, that's another story entirely.

ABOUT THE AUTHOR

Jamie McFarlane is happily married, the father of three and lives in Lincoln, Nebraska. He spends his days engaged in a hi-tech career and his nights and weekends writing works of fiction.

Word-of-mouth is crucial for any author to succeed. If you enjoyed this book, please consider leaving a review at Amazon, even if it's only a line or two; it would make all the difference and would be very much appreciated.

FREE DOWNLOAD

If you want to get an automatic email when Jamie's next book is available, please visit http://fickledragon.com/keep-in-touch. Your email address will never be shared and you can unsubscribe at any time.

For more information
www.fickledragon.com
jamie@fickledragon.com

ACKNOWLEDGMENTS

To Diane Greenwood Muir for excellence in editing and fine word-smithery. My wife, Janet, for carefully and kindly pointing out my poor grammatical habits. I cannot imagine working through these projects without you both.

To my beta readers: Carol Greenwood, Kelli Whyte, Carol Sutton, Linda Baker, Matt Strbjak and Nancy Higgins Quist for wonderful and thoughtful suggestions. It is a joy to work with this intelligent and considerate group of people. Also, to my advanced reading team, you're a zany, fun group of people who I look forward to bouncing ideas off.

Finally, to Elias T. Stern, cover artist extraordinaire.

ALSO BY JAMIE MCFARLANE

Privateer Tales Series

Witchy World

Guardians of Gaeland

Made in the USA
Middletown, DE
28 December 2020